© Faith Tilleray

Manda Scott's crime novels have been shortlisted for many awards including *Hen's Teeth* for the Orange Prize and *No Good Deed* for an Edgar Award. Her work has been translated into over twenty languages. Most recently, her bestselling Boudica series was optioned for television.

A Treachery of Spies has been chosen as . . .

Daily Telegraph Books of the Year

The Times Books of the Year

'Superb . . . a blend of historical imagination and storytelling
verve reminiscent of Robert Harris.' *Sunday Times*

'*A Treachery of Spies* is the equal of *Charlotte Gray* in
its insights into the period and, I would say, beats it for
sheer excitement . . . one of the most gripping spy stories
I have ever read. It's a clear-eyed and honest portrayal
of the potency of hatred and the endurance of evil.
But it also manages to demonstrate unsentimentally
the compensating power of love.' *S Magazine*

'This is a rich vein for fiction, and Scott does it more than justice,
with this beautifully imagined, beautifully written, smart,
sophisticated – but fiercely suspenseful – thriller.' Lee Child

'Ingeniously plotted and wonderfully written.'
Antonia Senior, *The Times*

'This book opened up and swallowed me whole – the
characters, the plot, the writing, everything. It's the most exciting,
involving thriller I've read in an age, and I can't recommend it
highly enough.' Mick Herron

'One of the year's best spy thrillers . . . the combination
of first-class writing, radical political engagement and
carefully husbanded but expertly deployed moments of
pure excitement reminded me of Le Carré at his best.'
Jake Kerridge, *Daily Telegraph*

'It's as hard for the reader as it is for Captain Picaut to guess what's going to happen next and where we're heading in this fast-moving, tightly-wrought thriller. The destination is in fact as unexpected as it is satisfying – and very thought-provoking.' Robert Goddard

'Lyrically told, the plot is peopled with real heroes and villains. None is quite what they seem.' Geoffrey Wansell, *Daily Mail*

'The most exquisite story of heroism, deception, love and treachery you'll find this year.' Simon Mayo

'Manda Scott has filled the grey areas of espionage with rich colour and written a thriller with a living pulse. *A Treachery of Spies* is so, so clever, I found myself wondering how on earth she does it. Simply put, this is a masterclass in thriller-writing and a cut above the rest. It is a heart-racing, heart-wrenching read, conceived with passion and executed with frightening skill.' Giles Kristian

'[Scott's] writing is as commanding as ever.' Barry Forshaw, *Guardian*

'In *A Treachery of Spies*, Manda Scott has written a novel of frightening intensity. Through Scott's deeply compelling, deeply damaged characters – police officers, spies, saboteurs, wartime resisters – we witness the desperate moral complexity of wartime covert operations. But then Scott does something more: she shows us those complexities reflected and remade for our own era.' Adam Brookes

'A multi-layered thriller that connects the Second World War to the modern day.' Sir David Bell in the *Times Higher Education Supplement*

'A brutally brilliant and extremely clever novel of espionage, heroism, love and betrayal. Bravo.' Anna Mazzola

A Treachery
of Spies

MANDA SCOTT

CORGI BOOKS

TRANSWORLD PUBLISHERS
61–63 Uxbridge Road, London W5 5SA
www.penguin.co.uk

Transworld is part of the Penguin Random House group of companies
whose addresses can be found at global.penguinrandomhouse.com

First published in Great Britain in 2018 by Bantam Press
an imprint of Transworld Publishers
Corgi edition published 2019

A CIP catalogue record for this book
is available from the British Library.

ISBNS
9780552169516 (B format)
9780552176491 (A format)

Typeset in 11/14pt Minion Pro by Jouve (UK), Milton Keynes
Printed and bound in Great Britain by Clays Ltd, Elcograf S.p.A.

Penguin Random House is committed to a sustainable
future for our business, our readers and our planet. This book
is made from Forest Stewardship Council® certified paper.

1 3 5 7 9 10 8 6 4 2

For Pat and Patricia Coles,
who showed me how to live
– with all my love

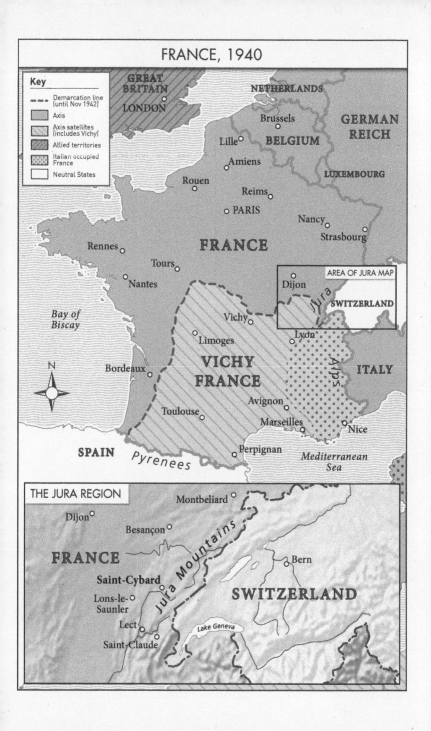

FRANCE, 1940

Key
- - - Demarcation line (until Nov 1942)
Axis
Axis satellites (includes Vichy)
Allied territories
Italian occupied France
Neutral States

GREAT BRITAIN
LONDON

NETHERLANDS

Brussels

Lille

BELGIUM

GERMAN REICH

Amiens

LUXEMBOURG

Rouen

Reims

PARIS

Nancy

Strasbourg

Rennes

FRANCE

Tours

Nantes

Dijon

AREA OF JURA MAP

Jura

SWITZERLAND

Bay of Biscay

Vichy

Lyon

Limoges

VICHY FRANCE

Alps

ITALY

Bordeaux

N

Toulouse

Avignon

Marseilles

Nice

SPAIN

Pyrenees

Perpignan

Mediterranean Sea

THE JURA REGION

Montbeliard

Dijon

Besançon

FRANCE

Bern

Saint-Cybard

Lons-le-Saunler

Jura Mountains

SWITZERLAND

Lect

Lake Geneva

Saint-Claude

I want to say to all young people . . . who do not know what it was like to be in the Resistance: It was one of the greatest times to be alive.

Jacques Chaban-Delmas
Prime Minister of France 1969-72
Former Member of the Resistance

AND THUS BY ACCIDENT WE BECAME AS GODS
BLYTHE CHILDREN OF THE MOUNTAIN
WARRIORS OF VENGEANCE
UNFORGIVING, UNFORGIVEN
UNFORGOTTEN

PROLOGUE

PARIS
June 1942

Y OU MAKE A MISTAKE, trust the wrong person, take a left turn at an alley's end instead of a right, and it is too late.

There are twenty of them, and one of you. You cannot out-run them and fear makes you clumsy so that you trip and fall and flail and are stamped on and kicked and brutalized in other ways. It was always going to come to this, and, as they hammer you into a van and out again, manhandle you up stone steps and down again, you swear that you will spit in their eyes and curse them as you die.

The Boche have other plans. They do not push you into rot-ting cells in the basements of Paris as they have done in the past with men – and some women – whose lives they wrested slowly. They take you out of town, to a big, mouldering farm-house, down two flights of stairs to a root cellar that is wholly insulated from the death and torment of others.

Here, it is cold. There is no light. The smell is of rotten tur-nips, wet sackcloth and rats. After the first slam of the door, the stamp of boots, the silence folds in, and it is this – more than cold and hunger and thirst; more than rats and their increasing boldness; more than bladder and bowels emptied after many hours of holding, so that the stench is no longer of putrid vegetation – more than all of these, it is the suffocating absence of sound that shreds your soul.

Come for me. Talk to me. Shout at me. Drag me out and beat me. Hang me by my thumbs from piano wire. Do you not care? Do I count for so very little? Christ on his Cross, I tried to kill you!

In the dark of the second day, or perhaps the tenth, they come: boots, voices, *light* and the blurry shapes behind it and a rush of cold-clean air.

You shrink from the light and the shame of your own stink. Go away. Go away. Leave me to die. Please, leave.

—Do you know me?

You are Kramme. I tried to kill you. How could I not?

—Then you know what I can do.

I don't care. Just kill me. Fast or slow. I no longer care.

—You deserve to die, of course. Many of your countrymen have done so, some with more dignity than others. But you are different. You have the potential to be useful. You have a choice, therefore: you may die here in darkness if you so desire, but I have come to offer you a proposition. Together, let us seize the day . . . .

CHAPTER ONE

ORLÉANS
Sunday, 18 March 2018
07.10

CHRIST, BUT THERE'S A lot of blood.

This is the first thing Picaut sees as she pulls to a halt in the Gare des Aubrais car park and angles her headlights onto the crime scene – that it is not a scarf at the dead woman's throat, but a sheet of blood, made black in the uncertain light, with spatter marks across the windscreen.

It's been a while since Picaut has seen blood. She has forgotten the visceral power of a violent death. This one jolts her, so that for a long moment she is locked as the woman in the car opposite is locked: eye to eye, face to face, life to death and back again.

The second thing she sees, the thing that stays with her as she steps out of her car and walks over to the gathering group of officers and scene techs, is how peaceful the woman looks amidst the carnage, how hauntingly beautiful, and old enough to be her grandmother.

Rollo is already here, standing by his own car, hunched against the dark and drizzle. He's grown more shadowed in

3

the past year or two, stronger. His hair is longer than it used to be, brushing his shoulders, and his black leather jacket has suffered far worse weather than this.

'Two to the chest, one to the head,' he says by way of a welcome. 'I know men who would kill for a grouping like that.'

From anyone else, this would be a joke, but Rollo doesn't make jokes about guns. So that they're clear, Picaut asks, 'Professional hit?' and Rollo, nodding, says, 'We'll see the details better when the lights are up.'

The lights are on their way. From deep in the dark, a generator heaves into life, arc lights fizz and pop, and, all of a sudden, liquid light pours over the car and the woman sitting behind the wheel, who has been—

Bloody hell.

From Picaut's other side, a younger voice says, 'Tell me they did that after she was dead?'

There is a brief silence. Lieutenant Daniel Evard, nephew to Orléans' fire chief, is the new graduate who joined the team while Picaut was in hospital.

There was a time when infants faced with scenes of wanton destruction retired behind a wall to vomit. Petit-Evard keeps his hands in his pockets where he won't wreak havoc with forensics, looks from Picaut to Rollo and back again, and says, 'You're not telling me she was still alive when they took out her tongue?'

'I sincerely hope not.'

Because this is what the lights have shown: that it is not lipstick around her mouth any more than it was a scarf at her throat. Someone, clearly, has been busy with a knife. Remarkably, it has done nothing to mar her beauty.

She has no name yet, this woman who shows such grace in death; Picaut knows nothing beyond what she can see through the windscreen, spectacular as it is. She takes her hands from her pockets and flexes her fingers. There's a particular

4

sensation in the first moments of a case that marks it for the duration and this one feels like standing at the edge of a high cliff in a thunderstorm with a hang glider strapped to her back. She has dreamed of this moment. It has not let her down.

Start with what you know.

The stationmaster discovered the victim when he came to begin his shift. In an otherwise empty lot in a sleepy northern suburb of Orléans, he parked his Renault behind the only other vehicle in the car park and strolled over to find out what train the lady thought she was going to catch at five fifteen on a March morning.

He is currently being interviewed by Lieutenant Sylvie Ostheimer, the final member of Picaut's new team, and the one who can best be trusted not to traumatize him further.

The car is an ageing Citroën BX, in nearly mint condition. The victim is sitting on the driver's side – which does not, of course, prove that she was driving – with her right hand on the wheel. Her left, on closer inspection, hangs down at her side. Most people neither sit nor drive like this, but the window controls are in the armrest and the window has been lowered (or raised?) to leave open a gap of around a hand's breadth.

Judging by the angles of the gunshots, they were all directed through this small space, which is the point Rollo was making about the skill of the shooter. This is not a blundering amateur.

The car door is closed, but it must, at some point, have been open because, while you might shoot through that gap, you couldn't reach in to cut out someone's tongue: that takes two hands. Picaut makes a note in her phone. To Rollo, she says, 'We need UV images of the blood patterns outside the car before anyone else goes near it.'

He gives half a shrug that might be an apology. 'We did that before the lights went up.'

Right. Rollo's a captain now and he's been leading his own

5

team for nearly a year. It's amazing, really, that he took the offer to come back and work with Picaut. He and Sylvie are the only ones from her old team who did. The rest have gone on to other things. In time, doubtless, Picaut's world will feel less truncated by their loss.

She turns back to the car. Freed from the need to preserve the scene, she moves round for a closer look. The woman has clear skin, not smooth, but with the translucent, porcelain quality that the fortunate carry into old age. The shots that so impressed Rollo have made neat, round, nine-millimetre holes and the one at her temple has faint powder burns tattooed at the margins. Whoever it was got very close. Does that mean they knew each other, shooter and victim?

For a time of death, Picaut eases her hand in through the open window to feel the old lady's brow. Her skin is cool, but not cold, and the muscles of her face, when pressed, are not yet rigid. An accurate time will have to wait for the pathologist, but at her best estimate the shooting took place in the first hour after midnight.

So the killer used a silencer. An entire estate of single-storey cottages nestles less than fifty metres away, inhabited by the kind of respectable, retired middle-class couples who head for bed at ten o'clock and sleep lightly: three shots in the middle of the night would have had them reaching for their phones by the dozen.

This close, it is clear that the victim had money and the taste to use it well. Her silver-grey suit is linen, cleanly cut. The pearls at her neck glow softly under the arc lights. Her hair is finely white, spun sugar rising sparsely from the pinked crown of her head. It's this that ages her, the sparseness of her hair; a bit thicker and she could be in her seventies. As it is, Picaut puts her closer to ninety. There's still something hauntingly familiar about the shape of her face, the fine, clear angles of her cheeks.

6

Thoughtful, she says, 'We need a name.'

Rollo bites the edge of his thumb. 'Car's locked. We haven't got in yet.'

To the waiting techs, Picaut says, 'Anyone?'

A blond forensic technician pushes through the throng and has the driver's door open in less than the time it takes Rollo to light a cigarette. The photographers step in to do their work and then Picaut is free to crouch down and study the damage done by the knife.

The incision to her throat is clean-edged, which gives credence to Picaut's hope that it was done post-mortem. She levers her pen between the teeth and confirms that the tongue has, indeed, been cut out and that yes, this too almost certainly took place after death; the blood is dark.

On a roll now, Picaut searches for an ID. The jacket pockets are empty, but there's a leather bag in the passenger footwell in which she finds, amongst other things, a passport and two credit cards. Standing, she says, 'She's Madame Sophie Destivelle until we find anything to say otherwise.'

Petit-Evard opens his mouth, thinks for a moment, then shuts it again and starts a web search on his phone. Picaut is beginning to like him.

Sylvie arrives from soothing the stationmaster. Her spiky hair is black these days, and she wears a short skirt, thick tights and big leather boots, relics of a year spent undercover in the anarchist networks south of the Loire.

Unless Petit-Evard is hiding more skills than he shows, she's the best they have just now with tech. To her, Picaut says, 'I want to know where she came from and where she was going. Get me anything and everything Sophie Destivelle has ever done.'

'On it.'

Sylvie departs. Petit-Evard says, 'She'll be lucky; there's nothing on Google. We could tidy up her image and put it out on Interpol? Somebody must know more about her.'

'I know more about her, if I could only remember.' It's like a fish, slipping through her fingers, her memory of this woman. She can feel the shape of it, taste the texture on her tongue. 'She's been in the papers. On the news. On Facebook. Something. She was sad. I remember thinking that.'

'So do we run her out to the news wires?'

'Not yet. I want to find out more about who was making what point and why, before we do anything rash.' Rising, Picaut says, 'Get her to pathology. Eric's got new software that makes people look more alive: we can run that through the databases and see what turns up. And check the car. If it's registered to her, that's our route in. If it's not, then we want to know where she got it because— Ah, fuck. Just when things were going well.'

A pearlescent white BMW rounds the corner and swings into the car park. Picaut feels her face stiffen; those parts that are not already stiff. She shoves the car door shut with her shoulder. To Petit-Evard, she says briskly, 'Head back to the office and start a search on the car registration. If Sophie Destivelle is not the owner, track down whoever is, and find out what they know about her. I'll be at the pathology lab. We'll meet there in half an hour and see if the post-mortem tells us anything beyond what we already know.'

He may be new, Petit-Evard, but he's fast off the mark. His car is reversing out of the gateway before the BMW has fully parked.

Rollo catches Picaut's eye. 'Want me to stay?'

Yes, but also . . . definitely not. Some things she needs to manage alone from the start.

She says, 'No, I'm fine. See if you can shake any trees that have assassins hiding in them. I want to know if there's been anyone of this calibre touting themselves around the dark spots of Europe.' And so Rollo, too, has gone by the time Ducat steps out of his car. The sundry technicians clear his path.

8

Pegged of tooth, squat of frame, with a lawyer's pedantry and an unreconstructed attitude to women, there was a time when the city's prosecutor, Maître Yves Ducat, barged roughshod over Picaut, trampling the fabric of all but her most solid cases. Tonight, he has a head cold, and arrives partially veiled behind a linen handkerchief. Nodding a greeting, he stares gloomily at the dead woman, the gunshot wounds, the car. 'Who is she?'

Picaut says, 'Sophie Destivelle.' And at his frown: 'We've drawn a blank on the name. Petit-Evard is tracing the car.'

Ducat pulls a face. He angles awkwardly at the waist to peer into the car. 'Professional hit?'

'That's the assumption.'

'Fuck.' She waits. Ducat is a man who chooses his words with care and this one is spoken with a distinct lack of inflection. He takes time to fold his handkerchief away. 'The Americans are not going to like this.'

Indeed. In an arrangement made under the old administration, the US security services have brought their oh-so-quiet anti-terrorist summit to Orléans. It's been running for two days now, and is due to go on for another three – unless they decide it's unsafe to continue.

Picaut says, 'Think they'll cancel?'

'If they do, you and I will join the queue of those trying to find work in poorly paid positions at minor security firms.'

And that, too, is true. A quite spectacular amount of effort went into persuading the CIA, the NSA and the many corporate-owned acronym-holders who populate the global espionage community, that they really wanted to come to Orléans for this year's conference. That choice was made on the understanding that the city was safe. A mutilated woman sitting in a car with two shots to the chest and one to the head is not, by anyone's measure, safe.

'Job share?' Picaut says. 'I'll take the nights if you take the days.'

Ducat pinches his lower lip. 'If, on the other hand, we can get the suits on side, they'll keep the press off our backs. The threat of the NSA rifling through a lifetime's emails should be enough to silence anyone who thinks they're going to make a name for themselves breaking a hot story. I'll take care of this. Just make sure to let me know what you've got when you've got it.'

Ducat is being unusually gentle. Picaut feels the touch of his gaze, which is novel enough to make her turn. And so she finds that he is not looking at her, but is, instead, examining her reflection in the wing mirror of the car. Thus, unexpected and unplanned, she sees herself clearly for the first time in . . . a long time.

She is thinner than she was, paler skinned and darker haired with none of the sun-bleached strands that used to lift the functional shortness of her hair. Too long without sun has made the freckles stand out across her nose, and her eyes are perhaps more hooded than she thought they were, more contemplative.

All of which is fine, but then this is her right side, her good side, the side she has been carefully keeping to the technicians, to Rollo, to Evard. Which is why Ducat is using the mirror. With it, he can see the other side. He is studying it, in fact. Her gaze slides to meet his.

'What?' She hasn't been angry recently. The jolt feels good. 'You think I'm not ready?'

'Not at all. Not. At. All.' Ducat smiles. He *smiles*. He reaches out haphazardly and pats her on the shoulder, more of a bear-paw batter on her upper arm. 'Welcome back.'

08.05

'She was beautiful, wasn't she?'

Cleaned of blood, Sophie Destivelle's naked body lies on

10

the steel trolley, while a photograph projected at twice life-size onto one wall of the pathology suite shows her as if alive: radiant and engaging.

In the past, Picaut would have had to wait for the victims' families to provide pictures of them as they were in life, but Eric Masson is experimenting with software that can take the lifeless face of a subject and warm it, brighten it, open the eyes and give them spark, return the smile to unsmiling lips – and this is the result.

Sophie Destivelle is the epitome of elegance and grace. Her gaze is frank, open, knowing, and she is laughing at something Picaut can neither see nor hear. This is a woman of intelligence and wit.

Picaut walks up to her image so that they are nose to nose, eye to eye. 'Why do I think I know her?'

'Half of France will think they know her. The software says her bone structure is a hybrid of Fanny Ardant's and Audrey Tautou's. I tweaked the colour of her shirt to match one that Tautou wore for a photo shoot last year; it's a better fit for your woman's skin tone. If I took forty years off her, she'd be in Hollywood, earning millions.'

'Can you make her look sad? Just subtly?'

'Sure.' A click of the mouse, a few keys tapped, and a new image appears beside the first one, in which the radiant smile becomes progressively more pensive until, in the tilt at the edge of her eyes, the lines about her mouth, is the grief that Picaut felt in the station car park.

'Stop.' It tugs at her gut, this look. 'That's her.'

Eric makes a series of images, all almost-but-not-quite-exactly the same. Looking up, he says, 'You OK if I put you down as investigating officer? If it has your name on it, the press will take a lot more notice.'

This is probably true. She has always been led to believe that the media have the memory span of a goldfish. In the lead-up to the fire, she discovered that where she is concerned, they can be remarkably tenacious. Today, this is not an advantage. She says, 'The press can't get near this. The conference needs to stay under the radar. We can't have the media sniffing round the city.'

Eric cocks his head. 'There's a conference?'

True to spook-ish form, the briefings are need-to-know and until this moment, Eric didn't. And now he does.

She says, '*Je suis Charlie.*'

'I'm sorry?'

'The attacks in Paris switched us from being cheese-eating surrender monkeys to the CIA's favourite new friend in the war on global terror. In demonstration of their undying love, they moved their annual meeting from Bermuda or Panama or whichever tax haven they normally sun themselves in and came to meet here instead.'

Eric whistles. 'Not a good time to have an assassination on the doorstep. Are they connected?'

Clever Eric. 'I don't know. The CIA certainly knows where to buy professional hit men. I don't want to think about the diplomatic fallout if it turns out they're involved, mind you.'

'What does Ducat think?'

'He thinks it's a catastrophe in the making and we'll both lose our jobs if we don't sew it up fast.'

'Better get going, then.' Eric pulls on a white coat that would look geeky on anyone else but makes him look distinguished. 'Help yourself to some coffee. I won't be long.'

He is a man happy in his work. Part of the negotiations that lured him to Orléans involved a re-tooling of his suite and now the white tiles and stainless steel that mark post-mortem rooms the world over also bristle with new technology, the use of which only Eric fully understands.

He starts with the photographic phase of his examination. A rail-mounted camera automatically takes serial images of

Sophie Destivelle from top to toe, left side and right. From this combination of multiple still shots a life-sized collage is built, then projected onto the wall alongside the life-like variation created by Eric's software and the crime scene pictures sent in by the techs. Joining them are various angles showing the gunshot wounds in her clothed, and then naked, torso. The entry and exit wounds are both small and neat.

Looking at their magnified images, Picaut says, 'Glock with suppressor?'

'Common things are common, so yes, that seems likely. Certainly it was a nine-mil of some sort. Ballistics sent an email just before you got here to say they've got the rounds out of the car. They'll give us something definite in an hour or two.'

'Is there any chance she was dead before the shooting?'

'Wouldn't have said so. You think it's possible?'

'Something doesn't feel right. She doesn't look the kind of woman to die without a fight.'

'I can run some bloods in case she was drugged?'

'Thanks.' They fall back into silence. Picaut heads to the table where the victim's clothes and personal effects are laid out in an order that becomes progressively more personal: suit, shoes, shirt, bra, stockings, underwear. It's all very clean. She pulls on some gloves and begins to check the labels.

After a while: 'What kind of Frenchwoman buys all her clothes in America?'

'A wealthy one?'

'Even the underwear?' This is not good. If she turns out to be American, Ducat will— 'Hello . . .'

Eric knows her well by now. His head comes up. 'What?'

'There's a business card sewn into the lining of her jacket. Have you got scissors?'

'Scalpel?'

'That'll do.'

'Wait. Let me take some pictures.'

13

Eric has a lens that magnifies by three orders of magnitude. Picaut holds up the lining of the suit, where she has felt the edges of a business card hard against the silk. Images of the suit lining appear on the screen. The silk is a deep, dove grey, the linen paler. The thread between them changes colour and count at the lower corner. 'Re-sewn,' Eric says. 'Good find.'

He wields his scalpel with natural dexterity, slips the thread into a specimen bag for analysis, eases out the card with tweezers and lays it on a tray. 'Don't touch.'

'I wasn't planning to.'

Together, they lean over to look.

ELODIE DUVAL
CREATIVE DIRECTOR
RADICAL MIND
ECD1@RADICALMIND.COM

Eric photographs the card with his macro lens and posts the image onto the screen beside the serial images of Sophie Destivelle's body.

Picaut says, 'See if you can get some fingerprints from that. I want to know if Sophie put it there, or someone else.' The skin along her jaw itches like it did in the car park. Unthinking, she lifts her hand to rub at it.

'*Inès!*'

'Sorry.' She jams her fists in the pockets of her jeans. Her jaw line is the surgery that keeps coming unstuck. Her arm, her shoulder, her neck – all of these healed after the second set of procedures. Her face is another matter. Her face is why she took six months to persuade various men – and a couple of women – in suits that she was fit to come back to work and didn't need, thank you very much, the oh-so-generous

14

invalidity pension they were offering her. Real work, if you please. Actual casework, not spreadsheet hell in an office.

Her face still itches, though.

Eric raises one brow. 'Ingrid said to remind you that you have an appointment at noon.'

Ingrid – her surgeon, his most recent lover – has the power to send Picaut back to the spreadsheets, or the indefinite hell of gardening leave. Simply to stand in her company is terrifying, which is why, obviously, Picaut has a habit of forgetting her appointments. She spreads her hands wide. 'Eric, I've got a case.'

'Nothing's going to happen that's so important you can't leave it to the team. Rollo's cool. He won't fuck up.'

Cool? Rollo? She is taking a breath to argue when a buzzer sounds and a screen lights up on the wall, showing the feed from the camera at the entrance. And here is the man himself, darkly dishevelled, grinning up into the CCTV lens.

Picaut leans over to the microphone. 'Got anything?'

'Nothing useful.' Rollo looks up into the lens. 'Nobody's acknowledging any hits for hire in the vicinity. And I checked the tapes. There's nothing on the station CCTV, nothing on the surrounding roads. Whoever did this knew how not to be seen.'

Picaut says, 'They put a head shot through a six-centimetre gap on an angle of thirty degrees to the vertical. It was expecting a lot to think they'd let themselves be caught on camera.'

She buzzes him in and listens to his feet, light on the stairs. As hers was, his attention is caught by the screen on the back wall and he whistles, softly.

'We're going with "striking",' says Picaut.

'Right.' As she did, he walks up to the wall and stands nose to nose with the dead woman for a moment before he passes to the images of the gunshot wounds. He says, 'The Americans . . .'

15

'Ducat is doing what he can to placate them.'

'I know. I've just had a conversation. They're feeling magnanimous, apparently. They're not going to pull out. I was asked to let you know.'

This is . . . novel. 'I hope you passed my thanks back up the line?'

'They got the message.'

To the best of her knowledge, Rollo has never actually been a member of any of the security services, but there's a reasonable chance that he could join if he wanted. Certainly he has more contacts among the acronym-suits than any normal human being.

'We'll have to be seen to be taking this seriously, though,' he says. 'And it might be politically astute to ask for their help.'

'They want in on the investigation?' There's always a catch.

'They won't throw their weight around, but they want to be kept in the loop, yes.'

Picaut winces. 'If that's going to happen, it goes through Ducat. We can't bring them in by the back door. Clear?'

'Clear.' Rollo takes one last look at the shots and heads for the coffee pot. In the new collegiate style that has emerged in Picaut's absence, he pours for Sylvie and Petit-Evard, both of whom follow him in, the latter with details of the car in which the victim died.

'It was reported stolen at eleven fifteen last night from Rue des Auberges, one of the residential streets south of the river. The owner is Monsieur Pierre Fayette, son of Daniel and Lisette Fayette—'

Rollo stares at him. '*The* Daniel and Lisette Fayette? Croix de Guerre, Médaille de la Résistance and Légion d'Honneur. That Daniel and Lisette Fayette?'

Petit-Evard glows in the light of reflected fame. 'The late Daniel and Lisette Fayette who each have streets named after them in Paris, Saint-Cybard, Lyon and Chinon – yes. Daniel died in 2002, Lisette ten years later. Pierre doesn't talk much about his parents. In fact, as far as I can tell, he doesn't talk much to, or about, anyone. He wasn't in when I went round, but I spoke to the neighbours on either side, who say he's a widower: his wife passed away a decade ago. He has a sister, Elodie, but she's not been around since their parents died. They fell out and—'

'Elodie?' Picaut lifts Eric's laser pointer and makes the red dot dance round the image of the business card. 'If Elodie Fayette married and took the name Duval, then Sophie Destivelle was carrying her card.'

Sylvie is already on her phone, fingers flashing. 'Elodie Duval, née Fayette, is a film director. She has pages on IMDb and Wikipedia.'

Picaut picks up a screen pen and draws lines joining the images on the wall. 'So Sophie Destivelle dies in Pierre Fayette's car with his sister's business card sewn into the lining of her jacket. We have a link.'

From links grow pictures and from pictures emerge suspects and cases. She writes *Pierre Fayette?* on the wall above Elodie's card. 'What else did you get on Pierre?'

'Not much. He used to work as an accountant for Rothschild in Berne, but recently retired and lives alone.'

Sylvie snorts. 'What kind of accountant drives a Citroën BX? That car went out of production in 1993.'

Petit-Evard is swift in defence of his contact. 'One who is, according to his neighbours, "very careful with his money". The car is a practical necessity, not a luxury. His father, the famous Resistance fighter, taught him that luxuries were the curse of the capitalist bourgeoisie.'

The team laughs, except for Picaut, who has caught, at last, the fugitive memory she has been chasing since the car park.

Something must show on her face. Rollo glances across. 'You OK?'

She says, 'The Maquis de Morez,' and then crisply, because they're all staring at her now, 'Daniel and Lisette Fayette were in the Maquis de Morez. Elodie Duval's film company, Radical Mind, is making a TV series based on them, billing it as the French version of *Band of Brothers*. They were all over the papers in the back end of last year: it's the highest-funded French series ever.'

'So, was Sophie Destivelle in the Maquis?' Evard asks. 'Is she in the show?'

Sylvie shakes her head. 'If she is, she's kept it off the net. She's kept everything off the net. As far as Google is concerned, she's the original invisible woman. She has a bank account registered in Lyon with five hundred thousand euros sitting in it – round figure, not a cent more or less. The passport and the driving licence were used to set up the account, and the two credit cards were issued from there, but we knew that already. Other than that, there is not a single record of her existence in any of the databases. She has no birth certificate; she hasn't paid taxes. She isn't registered as having married. She hasn't been in hospital or been to the dentist or the doctor. By any usual measures, Sophie Destivelle doesn't exist.'

Petit-Evard frowns. 'That's not possible.'

'Oh, but it is,' Rollo says, and there's a lift to his voice that Picaut recognizes.

Petit-Evard doesn't. 'How?' he asks.

'It's a cover name.' Rollo is as happy as she's seen him: his hair, his smile, his eyes, they shine. 'The Americans are going to hate this. Ducat is going to hate this. We may end up hating it, too. But if Sylvie is right, then Sophie Destivelle is the cover name for a very old, very elegant lady spy.'

February 1944: Supreme Headquarters Allied Expeditionary Force established in Britain. Plans for Operation Overlord – the Allied invasion of mainland Europe – begin.

SOE, F-Section: René Dumont-Guillemet and Henri Diacono dropped into Touraine to set up the Spiritualist network. Trainee operative Miriam Beaufort killed in a training accident at Ringwood airfield. No next of kin.

CHAPTER TWO

ARISAIG, SCOTLAND
28 February 1944

'CAN YOU TILT YOUR head to the left? Good. And if you could take off your scarf? No? If you could just push it down a bit? A little more ... Perfect. They shouldn't send you back. You've done your bit. I told them, but they never listen.'

The photographer chatters on in the whisky-soft burr of the true West Highlander. His room is small and lacks windows, dense with shadows from two arc lights. The camera is pre-war and smells of mildew and something else sharper – photographic chemicals, maybe – that overwhelms the scents of sea and heather. The shutter makes a distinctive dual sound: *snap-click*.

'Look straight ahead. Has anyone told you that you have beautiful eyes?'

'Several. Thank you. And they are not sending me. I go back because I choose it.'

She is sharp: too sharp. He takes a step back. 'I wasn't trying to pick you up.'

Of course you weren't. André, maybe, or Gregor, but not

me. She shrugs, a lift of two bony shoulders. 'I'm sorry. Too many—'

Stop. Unsafe. Too many hours standing near-naked under hot lights with English officers in SS uniform shouting in simulated interrogation, but she can't say that, obviously.

She is tired or she wouldn't even have started. Tired people make mistakes; it's why they kept the lights on, kept her cold and hungry, kept shouting questions, hoping for a mistake, and a reason to fail her.

They stripped her down to her shift, which was surprising: she had thought the English more restrained. They were trying to frighten her, and instead, she lost her temper. They weren't ready for that.

She bit her tongue and spat blood at them, and told them she had TB and they had it, too, now. For a moment, the older one believed her, the one with the guardsman's moustache, but the younger one laughed and hurled a bucket of iced water over her: the blond one who never took his gloves off. He looked thoroughly German even without the fake SS uniform. She hated him. Nonetheless, she didn't talk.

That was nearly a week ago, in a suburb of Glasgow. The whole exercise lasted three days. She is still tired.

The photographer looks more wary now. Tentatively: 'Can you smile at all?' She can. In the flaring lens she sees her solemn-cat face with the too-big eyes, the brief baring of teeth that barely changes it, the dark hair flopping over her brow, cropped short like a boy's at the back and sides, long enough at the front to hide the scar just below her hair line.

Snap-click.

'Thank you. You're free to go.'

No indication of what comes next, of why she is different, why she is still in Scotland, when everyone else was shipped down south weeks ago and has almost certainly been dropped into France. He may not know.

21

He packs up his kit: camera into bag, lights off and left to cool. Never move them when the bulbs are hot; she heard that somewhere.

She opens the door for him. Somewhere beyond is a window and beyond that, a sharp, bright winter afternoon slants towards evening. Clean light floods in; shows up the dust and the unclean floor.

Outside, crows squabble over something too-long dead to be worth throwing in a pot. A car clashes through the gears and stutters away. In the quiet it leaves behind, she hears men call to each other. The intonation is English, or rather, Scots. Her heart aches for it to be French.

The photographer nods his head to her at the doorway. 'You have a briefing with Flight Lieutenant Vaughan-Thomas in the morning. You're free until then.'

She walks back along a gravelled drive to the small cottage where they have housed her, within sight of the shore. A short distance away is the big manse, with its high, echoing ceilings and the smell of polish layered on damp wood, with ivy that is never silent, and windows loose enough that you could lift the putty with a kitchen knife and remove the pane, and nobody would know you'd been as long as you stuck it all back properly afterwards.

The officers live there, the ones who teach her the many ways to kill and stay alive. Technically, she is one of them now, a section officer in the WAAF; she can eat with them in the mess on the ground floor. Today, she prefers the solitude of the cottage with the wild sea splintering on the rocks below the windows.

A black telephone in the living room links her to the main house, so that she can order a meal. Thirty minutes later, a FANY orderly delivers mutton stew, potatoes, pie made from canned pears with a thin, watery cream on top. They are good to those who may die soon. Some days, you'd barely know there was a war on.

She washes up and then settles back in a rust-coloured arm-chair in front of a tiny, almost flameless fire and drinks coffee. She has an idea. She sleeps on it. It is an idea of darkness, and, in darkness, she rises and dresses in her darkest clothes.

As far as she can tell, the men who employ her here in Britain have infinite quantities of money, and they are anxious that their recruits, who may have their lives stripped slowly away when in France, should want for nothing while in training.

So for the first time in her life, she has new clothes. Not only new – these have been handmade to her size by a little Jewish tailor in a back street in London to designs current in France, using textiles brought over by men and women whose lives have been risked to get them here.

His designs, in her opinion, are less than perfect. As an alternative, she brought her own clothes. The tailor didn't want to copy them, but she is an officer; they have given her a rank. He makes what she wants.

Now, she wears blue-black trousers and a shirt that are modelled on her brother's. She has dark, rubber-soled shoes and an elasticated belt with a leather pouch that contains all she needs.

You have to make it true. So said the soft-voiced tutors, the ones who never relaxed. Whatever you are doing, whoever you are being, every part of you must believe it. Take the part of your heart that works for us and bury it so deep that even we are not sure it is there. The Boche are not stupid. They smell deceit the way a hound smells fox shit. So know what you are, and make it your truth.

This is her truth, therefore: that she is a cat burglar, a spy, come to steal secrets from the heart of the Firm, and they will shoot her if they catch her.

It is after midnight. The sky is a hard and brilliant black, cut through by the edge of the moon. The air smells of cold, salt, heathland. A fine frost lies like ground glass on the paths, the

23

turf, the chimneybreasts. Paris was never like this, never so quiet, never so night-shiny clean.

She keeps the moon behind her, and the sea. The cottage fades back into the gloom. She walks on the gravel, on the outer edges of her feet, heel to toe, heel to toe, feeling the stones press through the soles of her shoes.

Ahead, the mansion headquarters presses its high, hard angles against the sky. She has visited it twice in the three days since she arrived here and it is her opinion that the back door offers the easiest entry. In the starlit dark, she walks round the side.

In her pouch, she has a plastic protractor, the tool of a schoolchild: innocent. If she were caught with one of these in enemy territory (which is to say, her homeland), it would not give her away.

As she has been taught, she leans on the door, slides the curved edge between the lock and the jamb, feel-hears it push down on the snib and forces it back.

In.

And now up.

A set of servants' stairs leads up from the back door to the first floor. The third, fourth and twelfth treads creak. She steps on the very outer edges, letting her weight bear down slowly, evenly. She is quiet. She is not soundless. Nobody comes to stop her.

She reaches the head of the stairs. Her target is on the second floor, on the western side of the building. The falling moon spins long, lean shadows through the windows. Ghost-like, she follows them past locked doors behind which sleeping men may, or may not, lie. She presses her ear against the wood of the first two, hears nothing, carries on, turns left and comes to the corridor's blind end, and the final locked door that is her goal.

This one won't give to the protractor. In her pack are half a

24

dozen hairpins, a paper clip, a small pair of women's tweezers and a torch of a small enough size that she can hold it between her teeth.

The lock is harder than any of the test ones they gave her on the course, but not impossible. She thinks no lock will ever be impossible now, which is doubtless what she is meant to think: above all else, the English training fosters a sense of invincibility and immortality in those who complete it.

She has seen precisely this over-confidence kill them, but here, tonight, the lock yields to her soft insistence and she is in.

Into a heady fug of stale cigarette smoke, gun oil and sweat. Her torch stabs the dark. The office is not huge, but the only window is shuttered for the blackout and the resulting unlight is far denser than the night outside.

Closing the door, she resists the temptation to switch on her torch. She knows roughly where she's going. Four paces forward is the desk and to its left, set back against the wall, is a locked filing cabinet. She navigates to it by touch.

Still in the dark, this lock yields to the hairpin in under a minute. She gives a small hiss of satisfaction and now she does switch on her torch. She has taped cardboard over most of the face, so that the beam is pencil thin and will not give her away. Holding it between her teeth, she starts a method-ical search.

The top drawer is full of lecture notes; the middle contains plans for 'schemes' by which students may be tested physic-ally, mentally, emotionally. She knows them all.

Here in the bottom drawer, though:

STUDENT EVALUATION REPORTS

She riffles through the Fs. They're ordered by the date of their progress through the training, not by alphabet. Fleming:

'41, Fortuyn: '42, Fuentes: also '42, Fairburn-Drummond: '43 – ha! – Fabron: '44.

The other files have photographs; hers does not. The young man with the neat eyes has not developed the pictures he took in the afternoon. She feels naked, somehow, un-named. Her palms sweat.

She leafs past the front pages and the minutiae of her life story, past the chain of improbabilities that has brought her here.

And then, on the third page, this:

```
Fabron has demonstrated a satisfactory
degree of physical endurance compared
to the men of her group, but less
impressive in mental strength.

Shows a marked resentment of authority.
No vestige of military discipline. Does
not mix greatly with her peers, does
not socialize, does not take part in
the voluntary schemes of her cohort.
Dangerously solitary.

Displays an adequate quickness of
thought, but temper flares too readily,
particularly under pressure. At other
times, a tendency to over-confidence
and inclined to make elementary
mistakes.

Morse is adequate for the field, but
could be better if she applied herself.
Ciphers: good comprehension, but
careless application. Has neither focus,
nor patience to be a W/T operative.
```

```
Handling of weapons, explosives,
grenades: satisfactory. Unarmed combat:
exemplary.

Overall: this woman is too unstable to
use as an operative in the field.
Suggest she is sent to the cooler and
other work found, perhaps in ciphers,
at which she shows some proficiency.
```

Unstable.
Unstable? Jesus Christ . . .

Eyes closed, she lays the sheet down on the floor, rocks back on her heels. Words float past her half-closed eyes: adequate, satisfactory, elementary mistakes. Elementary?

Fuck them. This is not how it is supposed to go. This is her truth: she is a spy, and an angry one.

She could set fire to this place, then see if they like that. There will be cigarettes somewhere, and a lighter: no office is without them. She searches swiftly. Not on the desk, not in the top drawer, but – ah! – here, under a cardboard file, which in itself would burn swiftly if one were to crumple the top page and—

'I wouldn't, if I were you.'
Merde!

Spinning, her elbow . . . the edge of her hand . . . Nearby, a man's throat, low down: sitting . . . a blue-grey uniform . . . blue bands on the sleeves . . . Eyes that rest on her face, pale in the shine of her torch. They glance down and back up. She glances down with them, and sees a standard-issue Enfield revolver. Above it, sun-gold hair and a lazy smile that is burned on her memory.

All this in the time it takes to complete the turn. Her hand stops just short of his throat. She spits out the torch. 'You!'

'Who else?'

It's him: Laurence Vaughan-Thomas, the officer she is supposed to meet in the morning, but he is also – fuck you – the Aryan blond one of the two interrogators in Glasgow, the one who threw iced water on her. Here, the uniform is RAF, not SS. The difference is cosmetic. He still wears his gloves. Idiot.

Three feet separate them. A chair stands to her left, the door is to her right, easy on its hinges, but still pushed closed. He hasn't entered on silent feet; he was always here. She didn't check the room.

. . . inclined to make elementary mistakes . . .

Fuck them.

Archly, she says, 'You are a Boche spy?'

He runs his tongue around his teeth. 'If I were, I think Germany would have won the war by now. Certainly, we would have no functioning networks in France. So no, I am not a spy. I, in fact, have good reason to be here. You, however, are about to be an arsonist, which will certainly terminate your career.'

'What career? It's already over.'

'Possibly. You can certainly ensure that it is.' He nods to the file that lies on the floor between them. 'Were we unfair?'

That's not worth an answer. She has no gun, but there's a knife in the front of her pack. She leans back against the desk and lets her hands drift behind her.

He laughs, or perhaps it's a sigh: she can't see him well enough to decide. She says nothing, but, as if at her request, he stands up, strolls to the door and flicks on the light switch. The bulb is feeble and stained with fly dirt. The darkness doesn't recede much; the shadows just become less distinct.

Returning, he pulls a pipe from his pocket and devotes himself to filling it, tamping it, lighting it. Blue smoke blurs the air and she adds to her internal list of stupid mistakes the fact that the gun oil she smelled on the air was fresh while the smoke was stale, and it was not from cigarettes alone. Both should have told her he was there. This mistake is hers.

She is not the one making mistakes now. In the few seconds in which his back was turned as he walked to the light switch, she transferred her knife from her pack to her pocket. She is fairly sure he didn't see.

Back at his chair, he regards her, flatly. 'Shall we stop playing games? You are Amélie Fabron. You were born in Paris on the fifth of January 1926. Your mother was English. She served as a nurse near the front line of the Somme. Your father was amongst the many injured. She tended him back to health. Am I right so far?'

She doesn't move. This is like the interrogation practice. He sighs, noisily, and runs his tongue round his teeth again. The front two are very slightly crooked, his only flaw. She focuses on the place where they cross.

'What is not on the record is this: your parents were both active in the very earliest days of the Resistance. They were betrayed by an informer and shot during a raid on one of their first meetings. This was August 1941.

'After your parents' deaths, you were taken in by your neighbours, the Monins, who shared their views. You lied about your age and began to train as a nurse, in the way your mother had. You became close with their son, Alexandre, who was an active member of the Communist Resistance in Paris. He was convicted of taking part in the killing of Colonel Wolfgang Koch of the Sicherheitsdienst on the eighteenth of February 1942. He was put before a firing squad on—'

'March twenty-fourth.' Some things will make her speak and this is one of them. The date is etched on her mind, and the words of his last letter. *My love, today I will die. This is war. Many men will die, but I have the privilege of knowing the hour and the means. My joy is that I can think of you as I take my last breath. Do not give up the struggle . . .*

'Did you love Alexandre?'

Love? Do you even understand what that means? She is eighteen years old and knows without question that she has plumbed the full depths of love; that she will never love again. She spits on the floor.

He sucks on his pipe. 'Your romantic enthusiasms do not interest me. What I care about is your motivation. Let me go on. After Alexandre's death, certain members of the Resistance contacted you and certain arrangements were made. By the summer of forty-two, at the age of sixteen, you were an active member of one of the *équipes de tueurs* that ply their trade in the area around the Passy metro station in Paris.'

He leaves a gap. She doesn't say no.

He goes on. 'So, these *équipes* – correct me if I go wrong, our information grows a little hazy here – there are three of you in each team: young men and women, often students, highly motivated. You know only each other. Your names are not on any lists, for which you should be duly grateful because if one thing is killing your compatriots by the dozen, it's their habit of writing down long lists of each other's names in the mistaken belief that the Boche will never read them.'

'And what is killing your compatriots is their habit of sitting in Parisian cafés talking English amongst themselves in the mistaken belief that the Boche will never hear them.'

'Touché.' He looks down, and then up again. A smile is hidden in that movement. In her mind, her knife slices his throat and his blood wipes away all smiles.

'Anyway, those of you in the teams have no role in day-to-day Resistance work, and in this way, you remain above suspicion. You act only when someone brings information of a Frenchman who has betrayed one of your own to the Boche, at which point you kill him – or her – within the next forty-eight hours. Your team's score over the eighteen months of its activity, so I am told, was nineteen, two of them women. Six of these kills are attributed to you alone. You were proficient with a gun and our instructors inform me that you are one of the best shots they have ever trained. The knife, however, was your favoured weapon. You cut out the tongues of those who had informed against their countrymen. There is a rumour that you did so when they were still alive.'

He leaves another heavy pause. What does he want? An apology? This is war: you choose a side, you take a risk. In the cells of the Avenue Foch, they gouge the eyes out of living *Résistantes* with a fork to make them speak. Taking a tongue is nothing.

He is watching her, his eyes stitching the lines of her face. She wishes she knew what he was seeing. He says, 'Do you know how many kills you have to make before you're accounted a fighter ace in the RAF?'

Don't know. Don't care.

'Five.' He touches something on his jacket; it may be the mark of an ace. She doesn't care about that, either. 'Five Huns down and you're considered the best. There are not many aces flying the skies of Europe. Even in the army, half a dozen accredited kills is viewed as exceptional. There are men who go through an entire war and never draw blood. There are others who kill one man and never sleep properly again. Few and far between are those who can kill at close quarters without remorse or regret or recriminations afterwards. The army that can recruit such men – or women – to its side is the army that has an advantage. Just one, in the right place at the right time, can turn the course of a war.'

Something is happening beyond the words; beneath them; behind them. She is being tested. She doesn't know for what. She sits very still.

The blond Englishman blows smoke at her. 'You were doing well. Why did you leave Paris?'

Her mouth dries on old, bloody memories. She lets out a slow breath. Careful now, careful. Here is her truth. 'We were blown. Emile Gaubert brought us a new target. He had been caught and turned. That's what they're good at: find a weak one, take him, turn him fast and send him back before anyone notices he's gone.'

'Or her.' That's not worth an answer. He smiles at her obduracy. 'So Gaubert sold you? What happened?'

'The Boche were waiting. There was a shootout.' In her mind, the rattle of automatics, the crack and whistle of rounds on stone, the stench of blood, the feel of it, hot and slick on her hands. Run. Run. *Run!*

In the room, the cold, grey eyes, watching, testing her truth. 'Your two team members were killed in that ambush. Only you escaped. How?'

'I don't know.' How many nights has she lain awake, asking this question, searching for an answer that makes sense? 'I think they weren't expecting a girl.'

It works. He nods, dryly. 'I expect they weren't. Nor was Gaubert, evidently, when you went back two days later to cut his throat.' He takes another suck on his pipe. His eyes are the grey of the sea, and as flat. 'How did you get to England?'

Four weeks of hell, through autumn and into winter, nights spent lying in the open, waiting for boats that didn't come, days spent in terror, hiding in barns.

Does he want to know this? She thinks not. She says, 'My mother's cousin lives in Brittany. I went to visit her. She knew some men, who knew of a boat.'

He blows a thin stream of smoke down his nose. 'Look in the files. Go to D and find a Frenchwoman.'

She hunts through the file – Donaldson, Dupries, Danailov – until she finds a name that might be French: Sophie Destivelle.

Four identical photographs are fastened to it with tiny

paper clips. The face is familiar, framed in a lop of dark hair, the features cat-shaped, pale, too-big eyes—

She turns back, holding it up by her own face, as to a miniature mirror. 'What's this?'

'You.'

'I can see that. Why?'

His pipe has gone out. He lays it on the floor and leans back, hands linked behind his head. 'Amélie, think. If the Boche got hold of these files, would you rather they read glowing reports of agents we had sent into the field? Or reports of miserable failures who have been packed off into obscurity?' He tilts his head. She thinks he may be laughing at her. 'If any of what's on the first card were true, you would never have got this far. Trust us. We are neither blind nor irretrievably stupid.'

She has never thought that. Still, something is not right. He is watching her too closely, testing. She has passed all of their tests. She will pass this one. She has to.

He says, 'Everyone is given a cover name when they go into France. The owner of this one no longer has a use for it.'

A dribble of sweat slides down her spine. 'Who was she?'

'A Frenchman, like you. She ran an escape network down south, running out of Marseilles. When it was burned, she got out over the Pyrenees.'

His voice is edged in black, like a telegram.. *We regret to inform you . . .*

Thinly: 'How did she die?'

He has to think before he answers, sift through his words as if language is a forest with too many trees and not quite enough wood. 'She went through the same training as you, but earlier: she finished around the time you were sprinting up the hills out the back there, carrying big lumps of wood. She was good. She got as far as Ringwood and the parachuting. You'll remember, I imagine, how excessively careful the ground staff were about packing the chutes, to make sure none of them candled?'

Before her eyes, his hands make the actions: right hand high, fingers folded together, plummeting, and then *pouf*, left hand at floor level, fingers all spread open, for the impact.

'No.' She slides the file back into the cabinet, slides the drawer shut and makes for the door.

'Wait!' He catches her as she grasps the handle. He is fast and strong, but he has left his gun by the chair, and she may have made elementary mistakes with her breaking and entering, but her unarmed combat is exemplary.

She does throw her elbow to his throat this time, leans against his grip, all her weight down until he stumbles, off balance, choking.

She's kept herself between him and the door. With her free hand, she reaches again for the handle.

'Don't!' Quickly, he says, 'You know if you leave, you're finished?' His voice is muffled by the floor.

'I got out of France. I can get back in again.' It wasn't the original plan, but just now she's angry enough to do it, and deal with the consequences after.

She eases the knife from her pocket. Breathless, he says, 'Amélie! Don't be a fool. There are three men outside the door. You're good, but not that good. If you kill me, you're dead. Is that what you want?'

Fuck you all.

She lets go of the knife. She still has his arm locked across his back in a grip framed to cripple. She leans on it, harder. 'I don't work with liars.'

He doesn't scream yet, but she hears the change in his breath. Tightly: 'Every soul in this whole bloody war is a liar to themselves or somebody else.'

'Why did you kill Sophie Destivelle?'

34

'Why would you kill someone who wanted to work with you?'

That's easy. Why did she ever kill anyone? 'She was selling you to the Boche.'

She feels him nod. His breathing is becoming wetter. Hoarsely, he says, 'If we're going to talk, may I be allowed to sit up?'

He is slow to rise, rubbing his elbow and wrist. Back at his chair, he has the sense not to pick up his weapon. He does refill and relight his pipe. His hands are steadier than they have any right to be, steadier than hers.

Smoke blurs the space between them. She waits.

He says, 'Hitler is desperate to discover the date of the Allied invasion. If you had the Führer breathing down your neck demanding answers, what would you do?'

'Burn a line. Catch the organizers, turn one of them, and send him back as if he, himself, were escaping.'

'Exactly. Sophie Destivelle's line was burned. There was a shootout. She was the only one who escaped.'

Something sinks in her stomach. 'Like me.' Her throat is dry. Her hands are wet.

'Exactly so.' His gaze rests on her face. She keeps it still. She has played against more dangerous men than Laurence Vaughan-Thomas. 'And as we have recently established, nobody expects a girl.'

The silence stretches. When it is clear he is not going to break it, she says, 'At Ringwood, when we jumped, my parachute didn't candle.'

'It didn't, did it?'

'I don't understand.'

'We are making you an offer. Work for us, Amélie. *Actually* work for us. Let it be true.'

What is truth? A pack of cigarettes lies on the desk.

35

Without asking permission, she takes one, lights it, and blows a hazy smoke ring.

The taste unlocks her throat. Her hands are steady now. She *is* better than him at this. 'What do you want me to do?'

He gives a small, short laugh. 'Go back to Kramme, of course. What else?'

No! Thin, hot vomit hits the back of her throat. She swallows it down, burning, tastes the sour fat of the mutton, retches again. 'I can't go back to Paris. I *can't*.' She's not playing now.

'He's not in Paris any more. He's been posted to Saint-Cybard, in the Jura mountains.' She has never heard of it. He says, 'The trains come through it to and from Germany on their way to Paris and down to Lyon, or they used to. The local Maquis are proving quite effective at stopping them.'

'Maquis?' This is a new word. She frowns at him.

'The rural Resistance. The Boche started rounding up men to send to the slave factories in the east. In the cities, there was nothing they could do. In the villages, they took to the hills and lived off the land. They're making themselves useful, derailing trains and so forth.'

A handful of peasants hiding in the woods blow up the occasional bit of railway track and a Boche officer – *this* Boche officer – has been sent to torment them? There's only one reason that could happen. 'You are sending them weapons. They will hit the Boche in the back when you invade.'

'Well done. Very well done.' He smiles round the stem of his pipe, as if she has produced the proof of a knotty equation. 'Saint-Cybard may yet prove to be one of the most strategically important locations on the map. And Sturmbannführer Maximilian Kramme, as you know, is a past master at identifying those who hate him most and then bending them to his will. We are concerned that he may try to turn one of the Maquis. We would rather he believed he didn't have to, which he will if he thinks he has someone in place already. You would fill that role rather nicely.'

His words press themselves into the soft tissues of her liver. Her nails cut grooves into the flesh of her palms. 'How long have you known?'

He takes a long, long drag on his pipe. Then, sadly: 'We didn't. Until just now.'

Fuck!

He lays his pipe on the desk. 'I'm sorry. You really are very good. We had . . . uncertainties. We had to test them. If you had never come; if you had failed to break in; if you had not been so obviously good. But each has happened.'

Has he waited here every night since she arrived? Her mind is fractured. She seeks things to hold on to. 'Did Sophie Destivelle ever exist?'

'She wasn't called that, but the rest was accurate. I made the name up this morning. It would make a good alias for you to take back into France, don't you think?'

He is endeavouring to distract her and it doesn't work. She stabs a finger at him. 'You killed an innocent woman.'

'Perhaps.' He meets her gaze. She reads no regret. 'Our information is never wholly accurate. We knew Kramme had sent a woman up one of the escape lines but we did not know which woman or which line. It was possible there was more than one. When we met you, we thought . . . sometimes an opportunity arises to make a genuine difference. And you are so resourceful.'

He leans back and blows smoke at the ceiling. 'I'm sorry, but we need to know . . . what did he have on you? Everything we understand – every test, every measure of your heart rate, your blood pressure, your answers, your evident enthusiasm when it comes to killing anything in a grey uniform . . . leads us to believe that you hate the Boche. How did Kramme turn you?'

'Elodie.' In that one word is a bright flash of smile, a sweet sweep of innocence in a world of undiluted evil. 'They threatened her.'

'Elodie Monin?' That sad smile again. 'Alexandre's younger sister?' He stands, slowly. 'May I?' There is an envelope on the desk. He slides it to within her reach and sits again. 'I'm sorry.'

He's always sorry. She cannot open it: will not. He says, 'If you don't see, you will never truly believe us. And we need you to do that really quite badly. Please look. Rather a lot hinges on your doing so.'

Nobody told her, but over the past six months, if she has learned one thing about the English it is this: the more polite they become, the more serious they are, and the less likely to bend.

She opens the envelope and draws out the photographs inside.

And now she *is* sick, physically, on the floor, away from her feet and his. The smell hits them both.

Again, he says, 'I'm so sorry.'

'Why? *Why?*'

'I don't know. This is nothing to do with us, I promise you. But we thought she might be central to his hold over you, and so we took the risk of finding—'

'Tomas and Juliette? Her parents?'

'Both shot at the same time she was. And your mother's cousin, although, to be fair, she brought it on herself. On the evening you left, she stood in the town square cursing Hitler and the Reich. They had little choice. She was drawing their attention deliberately, I think.'

Yes, that was her way. And she couldn't know that nobody would ever have turned a machine gun on that particular dinghy as it rowed out from the shore.

So there is nobody left to be hurt. Nobody whose life

hangs on her behaviour. She is free. She feels light, as if her bones have grown hollow. But still. She says, 'Kramme will kill me.'

'Only if he knows you're working for us. Which he won't unless you tell him.'

'You don't understand. He's—' How to explain? Kramme is the stoat, she the rabbit; he the snake, she the small, lost thing, frozen. She thought she had buried this part of herself, but it is here now, quivering, and it has eaten her courage.

'We know how he is. He is ruthless, and he is driven. He inflicts pain for the sheer joy of it, and he plays games with the lives of others. But we play too, and you are our wild card, our chance to end his games for ever.'

'You are sending me back to kill him?'

Does he read the hope in her eyes, the desperate, driving need? Certainly, he laughs aloud, and it is a rusty sound, as if that gate has not been opened for many years. He pats the air with both hands, conciliating. 'Absolutely: for what he has done, and for the damage he may yet do, we want you to kill him. But not yet. That's the thing, Amélie. Not. Yet.'

'When?' Hope is dangerous. She swallows it.

'We don't know, only that there will come a time when his death may change the course of things.' The Englishman leans forward, bony elbows on bonier knees. 'Kramme is good; possibly the best. He runs a network of agents that stretches from Brittany to Belarus. He has moles in Stalin's cabinet. He has men among the French communists who, even now, are working to ensure that France will not veer violently to the left if – dare we say, when – the war goes against the Boche. He is a fulcrum around which many things turn and we can envisage a time when his death could change the whole course of the war.'

'You think I care about the course of the war?'

'I think you want to kill Kramme more than anything else

39

in the world. But I also think you want to live long enough to enjoy having done so. You are impetuous, we know that. You are not controllable; we know that, too – you could not be useful to us if you were.' He waits to let that sink in. His gaze scours her: eyes, mouth, soul. He says, 'Agents lead difficult lives. Double agents lead lives that are not just twice as difficult, but orders of magnitude more so. There will be times when you will forget who you work for, forget where your loyalties lie. You will hoard information to give yourself power. All of this is true, and we expect it.'

'Then how can I be useful?'

'We do not want information from you. We just want this one thing: that you get close enough to Kramme that you can kill him.'

'When you give the order.'

'Exactly so.' He leans forward, pokes the air with the stem of his pipe. 'You will be tempted before that. There may be times when you have the perfect opportunity to kill him. There may be times when he has tortured to death someone for whom, Alexandre Monin notwithstanding, you have come to care. But I tell you this: if you act too early, you will waste your life for no reason. If you wait for the right time, we may be able to help, possibly even get you out alive. Without our help, the Boche *will* kill you and everyone you care for. They know no restraint. You know this.'

She wants to say, I care for no one. I cared once, and look what happened. I shall not make that mistake again.

What she actually says is, 'You wish that I should hide like a slug beneath a stone and hope he does not recognize me?'

'Of course not.' He stands, paces to the door and back. In his own way, he is as agitated as she is. 'He will know you the moment he sees you. And you, of course, will know him, although you must each pretend this is not the case, at least in public. You will be a Maquis girl pretending to be a nurse, so

40

you will be afraid of him but trying to hide it. In private – and he will make sure you have private time together – you will become his agent amongst the Maquis.'

Her tongue curls over. This is what hope tastes like and it is bitter-bright. Cautious, she says, 'I will have to give him things.'

'Obviously.'

'Information about my training.'

'Tell him about the faked report cards. He'll like those. They're his style. It will also not do him any good. He could send someone to steal them all and how would he know which ones were real?'

'Names. I will have to give him names.' Real people, who will die real – and slow – deaths.

Laurence Vaughan-Thomas's pale gaze meets hers. 'Then choose those you give with care and do not grieve. This is war. A few must die that the many may survive. Two things he wants above all else, and must not have. The first is the date of the invasion. The second is the identity of the Patron of the Maquisards in Saint-Cybard. If you give him either of those . . .' He makes the folding shape with his fingers again. 'In the mountains, they have no *équipes de tueurs*. Instead, they have men who make Kramme look kind and each of them loves the Patron as a father. I would advise you not to risk their wrath.'

So this is their deal: walk a knife-edge for us, dance along a tightrope with death on either side, and we offer you a chance – a small chance: she is not stupid – to kill Kramme. Renege on our deal and we will see you skinned alive over a week by your own countrymen.

He is watching her. 'Can you do this, Sophie Destivelle? Will you?'

Can I lie to my countrymen, deceive them, pretend to be what I am not? Of course.

Can I betray those same countrymen for the chance to kill Maximilian Kramme? Really, you have to ask?

She finds that she is smiling, and he is not. 'I can,' she says. 'I will.'

With all of her heart, she believes this to be true.

CHAPTER THREE

ORLÉANS
Sunday, 18 March 2018
09.00

THE RAIN HAS CLEARED by the time Picaut parks her car in the expansive lot outside the film studio and presents herself to the door guard.

That this place merits a door guard is the first revelation. Passing through the soundless electronic doors and into the foyer, she finds herself in a whole new world.

The ground floor is an open-plan office, based on the model of every successful Californian start-up, designed to make the stakeholders – not 'employees' – feel valued, cheerful, productive, *creative*! All around are tall, toned and slender twenty-somethings, alive with early morning zeal that leaves Picaut feeling big and stolidly built, when she is neither of these things.

Already, the air is bright with the scents of green tea and citrus fruits. The decor is all clean lines, tinted in pastels, gold and sky blue over a floor of buffed naked wood.

Most of the desks are Walkstations, separated from the more traditional seated variety by a chest-high wall of zigzagging aquariums, wherein neon-blue gouramis soar through weed forests behind crystal-clean glass, and break-out areas at the margins of the room offer table tennis, table football, running machines . . .

Balancing these – so that nobody feels as if the sedentary are being judged – an array of computer consoles clusters behind a barricade of dragon trees. Here, a dozen youths barely out of their teens fight with silent, earphoned intensity.

Picaut taps the nearest on the shoulder. 'How would I find Elodie Duval?'

He shakes his head and shrugs, all in one fluid movement. Picaut hasn't flashed her card at anyone in far too long. She pulls it now, and holds it in his line of sight. With a sigh, he looks up.

'Elodie,' she says, 'Elodie Duval.'

'I haven't seen her.'

'Would you expect to?'

He runs his tongue round his teeth, takes a pull on a bottle of water and types a message under the action on the screen.

– Anyone seen Elodie?

Within moments, replies are scrolling down:

– Elodie's not here yet.

– Clinton's in though.

– Are you sure?

– Yes, I saw him.

– Bit early, no?

– Wake up, it's later than you think!

– So Clinton then? Can you take her?

– No, I'm heading into a battleground, get Martha. It's what she's here for. Text her.

– No, don't – she's here.

There's barely a pause before a hand falls on Picaut's shoulder and a bright voice says, 'Hi! I'm Martha. I'm an intern here at Radical Mind. We're not expecting to see Elodie until later this afternoon, if at all, but Clinton's upstairs. Please follow me.'

Martha is a strikingly blonde, mid-term-pregnant intern with an engaging smile. Picaut follows her through the buzzing creativity into a lift that carries them up one floor. A short, wide, blue-carpeted corridor stretches to left and right in front of her as the doors hush open.

Picaut steps out. To her left is a closed door: ELODIE DUVAL: CREATIVE DIRECTOR – RADICAL MIND.

To her right, ajar: CLINTON MCKINNEY: EXECUTIVE PRODUCER – RADICAL MIND.

Through the gap she sees more pale wooden floors, a wide open space, a Scandinavian desk near the back. A window stretches along the full length of the room, giving a long view out to the river, shining under the marbled sky, with the pinnacle of the cathedral behind. A lean figure sits behind the desk, his temple balanced on his closed fist. He has steel-grey hair, neatly cut, and glasses with barely tinted lenses.

Quietly, Martha says, 'Best keep to English if you can. He's Canadian. His French is . . .' She makes waveforms with her hands, and ushers Picaut through, alone. The door closes behind her. The air smells faintly of marijuana, which it did not downstairs.

45

'Elodie? You're early! I'm so sorry. We just heard about your godfather. If you want to take—' He looks up. 'Captain Picaut! What a pleasant surprise!' Clinton McKinney's eyes skate away from her face. She's grown used to this, but today he is the first: her team, and those around her, have learned better. He says, 'I have seen you, of course, on the television. Last year?'

'A little longer than that.'

'Of course. Time passes so fast these days, it's hard to keep up. So, are you here in a professional capacity? Or perhaps looking for alternative work? We could always use a woman of your obvious talent!'

McKinney is certainly Canadian, his accent fashioned in Montreal, tempered in Europe, with exclamation points added on the west coast of America and the Antipodean habit of slapping a question mark on the end of all but the most obvious statements of fact.

He says, 'I'm so sorry. I've just this moment had news that one of our contributors has died. One of those who fought alongside the Maquis in the war? I will have to tell the team, so if we could make this fast, I would be grateful. What can I do for you?'

This part of the job, she hates. She rushes at it, to get it over with. 'Mr McKinney, there has been a murder. We have reason to believe that the victim might be known to the studio.'

He blanches. His larynx spasms. His eyes spark wide. 'Elodie?'

'Not Elodie, although her name has come up.' Picaut opens her phone to the image of the business card and lays it on his gargantuan desk. 'A woman using the name Sophie Destivelle was murdered in the small hours of this morning at the Gare des Aubrais. Elodie Duval's business card was found among her personal effects. We need to understand why.'

She does not go into the bloody details of the murder, and

46

McKinney doesn't ask. It seems likely, in fact, that he doesn't care: his attention does not stray beyond his project. Frowning, he runs long, thin fingers through his long, thin hair. 'We can't stop filming now.'

'Nobody's asking you to stop filming. All I need to know is why the murdered woman had Elodie's business card sewn into the lining of her jacket.'

'I don't know. I mean, I don't know why anyone would keep a card in the lining of their jacket, but then, Sophie was a closed book; I really didn't know anything about her. She was Elodie's contact. Elodie found her. Elodie arranged the filming. The rest of us weren't allowed close?'

'You know Sophie Destivelle? You *filmed* her?' God, this is like pulling teeth.

'Not me. She was very elusive. Elodie persuaded her to talk on camera, but she had to get it all at once: the old lady wouldn't sit twice. And it had to be in Saint-Cybard. Where she fought in the war?'

Saint-Cybard. That rings faint bells. Picaut says, 'I would be curious to know how Elodie found her when we can't trace any record of her existence.'

'She's Elodie.' McKinney shrugs, and the angles of his shoulders make it look like some kind of muscular spasm. 'She never gives up. And her godfather gave her a lead, I think. Paul Rey. He's the one who died this morning.'

Picaut types notes into her phone. 'Who died, exactly?'

'Colonel Paul Rey. He was a major in the Jedburghs, the officers who were parachuted in behind the lines to make sure the Maquis kept to the script after D-Day? He became a full colonel later. Also, I think, Deputy Assistant Director of the CIA. The American agencies can be astonishingly arcane in their nomenclature.'

'How did he die?'

'He was ninety-six and he had lung cancer? It was his time.

He knew he was dying. It's why Elodie went to visit him. A last goodbye, so to speak? And he wanted to give her an old ciné film he'd found of the wedding of a German officer that was taken during the war. We're going to use clips of it in the show.'

'Wait, you're telling me Elodie Duval was in America?' Jesus Christ . . .

'Two days ago.' He nods. 'She's due back into Charles de Gaulle just after noon. She texted me last night to say she was on schedule, but then when you came in, I thought she had changed her mind and come back early?'

'I'll need details of her flight.'

'But she can't be a suspect, when she—'

'Mr McKinney, we have a dead woman who died in Pierre Fayette's car with his sister's card sewn into the lining of her jacket. Beyond that, we have very few leads. So I want to talk to Elodie Duval the moment she lands. Look on the bright side: she'll get through customs faster than you'd ever believe.'

'Martha will give you her flight details.' He presses a button on an intercom and Hi-I'm-Martha confirms that Elodie Duval boarded the red-eye from JFK and is due to land at 12.40. Picaut texts the flight number and landing time to Ducat, with a request that he talk to immigration and lubricate Duval's passage through customs.

Martha is considerably more useful than her employer. Without being asked, she also supplies details of Sophie Destivelle's address in Orléans: an apartment on the north side of the river. This proves to be registered in the name of one Céline Sutherland, who does not, as far as the records are concerned, exist. Sylvie and Petit-Evard are dispatched to look into this.

McKinney watches Picaut issue instructions. When she's done, he leans across his desk, fingers locked. 'It was Colonel Rey who first proposed the idea for the show. Elodie was devoted to him. So we absolutely must keep shooting, you see?'

'Mr McKinney, I'm really not arguing about your schedule. I just need to speak with Elodie, to find out what she knew about Sophie Destivelle. In the meantime, if you know of anyone else who might have information about Sophie that would—'

'Oh my God!' McKinney's whole body jolts. 'Laurence! He mustn't hear this from anyone else!'

He is up and out from behind his desk, all angular limbs and long, fast strides. Picaut has to run to keep up. They eschew the lift and take the stairs, bounding down to the floor below where McKinney turns, running backwards with an unexpected athleticism. 'Don't tell anyone, please? We are family here. I must tell them in my own way?'

'Of course.'

She follows him, to see the family and how they respond to the news. They turn right at the foot of the stairs and through the doors into the open-plan meta-space where the interns gather like so many hens in a coop. McKinney winnows through, nodding a lot, smiling thinly, not really connecting. They pass the zigzag aquarium, the Walkstations, the table tennis. McKinney's flickering gaze alights with relief on a figure who is twice the age and three times the body mass of the starved-slim post-teenagers who flit from desk to Walkstation to console and back.

He sits at a desk with his back to the window, and rises with muscular ease at McKinney's nod. Picaut recognizes his type, and he's not the kind of man she'd expect to see here.

'Martin?' To Picaut: 'Martin Gillard is our stunt advisor in the historical action sequences for the film; which is most of it, really: the action. The talking heads take up, by necessity, less than ten per cent of the running time. Of course we introduced the actors to those of the Maquis still alive: to Laurence

49

and JJ and René; to Paul by Skype. The scripts will be based entirely on their testimonies— Martin, I'm sorry, I'm being hopelessly rude. This is Captain Picaut of the Orléans police force. You'll have seen her on the news? Captain, this is Martin Gillard of the—'

'Foreign Legion. BlueSkies. Hollywood. And yes, I have seen you.' Martin Gillard's smile is functional: this is me; my biography in three short words and you can fill in the gaps. His grip is carefully modulated: I could crush your hand effortlessly, but see, I choose not to. And I do not speak in queries.

Picaut works through the sequence. The Foreign Legion takes the hardest men it can find and makes them harder. She has no idea what the entry criteria are for BlueSkies but if Rollo is half right, they take the kinds of men the Foreign Legion has shaped and make them rich doing work even the Legion would not touch. But then *Hollywood*? What kind of man trains with the hardest male bonding units and then steps sideways into the world of air kisses and frippery? He's not joking though. Martin Gillard does not look like the kind of man to make jokes.

Martin Gillard, frankly, looks like the kind of man who could kill half a dozen old ladies before breakfast and not break a sweat. His eyes meet Picaut's with a kind of focused curiosity that makes the hairs on her forearms prickle. He is Caucasian, but his skin is tanned deep as shoe leather, as if he has spent a long time in hot countries with a wind that scalds. His hair is cropped close after the fashion of the US services, but he's a sandy blond, heading towards silver.

He wears jeans and a maroon polo shirt tight enough to demonstrate two things. First, he may be twice the age of the marathon-running interns, but he's easily twice as fit. Second, he is not currently carrying a gun, but he could, without question, put two to the heart and one to the head through a six-centimetre gap with his eyes shut balancing on a unicycle.

In his presence, McKinney deflates. He says, 'We had some bad news from America. Colonel Paul Rey—'

'Is dead. I heard.' A fine white line frames Gillard's lips as he says this. Rey's death has moved him, and he doesn't want to show it. Given his history, it is likely that he knew Deputy Assistant Director Rey of the CIA long before he came here: BlueSkies may be a private firm, but in America, even before the current president took office, the walls between private companies and public institutions were growing porous. Hidden connections are Picaut's investigative lifeblood. Somewhere, there will be a paper trail or its electronic equivalent. Rollo will find it. He's good at that.

McKinney says, 'There's something else. If you'll come with us to the shooting room? I need to tell Laurence the news.'

They reach the back of the open-plan area, where there is a wide, dark double door. A notice pinned above the handle says: SHOOTING ROOM: FILMING IN PROGRESS – QUIET PLEASE.

Picaut has the sense of things running away from her, not yet controlled. She asks, 'Who's Laurence?'

'Group Captain Laurence Vaughan-Thomas, formerly of the British MI6 and before that of the SOE. He was one of those based in the Baker Street London headquarters who sent agents and supplies to the Maquis de Morez, so he had a unique view on their existence. And he's the one who trained Sophie before she was parachuted into France. He's been immensely helpful. Really, finding him was our first real break. He's given such heart to the project. Without him we'd— Laurence! So good to see you!'

The doors spring apart on magnetic rollers. Inside is a small, starkly monochromatic studio. The walls, floor and ceiling are all black. At the back is a black stage with black curtains draped on three sides. A pair of hooded television cameras stare at it, poised, as if over prey.

And there, flooded in artificial light, sitting upright in an armchair, is a tall, lean, ice-haired gentleman – there is no other word for it – dressed for the part in a mustard yellow V-neck sweater and buff corduroy trousers. Every part of him, from the straightness of his spine to the well-combed hair, to the hands laid flat on his thighs, screams his Englishness.

When Group Captain Laurence Vaughan-Thomas stands, stiffly, it is to bow in Picaut's direction: nothing grandiose, but a definite nod of the head. His handshake is firm and feels like a test: weight, muscle tone, balance. He is stronger than his age might suggest. It wouldn't surprise her to find he does fifty press-ups in the morning before a cold shower. He looks like a well-worn seventy-something, yet he cannot be less than ninety years old.

He gives her hand one final squeeze and drops it. 'Captain, what a very great honour. I have seen you on the television, of course, but it is a delight finally to meet you in person.' His smile is careful, hiding teeth that are no longer perfect. As with the dead woman, so with him: there is a patina of grief laid over his features, something about the angles of his lids that suggests he has never known real joy. He switches to French, with the accents of age, of money, of Paris. 'Are you here to see the filming? Or is there a professional reason?'

He's brighter than Clinton McKinney, but then, if he was in MI6, that's to be expected. Picaut draws in a breath. 'Captain Vaughan-Thomas, I'm so sorry—'

August 1940: The Battle of Britain begins with Adlertag – an assault by the Luftwaffe against British ports.

SOE: Special Operations Executive officially formed with orders to conduct reconnaissance, sabotage and espionage behind the lines in occupied Europe. Personal instructions from Churchill: Set Europe ablaze!

CHAPTER FOUR

Warren Road Hospital, Guildford, Surrey
October 1940

He wakes to sun on his face, too much like fire. He flinches away from it and tears at the sutures. Pain makes him mute, holding it in, tight, hard, solid. Don't speak. Hell, but my shoulder hurts. My arm. My *hand*. Don't move. Don't move. Don't bloody move.

'Laurence?' Something touches his face. The back of someone's hand? Gentle. Cool. He opens his eyes, then shuts them tight. Too bright.

'Draw the curtains, will you?' The voice is a man's, cultured, echoing, too big for the room. Soon, the swish of curtain runners, the light, peppery smell of dust and a woman's scent and wine; things from before.

'Laurence? Can you hear me? It's me, Jeremy.'

Jeremy. He has run through the entire squadron, dead as well as living, before other memories line up in his head. Near the top, amongst his father's cousins, is Uncle Jeremy. Not a flyer. High up, though, greasing the wheels that turn. Brigadier Sir Jeremy Vaughan-Thomas, OBE.

'Hello, Uncle.' He sounds like a crow. When did he last

speak? *Chris! Chris! Behind you! Climb! Climb, for God's sake . . .*

'Laurence? Listen to me, it's over. I swear, it's over. No more flying. I promise you.'

But I live to fly.

He opens his eyes.

There is no sunlight now, only a fly-specked electric bulb, and, closer, silvering hair, silvering moustache and silvery-grey eyes, so like his father's – the same long, lean, weathered face that shows nothing and gives nothing and somehow is home.

Jeremy was the younger by eighteen months, the baby of the family. The Vaughan-Thomas cousins were tight as brothers; tighter, possibly. Five of them, and eight in the next generation, all one big brood of second cousins. Seven now that Chris has gone.

Chris.

'I didn't save him. I saw him go down, and I didn't save him.'

'You tried – that's what matters, everyone saw. You're slated for a DFC.'

'I don't want it.'

'Which is why it's not your decision to make.' Astonishingly, the Brigadier leans over and presses a tight, dry kiss to his brow. 'Your father would be proud of you, Laurence.'

I doubt that. 'He didn't tolerate failure.'

'Four kills is not failure. You got the 109 before you went down.'

'And I got this.' He lifts his arm. At the end of it, his hand, which is not his hand, but a claw, clamped round some imaginary toggle. He lets it drop and knows that while this is what he can see, it's the damage to his lungs, the flame-seared fabric of his alveoli, that will invalid him for life if he's not lucky.

His uncle shrugs it off. 'They say the meat and the bone are intact. Your hand will relax in due course and your lungs . . . they should heal, given time. So what you have is a war wound and there have been a lot of those, and there will be plenty more. It's not an excuse for self-pity. It's not as if it's your right hand. You'll be perfectly fit in a month or two. Maybe three.'

This is more like the family rhetoric. There's a relief in returning to normality. The medics said a year, but the family never did believe in the limitations of medicine.

With his good hand, Laurence plumps the pillows and pushes himself upright.

Uncle Jeremy pulls up a chair, screeching iron across the linoleum. Sitting, he looks younger, too young to be a brigadier. War makes things happen faster than they should. He stares down at his hands while he settles on what he needs to say. 'On the topic of which, did you know you spoke German in your sleep?'

Seriously? *Schweizerdeutsch*, if anything. Swiss, not German. The Brigadier has not moved. His gaze is flat, open. It may possibly be hostile, there's no telling.

'Uncle? You *know* I'm not—'

'Lie back, you'll do yourself an injury. Of course you're not. But with your looks and your linguistic capacity, you could pass for the Hun and just now, we have need of that. We might have asked you anyway, but the sleep-talking makes you a perfect fit.'

'For what?'

'For some underhand, undercover work, of exactly the sort your father loved and you loathe. No, hear me out. There's no escaping biology: you are your father's son. And your mother's.'

And there's the rub. From his father come his sharp edges, his failure fully to fit in the world, always the jagged peg never quite settled in the round hole. And from Mother, his polyglot languages, the brilliance of his hair, his unfailingly Aryan looks; none of these is an asset in this war. Alicia Vaughan-Thomas is still alive. One has to imagine she knows her only son is here, wherever 'here' is. She hasn't been to visit.

Uncle Jeremy is still talking. Or asking. Or ordering. By the time you're a brigadier, the two are indistinguishable.

'So this is a straight request, and if you say no, we'll speak no more of it. Would you be prepared to sleep for a night or two in a ward of POWs? They're all airmen: bombers, mostly, two fighters, all in various stages of injury. Duncan Hammond's boys brought down a 109 near Lincoln three days ago. All on board dead, but we'll say you're from that, and we'll make sure you're sporting a few more bandages, make out you've been burned worse than you have. You won't need to talk to them if you don't want to.'

'But I can listen?'

'Precisely.'

'What for?' He has said yes. He was never going to do anything different: that's not how these things work.

'If we knew that, we wouldn't need you. We picked up some radio chatter linked to the hospital, but we can't work out how or why. So just keep your eyes and ears open. I'll see you've got a bell within easy reach. If things get sticky, ring it and we'll pull you out. If you pick something up and want to talk, tell the surgeon your hand is going bad, he'll know what it means.'

His uncle stands, picks up his briefcase, his umbrella. 'We'll get you some reading material so you're up to speed on the Luftwaffe, but don't speak if you're not confident. The more ardent ones have a habit of smothering those of their compatriots who don't say their *Heil Hitler*s with sufficient enthusiasm.'

Two weeks pass, in which time he progresses to the point where he can sit up, can hold his own mug of tea. Being on the ward is harder than he had imagined. He hasn't been in German company since he was fifteen and two years is a long time when there's a war on. His memories of summers on the Rhine are viewed now through lenses of blood.

In poor English, he complains of his hand to an RAMC surgeon who pretends to know no German and the next day, the surgical orderly withholds his breakfast.

An hour later, stomach grumbling, he is wheeled out of the ward and along a corridor to a small, well-lit office which – glory be – doesn't smell of gangrene, burned flesh and antiseptic. The curtains are of heavy maroon velvet, drawn shut. The electric light bulb in the centre of the room is brighter than he's seen all war.

The orderly departs. There are no papers on the desktop, nothing else to see, but in a drawer is a half-empty pack of Player's. He hasn't had one since the accident. His lungs, apparently, are not fit yet, but some things are worse than dying and being smokeless is one of them.

He is bending down to light up when his uncle walks in. 'I'm not sure you should be doing that.'

'Are you going to stop me?' His voice has all the dry rustle of a turpentined rag.

His uncle shakes his head. 'It's your life. I'll have one if you are.' They light from the same flame, share the first, beautiful, cool-hot smoke. It makes him cough, but there is no blood. He doesn't stop.

Sir Jeremy is tired and making no effort to hide it. His skin is grey and taut. The whites of his eyes are cross-hatched in red.

'Got anything?'

Laurence says, 'Gerhard Lange, the Jagdwaffe pilot at the far end of the same row as me, has been passing messages in cipher to one of the orderlies: Whitaker.'

'Whitaker.' A note, scribbled in a small book. 'Conscientious objector?'

'I imagine so, or he'd be in uniform, not mopping floors. He pretends not to understand German. I haven't spoken to him.'

'How does it work?'

'Gerhard attempts *The Times* crossword, leaves it half done. Whitaker picks it up and finishes it. They work out anagrams on the page. Some of the letters are written slightly stronger than the others. If you bunch those together in a grid, they make a Playfair cipher. In German, obviously.'

'Playfair?'

'It's a pretty basic digraph substitution cipher, and not at all secure, but it has the advantage that you don't need a shared key if you have a word.'

'A digraph substitution cipher?'

The Brigadier looks at him as if he's speaking Greek. Laurence says, 'It's harder to crack than single letter subs, but not as hard as the Vigenère. I can sketch it out for you if you like?'

'Not at all. I'm sure you're right. How do you know this?'

'Father taught me; he taught all of us. Chris was just as good.'

'Was he, by God? I never thought that Archie so much as gave him the time of . . . never mind. What does this one tell us?'

'A time and a date and a code phrase: WARM, BRIGHT NIGHT. If I'm right, someone else is coming to meet them both, some kind of organizer.'

'Any idea who this organizer might be?'

'No, but the meeting is on Friday at fifteen forty-seven on the lane that runs behind the hospital. The men are allowed out to walk around without much of a guard. That should be stopped, too.'

'Splendid, I'll see to it. Anything else?'

'The bomb aimer from the Heinkel in bed three, the one with the broken ankle. You might want to pull him out, give him a cup of tea and a biscuit, and bring him back.'

'And why would we do that?'

'Gerhard and the others already think he's a spy. If you give them a good enough excuse, they'll kill him.'

'We'll take a look at that.' The Brigadier stands. 'The medics say you're fit to leave the ward and head back into the outside world. A spot of convalescence in the bosom of your family and we'll have you fighting fit. Lydia is making up a bed for you at Ridgemount as we speak. We're the last men in a family of women, you and I. You'll be mothered and sistered and cousined back to health. After that . . .' There's a spark in the Brigadier's eye: mischief, or something darker. Different, at any rate.

'What?'

'There's a new outfit that has need of your skills.'

'Even with this?' Laurence holds up the wreck of his hand. His German wardmates have been most sympathetic.

'Wear gloves. Nobody will know. And don't smoke too much. I want your lungs back to fighting fitness. But really, it's your brain we need, and your other skills. We'll send you up north for a spot of training, just to make sure you're fit, and then get you where you're needed and put your mind to work.'

CHAPTER FIVE

G OD, IT'S WET. IF it rains any harder, half the bloody mountainside will sweep down and punt Mallaig into the sea.

'Vaughan-Thomas?'

'Here.' Flight Lieutenant Laurence Vaughan-Thomas is lying prone on a rocky shelf halfway up said mountainside. The top third is lost in the cloud layer and has been since he arrived, three weeks ago.

The ghillies said the peak wouldn't be visible this side of midsummer and Laurence, not believing this could possibly be true, took a foolish bet with Captain Patrick Sutherland that they'd see it before they left. With a little under thirty-six hours remaining before they take the train south, he is going to lose.

Captain Patrick Sutherland, late of the Black Watch, is out of sight, over in the bracken to his left. Sutherland was finishing his training as a medic when the war broke out. He could have served as an army physician, but signed up instead in his father's regiment and proved far too valuable to waste his time winding bandages and hacking off limbs. He has seen action in France and was mentioned twice in dispatches during the mayhem of the evacuations the year before, then followed that up with something else more subversive he's not allowed to talk about, but which seems to have involved inflatable rubber dinghies and plastic explosive: certainly he is adept at handling both.

He is the best saboteur Laurence has ever seen, skilled in this mud-soaked squirming over open ground, with a Sten on his back and a long-knife in his boot and earth plastered over his face so that the pale skin doesn't show up; not that anyone can see more than a dozen yards in this murk, but still . . .

He, Laurence, can barely see the rock from whence the call came. He slides over, belly to the heather, breathing in the heady almost-eucalyptus scent of bog myrtle.

And here is Sutherland, crouched in the lee of a rock, alert, cheerful, eyes a-shine, his receding hair line lost beneath a grubby woollen hat that is certainly not standard army issue.

Nothing he wears is army issue: the little tailor of Jermyn Street has done them all proud, and Sutherland has taken to heart the injunction to make the clothes look worn, to the extent that the left knee is already patched and both elbows of his jacket have holes in. He doesn't reek of garlic and Cognac, or have a Gitanes drooping from his lip, but if ever a British officer stuck halfway up a Scottish mountain could look authentically French, Sutherland is doing so. He has rust-red hair, which spoils the illusion a bit, and he doesn't sound absolutely French. His accent, in fact, is decidedly Belgian, but nobody has yet said this puts him out of the running.

At Laurence's stealthy approach, he lifts his hat in salute. 'Fine weather for the time of year.'

Two can play at that game. Laurence forces a cheerful grin. 'Keeps the midges off, at any rate.'

'Right enough.' Sutherland works his way forward a yard or two, takes a look over the edge, down towards their target at the foot of the hill, then edges back again. 'We've got ten minutes, I'd say. They were slow to start.' He fumbles under his jacket. 'Cigarette?'

After seven months' convalescence, Laurence's lungs have been given the all-clear. He smokes now more than he ever did when he was flying. 'Got a match?'

They share the intimacy of the flame, close enough to breathe in each other's sweat, last night's whisky, this morning's coffee, the last breath of bacon.

The last time he was this close to a man was with Chris, on the morning before—

'You all right, Thomas?'

'Fine.'

Sutherland huddles back under the rock. 'Got the Talisker?'

'Of course.' He hasn't. He hasn't worked out how he might get it, either, short of sending down to Uncle Jeremy in London and getting him to ship one up from White's on the overnight sleeper. 'But I won't need it. It'll clear in the morning, McGillivray said so.'

There is a pause. Somewhere, a sheep bleats, lonely in the rain. Sutherland smiles, thinly, round his cigarette. 'Don't ever let the Boche ask you questions. You're a terrible liar.'

He's right, probably. Laurence says nothing. After a moment, Sutherland gets up again, pokes his head out for a look. 'Where are the others?'

'Back at the saddle of Càrn Mòr, where you said.'

'Think they'll hold?'

'Castlemaine might be sticky. He's not keen on the rain.'

'Nor loud bangs, neither. He'll hide in a hole as soon as the plastic goes up. His language is good, though. He'll do well if he's put in a city somewhere, with good roads and a half-decent bicycle. The others? Hughes-Symmonds and Cartwright?'

'Solid. They understood what you wanted.'

'And in France? Think they'll hold?'

France. They're not supposed to talk about France. There's a fiction that the ten of them don't know why they're here or what they're training for. In reality, France is the Promised Land, the place where dreams and nightmares may both come true. Laurence says, 'They'll hold.'

'What about you?'

'I'm sorry?'

'How does it feel slogging through all of this and knowing you're not going at the end of it?'

Again, that stabbing pain in his chest. 'What do you mean?'

There's a silence, jagged at the edges. Patrick Sutherland has grey eyes, the colour of pewter. Here in the water-light of the West Highlands, they are flecked with green to match the lichened rock around them. They can be damned inhuman at times.

He blows out an irregular smoke ring. His gaze is fixed somewhere in the middle distance. 'You don't know, do you?'

'Know what?'

'You're not going.'

'*What?*'

'I don't know why you're here, but it's not to get you ready to jump into France. They won't send you. They can't.'

'Screw you, Sutherland.' He'd leave, but there is nowhere to go, and there is an exercise to finish and he will *not* accept . . .

And yet— He lifts his hand. Bitterly: 'Because of this?' Even here, now, in the middle of nowhere, the curled claw is gloved. 'I can still—'

'Shoot. I know, I've seen you. And swim. Run. Climb rocks. Use a knife. But in France, we not only have to do that, we also

64

have to be invisible. We can dye our hair or cut it short, we can grow beards and shave them off again, we can pad out our clothes to look fat as a goose . . . hell, we can wear a dress if we have to, and look good in it. But if you have a hand that won't unwind, and the Boche get to hear of you, you're finished. The high-ups won't send you. Besides, your uncle won't let them.'

'My—? You utter bastard. Leave my family out of this!'

'That's tricky when your uncle is third or fourth in line to the throne of the Secret Intelligence Service. Add to that the fact that he lost his only son in a downed Hurricane and you're his sole surviving male heir. I'd say he's highly unlikely to send you out on work where the average lifespan is six weeks after landing.'

'My uncle is in the Ministry of Works and Buildings. He has no say in this.'

And at last, a kind of eye contact. Here, in the rain, with his world turning over, it may be hateful, but it is better than before. Except that there is pity in the cold, grey gaze. And truth. It slides, cold, into his belly.

'How do you know who my uncle is?'

'I took a look at our personnel files when everyone else was enjoying the Drambuie the other night.'

'You said you were feeling ill.'

'So I'm a better liar than you are. Or else they expect us to break in. I rather suspect they do.'

'They wouldn't write "SIS" on anyone's file.'

'Naturally. Nor "MI6", which is the preferred title these days, I gather.' The cigarette is pinched out, slipped into an inside pocket. 'I went to college with a chap who really does work in the Ministry. Your uncle has an office there, but he's never in it. All his mail is forwarded. He's in something so hush-hush that my contact was nearly cashiered simply for asking. He had to pretend he was a schoolfriend of your late cousin's, trying to find a way to send condolences.'

'You will leave Christopher out of this.'

There was a time when he thought he couldn't kill. Then the 109s flew out of the horizon line, and he knew he could kill at a distance. Now, he could kill this man with a knife in his throat, and not care for the consequences. He keeps his hands rigid by his sides.

'I'm sorry.' Sutherland raises a placating palm. 'Genuinely sorry. I thought you were—'

'My uncle's stool pigeon.'

'Something of the sort. And you're not, I see that now. And I've spoiled your day, for which I apologize without reservation.' Sutherland eases out from the shelter of the crag, worms forward to the edge and back. 'They're there. We have to go. You can keep the Talisker as a gift from me. Drink it if you hear I've been picked up. Now I think we should show young Devereaux and his friends that we're the better team, don't you?'

HAMPSHIRE AND SURREY, ENGLAND
August 1941

Three months on and the rain-soaked mountains of Arisaig are a distant memory. Between then and now has flowed a sequence of ever more implausible, daring, demanding – technically, physically and mentally – jaunts, each one successful.

The final 'graduation' took them to Cambridge where Laurence Vaughan-Thomas, Patrick Sutherland and 'that youth' – the implausibly young Alain Devereaux – succeeded in blowing up the railway line, at least in theory. The dummy charges did not actually explode, but the local police and the chase team of their fellow students singularly failed to stop them. Celebrations began on the way home and here, at Beaulieu, the Mess has an end-of-term feel to it. Nobody is sober, not even the trainers. Especially not the trainers.

Laurence Vaughan-Thomas and Patrick Sutherland are a team, welded, bonded, tempered to perfect union. They have seen the worst of each other and discovered the best in themselves and there is nothing sweeter than either. They think as one, move as one, drink as one. Elbow through elbow, they are currently doing their damnedest to drink the Mess dry while the boy Devereaux is up on a table demonstrating, with much swinging of arms, the sword dance taught him by his Scottish Highland grandmother. For the first time in many months, Laurence is warmly, giddily happy.

Patrick's face gives him the clue. Patrick, suddenly and disconcertingly sober. 'Thomas. Look left.'

And so Laurence, too, is verging on sober by the time the orderly stamps to attention and snaps his overly crisp salute. 'Beg pardon, sir, but the Brigadier would like a word.'

Oh, God. 'Now? Are you sure?'

'Brigadier's orders, sir. There's a car outside.'

Damnation. Laurence won't show distress, though, not here. With a wink, he throws back his brandy, claps Patrick Sutherland on the shoulder and shouts, 'I'm off to France! See you all in Paris!'

The energy of this keeps him buoyant, humming all the way down the road towards Surrey. Even when they turn off towards Godalming, it is possible to imagine that they are heading for yet another of the anonymous stately homes the Firm has requisitioned for their comfort and delight.

They head over the Hog's Back, past Thursley to the Devil's Punch Bowl, and then it is impossible any more to pretend.

'We're going to Ridgemount?'

'I couldn't say, sir.'

Of course not. He grips the last shreds of hope until the car turns off the road and sails between the tall sandstone gateposts.

He's known these since childhood. The family crest is

carved in weathered relief on each: a pair of wyverns erect embracing the motto: *Familia Supra Omnia*. There has never been anything subtle about the Vaughan-Thomases, even as they made the move from the Welsh border reivers to the core of the English Establishment.

A long avenue of poplars leads to the house itself. Bigger, older, kept in better condition than any of the Firm's mansions, there is no likelihood that this one might ever be requisitioned.

There is, however, a gang of men digging up the croquet lawn to the right of the main drive. The Brigadier is there, in boots and mackintosh, overseeing the mixing of concrete. Clearly, then, this is not some vanguard of the German invasion, shipped in by U-boat to assault the heart of government. Still, it's quite a shock. Gardeners of ancient standing have been given notice for failing to keep this lawn pristine.

Laurence steps out of the car and comes to attention.

'Sir.'

'At ease, Larry, no need to play toy soldiers at home. What do you think of our excavations?'

'Seems a bit drastic, sir. Aunt Lydia won't be amused.'

'Most perceptive of you. She's gone up to town to escape the horror. Won't you come in? Unwin has the coffee ready.'

Laurence surveys the scene as they pass: eight men, a reel of cable of the kind he has been learning to cut. The trench they have dug is twice the height of a small man and concrete is being mixed on the drive.

'Might I ask why you need to bury your telephone line ten feet deep under reinforced concrete when Uncle Charles has his going in from a telegraph post outside the house?'

The Brigadier keeps walking; a man in a hurry. 'What do you think?'

In the drawing room, with the butler gone and the coffee

rich, sweet and hot, Laurence answers. 'I think Uncle Charles is not in the Secret Intelligence Service.'

'Ah.' His uncle looks down at his hands and back up again. There's a weight of sorrow in his eyes. 'Did your father tell you?'

'Father told me very little, as you ought to know. I was informed by a particularly resourceful colleague, Captain Patrick Sutherland, formerly of the Black Watch, now of the Firm.'

'The Firm?'

'The Outfit. The Thing. The training section that nobody will name, that we thought at first was shaping us up to be a commando unit and increasingly appears to be fitting us out to be *Boys' Own* saboteurs in France. Father would turn giddy cartwheels in his grave, but I imagine we are, in fact, all now members of the Secret Intelligence Service, of which you are a senior member?'

'Correct in the last part, not in the first, unfortunately. Would that you were.' The Brigadier makes a foray to the window and stands there, framed in the light, hands clasped behind his back. 'You know, I could have brought a dozen of your contemporaries here, and I don't think they'd have made that link.'

There's a warning in his voice. Laurence feels the kick of it, and straightens.

'You underestimate us, sir.'

'I sincerely hope so.' There is a moment's wretched silence, a last shard of hope, breaking his heart. Then, turning: 'I'm sorry, Larry. You do realize France was never an option?'

'With respect, sir, I feel it could be. I have passed—'

'Of course you have. That was the point. Neither you, nor any of your instructors or teammates, will ever be able to say you didn't cut the mustard. For you and for them, this was

69

essential. But we cannot send you into France. You're too valuable to us alive.'

'To be honest, sir, I think Theo would make a better heir.'

'I beg your pardon?'

'Theodora. Uncle Charles's daughter. She joined the Nursing Yeomanry three months ago and they have already deployed her.' His mother, source of all information regarding the family, was most displeased, but not, apparently, as much as Aunts Lydia and Dorothea.

'I know who she is and what she does. I fail to understand her place in this conversation.'

'She'd be a better vehicle for the family name. A more worthy heir to . . . all this.' Now that Chris has gone. He doesn't say this. He thinks it is obvious, although, by the way his uncle is looking at him, he is evidently wrong.

'Larry, sit down and drink your coffee. This has nothing to do with the family name.'

He hadn't realized he was standing. He does not sit down. 'Then let me go to France.'

The Brigadier sits, heavily. 'Dear boy, you just sailed through a course that has crippled standing members of the land regiments. You took the coding apart and rebuilt it. You speak French, German and Italian fluently, and your Spanish, I gather, is passable if we said you were Minorcan. We do not need you to end your days hanging by your thumbs in a Gestapo cell in Paris.'

'Sir, I—'

'Laurence, sit down and tell me what you thought of the ciphers you were given to use in the field.'

He can't sit; sitting would be surrender. He stands behind the chair, gripping the back with both hands. 'They are insanely easy to break.'

'They look like blocks of numbers to me.'

'They are blocks of numbers; it's the way they are generated

70

that's beyond stupidity. The agent picks a poem that he knows by heart and lets his controllers know what it is. In the field, he chooses five words from that poem and uses them to form the basis of the cipher. Provided the people in the cipher unit back home know the correct five words, they can reverse the process and arrive at the plain text.'

'As long as he gets the numbers right. They're having a devil of a job with the ones that come in jumbled because someone got a letter wrong.'

'Yes, but that might at least be safer. How many of Hitler's cryptographers do you suppose know the words to the first verse of "God Save the King"?'

The Brigadier's face freezes in surprise. His eyes narrow. 'Dear God, tell me nobody has used—?'

'Hughes-Symmonds reckons it's the only thing he can reliably remember under duress and that composing double transpositions in the field when the Hun might be breathing down his neck is the very definition of duress. Castlemaine is going to use lines from *Hamlet*, and yes, they do begin, "To be or not to be". Young Devereaux at least allowed himself be talked out of "Sur le Pont d'Avignon".'

'And the Huns—'

'Have some very, very bright chaps. I know, I went to university with several of them. They have their Shakespeare by heart and anything they may be unsure of can be found in any good compendium of common English verse. You may as well write out the plain text and telegraph it to them clipped to an arrest warrant.'

'Good God.' His uncle is up again, pacing. Half a room away, he turns. 'Laurence, you will sit. That's an order. And drink the coffee. Unless you need some made fresh?'

So we're not playing soldiers until we are. He sits. The coffee is still perfectly hot. He drinks. He feels sick.

'Sir, I can at least begin to solve that problem. All you need

71

is to make up a new poem for each agent, something easy to memorize, but not in the common canon. The more risqué you can make it, the greater its chance of being remembered. The result won't be unbreakable, but it's a decent start. And now that you know this, there is no reason to keep me from going to France.'

His uncle returns to the table, places his elbows upon it and steeples his fingers.

'Let me be clear. You are not going to France. You are not going anywhere near the line of battle. This, too, is an order. You are too valuable to us alive, and your compatriots, I am sorry to tell you, are very unlikely to survive. No, listen to me. There are times when the war effort is better served by keeping people of your calibre in places where they can do the most good. Tell me honestly, what do you think of the men who trained you? Not the ones in your unit – the ones who taught you?'

'They were charming. They were very well meaning. By and large, they were amateurs.'

'So we are in agreement about this, if nothing else. The Firm needs an injection of professionalism. You shall provide it.'

'With respect, sir, I'm as much of an amateur as they are.'

'With respect, Laurence, you are not. You are Archie's son. Whether you like it or not, you've been training in this game since the day you were born. Accordingly, you will go from here to Bedford where the chaps in the government codes and ciphers department will give you eight weeks' training in cryptography, most of which I suspect you will already know, but you need to have the right pedigree on paper. At the end of this time, you will take up a position in the Signals Unit of the Special Operations Executive, that outfit you call the Firm, and which is most certainly not a part of the Secret Intelligence Service.'

Of this whole great catastrophic bombshell, he fastens on

the last fragment: his Firm is not a part of his uncle's firm. 'Why ever not?'

'Those higher up, in their wisdom, wanted to give the Labour Party a bite of the intelligence cherry as a thank you for entering the government, and none of the rest of us wanted to be run by a bunch of socialists. In his infinite wisdom, therefore, our prime minister magicked up the SOE so he could give them something that at least had three letters to its name.'

In his perambulations, the Brigadier pauses by the window, standing so that he can be seen only in silhouette.

'The problem is that the orphan child is rapidly outgrowing its origins and making a nuisance of itself. It needs chaps like you to make sure that the chaps they send into the field have at least half a chance of returning alive. Or at least, have a chance to die cleanly when they are caught. More importantly, we need to make sure they don't interfere with the business of winning the wars.'

'Wars? I wasn't aware there was more than one.'

'There is always more than one war, Laurence. It's just that some are briefly more pressing than others. Hitler is an inconvenience, I grant you, but Stalin may have more staying power in the long run and none of us wishes to wake up one morning and find ourselves staring across the Channel at a soviet of socialist republics, of which France is a willing part, allied to a communist Greece and an Italy led by partisans who care for nobody who isn't immediate family. So yes, we are fighting on many fronts and I would prefer it if your Firm was prevented from throwing too many spanners into the works.'

'I don't see—'

'You will answer to whatever passes for their usual chain of command. If you have any sense at all, you will never mention my name in the hearing of your new colleagues. They don't

73

like us. We don't like them. It would be unfortunate if they believed you to be a stool pigeon.'

'Which I will not be. And to suggest otherwise is—'

'Larry, I am not impugning your honour.'

'Then what will I be doing, exactly? Assuming they are going to give me a real job and not just a desk to sit at so I can spy on them in comfort for the duration?'

'You'll be making up workable ciphers that aren't a liability to the men that use them. And doing your damnedest to unscramble the most badly scrambled of those coming in from the field, so your erstwhile colleagues won't have to send them twice. That's what most of the Signals people seem to do. And while nobody is looking, you and I will make sure that our respective services actually cooperate and there are no snarl-ups in the field. I don't want your friend Sutherland to be shot by a British agent because he's in the wrong place at the wrong time. You, I imagine, do not wish it either. We shall collaborate. We shall prevent disaster. It's what our family does best. The car you came in will take you directly to Bedford. Your kit will follow from Hampshire. You may go.'

At the door, he turns. 'What about the others, sir?'

'They will jump as soon as conditions permit. I'm sorry, Larry, but you are better off like this, I promise you.'

CHAPTER SIX

GROUP CAPTAIN LAURENCE VAUGHAN-THOMAS is a man who husbands his grief with the skill of long practice. It shows in the increased stiffness of his neck and a flat tension about his eyes, but even these might as easily be age. He has set his mind to an unburdening, to a telling of long-harboured truths, and he will not let one more death dissuade him.

He says this: one more death. There have been many of those in his past, too many to count. As with McKinney, Picaut has not told him the details of all that was done to Sophie Destivelle, but nevertheless, he is, she thinks, deeply upset. She sees an undertow of anger, particularly when Clinton McKinney drops in the fact of Colonel Paul Rey's death – Laurence's former comrade in arms – as an afterthought. She meets the old man's eye and they share a moment's despair. She asks, 'How well did you know Sophie?'

'In 1944, I trained her for her role as an agent of the French section of the Special Operations Executive. She was eighteen, and about to return to France to undertake one of the most

75

dangerous assignments of the war. I was in awe of her courage. Some months later, I was a member of the Jedburgh team that aided her Maquis, but we were never close. In those days, it wasn't a good idea to get to know people too well.'

Laurence purses his lips against old, remembered pain. His gaze flickers to Clinton McKinney and back. 'Paul Rey – he was a major then – was in my Jedburgh team. I knew him much better.' Briefly, he looks away.

Picaut says, 'I'm sorry for your loss.'

'Thank you. Paul's death, at least, was not unexpected. If you would excuse me? I ought to talk to Clinton.' He leaves her with Martin Gillard, who is far harder to read.

Gillard is deeply unhappy at the news of Sophie's murder – of this, there is no doubt. His gaze is still flat and holds hers without tremor, but there's a rage that rolls off him and seethes across the floor. She thinks he might call the CIA: certainly he will know they are in town. She wants to put a tap on his phone but has not yet got a good enough reason. Instead, she invites him to join the queue to have his fingerprints taken when the technicians arrive, and submit his gun for ballistics examination.

This, at least, gets a reaction.

'You have a suspected weapon? It will not be mine, I assure you.'

'We have no details yet. This is a routine. Everyone who is armed will be treated the same.'

'Still.'

'There are no exceptions, Mr Gillard.'

She raises Gillard several notches up her persons of interest list. His anger is not all counterfeit, but there is a current beneath it of something else he does not want to show, and she wants to see.

The rest of the Radical Mind team is broken. Even before McKinney stands on a chair by the window to address them, a sense of tragedy spills out into the main room. When he gives them news of the two deaths, they weep, although it is unclear whether this is for Sophie Destivelle's murder – she is, after all, a hero of their film even if none of them has ever met her in person – or the death of Paul Rey, whom they regard, evidently, as their own surrogate grandfather.

Back upstairs in his office, McKinney is restless. 'I must call our backers. Elodie is in the air and cannot be reached. I am alone with this and it's all a mess. Captain Picaut, if you'll excuse me?'

'Of course. But I need to start collating details from your employees. Is it possible to use an office? Just temporarily?'

That stops him. He chews the edge of his thumb. 'I am not fully familiar with police powers in France, but I expect you could commandeer the entire building if you felt like it.'

'I'm not here to destroy your business, Mr McKinney, I just need somewhere to sit down, preferably with a phone line, an internet connection, a desk and four chairs.'

'The office next to Elodie's is empty? It won't take long to fit it out.'

The office next to Elodie's is a plain space with a vast window looking out over the parking lot. Martha conjures up an office desk and chairs that look as if they cost thousands, while one of the gamers comes to set up the broadband connections for her phone and iPad. Picaut tests out the biggest of the chairs, which feels every bit as expensive as it looks.

Martha makes coffee that jolts a kick from halfway across the room, although, when McKinney decides he has, after all, got time to join them, she brings him green tea in a tiny fluted cup the size of a shot glass and the colour of mutton fat jade. The scent is light, airy and pleasingly acerbic.

McKinney has brought his iPad with him. 'I have some original stills of Laurence that I thought you might like to see.

77

And our first action sequence. We only shot it last week; the rough edits just came through. It's not long, a couple of minutes at most, but it shows our band of brothers in their best light, I think. You can feel the bond that they had.'

He's like a child bringing a gift to a difficult teacher. The early images are sepia-toned stills of a young man with a ready smile, wide, pale eyes and shining blond hair. One shot shows him to the left of another young man; the pair stand with their arms over each other's shoulders in front of a wartime plane with RAF roundels.

Later, he is older, more lined, wearier of the world and all that's in it, sitting in an office chair. In the third, he is flanked by two other men: one smaller, dark-haired, with an intense stare; the other taller, freckled, fair-haired, with a wide, strong smile and good teeth. According to the caption, they are Lieutenant Toni Gaspari and Major Paul Rey.

'Rey was a good-looking man,' says Picaut. 'They all were.'

McKinney regards her warmly, as if she has complimented his children. 'I thought you'd like them.'

She says, 'Who's Toni Gaspari?'

'He was Italian, I think. They don't talk about him much.'

The things people don't talk about are piling up. Picaut adds his to her list of names to check. McKinney says, 'The video isn't finished, but it'll give you an idea of where we are heading.'

The moving sequences are shot in the low-saturation colours beloved of period dramas where the past is another country, the grass was never fully green, the sky never fully blue, and the people all quirkily mannered. Laurence is played by a blond young man with a long face and a habit of waving a pipe stem to emphasize his points. He is surrounded by startlingly attractive young women in uniform.

McKinney tilts his head at her, questioning. 'What do you think?'

'It's good,' Picaut says, which is true. 'The actor looks the part.'

McKinney pulls a wry face. 'The auditions took half a year. We narrowed it down to three for each of the surviving Maquisards and then had them spend a week in the company of the people they were representing. At the end, we let the veterans have the final say on who would play them.'

This has the feeling of a story destined to be told often, and at length. Picaut guides him elsewhere. 'And the locations? Did you shoot these in England?'

'For the early sections, yes. Several of the old mansions have been demolished and others are closed to us, but we've been able to find enough to improvise and we were given full access to Beaulieu in Hampshire, which is an SOE museum now. The Scottish shoots are all on location in Arisaig. It's wild up there, but very beautiful.'

Martha taps on the door with news that other police officers are here: Rollo, coming from the conference, catches Picaut's eye and shakes his head. She wants to know more, but she sees his gaze flicker to Martin Gillard, and so is witness to the infinitesimal moment when each gauges the other and yes, she was right: for all that Rollo may be a gun-crazy psychopath, he is her psychopath and there is nobody she would rather have at her side when the shooting starts. But Martin Gillard is better: he is Foreign Legion and BlueSkies; he has been to the places Rollo dreams of.

Which leaves a question: Why did Elodie Duval need a man of his calibre (and, Picaut has to assume, his cost) to advise on the stunts for her forthcoming action film? He remains at the top of her sparse list of suspects and Picaut doesn't know why.

Sylvie catches her eye and nods her over to the side. 'Nothing at Sophie Destivelle's apartment. It's clean.'

'Clean as in no useful leads?'

'Clean – as in, it looks like a five-star hotel after a team of maids spent an hour on it half a year ago and nobody's touched it since. There's a couple of hairs on the back of a sofa that we've sent to Eric for matching, but the rest doesn't look like it's been inhabited for months.'

'Her clothes were all from the US. She could have been living over there. Her passport had no stamps in it, so she must have used another identity. Get the CCTV from the airport for the past two months. We might be able to get some facial recognition software from the Americans if we play our cards right. What else?'

'Pierre Fayette is home now. Someone needs to talk to him.'

Picaut makes some quick calculations, starting with her own need to be out and active. 'I'll go. I want to meet him. You stay here. We need names, addresses, locations of all the staff last night and fingerprints from everyone in the building: get the tech team to do that. Plus, we need full ballistics on Martin Gillard's gun.'

'The grunt who thinks he owns the room?'

'The very one. Get Rollo to take it off him; he'll enjoy it. And be kind to the boss. He may be an arse, but he's more hurt than he looks.'

The house of Monsieur Pierre Fayette, owner of an aged Citroën BX, is a late twentieth-century brick box painted cream with a red pantiled roof and shutters stained an unfortunate shade of fake-wood orange. The front garden is mostly laid to paving, with some over-tended perennials in a border. A glisten of oil on the drive marks where a car lately stood.

Fayette meets her at the front door. A man readily lost in a crowd of two, he is of medium build, with mousy, unremarkable hair, thinning on top; well-worn, unmemorable features; fussily neat in a polyester suit with a dark-blue tie marked with a small silver Cross of Lorraine in a repeating pattern. He wears reading glasses on a cord around his neck.

'Captain.' He offers a small stiff-necked bow. 'Your fame precedes you.'

She smiles. It pulls at her jaw line. He says, 'You are recovered now, from the . . . excitement of the fire? Good. Excellent, in fact. We need more of you in Orléans, not less. How can I help? You have found my car, perhaps?'

And again, this, the breaking of news. Her face aches. 'Can I come inside?'

'Ah.' Wary now, he leads her through to the living room and yes, the inside is as uninspiring as the outside; everything is clean. On the walls are photographs of family members, no art. The furniture is aged, but not antique. Most of it looks as if it was bought when francs were the unit of currency and mobile phones were the size of bricks; nothing has any value beyond the utilitarian and there is no sense of style or taste.

The television is at least flat screen. Pierre Fayette mutes the sound, leaving the rolling news to roll in silence. He folds his arms across his chest. 'An officer of your stature would not come to report the discovery of a stolen car. You have news you are unwilling to convey on the doorstep. Both my parents are dead, as is my wife, so that leaves—' His smile freezes. 'Not Elodie?'

She says, 'Not Elodie. And yes, we have found your car. Can we sit down, perhaps?'

'Of course.' The sofa is covered in dark-green velvet that can only have been chosen by a colour-blind individual who didn't think to ask for help. The contrasting cushions are laid at precise angles. Pierre Fayette is not only dull; he is also ferociously neat. Everything is in alignment – squared edges or perfect perpendiculars. On a sideboard of cherry veneer rests an elegantly carved music box that is by far the most interesting feature of the room. It stands with its lid up, the hollow filled with dried lavender so ancient it barely scents the room.

Baldly, he says, 'Who has died, Captain?'

On Picaut's phone is the life-like image of the victim created by Eric's software. She lays it flat on the table. 'A woman was shot in the early hours of this morning. She was using the name Sophie Destivelle. We believe she may have been known to you?'

He blinks, slowly, and turns. Old photographs line the sideboard, most of them black and white: various poses of proud parents with their children. One image stands out: an action shot that has the patina of age. Here, it is high summer. In the background, a mountain shrugs snow from its shoulders. In the foreground, beneath leafy trees, a group of men – and two women – jump a low stone wall, cradling machine guns, firing, it seems, at the camera. They are united in their savagery, in the hate, the anger – and the joy that drives them. The names are strung along the footer in a strong, cursive hand: Céline, Paul, Daniel, René, JJ, Laurence, Sophie.

'Is this the Maquis de Morez?'

'That McKinney is calling his "band of brothers"?' He pulls a wry face. 'Yes, I'm afraid it is.'

'Afraid?'

He shrugs. 'It is not fashionable these days to be proud of one's parents, particularly not if they fought in the war. We are too aware of the ambiguities of the time.' He picks up her phone between thumb and forefinger, and holds it next to the image. 'Third along from the left. Does this look like your victim?'

The woman is small, neat, dark-haired – and ferocious. She holds her weapon as if, alone, she might kill the whole world. It is possible that, seventy-odd years on, she is currently lying on Eric's pathology trolley.

'Is this an original?'

'Shot in September 1944.'

Picaut retrieves her phone from Fayette and takes three pictures, varying the distance and the light. 'How well did you know her – Sophie?'

'She was a friend of my parents. She came to my wedding. She sent a card expressing her regrets on the occasion of my wife's death. She spoke at the funerals of both of my parents. Beyond that—' He spreads his hands. 'Mother and Father spoke of her often. They were in awe of her, or afraid: it can be hard to differentiate between those two when one is young. There was a betrayal in the Maquis, and she was involved, that much I know. And they believed she could kill. If you had found one of the others dead today, I might have suggested that you seek her out as the likely culprit. But if she is the victim . . . It wasn't me, I can tell you that.'

'And yet she died in your car.'

'*What?*' He spins, eyes bright. Is he angry? Certainly he is shocked. 'That is not possible.'

'She was found in your car in the car park of the Gare des Aubrais at five fifteen this morning. She had been shot twice in the chest and once in the head.'

It's there, a flicker: he knows this pattern. He looks at her and for the first time she sees the true speed of his mind. Thoughtful, he says, 'So this was not a passing drug addict.'

They are in a new place; he looks the same, but he feels different, sharper. She says, 'We have reason to believe Sophie Destivelle was a cover name. Did your parents ever call her anything else?'

'Not in my hearing.'

That sounds true. Picaut asks, 'Did she have enemies that you know of?'

'Of course.' Pierre Fayette laughs, tightly. 'She fought in the war. If the stories are right, she killed people, a lot of people, and they will have had brothers, sisters, parents, cousins. The past is not just another country, Captain, it is another universe, a parallel reality that we enter at our peril. Some things are best left undisturbed.'

'Did you say that much to Elodie? We heard you were . . . estranged.'

He pinches his lip, pulls at his nose, all of the things a man would do to show he is thinking. 'My sister changed her name, you will have noticed?'

'We assumed she married a Monsieur Duval?'

'As one does. But no. If she has married, I have not been told of it.'

'Why, then, did she change her name?'

Pierre Fayette's shrug is far more eloquent than Clinton McKinney's. 'All I can tell you is that she did it the day after our mother's funeral. And that Sophie Destivelle was instrumental in her decision.'

Something in his voice . . . 'You didn't like Madame Destivelle?'

He smiles. It is not a kind smile. 'She was a hero. I respected her.'

'And yet you lent her your car.'

'No, Captain Picaut, I did not.'

'She took it?'

'She must have done.'

'Why?'

'I truly have no idea, but the real question we should ask ourselves is "How?" Because I did not help her.' He is brisk now, commanding, almost. 'Come with me.'

He leads her through to a kitchen whose cleanliness is on a par with the rest of the house. Above the cooker is a key board shaped like a house, with labels beneath the hooks: *Front Door, Back Door, Cellar, Loft, Car, Shed.*

A set of keys with a Citroën fob dangles from the hook above the *Car* label.

Fayette says, 'These ones, as you see, are in place. There is a second set in the garden shed.' He lifts the shed key from the final hook. 'If you will follow me?'

The back garden comprises two square metres of perfectly flat lawn framed at the far end by three cherry trees just coming into bloom, and on the left-hand side by a small wooden shed stained in the same unfortunate orange-tan as the window shutters.

The substantial shed door is closed with a hasp, which is in turn secured with a padlock, which Fayette unlocks. Swinging the door open, he reveals an interior that is as neat as the house: a lawnmower, a ladder, three cans of the orange wood stain, a closed carpentry toolbox – all in perfect perpendicular order. Picaut can smell a trace of gun oil, but cannot see any weapon. There is no panel of key hooks.

'The keys were in here.' Fayette lifts a chisel from a row of five in the toolbox and slides it under one of the floorboards, which looks perfectly secure but is, in fact, not fixed down.

Levered up, it reveals a cavity, within which rests a small cash box with a combination padlock. She watches as he spins the wheels. The combination is 6644: 6 June 1944.

'Was this your father's lock?'

'Thank you. Yes.' He is pleased. These days, not everyone remembers this date. For those who fought in the war, the day the first landing craft touched French soil is engraved on their livers in letters ten centimetres tall.

Opened, the box contains two sets of small keys, as if for other padlocks. There is room for a set of car keys. An old, post-war Colt semi-automatic lies beside them: the source of the oil she smelled. A spare magazine lies beside it, full.

She looks up to find his gaze waiting for hers. 'I have a licence,' he says, and Picaut believes him: it would be too easy to catch him out if he were lying.

'I'm sure you do. Who else knows the keys were here? Elodie?'

85

'If Elodie knows, I didn't tell her.' He rocks back on his heels, thinking. 'My father knew, of course, and it is possible he may have told his friends. The Maquis . . . they were very close, those who had fought side by side, even after the war. They had no secrets even then, and there are so few of them left that they have few now.'

'How many are left?'

'Three.' Of course, there is a pen and paper hanging from a hook on the wall of the shed. He pulls it down and begins to write. 'Laurence, obviously. You'll have met him at the studio.'

'Captain Vaughan-Thomas? I thought he was a Jedburgh, not part of the Maquis?'

'Yes, but he was one of those who jumped the cemetery wall at Kramme's wedding. In the eyes of those who survived, that made him Maquis. The other two were there from the beginning, though, so they knew her better. They are all that is left now: three old men, joined by bonds that only death can break. For a while, they were spread around the country, but now in their dotage, they have retired together to Orléans, where their fame is less and they can live quietly within reach of each other without constantly being stopped in the street. I can write their addresses for you.'

His pad has perforated pages, so that the line of the tear is perfectly straight.

Laurence Vaughan-Thomas: In England: Ridgemount, Strawberry Lane, Nr Godalming, Surrey. In France: 89 Rue Parisie, Orléans

René Vivier: 17 Rue du Château Gaillard

Jean-Jacques Crotteau: 93 Rue de la Guillaumière

And there's a name she wasn't expecting to see. Something must show on her face.

'You know them, Captain?'

God, yes. He waits. She says, 'Old René Vivier. His grand-daughter stood for the *Front National* in the last mayoral elections.'

'Before the fire. Of course. I had forgotten. Forgive me.'

'No reason you should remember.' She does, though: René Vivier was, in part, responsible for her coming through the fire alive. She has never been to thank him, which now looks like an unforgivable oversight.

But his was not the name that jumped at her first. That was JJ Crotteau, whom she knows rather better and in an entirely different context. Already, the complexities mount.

'You don't happen to know where Sophie Destivelle lived?' she asks.

'Saint-Cybard, I think, or the mountains just outside, where the Maquis were. I heard she had a cabin there, but I've never been.' Pierre Fayette walks her out. They part at the front gate.

Picaut says, 'If you remember anything else, let me know.'

He gives his small bow. It feels different now. 'I will rack my brains on your behalf.'

Picaut hits the commuter traffic as she drives back across the river. Slowed to a standstill, she texts the image of the photograph to Eric, along with a message.

– Can you check bone structure to see?? Sophie Destivelle?

– I'll try. Where will you be?

– Conference. Have to check the temperature.

– OK. Will call u there.
– PS: There are no fingerprints on the card in her jacket. Interesting, no?
– PPS: Don't forget your appointment.

87

CHAPTER SEVEN

10.35

ALL IS QUIET AS Picaut drives down the tree-lined avenue to the conference venue. The Château d'Alençon is neither large nor outwardly ostentatious, but it is famously discreet. Standing at the heart of a small estate about ten kilometres south and east of the city, its walls are impressively old, and show the scars of battles fought over centuries with battering rams and pikes, with powder and shot, with machine guns, tanks and bombs – all of which gives it an air of impregnability that the Americans liked in their preparatory explorations.

Not that the interior is outdated, far from it: if there is anywhere in the world where the intelligence agents of the major powers might feel at home, it is here. Most of the details of the defences fall outside Picaut's security clearance, but she has been informed about the high-frequency shielding paint on the interior walls that keeps delegates safe from keystroke loggers and the sundry other tools of enemy hackers, and the ultra-fast broadband and conferencing facilities that enable whatever connectivity they might choose – or not choose; everything can be shut down at will.

All the modernization has left this place creepily quiet. Leaving her car to be driven away by a security guard, Picaut mounts the steps to electric doors that flow open without so much as a hiss of compressed air.

Inside are only the murmurs of the professionally quiet. The carpets are not particularly thick, but there's a resilience to them that sucks in sound. There is no traffic noise, and nobody is so crass as to let a mobile phone ring aloud.

Nobody wears a name badge, either. Here, if you don't know who you're speaking to, you don't belong. Picaut, of course, knows nobody. She stands to one side and scans the room. Men built like Martin Gillard hover at the edges with their hands free and their weapons bulging. There are some women, too: armed, fluid, dangerous, which shouldn't surprise her, but does. The irony of this leaves her smiling and she has no time to wipe the look off her face when a bulky, square-cut figure pushes out of the crowd towards her. 'Inspector Picaut?'

He's a big man, with a square all-American jaw and short, straw-coloured all-American hair, but it's his face that draws her attention. His nose has been broken and left to set with a strong leftward list and there's a thick, white scar across the bridge as if someone, long ago, has smashed his face with an iron bar and nobody was on hand to straighten things up afterwards.

She has to fight not to stare. He seems to be having the same problem with her jaw because his gaze clashes with hers and there is a frozen moment when each is not-staring at the other's scars and the effort of that is too great to let them erect the usual shields that keep first meetings bland.

Thus, she sees him unguarded, and he her. He breaks away first. 'Sorry. That was rude.'

'Then we were both rude. But actually, I think it was quite refreshing.'

'It was, wasn't it?' When he smiles, it seems the iron bar affected more than his nose because his lips are crooked, reaching higher on the left than the right. She offers her hand and he grasps it in a double-bear-paw grip. 'Conrad Lakoff at your service, Inspector.'

He's fifty, or thereabouts, with pale grey eyes lodged deep in the same been-to-hot-war-zones tan as Martin Gillard. His grip is firm and dry. He's fit, but not in the same league as the security men, and he's not carrying a weapon. Despite all of this, there's an air about him that speaks of power, even in this place where power is the common currency. In the short time since she passed through the so-silent, utterly unassuming front door, Picaut has watched for the centre of gravity in the crowded foyer and she thinks it hovers nearest to this man.

She says, 'Captain, not Inspector. Am I allowed to know your rank?'

His lopsided smile stretches. 'I'm the Strategic Operations Director of my research group, but the acronym for that is so unfortunate that I'd be grateful if it was never mentioned aloud. I answer well enough to Conrad. Or Lakoff if you're desperate for formality, but I think we've progressed beyond that by now.'

'I'd say so.' She feels cheerful, which she wasn't expecting. 'In that case, do you have a name yet for the woman who called herself Sophie Destivelle?'

He laughs aloud, which in this place is enough to cause the murmuring silence to trip on itself and fall into the carpet. 'They said you were fast.' He looks over her shoulder, checks left and right, all with an effortless subterfuge that makes it look as if he is adding her contact details to his phone.

Evidently there are too many people nearby because, looking up, he says, 'Perhaps you'd like to see some of the memorial display? It's in the second-floor suite. I imagine it will be empty at this time in the morning.'

If it wasn't before, it is by the time they reach it. The second-floor suite is a good-sized room, with high ceilings and careful lighting. The window looks out over a formal garden, with espaliered apple, pear and cherry trees trained in rows along red-brick walls and herbs planted in horological designs.

The room has been transformed into a temporary museum. Every wall is covered in the sort of sepia-toned photographs Clinton McKinney showed Picaut at the Radical Mind studio.

On the left as Picaut walks in are black-and-white images of young men in army fatigues, grinning for the camera. The caption above the first says, SARPEDON RAID: DECEMBER 1941. The images below are aerial shots and computer-generated mock-ups of a hydroelectric dam. Running beneath are tele-printer outputs of text in five-letter cipher blocks.

Picaut says, 'What's special about this?'

'It was the first big raid of the Special Operations Executive behind enemy lines,' says Lakoff. 'They were sent to destroy a hydroelectric dam in the east of France, near Saint-Cybard.'

And this is the second time today she has heard the name of Saint-Cybard. She doesn't believe in coincidences. Carefully, she says, 'So it either went textbook right, or spectacularly wrong, or it wouldn't be worth your attention.'

His gaze rests on her face. 'If you'd ever like a job as an operations instructor, please do let me know.'

'Which was it?'

'Both, after a fashion. The Sarpedon raid itself turned ugly soon after the dam blew. Only one man survived, and he went on to be the patron of the Maquis operating out of Saint-Cybard, from where the Brits ran one of the most important double agents in the whole war.'

Her jaw itches, savagely. 'Sophie Destivelle?'

'No. At least, not that we know of. This one had the code name Icarus. He came over to us eventually and went on to be useful in the Cold War against Soviet Russia, but actually . . .'

Lakoff pauses and Picaut watches him redact the things that still cannot be spoken. 'There have always been rumours of a second agent, a double. One of ours who became one of theirs, or perhaps the other way around. The code name was Diem. His handler was Carpe.'

'So together, they seized the day?'

'Indeed.'

'Why is he interesting?'

'Because we're not sure he existed. Like with the *Mary Celeste*, or Bigfoot, there were rumours – some of them really compelling – but no proof. Which is the thing, you see?' His lopsided smile stretches with enthusiasm. 'The disinformation and double disinformation surrounding the Diem operations have become the stuff of espionage textbooks and legends. That's the real story here. Our younger, more technocratic, colleagues tend to live in a world where everyone gathers everything about everyone else and keeps it for ever. Once in a while, it's useful to remind them that sometimes one individual in the right place at the right time can change the course of history.'

Picaut walks down the line, and learns of ciphers and radios and very little about the ghost called Diem.

She crosses to the far wall, where the real people are. 'Is this Paul Rey?' She taps a photograph on the adjacent wall. 'Standing next to Sophie?'

'I'm sorry?' Lakoff fishes spectacles from his pocket and leans in to peer at the image. 'You're right. I'd forgotten he was here. I should have remembered when we got the news of his death this morning.' He steps back, tugging on one ear lobe thoughtfully. 'I suppose I should take that down. Your countrymen will be most upset: Rey's something of a hero here.' He turns to her, frowning. 'I am surprised you recognized him. Knowledge of the local war is something of a specialist subject.'

92

'I was shown his picture at the Radical Mind TV studio earlier. You know of it?'

'Hard not to.' He views her askance over the ruined crest of his nose. 'My daughter is McKinney's intern. Martha. You may have met?'

'I thought Martha was French?'

'Did you?' He looks pleased. 'My mother was French. We spent a lot of time visiting with my grandparents. Still do, as a matter of fact.' His pager bleeps. Lakoff hisses a sigh. 'I'm sorry, I have to go. In answer to your original question, we are certain, as you are, that Sophie Destivelle was a cover name, but I have no alternative to give you. We also have no idea of who might have shot her and then enacted on her such specific mutilations. If we find anything relevant, I will let you know.'

'Thank you. I will share what we can. All we have so far is that she was driving a car owned by Pierre Fayette, Elodie Duval's brother.'

'You have the registration?' He makes notes with a fountain pen on a small notepad. In the world where everyone gathers everything electronically, this may well be the only sane way to protect information. 'Is there a number I can reach you on?'

She is tempted to tell him to ask his young technocrats who doubtless have it on file, but that one probably ran out of steam about a decade ago. She gives him her business card, the first time she's handed it to anyone since she came back to work. It feels good that it's him.

He escorts her back to the front doors. Out in the weak spring sun, his angled nose casts a mountainous shadow across his face. Picaut shakes his hand under the gaze of a dozen discreetly armed guards. One of them fetches her car and parks it at the foot of the steps.

'Enjoy France,' she says, as they hold open the door.

Conrad Lakoff gives a dry laugh. 'I was planning to. Let's see if we can still make that happen, shall we?'

The last time Picaut ran a case, her office was a glass fish bowl in an otherwise open-plan space.

This has changed in recent months, and today, for the first time, her team convenes in the department's new, windowless incident room in the basement of the police department. The paintwork is magnolia-boring and the air conditioning is set too high, but they have privacy, superfast broadband that doesn't drop out every ten minutes, and office chairs that have the full complement of castors.

One wall has a tall, touch-sensitive screen that links directly to Eric's lab. Already the images of Sophie Destivelle are spread across it, with the black-and-white shot that Picaut took in Pierre Fayette's living room. The wall by the door has an interactive white board that stores everything written on it to a central server, and screens that link to Interpol and other national agencies. There's a hook for her jacket, a station for her phone and her iPad, and when she docks these last two, the notes she has made are added to the screen.

Her team is here ahead of her: Rollo, Sylvie, Petit-Evard. On a table is a plate of hot croissants. Croissants. Really, the world has changed out of all recognition, but they are warm and Picaut is hungry and there is coffee in the filter and Rollo is perched on the edge of a chair with his jacket hooked over his shoulder in a way that radiates good cheer.

As she sits down he passes her a Post-it note from Eric.

Bone structure match w your picture = 100%
Chance of false positive < 1/10,000,000
Your victim **is** the girl in the picture
Well done!
PS: Ingrid. Noon. Be there :)

Picaut folds it in four and slides it into her pocket. 'OK, so Sophie Destivelle in 2018 is the same Sophie Destivelle from 1944. So far so good. And you have even better news,' she says to Rollo. 'I recognize that look.'

And he has. 'Sophie Destivelle worked for the DGSE when it was still the Deuxième Bureau. She used at least two other aliases: Lisette Thomas, Céline Vivier—'

Picaut says, 'There was a Céline in the Maquis picture. And Lisette Fayette was Pierre's mother.'

'Exactly.'

'How come the Americans don't know this?'

'Maybe they do.'

She doesn't want to think that Conrad Lakoff might have lied to her. Or rather, she doesn't want to think he could lie to her easily without her noticing. She says, 'What do we know about Strategic Operations Director Lakoff? I met him for the first time today and he acted like he owned the place.'

The smile falls from Rollo's face. 'If he's harassing you . . .'

'He was the soul of courtesy. I just need to know who he is.'

Rollo fixes his gaze somewhere in the middle distance and she can see him unpacking an internal file. 'He's a legend, a genetically engineered spook. His parents were both CIA from back in the sixties when it was at permanent war with the KGB. Young Conrad was their only child and they gave him everything they could. He went to MIT and then Caltech and then straight into the CIA where he cut his teeth in Europe in the year before the wall came down. He did some pretty wild stuff behind the lines in the chaos of those last few months, then stayed on at the Soviet desk when it wasn't fashionable any more, but still turned up useful stuff. Eight years ago, he stepped sideways into the Joint Tactical Analysis Research Group, which is a private hideout for ex-CIA operatives who want more money than their government is prepared to pay them, but he's slated to come back into government service as the new Deputy Director of the NSA, which is about as high up the tree as it gets. We'd be well advised to keep on the right side of him.'

Picaut says, 'I'm doing my best.' And then, to Sylvie, 'Anything on Pierre Fayette?'

'Am I looking for anything in particular?'

'I want to know if he had a phone call from the US earlier today. Either he can't count, or he already knew that Paul Rey was dead.'

'He's an accountant. He can probably count.'

'Exactly. So find out if Sophie Destivelle ever wore a dark-red scarf in watered silk, because there's one hanging on Pierre's back door and he didn't look the type for silk scarves. And we need to find out how Sophie got to his place to steal his car. She might have taken a taxi, in which case, I want to know where she picked it up and what time she got there.'

Picaut turns to Petit-Evard: 'You're on that. See if you can trace Sophie's movements yesterday before she "borrowed" his car. Take a picture with you, but be subtle about it. I don't want to read Facebook posts about a dead woman from some bored taxi driver.'

'On it.' He is learning the Teamspeak. 'Do I go now?'

'No.' Sylvie catches his arm. 'Wait until we're done.'

Picaut is already writing on the white board, trying for neatness now that the software stores everything for posterity. It occurs to her that if she were Conrad Lakoff, she'd probably use a flip chart and burn the pages in an incinerator every evening. Still, there's nothing she knows that he or the NSA can't safely know, as long as they don't broadcast it.

Sophie Destivelle: Who is she? Who killed her? Why?
Elodie Duval/Fayette: Why did she change her name?
Elodie Duval <—> Sophie: How much of a link?

*Pierre Fayette: How does he know that the shot pattern is
    professional?
        (Colt M1911 – check registration)
Radical Mind: What has all this to do with their film?
        (Why is it called WILD CARD?)
In the frame: Martin Gillard. Anybody else?*

Combining Pierre Fayette's list with the images McKinney
showed her, she writes:

> *Maquis de Morez:*
> *Sophie Destivelle*
> *Laurence Vaughan-Thomas*
> *Céline (surname?)*
> *René Vivier*
> *JJ Crotteau*
> *Paul Rey*
> *Toni Gaspari*
> *Daniel Fayette*

Rollo blinks. 'The JJ Crotteau?'

Picaut laughs. Before he can ask, she says, 'I'm going to see
him. You can go later if we need a follow-up. If you're good.'

'Then you need to know that he's Conrad Lakoff's
grandfather.'

'What?' It's her turn to gape. 'How?'

'JJ Crotteau had a daughter who moved to the US, joined
the CIA and married a senator, except he wasn't a senator
when she married him – he was on the staff at Langley working on the Soviet desk. This is the couple who produced the
infant prodigy, Conrad Lakoff.'

*My mother was French. We spent a lot of time visiting with
my grandparents . . .* Picaut sketches a quick family tree on the
white board.

JJ Crotteau's daughter m. Senator —> Conrad Lakoff
—> Martha – intern

'In which case,' she says, writing it in, 'Martha the intern at Radical Mind is JJ's great-granddaughter.'

Rollo chews the edge of his thumb. 'That's a bit close to home.'

'I'd say so.' She adds Conrad Lakoff to her list of relevant individuals and stands back, tapping the end of the pen to her teeth. 'What do you know about the Sarpedon raid on the hydro plant at Saint-Cybard?'

'Not much. It's used as an example of how to turn disaster to your advantage. There's a kind of hero worship of the men who died on it: that sense of doomed courage shown in the face of overwhelming odds.'

'That's what Lakoff said.' She writes a question mark beside Conrad Lakoff's name. 'Do you think the NSA reads this in real time?'

'Probably.' Rollo leans over and writes, *Colonel Paul Rey?* 'He could do with a closer look, too.'

'He's dead.'

'Yes, but under the circumstances, I think we ought to check whether he died of natural causes, don't you? Because otherwise, the last person to see him alive was Elodie Duval.'

Picaut writes, *Paul Rey? Murder? (Ask Elodie Duval.)*

She lifts her jacket from the hook and her phone from its cradle. 'Petit-Evard, I need you to check on Pierre Fayette's gun. I'm pretty sure it's registered, but it's older than he is: see if you can find out who had it before him. Rollo, I need you to touch up your contacts on the dark side and get me more background on Martin Gillard. Anything he is, was or ever has been. Sylvie, get to the airport. Immigration is already primed, but I want Elodie Duval in a car on her way here before the wheels of her plane hit the ground.'

'Where are you going?' Sylvie asks.

'To talk to Laurence Vaughan-Thomas. He said he was a Jedburgh, but Pierre Fayette put him on the list of Maquisards who used to know his parents and McKinney said he was MI6. He has his fingers in a lot of pies. One way or another, he has to know more.'

'He went home soon after you left the studio,' says Petit-Evard. 'He looked pretty wrecked.'

'Then I'll visit him at home. Let me know when you've got something else useful.'

7 December 1941: Japanese attack on Pearl Harbor ends US neutrality.

8 December: The United Kingdom, Australia, New Zealand, the Netherlands and the United States declare war on Japan.

SOE, F-Section, 12 December: Alain Remplin, code name Oberon, arrested while making a radio transmission to London. Whereabouts thereafter unknown.

CHAPTER EIGHT

BAKER STREET, LONDON
27 December 1941

L AURENCE'S OFFICE IS SMALL, badly lit and windowless, and any oxygen has largely been replaced by tobacco smoke. Since coming here, he has taken to smoking a pipe of Navy Cut, a habit of his father's that he had previously sworn never to emulate. It is not the only one of his personal oaths he has broken in the past six months, but it is the most outwardly evident.

It is also the most trivial. There are entire days when he can't remember filling his pipe or lighting it, only that at the end of the day, the pouch is empty and it's time to touch one of Uncle Jeremy's shadier contacts for a refill. In between, he has drunk over-sugared tea, eaten sandwiches whose component parts it is safer not to identify – and he has stared at line after line of teleprinted characters and endeavoured to make sense of them.

Thanks to his uncle, the Brigadier – or possibly no thanks at all to the Brigadier – this is Laurence Vaughan-Thomas's contribution to the war effort.

The eight weeks of training at the cipher school in Bedford

passed far too fast. He came away thinking he'd learned more than he knew there was to know. In the few months since, he has been discovering how much he still has to learn.

In the life cycle of a ciphered message, an agent in the field has a brief timespan in the day that has been allocated to him and he must send his missive within his scheduled slot.

If the conditions are good, his Morse will reach the south coast, where immensely secret listening stations will be tuned to his wavelength and a listener with (hopefully) good Morse code skills will be ready to take down his ciphered message.

The result is sent by teleprinter to the Baker Street offices where the cipher clerks – FANYs to a woman: all around twenty, all with good breeding, good looks and exceptionally sharp minds – will decipher it using the same agent's poem.

This is the theory.

In practice, there are any number of ways in which the system falls down and Laurence is the one who must put it on its feet again. He is not, thank heaven, a cipher clerk, but he is the one who takes their output and makes sense of those messages that have no obvious meaning. He sorts out the misprints, the moments when, say, the listener briefly lost focus and heard an A (*dit dah*) in place of an N (*dah dit*) or the sender slurred a *dah* into a *dit* and the receiver heard a K instead of a P, an M instead of an S, or any of the thousand other mistakes of mutilated Morse.

None of this would matter in straight text. If someone writes A VERY MERRY CHRISTMNS TO YOU ALL, it isn't hard to correct the mistake, however improbable merriment might be in the current climate.

But when the text is HKIQN PRRUF WINDO FRLLK NMWSA and so on for a minimum of two hundred characters, and there are ten such missives arriving throughout the day, from Norway, France, Holland and occasionally, in brief, urgent stutters from Germany, it is harder. When the sender

103

of this gibberish has to be identified, their poem code located, their bluff and true checks codes verified, and the double transposition performed in reverse to turn it back into plain text before their next scheduled slot . . . then it is very much harder.

But not impossible. One letter wrongly transposed doesn't ruin an entire message; it just makes some of the finer detail less transparent.

What makes it impossible is when the listeners at the secret, unmentioned stations along the coast lose the signal and half a message is gone. Or when the coder has lost or forgotten or misremembered his poem or, more charitably, has been coding in a cave or a barn or an attic in the midst of a Dutch or Norwegian or French winter (Sutherland, are you there? Are you still alive?) on his second day without food because nobody can safely deliver supplies, is without gloves, without heating, without any means of boiling a kettle, and the Gestapo direction finders are closing in with every group of letters sent. Then, understandably, the double transposition cipher may well be less than perfect and the FANYs, who man the stations and prepare the telegrams for the heads of station to read and respond to, can make no sense of it.

Which is when they bring their slips of paper to Flight Lieutenant Laurence Vaughan-Thomas, RAF, DFC (pending), who has friends out there, men he trained with who, however much he may hate their arrogance – and he does – however much he may envy their contact with the enemy – and he does – do not deserve the kind of deaths that await them if they are caught.

Their names are etched into the parenchyma of his liver: those he trained with and those he has met since. He will not give up on them while there is breath in his body. He has been known to work around the clock without pause to break a ruined code, and perhaps six times out of ten, he succeeds.

But not today. Here, now, at something after six o'clock in the evening on the day after Boxing Day, in the war's third year, he is stuck. He has tried flipping As for Ns, Ks for Ps, all the other common errors. The coder's key is not the National Anthem, so the easy fixes, like spelling 'reign' as 'rein' or even 'rain', and 'knavish' with an 'e' do not work.

He has had this problem before. Sarpedon, whoever he might be, is not, evidently, a native English speaker; more of a hybrid, or from one of the colonies: Scotland, maybe. Or Wales. This is a joke. He made it to himself around lunchtime and has waited ever since for someone with a suitable national brogue to drop by so he can speak it aloud.

Nobody has come, which is probably as well because he's looked at the files and found that Sarpedon is, in fact, a major, and his combat history thus far suggests that he is not a careless coder, quite the reverse. He and three others of similar calibre have been sent on a *coup de main* operation against a hydroelectric dam in the eastern Jura: a quick in and out with a big bang in the middle and the Reich's war machine will be encouragingly short of power afterwards.

The incoming commando is to be helped by three British agents from the Firm, plus one Paul Mignon, known as Caesar, a French agent who has managed to gain employment as an inspector of trains, and who can therefore travel with impunity and issue valid travel passes to his friends.

The dam should have blown last night. It is likely that the mangled message – has it been jammed? Laurence has never seen a jammed message before – confirms destruction and requests a Lysander to take them out. It should have within it the name and coordinates of a suitable pick-up site, together with major local landmarks, although it could as easily be calling in an air raid, or asking for more supplies, or giving information about new defences that made their target harder to hit.

Laurence has not been specifically briefed on any of this, but he has pieced together the detail from the jumbled ciphers he has had to mend. If he were an Abwehr spy . . . best not to think about that. The threat of an enemy agent inside the Firm is real and terrifying but frankly, if the high-ups were to clamp down on security to the extent that all the operations were actually secret, the whole outfit would grind to a halt in a matter of minutes. Thus everyone pretends not to know anything, until they are required to know something, at which point they know everything (within reason).

This Christmas, few people know what's going on because few people are around. As far as he can tell, barring a handful of guards, Laurence is on his own in the Signals Unit. Technically, he shares his shift with the FANYs who man the incoming and outgoing lines, but they are in a dungeon across the road. To get a message to them for sending, he will have to go up to road level, out and down. He's been avoiding this for an hour, hoping for a breakthrough. Defeat is bad enough. Having to brave the cold outside does not make it sweeter.

He reaches for his pipe and finds it has gone out. He pulls on his coat and heads into the lightless night.

The sirens are silent. Laurence was never a night fighter, but it's not hard to imagine the bombers waddling along like herds of pregnant sows, concealed from the ack-acks below, but for those above, picked out in perfect silhouette against the silver upsides of the clouds.

Up at street level, his breath crystallizes around his head. He hurries across the road, leans on the swing door, nods to the guard corporal's salute – 'Evening, Brian.' 'Evening, sir. Bit chilly out there.' 'Certainly is, Brian.' – and heads down the stairs.

He lights up as he goes and draws in the first rush of heat against the chill of the coding room. Eight girls work each shift. None of them look up as he enters. They are dressed in their outdoor coats with fingerless gloves on, hats and scarves. Their breath colours the air. A single-bar electric fire hung up on one wall struggles against impossible odds. It is colder in here than it was outside. But not colder than the seas off France.

He writes his chit: RESEND PREVIOUS MESSAGE STOP REPEAT RESEND PREVIOUS MSG/ENDS

It takes him roughly twice as long to encipher the message as it does to write out the plain text. Six months ago, it took him an hour and three sheets of shorthand pad. Now, he can do it in his head. He throws the result in the tray. Failure tastes like this.

He stands back against the wall and waits to see it go, an unnecessary superstition that has evolved over the past two months, as if by willpower he can get the message securely through to the other side and draw a clear cipher back by return.

One of the girls in the front row stubs out her cigarette and comes back to empty the tray: she's tall, brunette, extraordinarily good looking, but then they all are. The high-ups don't like ill-favoured girls. Patrick Sutherland called them the Intelligent Gentlewomen, which just about covers it.

The Firm has access, it seems, to a ready supply of girls like his cousin Theodora, who have been waiting for something like this to let them off the leash.

He doesn't pay much attention to the one who collects his chit, and a couple of minutes later he pays even less attention to the equally tall ice-blonde who walks across the room towards him.

'Hello, Larry.'

'Theo? Cousin Theodora? Good God, I heard you'd joined the FANY, but I never . . . Wait . . . Does Uncle Jer—?'

He sucks back the name before it hits the air. There are mines here, wherever he puts his feet. He snaps his mouth shut and refuses to look around to see who might be listening.

Laurence's memory of his cousin is of a prissy youth, rather taken with her own good looks.

She looks tired. She also looks immensely competent, but then that applies to all the women in his family: the true brains are all, as his father once said, on the distaff side.

She smiles, thinly. 'My shift finishes in an hour. Would you like a drink?'

'Where?' He's thinking White's, but she's a woman so that's impossible, obviously. Maybe The Strand, or—

'The Queen's Head?'

His cousin knows the name of the local public house. Wonders never cease. 'One hour. I'll see you there.' He nods in the direction of the stunning brunette who is typing his cipher into the teleprinter. 'See that gets out cleanly to Sarpedon. And pray that what comes back is intelligible.'

He doesn't have much experience of drinking beyond the club and he has certainly never been in the Queen's Head. It's warmer than his office; this much is in its favour. It's relatively quiet and the air smells more of tobacco than sweat.

'You really shouldn't have gone for the gin. I don't know what it is, but if you tried to strip walls with it, they'd dissolve in puddles at your feet.'

Theodora stands over the table he has found in the corner booth. In this light, it is apparent that she inherited all the family's most attractive features. She smiles and becomes Chris, but with a leaner face, and long, iced-moon hair piled up on top in a way that adds to her height. Her out-of-work make-up is wildly iridescent. You could target a bomb strike from three thousand feet on the hot, bright red of her lips.

She says, 'I should have warned you. I'm most terribly sorry. About everything. Abandon the gin; truly, it's vile. The beer is passable. Shall I get you one?'

'If you like.'

108

Life is full of new surprises. She brings it back, foaming, bitterly cold. It slides down in a welcome fashion. Theodora drinks it with him, a half to his pint.

With a grimace, he says, 'It's an acquired taste.'

'One could acquire it, though.'

'Looks as if you have. Uncle Charles won't be pleased.'

'On the scale of my father's displeasure, I suspect my drinking beer will rank relatively low.' She rearranges her face and she is no longer the gamine version of Chris, but Charles, the business head in the family, older, more clipped, prone to unheralded bursts of anger that leave the company silent, staring at their plates. He can calculate profit and loss in a heartbeat, and carries his skill as a chip on his shoulder.

In his voice, stentorian and aggrieved at once, she says, 'Are you seriously trying to tell me that you're planning to serve in the company of the *other ranks*?'

Laurence laughs, loosely. If he closes his eyes he's back in Cambridge, the Christmas before the war, Aunt Lydia at one end of the table, Aunt Dorothea at the other and Charles in between them, pontificating.

And Theodora, the irritating prodigy, declaiming some obscure lines of Troilus to Cressida or the other way about, thinking it will impress—

He opens his eyes. 'How was the Christmas-fest? Wiltshire, this year, wasn't it?'

'I expect it was. I didn't go.'

'In case you drove your father to kill his last surviving brother?' It's as close as he can get to asking the question he bit off in the coding room. Neither of them can mention the Brigadier in here, or what he does. If she knows, which she might not.

She relaxes her face and shakes herself briskly, like a hound stepping out of a river. As herself, she says, 'He doesn't know that part, only that I'm here.'

So he was right: the Brigadier recruited Theo, too. 'When did you start?'

'October. And yes, I should have told you, but I was finding my feet and I didn't want to be in your shadow. Actually, that's not quite true. I wanted to make it in the cipher room on my own, without anyone thinking I'd had a leg up from you.'

'How is it?'

'Good at times. Deadly at others. The night shifts are grim. And then something comes in when you just know that . . .' Her gaze travels from the bar to the door via the three other couples making desultory conversation. They don't look like walls, but they all have ears and word is coming back, slowly, of what happens to those caught by the Sicherheitsdienst, or worse, the Geheime Staatspolizei. The rule for agents going into the field is: if you have any kind of choice, be caught by the Abwehr, the army intelligence. They at least understand the rules of war.

Finishing her thought, Theodora says, 'When it matters.'

'Like tonight. That last chit.'

'You didn't break it, did you – the message from this morning?' She winces at the change in his face. 'I'm sorry. They think you're some kind of boy wonder, that nothing is beyond you.'

'They?'

'The cipher clerks. My friends.'

'Just for a moment, I thought you meant our illustrious superiors.'

'The day I know what they think . . .' She laughs, relaxed, and tilts her beer in salute to the absent officers. She is so very like Chris. Perhaps all the cousins are pressed from the same mould; he just hasn't spent time with any of the others since he finished school.

He looks past her. There's a piano in the corner; an ally. 'Can you still play?'

One plucked brow soars. She looks like her mother now, or his. They were bred differently, but are very alike. 'Here?'

'Why not? It's Christmas. More or less.'

And so she does, but not the Christmas fare of the Family-Fest, nor the piano concertos and sonatas of an expensively tutored girl who has worked hard on her fingering. Tonight, she plays fast American band music, and within a dozen bars the desultory denizens of the Queen's Head are desultory no longer, but have found the mood to swing.

Laurence Vaughan-Thomas orders another beer, and then a Scotch, and this time they do not serve him barely disguised turpentine, but the real thing – Talisker, decades in the ageing, and he finds that he is not immune to warmth, and that he can laugh, and smile, and sing and, wonder of wonders, dance.

Happiness is not impossible. Duller than it was, perhaps, but this is war; it could be so much worse.

Sarpedon is scheduled to resend his newly encrypted message at 08.45 the following morning and Laurence is in the cipher room early, drinking coffee, staring at the teleprinter.

Theo stands beside him, delicately green beneath her powder. Her working lipstick is several shades less brilliant than the one she wears at night. He prefers it.

At 08.33, the teleprinter snaps and chatters and spits out a string: sender's ID, wavelength, signal strength and sked times, followed by the cipher index and the first few groups of code.

SARPEDON QRI4 0830 28.12.41

L3W25 L6W3X L7W14 JKIID QSURT VFGGO KLSPY

Theo says, 'They're sending early. Different wavelength, different cipher. If the last one was jammed to order, this one might get through.'

Laurence is already writing. The line numbers are there, and then the word numbers. Sarpedon uses an unpublished poem of W. H. Auden's that Laurence can recite in his sleep, more or less.

Line three, words two and five: ORDER, MANIFOLD; line six, word three: GRATEFULLY; line seven, words one and four ... Some people pick their shortest words. Sarpedon, whoever he is, picks the longest, presumably on the grounds that it's more secure. It's also harder to code and to decode. Laurence hasn't brought squared paper. The stunning brunette FANY hands him some. He is growing used to the fine, chiselled edges of her features.

Swiftly, he lays the words out, numbering them in alphabetic order, then creates the grid. Beside him, the FANY is doing the same. He thinks her name is Jane, or Jean, or Janet. It begins with a J, anyway.

Theodora says, 'The signal's good.'

At four out of five, the signal is excellent. It will be for the Gestapo as well, and their French bloodhounds. They'll be onto him by now. Hurry up. Hurry up. Forget the two hundred characters. Just send the bloody thing.

JKIID QSURT VFGGO KLSPY KATTG
WIDNC KIOER RTGQU

The plain text emerges, letter by letter:

NEPTU NEHIP PYREQ UELTP ICKUP
DQMIK E2812 42BBC

Neptune Hippy. Sarpedon's true check is a spelling mistake every ninth letter, so HIPPY becomes HAPPY and the dam is out of action. Nicely done – this is what the SOE was first created for, the quick in and out of a *coup de main*. Show the bastards we're not done yet. An L becomes an S and he is requesting a pick-up at . . . Q to Z and DQ becomes DZ, so the location is dropping zone Mike on the twenty-eighth, which is cutting it fine, with a BBC message on *Radio Londres* to confirm that says . . .

He has no idea what it says; the teleprinter has stopped. Come on, Sarpedon. Keep going. This is perfect, clear as day.

He says it aloud. 'Come on.' Beside him, Theo is biting one perfect nail. The J-named brunette is leaning over, gripping both arms with fingers gone rigid. She says, 'Here!' and the teleprinter stutters. Rapid as gunfire, it spits out three fast groups.

QUG QUG QUG

'Strewth.' Last night's alcohol gathers at the foot of his gullet, churning. Laurence holds himself tight, as he did in the cockpit.

Theodora asks, 'What is it?'

'Q-code. Three-letter abbreviations to keep the channels clear. There are pages of them they have to learn before they go out.' Fire blossoms around him. It cannot be real. He shuts his eyes.

'I know what a Q-code is. I've just never seen QUG. What does it mean?'

'I am under assault and must cease transmission.'

And Sarpedon does, except for one last burst in plain text.

SLAINTE

'Oh, Christ Almighty.' Bile hits the back of his throat. He retches, clutching the chair.

'Larry, what is it?'

'It's a Scottish toast. In Arisaig, he . . . we— I'm sorry. I have to go.'

He makes it up past the unsaluted guard, and out into the grey and silent street where he pukes violently into the gutter.

He has never wished death on anyone before – not someone he knows, not a man whose breath, laughter, courage he has shared, whose hand he has shaken. But he wishes death on Patrick Sutherland now; a swift, clean, glorious death in battle, and no chance for anyone in a grey uniform to demand answers to questions afterwards.

He goes back to his office, takes out the uncrackable gibberish of the day before and spends the rest of the morning beating his head on its intransigence. He fails.

CHAPTER NINE

12 MONTAGU SQUARE, LONDON
2 January 1942

'HAPPY NEW YEAR, LARRY!'
The Brigadier barges into the maisonette at six seven-teen, bearing a bloodied parcel wrapped in butcher's brown paper. Laurence is in his dressing gown and slippers, contem-plating his first real coffee of the new year. He is doing *The Times* crossword, but the possible proximity of real meat is hard to ignore. He looks up, warily.

'Did I forget to lock the front door when I came in with the milk?'

'I have a key.'

'Of course you do.' Nothing, really, should surprise him. It was the Brigadier, after all, who magicked up a fully furnished two-bedroom apartment on Montagu Square, barely a five-minute walk from work, when almost everyone else is living on the wrong side of Hampstead Heath, or, worse, south of the river.

Laurence has been here slightly less than a month and it has taken him this time to come to appreciate the angles and curves, the subtle earth-and-turquoise colour palettes that are so different from the big, bold colours of his youth. He has not dared ask whose apartment it is, or was. He suspects the latter. Were it his, he would not willingly have left it and in default of ownership, he has come to see himself as its warden. At times, when the bombing is at its worst, he stands in the absolute dark of the blacked-out living room and offers an urgent, unfocused yearning that it might not slide to dust and rubble as has so much of London. By a miracle of chance, or the power of his fervour, it has remained intact so far, and he intends that it remain this way.

He lays aside his paper. 'Happy New Year, Uncle Jeremy. Perhaps I should say "Happy Hogmanay" in honour of our late friend?'

Five days have passed since he found out that Sarpedon was Patrick Sutherland, and that his raid had gone down in the most disastrous circumstances. He remains explosively angry, mostly with himself.

The Brigadier says, 'It wasn't your fault.'

'I should have cracked Sarpedon's first transmission.'

'But you couldn't have done. Nobody could. The Frenchman who keyed it had been turned. He was sending gibberish. There was nothing to decipher.'

'Who turned him?'

'You've heard of Maximilian Kramme?'

The name is vaguely familiar. 'I thought he was in Paris?'

'He spreads his net wide.' The Brigadier sits without being asked. His nails are shorter than they have been. He has a cold sore on one lip. In a man of imperturbable bonhomie, this comes as something of a shock. He lays his bundle of meat on the table. Laurence stares at it.

Gently, his uncle says, 'Open it, Larry. It won't bite.'

There's something wrong here. Laurence opens the parcel, peels back the layer of greaseproof paper and lifts out—

A file. Not sirloin, or even a lump of gristly stewing steak, but a file, rolled and bound with string. Beyond the subterfuge of the outer wrapping, there is no blood, only a profusion of red type that is far, far more dangerous.

He steps back. 'I really don't think—'

'Trust me, I don't take risks of this nature without reason. You do want to read this.'

He does. Against all sanity, he does. Because he has seen the smaller black type beneath all the fatal warnings: Sarpedon.

He may be sick. He opens the file. He reads the first page. And thus does he discover that one man survived the carnage of the raid.

Hope is such a dangerous thing, and fickle. 'Patrick Sutherland is coming home?'

'He is already home.'

'In one piece?'

'Yes.'

Laurence sits, heavily. His hand is shaking. He lays the file down on the table and stares at it until the type is no longer blurred. Raising his head, he asks, 'Who betrayed them?'

'Paul Mignon.'

'The train inspector.'

'The very one. He had sold them to the Boche before they ever landed, apparently.'

It is war. These things happen. On the gas, the kettle screams. Laurence pours for them both. This is not coffee, but it is not as bad a substitute as some he has tasted.

'Where's Mignon now?' he asks.

'That's the interesting thing. According to your man Sutherland, the French cut his throat. They have teams of youths, apparently, whose sole function is to dispose of collaborators. He was dead before Sutherland left the country.'

'But?' There is always a but. His uncle never gives gifts without strings attached.

117

'But his radio continues to transmit on the same schedule.'

Laurence finds he is smiling, thinly. 'So the Boche are running it.'

'Quite so. And if they are, there is a chance that they don't know that we know he's dead.'

'We can test that, though, can't we?' Already he can think of the ways. The morning is brighter. The coffee tastes . . . never mind. He watches his uncle and tries to think three moves ahead. 'You want me to work on this?'

'I want you to coordinate it.'

'Why not someone from Six? It's more their bag, surely.'

The Brigadier stares at the swirling surface of his coffee. 'What do you know about the Service?'

'I've heard a persistent rumour that they are trying to shut down my Firm: that Claude Dansey, in particular, hates us.'

His uncle nods. 'True on both counts. Dansey is a vicious, bitter, foul-minded bastard who should never have been given charge of a scout camp. How he manoeuvred himself to the position of power he currently holds is quite beyond me, but there is no doubting his hatred for anything that isn't under his personal and total control. If he is given any excuse at all, he will shut you down. There are . . . individuals in higher positions who would prefer this not to happen. This potential ploy with the radio might give him just the excuse he needs. Therefore, we would rather he did not discover its existence. Therefore, we would like you to run it.'

We. It's impossible, really, to imagine the power of men who can give orders to the likes of Uncle Jeremy.

It's not quite as impossible to imagine the turf war in which he is caught, though it sticks in his throat. 'Have we forgotten that Hitler is the enemy?'

'I do believe some of us have, yes. At the very least, the corporal is considered a lesser threat in the great scheme of things, particularly now that our colonial friends have scented blood and joined the chase.' The Brigadier leans back and stares at the ceiling. 'Someone in Washington has realized, a little late, that Germany is twenty years ahead of us in all things scientific. I rather think they plan a spot of intellectual larceny when the shooting stops. And, as we have already discussed, they are a great deal more interested in the Russians than they are in the Boche. That way lies the longer war. This one is all over bar the small matter of a successful invasion of the continent.'

Dear God.

He has always thought himself a small cog in a vast and crushing wheel, although when he was a pilot, up above the cloud layer, it was possible to imagine himself king of the skies. Down here, he sees himself as a joker in an entirely disposable hand. He says, 'Men are dying in the most appalling circumstances to win this war. You do know that?'

'I do.'

'Eyes gouged out with kitchen forks. Limbs smashed with iron bars. Hung from rafters in handcuffs until the bones of their wrists come apart. Nailed to—'

'*Laurence!*'

He stops. 'I'm sorry.'

'Don't mention it. We're all under pressure.' His uncle stands, glances at his watch and makes a show of departing. 'But your man is back. He is alive. He is being debriefed at Beaulieu. Your cousin Theodora is visiting us at Ridgemount. Lydia asked me to invite you to luncheon. If you were to drive down, it wouldn't be too much of a detour to pick Sutherland up on the way back.'

Chance would be a fine thing. 'I have no fuel.'

And here is a smile that he hasn't seen in years. 'I believe your Firm's Daimler is free. I believe, also, that if you mention my name to Walkinshaw, the commissar of the car pool, it will be made available. Don't get up. I'll see myself out.'

*

Which is how, sometime after four o'clock, Laurence finds himself driving a Daimler – a *Daimler*, dear God – south and west from Ridgemount with Theodora in the passenger seat. Luncheon was probably good, but he didn't particularly notice. He feels oddly light-headed, unburdened, even happy. The evening sky is clear, the sun is setting and the full moon hangs fat in the eastern sky.

He drives through snow-huddled villages on roads mired with slush and makes small talk with Theo about the family. Somewhere on the far side of Selborne, he says, 'Where are you living?'

He asks in French, to keep in practice. She answers in kind. 'In town.'

'Yes, where?'

'I have digs on Old Compton Street.'

'Soho? Really?'

'It's fun. I share with Julie Hetherington.'

'Another cipher clerk?'

'Who else do I ever meet? You'd recognize her if you saw her. She's dark-haired, tall—'

'Legs like a Tattersalls filly and a penchant for coding?' The J-named beauty. She has beaten him to three ciphers. Julie. He really did think her name was Joan.

Theo says, 'She has an uncle in the Admiralty; he got us the flat. Where are you?'

'Closer than that. Uncle Jeremy got me a maisonette at Montagu Square, and it's too big – I was thinking we might share.'

'Can't, sorry. Julie would have a fit.'

'Really?' He glances at her, sharply. She lifts one wry, dry eyebrow in a look that is so like Chris it should hurt, except it doesn't; it trips a final wire in his head and he is laughing, laughing so hard he can barely see the road, and Theo is laughing with him, hanging on to the door handle for dear life as he puts his foot down and throws the Daimler into a bend and loses the rear wheels coming into the straight again. Wresting back control, he changes up a gear and shouts a whoop to the skies, and they make the next twenty miles before either of them really returns to normality.

He misses the turn to Beaulieu and has to reverse back, peering through a misted rear window, which is enough to bring him down to earth. A little breathless, he says, 'Does it run in the family, do you suppose?'

Theo is still holding on to the door with white-knuckled fingers. 'Julie asked that,' she says. 'We decided it probably did. Aunt Lydia, obviously.'

'Obviously. And cousin Roderick who moved off to the back of beyond too suddenly to be normal. But I always wondered about your father, frankly.'

'I'm not sure I want to think about that, thank you.' Theo contrives to sound arch.

Laurence grins at her. 'Sorry.'

'Don't be.' She lets go of the door and leans back in the passenger seat. More soberly, 'I'm sorry about Chris.'

What is there to say? He says nothing and then, because nothing is not enough, 'Thank you.'

He drives for a while. The silence is not unfriendly. Presently, she says, 'Did Uncle Jeremy say something pertinent?'

'Many things, but not in this regard. He'll know, though. He knows everything.' So saying, Laurence parks the car at the gates to Beaulieu, the stateliest of the Firm's stately homes. In the guard room, a man is waiting.

Laurence steps forward, the conversation still a-buzz in his head. 'Sutherland! Christ, it's good to see you!'

'Thomas. I hoped it would be you.'

Patrick Sutherland is not the man he was. He looks harder, his features more drawn. He is wearing the dress uniform of the Black Watch with a crown newly sewn on his shoulder, and pale spaces where the pips used to be. 'And your cousin. Mademoiselle, *enchanté*.' He bows. She offers her hand. He kisses the back of it.

Sutherland may be brittle, and jagged at the edges, but he is alive. Laurence stands in the part-frozen snow and feels his heart rise like leavened bread until it jams his throat and he cannot speak.

'Let me take you back to London,' he says, at last. 'You've been too long away.'

With darkness the frost has set in, hard and crisp, and Laurence drives back along roads of polished glass that send the Daimler whispering round corners with the rear wheels making graceful balletic movements across the tarmac. Theodora is in the front seat: Patrick Sutherland has insisted. Sutherland himself is fast asleep in the back, his face peaceful. Laurence and his cousin do not speak for fear of waking him.

In London, the roads are less obviously lethal, but there's a raid on somewhere south of the river and the searchlights send an eerie, translucent glow across his path, overpowering the blade of his blacked-out headlights, so that it is impossible, really, to be sure where he's going or what's in front of him. By sheer fluke, Laurence finds himself driving north, up Charing Cross Road. Halfway up, Theo taps his arm.

'I'll get out here.'

'You sure?' His face is frozen, his lips rubbery and numb.

'It's faster to walk. And probably safer. I'll see you tomorrow.' She shoves open the door, unfolds herself. He forgets how tall she is. She leans in towards the silent figure in the back. 'Goodnight, Major Sutherland. You are an inspiration to us all.'

Sutherland wakes, if he was ever truly asleep. He stretches out one long arm and shakes her offered hand. 'Thank you,

Warrant Officer Vaughan-Thomas. It's a pleasure to know you.'

His gaze follows her as the Daimler eases away. The silence might suffocate them both. In the background is the low hiccough of an anti-aircraft gun. Still, Laurence can hear no planes. 'Was it hell?' he asks.

Sutherland says, 'Not at first.' There is a pause, and Laurence thinks that might be all there is to say, possibly all there ever has been, but then, 'All that running up hills in Arisaig paid off. You'd have loved it.' Then, as they turn west along Shaftesbury Avenue, reflectively: 'It was hell. It *is* hell. Every single German on French soil is an offence against humanity and the French who collaborate with them . . . they are worse. I saw Castlemaine take his L-pill after his Sten jammed. If it's any consolation, the death is swift, and not too grim.'

God.

Laurence drives another mile before he dares ask, 'How did you get away?'

'I was ordered to run. Pitt-Williams was with me at St Andrews. I beat him on the cross-country course three years in a row. He was a colonel. I was not. I ran.'

And again: God. So much pain. So much . . . Did he argue? Of course he argued. Any man would argue and Patrick Sutherland most of all. 'Dying with them wouldn't have helped,' Laurence says. 'As it is, we know Paul Mignon is dead and yet his radio is still running, which means we can feed things to the Boche: stories, falsehoods, ideas. Things like that can change the course of a war.'

'I know. That's what makes it worth it, the feeling that we might have done some good. You know – maybe you don't know; flying Hurricanes has an obvious point – but in the ground war, you spend an eternity hanging around waiting for something to happen, and even when it does, you're not sure if you're actually being useful or if someone, somewhere is just sticking pins in a bloody map and likes blue, so the blue people move up a bit, and that's you, and men die, and you take a hill, and then you lose it and it's all a complete waste of time and life and pain and blood.' He stops, abruptly. 'Sorry. I think I may be a trifle jaded.'

'You're entitled to be.'

'No. You can be jaded when you're dead. And if you can keep us out of the way of the falling ordnance, we won't be dead for a while yet.'

There's a warning under the words. Laurence says, 'You're going back?'

In the dark, he feels Sutherland nod. 'I have a contact who hasn't turned and will never do. A physician in a small town in the Franche-Comté. He's about to retire and he's agreed to sell me his practice. My French is accented, but if I grab a textbook and touch up on my general practice, I'll pass as a Belgian doctor. All the records are a mess. Nobody will be able to prove otherwise.' There follows a pause of about half a mile, in which Laurence cannot find anything useful to say. Patrick Sutherland says, at last, 'I can do this. Don't try to talk me out of it.'

'I wasn't going to. I'd give my eye teeth to go with you. But you'll be a village doctor for exactly as long as it takes the Boche to capture one of your men and make him talk. Then you'll have to take to the hills.'

'I know. But that's the point, don't you see? Out of the cities, it's the men who take to the hills who will do the most good. There are hundreds of them out there already. The Boche made his big mistake when he started shipping Frenchmen east for the slave factories. A lot of men who might otherwise have buckled down and collaborated are now living like bandits in the forest. If we arm them, we have an army, just waiting to fight, and they hate the Boche.'

'Have you told anyone this?'

124

'It was the first thing I put in my report. It's the reason Pitt-Williams ordered me to leave. Someone had to come back and persuade the chinless wonders who congregate around your uncle that they actually need to do something.'

'Did it succeed?'

'I have no idea. If I never get sent back, we'll know not.'

They are at Baker Street. Laurence pulls in to the kerb. He has been postponing this decision and finds that, effortlessly, it is made.

'Do you want to stay in a hotel?' he asks. 'Or would you like to sleep in a real bed with real cotton sheets and your own bathroom complete with water closet and bath? There's a boiler, obviously. Hot water on tap.'

Silence. A long silence. 'You have such a thing?'

'I have two: a maisonette with two bedrooms. It's too bloody big. If you wanted to share it while you're in London, you're welcome. And while you're here, you can help me find a way to make things easier for your coding in the field.'

CHAPTER TEN

ORLÉANS
Sunday, 18 March 2018
12.00

LAURENCE VAUGHAN-THOMAS'S HOME address is in Surrey, England, but for the duration of the filming at Radical Mind, he has rented an apartment at the expensive end of the Rue Parisie. One window looks out over the cathedral, and the other overlooks a narrow cobbled street that hasn't changed significantly since the time of Jeanne d'Arc. By chance – or more likely, not at all by chance – he lives two streets away from Sophie Destivelle's never-inhabited apartment.

'Hello?' He answers briskly as Picaut presses the buzzer. Age has pared back his voice, but there's still a martial vigour that makes Picaut stand straighter.

In his honour, she practises her English again, leaning in to the speaker. 'This is Captain Picaut. We met earlier. I have a few more questions. May I come up?'

'Yes, of course. Take the lift. Third floor. Green door.'

She takes the stairs. At the top, pipe in hand, Laurence Vaughan-Thomas is waiting with the door open.

'Captain, welcome. Forgive me. I am still somewhat . . .' disconcerted by the morning's news. Sophie was an extraordinarily courageous woman. I did not envisage this end for her.' A Frenchman would sob on her shoulder. Laurence is red about the eyes, as if he's had a recent bout of hay fever.

She follows him into a so-English living room with high-backed armchairs on either side of the window, and an entire wall given over to calf-bound copies of Kipling, Shakespeare, Austen on one side and an eclectic selection of poetry on the other: Auden, Rilke, Emerson, Hilda Doolittle, Stevie Smith, Mary Oliver, Jean Atkin. A radio speaks tinnily from a corner: the BBC World Service, or something that sounds remarkably like it. He switches it off.

On the marble mantel, a walnut music box stands open, a bowl of dried lavender in the centre, just as in Pierre Fayette's house. The difference is that here, it is fresh enough for the scent to fill the room, bringing the aroma of the countryside into the city, balancing the lingering smell of pipe tobacco that lures her back to a forgotten childhood of elderly men, arguing.

To either side is a clutter of framed photographs, and again, as in Pierre Fayette's house, pride of place is given to a string of young Maquisard warriors leaping a wall with a mountain in the background.

Here, though, opposite and balancing it, is a newer version of the same shot in colour – brighter, sharper, the tone cleaner – staged, one has to assume, for the Radical Mind marketing department, in order that they might encourage the big backers to part with their money.

'They look good,' she says.

Laurence replies, 'You'll have heard they let us pick our own actors. I gather that was considered "courageous", which is industry code for hopelessly naive. Nonetheless, I think everyone is now agreed that it was the right choice.

Paul Rey was the hardest. It took an age to find the right mix of intelligence, brash bravery and erotic appeal to the womenfolk.'

He laughs at the expression on her face. 'He had five wives, all told. I'm reliably informed that his colleagues in the intelligence services called him Henry the Eighth minus one. It's a lot to live up to. You'll have time for tea?' He is standing near the window, teapot in hand. Beyond, against the far wall, a round oak table is laid with a chequered cloth and linen napkins.

He gives a wry smile. 'My late mother was of the opinion that any good Englishman held himself and his house in a state of perpetual readiness in case the king should make a personal visit unannounced. All these years and I have never managed to shake off the fear that a royal visitation might find me wanting. These days, I'm sure there are talking therapies specifically intended to resolve this inner conflict, but I am much too old for that kind of extravagance. Do you take milk?'

'No, thank you. Just black. No sugar.'

'Goodness, that's barely worth the effort. Still . . .' She accepts cake and smoky tea, and turns back to the prints on the sideboard. They are cluttered, overlapping, more colour amongst them than Pierre Fayette's equivalents. Here, once again, is the brilliantly blond Laurence in his youth, leaning on his plane.

'Is that a Hurricane?'

'Well done.'

And later, older, leaning on a little open-topped MGB Roadster in British racing green. There are pictures of a red-haired girl, growing up: at school, at university. 'This is Elodie?' The woman is vivacious, dressed in a powder-blue T-shirt, jeans cut off mid-calf, sandals, painted toenails. Her hair is wildly buoyant, pulled back in a scrunchie. She is laughing. Beside her, relaxed, happy, one arm flung around her shoulders, is a young Pierre Fayette.

She asks, 'Which one is the elder?'

'They were twins. Not identical, obviously, but born together.'

'I've just come from interviewing Pierre Fayette. He didn't tell me.'

'Perhaps he thought you knew? Or perhaps it is too painful. They were as close as any two people can be.'

'And yet now they don't speak?'

'Family is complicated, Captain. Those of us on the outside endeavour not to take sides and to support each of them. With luck, they will reconcile.'

Picaut takes a picture with her phone and texts it to the incident room. Petit-Evard responds with a thumbs up. She says, 'Are you close?'

'I have no children, and I owe much to her parents. Elodie is both my apology for the past and a promise to the future. I paid for her education, or at least, the European parts of it. Paul Rey funded Stanford and Caltech.'

'She's clever?'

'Very. You'll meet her soon, I'm sure. She doesn't throw her intellect around, but it's there to be seen.'

There are layers here that Picaut didn't expect. She lifts the image of the wartime Maquisards from the mantel. 'How well did you know Sophie?'

She has asked this before and he has answered. Asked a second time, he reconsiders, sucking on the stem of his pipe. 'I'm not sure any of us could claim really to know her. Paul, I think, knew her best.'

'You kept in touch after the war?'

'For a few years. Not recently. She contacted me a year ago, telling me that Elodie's film was underway, and I agreed to help. I suspect in hindsight that may have been a mistake.' He pulls a wry face. 'The war was complicated, Captain. Many of us prefer not to remember our roles in it. I remain to be convinced that informing the younger generations of the blood spilled by their forebears is of benefit to anyone.'

He is older than he seemed at the studio; his gaze is milky, his face a landscape of past remembrance. He gazes past her, staring at the wall, lost in times and places she will never know. Softly, not to intrude, Picaut says, 'What was Sophie's real name, do you know?'

'I did once.' He abandons restraint and lights the pipe. The first billow of smoke is sweet, and not unpleasant. 'Emilia? No. Amélie. Amélie Fabron was the name under which she came to England, although that, too, may have been an alias and I think you will find very little record of it.'

Picaut is already typing the name into her phone. She stops. 'It was erased?'

'I think so. Are you familiar with JJ Crotteau?'

That name again. 'I am, yes.'

'JJ and Sophie were very close during the war. After it . . . some people wanted a fresh start. Sophie was one of those.'

'We haven't found any record of a Sophie Destivelle, either.'

He smiles, thinly. 'JJ was always very thorough.'

'Do you know who she became?'

'I'm sorry, I don't. We met once or twice in the forties before reunions became a source of shame, but she was always Sophie to us. You understand, we did not pry into each other's lives. If you trusted someone to fight at your side, to give his or her life for you, then that was enough.'

'And did you trust her in this way?'

'Absolutely. Without question.' This is true. She is beginning to get a feel for the times when one or other of these secretive men tells her something utterly beyond doubt. It sets everything else in contrast. 'We have reason to believe Sophie didn't spend much time at the apartment in Orléans,'

Picaut says. 'Do you know of anywhere else she might have lived?'

'I heard a rumour that she had a cabin of sorts in the mountains east of Saint-Cybard. I can't confirm that.'

Can't deny it, either. Picaut pushes on. 'Did you know she worked for the Deuxième Bureau, too?'

'Or as we call them now, our colleagues in External Affairs? Yes, I knew. If you're asking, did she make enemies after the war as well as during it, then of course, it's possible, although I suspect most of them are dead. She was—'

'An assassin.'

'I might not have put it quite so bluntly, but yes. Some of us were relieved to relinquish our weapons at the war's end. Some were not, but did it anyway. A rare few had found a vocation. Sophie was one of them.'

Picaut waits. When he offers nothing more, she says, 'We know you worked for MI6.'

He gives his shy smile, and sucks again on his pipe. 'There is a lot to be said for inter-agency communication.' Smoke fusses past her; it is sharp now, and drags at her throat. She watches him through the haze, sorts through her questions, trying to assemble priorities. 'Elodie called the film *Wild Card* – where does that name come from, do you know?'

'That's a good question.' He spreads his hands. 'I'm sorry, I truly have no idea. You'll have to ask Elodie when her flight lands. Until then, it remains a riddle wrapped in an enigma inside a conundrum.' Another smile. 'Churchill. Speaking of Russia. Whatever one thought of him, one cannot deny that he had a good turn of phrase.'

He stands, stiffly. He has said nothing, but it is clear she has outstayed her welcome. She sets down her cup and follows him to the door. There, he turns. 'The first few hours are crucial to an investigation, so I'm told. Are you able to share such clues as you have?'

'Probably not if I had any, but I don't. Only that Sophie knew whoever it was well enough that she wound down the car window. And they were good with a gun. Without DNA or a ballistics match, we could have some trouble proving anything.'

They shake hands. He says, 'If you have any more questions, please don't hesitate to come back.'

'I won't.' She takes the stairs fast and lightly. Walking back to her car, she Googles Churchill's quote and finds: *I cannot forecast to you the action of Russia. It is a riddle wrapped in a mystery inside an enigma.*

A needle pricks at the back of her mind. She cannot imagine that Laurence Vaughan-Thomas is the kind of man to misquote anyone, especially Churchill. The question is whether it was deliberate or a sign of fractured composure.

He hasn't asked her how Sophie died, which, the more she thinks about it, seems surprising. She puts two question marks next to his name in her notebook.

12.15

Picaut walks the two blocks from Laurence's apartment to her car. The rain has stopped, and she needs the fresh air.

She calls the incident room as she goes. Petit-Evard answers, speaking over the hum of the air conditioning. 'Nothing from the taxi drivers. None of them recognize her.'

Picaut says, 'So we still need to find out how she got to Pierre's house. In the meantime, I want to know why Elodie Fayette changed her name. See if you can find a Duval among the Maquis. And while you're at it, look for a cabin in Saint-Cybard registered to any of the aliases Sophie Destivelle might have used. Run through every combination of women's names and surnames from the Maquis as a starting point.'

'We've got another one, which isn't Maquis. You asked about a Colt M1911 – the gun that Pierre Fayette has in his shed?'

'I remember. Is it legal?'

'Definitely. It was his father's and the registration was changed when he died: all above board. But it's not the only one. There's a whole series that were registered at the same time to Laurence Vaughan-Thomas, René Vivier and JJ Crotteau. The last of them is registered to Amélie Fabron. I'm thinking it could be an earlier alias? One with more of a history attached, perhaps?'

Really, the boy has promise. Picaut says, 'It's the name Sophie Destivelle used when she first went to England. I want everything we can get on it.'

'I'm trying. There's precious little.' There's a pause. He says, 'If our victim knew she was going to die, is it significant that she chose to leave us with ID for Sophie when it clearly isn't her name?'

Picaut says, 'It must be. We just don't know why. Well done.'

'Thanks.' She can hear him blush. In a thicker voice, he says, 'Rollo's gone to see a man about a dog. He says to tell you that Martin Gillard rocks a SIG Sauer, standard police issue.'

'Rocks?'

She can hear the grin. 'Myself, I think he's been watching too many American cop shows.'

Picaut finds herself grinning and only afterwards notices that it didn't tug at her face. Still cheerful, she says, 'Keep an eye on Gillard. This doesn't rule him out, but it doesn't push him any higher up the list, either. Does Rollo have any other gems to share?'

'He says you'll want to know that Sophie Destivelle was working for the Deuxième Bureau in the eighties when JJ Crotteau was in charge.'

'He's jealous.'

'And one day someone will explain to me why.'

'You need another twenty years on the team for that. Tell him I'll send him a selfie.'

JJ Crotteau lives in a three-storey town house opposite a gated park, a few doors up from a celebrated school. The balconied windows face west, towards the trees and children's play area. This is Orléans-chic and unless he inherited it, it did not come cheap.

The door unlocks electronically as Picaut approaches. A leathery voice draws her in. 'Captain Picaut, welcome. You find us at a loss. We just heard the news. Paul and then Sophie gone on the same day. It's too terrible for words.'

JJ Crotteau is waiting for her in the hallway, bent over, leaning on two sticks. In his prime, he was the biggest man Picaut had ever met: not overweight, but big boned, big voiced, a giant presence in any room. Now, although his voice still has its old power, he is stooped, as if his chest has caved in under the weight of such bigness, so that the only way he can look her in the face is to raise his head up and back; otherwise, he'd spend his life staring at his shoes.

'Come in. You have met my grandson, Conrad, and Martha, his daughter. Now is the time to meet the rest of the family.' He shuffles ahead of her, through to a living room that is as French as Laurence's is not.

Instead of calf-bound books and tea set ready for the queen, a clutter of children's toys is scattered through a room that boasts Picasso and Matisse on the walls. If there is a music box containing lavender flowers on a mantel somewhere, it is hidden and its telltale scent swamped by rich coffee. The remains of a late breakfast litter the table.

On the other side of the table, a hawk-nosed man in early old age rises, fluidly. 'Captain Picaut, you find us in the midst of a family reunion. Were my son here, we would be four and a half generations united under the same roof.'

JJ reaches out an age-mottled hand. 'This is my son-in-law, Edward Lakoff. You may know of him as Ted Lakoff, formerly a senator for Illinois.'

Edward Lakoff, who married JJ Crotteau's only daughter, is a dapper man, neat and strong with white hair swept back from a broad brow.

A new piece falls into place. Picaut says, 'You used to chair the Intelligence Select Committee.'

'I am impressed, Captain.' His eyes are blue-grey. Behind his glasses, they seem large in his head. 'Not in this administration, of course – but in earlier, saner, times, I had that honour, thank you.'

So three generations of this family served in the security services of one nation or another. And then Martha, fourth generation, decided to go into the movies. Picaut is digesting this change of tack when the door opens, and here is Martha herself, startlingly blonde, emphatically pregnant. There is something primordial about the two men's response.

Fondly, JJ says, 'My great-granddaughter, who, as you can see, is on her way to bringing us a new generation of Lakoffs. We learned today it will be a boy. We shall call him Paul, in honour of our departed comrade.'

'Congratulations,' Picaut says. And, to Martha: 'You didn't tell me you were related to the Maquis?'

'I'm sorry.' The girl pulls a face. 'Elodie got me the job. Or maybe Gramps leaned on Clinton who leaned on Elodie. I hate the stink of nepotism, but it's the way the world works and I genuinely do want to be a director. It doesn't feel good, though. I don't crow about it.'

Her French is faultless. Her English is mid-Atlantic, not tied to any particular geographic location. Now that the family is all together, it's easy to see the resemblance. Martha is a younger, blonder, considerably more symmetrical version of her father.

She leans over and kisses JJ Crotteau on the brow. 'I need to get back. Clinton'll be going crazy.'

Picaut says, 'I won't stay long. You all knew Sophie Destivelle, obviously, although I'm assuming that if you knew her original name, you'd have told me by now. We have an address for her in Orléans, but she hasn't been there recently. I wonder if any of you has an alternative. In Saint-Cybard, maybe?'

The men both look at Martha, who shakes her head. 'I gave you everything we have. If there's more, only Elodie has it. We met Sophie at the Hôtel Cinqfeuilles in Saint-Cybard. It was the Gestapo centre in the war and Sophie wanted us to film there.'

'You actually met her? You, personally?'

'I was the researcher for this segment. We met twice ahead of the shoot and then the third time, Elodie filmed her. That was last week.'

'Just Elodie?'

'That was the deal: it was to be completely private – no live feed. We set up the camera and the lights and left them to it. There are not many directors who could manage that, but Elodie knows how to handle the kit. They were alone the entire afternoon.'

There's something in the way she says this. Is it pride? Envy? Both? 'Can we see the footage?' asks Picaut.

'Elodie has it. We filmed the day before she went to the US. She went in a hurry when she got the news that her godfather was dying and took everything with her. It's all on her laptop.'

'Then we'll wait until she's here. Someone's gone to pick her up now.' Picaut pulls out one of her new business cards and lays it on the table. 'If any of you has any thoughts, please let me know. I can see myself out.'

Departing, she catches a scent of lavender in the hallway, but cannot see its source.

Of the three old warriors, bound by bonds stronger than blood, Picaut has one left to see.

René Vivier, the last and potentially most difficult – at least for her – lives alone in a single-storey, mid-terrace, south-facing cottage north of the cathedral and west of the railway line. The exterior is white pebble-dash, gone slightly to seed, with decorative red-and-white brickwork in fans around the windows.

He doesn't answer her first two knocks, and Picaut is beginning to consider the wisdom of a kick to the door, when stockinged feet shuffle on wood and a key turns in a lock.

A chain chimes, then two bolts, and a second key. The door opens to the width of her hand, edge-on. She sees the barrel of a gun.

'You?' René shoves the door shut, which is not entirely unexpected. Picaut leans her shoulder against it and keeps it open by perhaps half a centimetre and speaks through the gap. 'Sophie Destivelle was shot twice in the chest and once in the head sometime early this morning.' She doesn't mention the cut throat and the missing tongue.

After a while, he says, 'It wasn't me.'

'Because you lost the fingers of your gun hand in your teens. I know. So do you think you can shoot them now if they come for you, whoever they are?'

She may have pushed too far, or in the wrong direction. For a long half-minute she thinks this, before she feels the door give and manages to shift her weight onto her back foot before it swings wide open.

René stands before her, short, wiry, angry, his hair stained with a lifetime's nicotine. He keeps his arms folded across his chest, his ruined hand on the outside. The fingers of his right hand were crushed, one joint at a time, to make him betray his Maquis comrades. He didn't talk. He got away and fought on. He is not as famous as Daniel and Lisette Fayette, heroes of the battle of Saint-Cybard, but even so, two separate villages in the Jura mountains now have residential streets named after him.

His eyes are small and bright and hard. He lays the gun down on the side table and takes a step away. 'Was anything else done to her?'

That's an interesting question. Picaut says, 'Would you care to tell me what else might have been done?'

'Not if it makes me a suspect.'

'Not only is your hand damaged, but, forgive me, you're also too short. You'd have had to stand on a box to make the shots at the angle they were fired. So no, you're not a suspect, but I am interested in what you think might have been done to Sophie Destivelle.'

'I think she will have had her throat slashed and her tongue cut out.' He smiles, tightly, at Picaut's reaction. 'It's what she did in the war. She cut the throats of traitors and ripped out their tongues. You are looking for someone who knows that.'

'And has reason to do the same to her in return. Do you know of anyone who might feel as if she had betrayed them?'

He tugs thoughtfully on his ear. 'You'd better come in.'

She follows him down a narrow hallway to a small kitchen and adjoining day room that are neither as pathologically tidy as Pierre Fayette's, nor as family-chaotic as JJ's.

René, it seems, is just untidy. Newspapers litter a sideboard. Old coffee cups line up by the sink, waiting for time to wash them. His last meal was a goulash of sorts, which bubbled over onto the surface of the cooker. She smells lavender again amongst the warm burnt-toast smell of a tumble dryer, and the layers of coffee and cigarette smoke, and, yes, a music box stands open on the mantelpiece. This one in a rich red colour;

mahogany, perhaps, or cedar, with the inlaid script almost sulphur yellow on the top.

René sees her looking. 'Patrick made them: Patrick Sutherland, Patron of the Saint-Cybard Resistance. He carved us one each, those of us who survived.'

'Pierre Fayette has one.'

'He inherited Daniel's. Sophie's will be somewhere. Elodie has Céline's. She got everything of hers when she was twenty-one. You'll take coffee?'

She can't refuse, although his coffee looks like tar and she is already near the toxic level. Passing her a mug, he says, 'How is Laurence?'

'Sad. English. We didn't discuss mutilation, which may have been an oversight. When did you last see Sophie Destivelle?'

He tilts his head back and blows smoke at the ceiling. 'I spoke to her by phone five days ago. She called from a mobile and no, I don't have the number; although if you search my phone records, I'm sure it will be there. She was in America. That's all I know.'

She could say, *We won't search your phone records*, but they would both know it for a lie. Instead, she asks, 'What did she call about?'

'Paul Rey was dying. She wanted to know if I had any messages for him.'

'Did you?'

'Only to keep me a warm seat by the fire.' At the sharpness of her look, his grin fades. 'I'm sorry. But we were bad men, Captain. Heaven will not have a place for us.'

'Paul Rey's dead now, did you know?'

His nod might also be a shrug.

'You don't seem sad.'

It is definitely a shrug. He holds up his ruined hand. 'I should have died when this was done. Every day that passes since then has been a gift. I live each to the full and will have no regrets when the last one has passed.'

'You were courageous.'

'I was young and very stupid.'

'You kept silent while men with a terrifying reputation smashed your fingers. That counts as unbelievably brave to me.'

'Of course it does, you were not there. But I know the truth, which is that I was more afraid of betraying my Patron than I was of the Boche.' He makes a circle in the air with his cigarette so that the glowing loop hangs for a moment amidst the smoke. 'Some people will inhabit a much deeper pit of hell than us.'

It would be good to think so. 'Who do you think would want to kill Sophie Destivelle?'

He looks at her, narrowly. 'Are you sure that's the right question?'

'What would the right question be?'

'You have seen this photograph?' Like Pierre and Laurence, he has on his mantel the print of a Maquis war band leaping a wall. He waves at it. 'Look at us. What do you see?'

'Maquisards at war?' He stares at her. She looks again, more closely, at the faces, at the guns, at the shine of their eyes. 'I see young people who hate their enemy and love their own strength and the power of their weapons.'

He lifts his eyes to the skies and back with exaggerated patience. 'You are not a film maker. Elodie saw it straight away. Where are they looking, Captain Picaut? What is their target?'

From either end she studies them: Laurence, Paul Rey, Daniel, René, Sophie and— 'All of them are looking to the left, except Sophie. She's looking over to the right.'

He nods. 'And what is there, Captain?'

'How should I know? What *was* there?'

'I don't know. I have never known. The rest of us had eyes

only for the church door where Maximilian Kramme was stepping out with his new bride. I did not look to my right. I had no idea that anyone had done so until I saw this photograph a couple of months ago when a copy was sent to each of us. I have wondered every day since then. What is she looking at? Or who?'

'Who sent you the picture?'

'That's the question, isn't it? I'd bet on Paul Rey, but he never acknowledged it, and we can't ask him any more. I am told Elodie Duval went to America to get the original ciné film from which this still frame was taken. If you can locate that film, you will learn more about our late friend Madame Destivelle.'

Something in his voice makes her ask, 'Did you love her?'

He laughs, and it becomes a rattling smoker's cough. When he can breathe again, he says, 'You have seen her in old age, and she is beautiful, no? In her youth, she was like a magical being, strong and fragile at once: dangerous and beautiful, with a core of such vulnerability that every man who saw her promised himself in his heart that he would give his life to save her from harm. So yes, from the moment she first fell from the sky, I loved her. We all did.' He traces the nub of a ruined finger along the mantelpiece. 'This may have blinded us to aspects of her character that were ... not what they seemed on the surface.'

'Pierre Fayette said there was a betrayal and Sophie was involved. Was she a traitor? Is that why she died the way she did?'

'I hope not.' The deep lines about his mouth deepen further. His eyes grow sad. 'She was something she should not have been, that much I can tell you. But she hated the Boche, that also is true. I never saw anyone so desperate to kill them.'

April, 1944: Allied bombers target Budapest and Bucharest ahead of the advancing Soviet Army.

SOE, F-Section: Maurice Southgate, aka Hector of the Stationer network, arrested in Paris. Believed alive.

Hélène Lymond, aka Astraea of the Troubadour network, arrested in Saint-Cybard. Presumed dead.

Sophie Destivelle, aka Keres, dropped as replacement together with supplies as per request.

CHAPTER ELEVEN

Cipher Message from AJAX
of TROUBADOUR network

1.3.44 1522 GMT

REQUEST URGENT REPLACEMENT W/T
OPERATOR STOP ALSO NEW DEPUTY AS
PROMISED LAST MONTH STOP ALSO THREE
PANSY, THREE (MIN) COWSLIP, TWO ASH,
ONE SPIDER, ONE MIRANDA, ONE LONDON,
ONE GRUB INC COFFEE CHOCOLATE TOBACCO
STOP STORES ALL LOW AFTER RECENT
SUCCESSFUL OPERATIONS STOP DROP ZONE
HERON STOP BBC MSG LA JEUNESSE EST
L'ESPOIR DU PAYS STOP LETTER U STOP
MOST URGENT STOP A BIENTOT A

Bluff check: NEGATIVE

True check: GIVEN

Note from cipher clerks:

PANSY = 1 container holding 10 x 7.9mm
German-made Rifle plus 1,000 rounds
ammunition

COWSLIP = 1 container holding 6 x 9mm
Auto Beretta plus 3,000 rounds

ASH = 1 container holding 1 x BREN .303
Light Machine Gun plus 1,000 rounds
(not available. Will substitute STEN: QM)

SPIDER = 1 container of 1 x 3" mortar

MIRANDA = 1 x 70lb 808 type plastic
explosive

LONDON = standard basic surgical kit
(2 canisters)

GRUB = work it out.

Total = 12 canisters inc. one for agent

NOTE from B: Drop to go ahead w agent S.
Food supplies to be given priority.

RAF TANGMERE, WEST SUSSEX
8 April 1944

L ATER, SHE REMEMBERS THE floodlights, the liminal quality of the light on the plane's fuselage, the damp shimmers
on the tarmac where the afternoon's rain has not yet cleared.

At the time, she is bound up in the unreality of it. She hangs
on to the press of the dense, cold air and the taste of coffee,
thick at the back of her throat. These things are real. England
is not. She is in France, she must think only of France.

I am Sophie Destivelle. This is my truth.

My contact is François Duval, a Belgian doctor. I am his nurse, come from Paris. The good doctor wrote the advert and passed it to the mayor of Saint-Cybard, Raymond Vivier, who sent it to his cousin, Victor, who works for the Milice, who passed it to his neighbour, Madame Aubrais, who showed it to me. I have just completed my training. Here are my certificates . . .

'Kramme will know this is fake.' She said this at the first briefing after the night of her undoing.

'Of course.' Laurence Vaughan-Thomas is her case officer. She doesn't like him, but she can't imagine it being anyone else. 'But it is a very good fake and he will want to accept it. He's hardly going to have you arrested, is he? You'll be his greatest achievement.'

'Do they exist, Raymond Vivier, Madame Aubrais, the others?'

'Of course. They have no idea that what they were doing was anything other than their civic duty, so Kramme can break their every bone, and still they won't be able to tell him anything.'

'But if he does . . .'

'He won't. No case officer would want to risk alerting the enemy to any hint of duplicity on your part. So actually, I rather think these four people are amongst the safest in France just now.'

Nobody else is safe, though. Not Sophie, certainly not her contact – the doctor François Duval, who is also Patron of the Saint-Cybard Maquis. He is other things, too, as yet undiscovered. She does not know Laurence Vaughan-Thomas intimately, but she knows him well enough to read fear on his face, in his eyes, in the too-careful use of language. Three times already he has told her that the one person who matters above all others is the Patron.

'At all costs, you must protect the Patron of the Saint-Cybard Maquis.'

So perhaps I shall. Or—

A figure waits at the tail of the Stirling. This newcomer is taller than Vaughan-Thomas, bulkier, dressed well for the cold. His hair is a white hedge, growing out at unkempt angles. He offers his hand in the way of the English officer class who are not used to shaking hands with civilians.

'Mademoiselle Destivelle. I'm sorry we haven't met before, but I have heard much of your progress, and all of it good. Laurence has, I am sure, let you know that we three are the only ones who know who and what you are. Nothing is written down, no conversations have taken place where there was any risk of our being overheard. We shall not betray you. You have my word on that. We count on you not to betray yourself.'

Is she supposed to be grateful? She stares past him into the night. She is beyond fear. She tells herself this: beyond it. The officer has come for a reason; men like him never make journeys like this just to shake hands.

She adjusts her scarf, and waits. He smiles a little, blows on his hands, and says, 'We have an agent somewhere in the region of Saint-Cybard, with the code name Icarus. There may come a time when he requires our aid and you may be the only person on the spot. If that call comes, it has absolute priority. If you have Hitler himself in your sights and that call comes, you leave the kill and you give whatever help you can to Icarus. Is that clear?'

She nods. A silence arises, which she must fill. She says, 'Icarus. Whatever help he needs, if I wish to retain your good will, I am to give it.'

The Brigadier smiles, showing yellowing teeth. 'Splendid. I'm told it's not wise to offer luck. And you will not need it. You will need strength of mind and sharpness of wit. I wish you both of these, Wild Card. A great deal rides on you.'

Wild Card. This is the first time she has heard the name spoken aloud. It does strange things to her head and her heart, like a tuning fork finding its note. She smiles at him, and his eyes widen a little in surprise, or surmise; she can't tell which, then he touches his brow in a half-salute and is gone into the cold night.

She was expecting more. Rumours run rife of the parting gifts of gold, of the weight of them. You can tell how much you are valued by how much they spend. A name costs nothing.

The pilot beckons. The moon waits for no one. She has mounted two steps when a hand catches her arm.

She sees him clearly, the sharpness of his cheekbones, the steel of his eyes, the way they sparkle in the strange, cold light. He wears a hat that hides his Boche-blond hair.

'Captain Vaughan-Thomas.'

'Sophie.' He lets go of her arm. He still wears his gloves. 'Wait a moment.' He is wearing a heavy overcoat against the cold. He undoes the top three buttons, fishes in his inner pocket and passes her something solidly warm; a make-up compact, in gold. 'For you.'

The weight is all she could have asked for. 'A necessary part of my cover?'

His smile is as dry as she remembers, but sad now, at the edges. 'That doesn't stop it being useful. Or any less heartfelt.'

She is turning away, made clumsy by the parachute suit. He says. 'Troubadour's patron—?'

'Is the Belgian doctor. I must not give his name to the Boche. I heard you the first time you said it and every time since.' She wants to know why he matters so much, but she cannot ask and even if she did, nobody could tell her.

He chews on his lip. Even now, he is deciding what he can say. At last: 'He can be prickly. And a stickler for protocol. He also thinks . . . that is, he will not want to put a woman at risk. It is part of who he is. You will have to prove yourself worthy, but once you have done so, he will give his life for you, and more.'

He does not give a name. It may be that she is never allowed to know it, only that, in her opinion, this one man matters more to Laurence Vaughan-Thomas than does winning the war.

She says, 'I shall protect him. I give you my word.' She offers him her hand, and he shakes it, as if she were a man. In many ways, it is the most encouraging thing he has ever done for her.

Climbing the ladder is the hardest part: her parachute harness holds her in a half-crouch and stepping up is virtually impossible. Nonetheless, at the top, she turns to look back into England, and he is still there, looking up at her. He has taken his hat off. His hair is silver in the light. He tilts his head back, salutes her. *'Merde, alors!'*

It is the first French of the night. She salutes and turns away before the light can shine in her eyes.

SAINT-CYBARD, FRANCHE-COMTÉ

Red to green: the light above her head.

Hot brandy tea catches at the back of her throat, sloshes about her heart. The controller's hand swipes down, hard.

'Go!'

The square space in the floor is black and beyond is the cold, cold night.

Slip-slide out, into the sharp, clean air. Fall. And, falling, pray that the static line was clipped in, that the parachute was properly packed, that this is not an elaborate murder, planned to send you diving five hundred feet to earth. Kramme is somewhere down there.

The tug wrenches her groin, snaps her shoulders back. The air rips open above her, her head tears a white hole in the black sky, and she is falling less fast, but still too fast, too fast, too fast . . .

The correct posture to brace for landing keeps the feet

parallel to the ground, knees together, flex the hips, roll into the impact.

But this is nothing like the practice. An unploughed field hurls up to assault her. The turf bucks and heaves and she falls on her side, and hits rocks, and rolls down a slope until she is jammed at the foot of it with a stone wall to one side and earth to the other and her pack wedged beneath her and her parachute snagged somewhere over her right shoulder. *The landing ground should be flat and free of obstruction.* She cannot breathe.

'You look like a beetle trapped on its back.'

The shadow looming over her speaks in the English of the officer class. From behind him, where she can't see, men are shouting at each other in French. Even so, it may be a German trap.

Nobody shouts at her. The figure waits. She says, 'They say the asparagus is best picked under the full moon.'

She speaks French. The shadow answers back in the same tongue. 'And Churchill's cigars are green in its honour, but the Boche know that by now, so you want to watch where you say it aloud. London should have told you.'

So this is her new Patron. This, *this* is the famous François Duval, friend of Laurence Vaughan-Thomas, whose life she must preserve above even her own. Welcome to France, Sophie.

He can be prickly ... You will have to prove yourself worthy ...

Fuck that.

She spits out a mouthful of dirt. 'I am not responsible for London's mistakes.'

His face is visible now; long and lean and tired. He is staring at her, fixedly, so that she can see the white rims of his irises. Their eyes meet and she thinks he may be about to say something kind, but he turns away. His voice slides down to her. 'Your papers will be out of date, too. We shall replace them in the morning.'

'Are you going to help me up or did I come here to die on my back in a ditch?'

Sighing, he turns back, reaches down and, one-handed, hauls her up – pack, chute and all. His fingers make dents along her bones.

As soon as you stand, check the wind.

She turns to face into the breeze. It isn't strong, but enough to lift the chute, and drag her across the meadow. She thumps the catch on her chest, wriggles out of her harness and wrestles in the silk, rolling it up until she can hold it bundled in her arms and look around at this place she has fallen into, this part of her land that she has never seen, and does not know.

At the top of the field is a thick hedge, and beyond that, a road on which stand a pair of two-horse carts and a monstrous truck with a frayed tarpaulin pulled over its frame and a man-sized cylinder welded behind the cab.

In the meadow, men run, shouting, carrying the other dropped cylinders, four to each, with poles stuck through the carry-slots. A man at the head of each team is brandishing a torch, hollering orders back and forth, across the field, into the woods on her right, out onto the road. All about is a noisy, bright-lit Gallic mayhem.

All reception committees are to be conducted in absolute silence.

Christ, if Kramme had half a clue . . . Why is he not here?

She turns, watching, and stumbles on the uneven earth. The Patron catches her before she hits the ground. He says, 'We are silent when we need to be. The rest of the time . . . this is their country. They need to be allowed to remember that. And yes, your landing would have gone better with a flatter landing site, but the two best ones are blown and we thought you'd rather not meet the Boche your first day here. Our local commander is Kramme.'

He is taller than she is. He looks over her, not at her. His hair shimmers under the silver moon. If the night offered any colour, it might be red.

He looks beyond her, signalling to his men. She is of no consequence: of this, she is sure. Bored, he asks, 'Can you bury that chute on your own, or do you want help?'

She takes a step or two up the slope until her gaze is level with his. 'Have I angered you?'

'Not yet.' He nods into the dark. 'The Gazo is up on the road. When you're ready, I'd be grateful if you'd wait in it until we've finished collecting the drop. How many cylinders came with you?'

'Twelve.' One and a half sticks of the big six-compartment cylinders with their bounty of weapons, ammunition, food, money and medical supplies for this man who claims to have been a doctor.

She didn't pack them, or decide what they contained, but they are here because she is here. Available aircraft are rare and even more so are pilots capable of navigating by rivers and roads under a no-longer-full moon. There is an invasion on its way. Everyone knows this. It follows, therefore, that in the overall list of London's priorities, sending food, fuel and munitions to the middle of the French border with Switzerland does not rate highly. She didn't expect gratitude . . . well, no, actually, she did.

She tilts her head up, makes him meet her gaze. 'How many men have you killed?'

'What?'

She asks in English and he replies in kind and she thinks his accent is similar to that of the local men at Arisaig. For certain, he is not French.

She says, 'Not at a distance, but by your own hand, knife to the neck, hot blood on your hands, in your mouth, up your nose. How many?'

He blinks, twice, hard, opens his mouth to answer, thinks

better of it and turns away. 'Deal with your own debris, then count the canister chutes and make sure they're all buried, too. If someone takes home a bundle of silk, I'll hold you personally responsible.'

He is gone into the dark, striding.

Her training was good. Every fibre of her being yearns to unbuckle the spade from her leg and dig a hole. But first, there is a promise she made to herself last year, when she left French soil.

She fumbles a crushed packet of Gitanes from her inside pocket and, turning away from the wind, lights up.

'Got a spare?'

He could be anywhere between sixteen and twenty-five, the one who stands at the top of the small rise, his body arced against the wind. He's big, not in the way of the Boche officers, who waddle their fat up the streets of Paris, but in the way of farmhands, who are born with bones like mammoths and sometimes brains to match.

He grins at her, and she thinks he might be brighter than average. He's good looking, in a roguish kind of a way, with the beginning or end of a moustache on his upper lip. His hair is sandy-pale, wind-scattered, in need of a cut. His smile is a flash of teeth in the dark, seen and then gone. At least he doesn't hate her. She flips him a cigarette and brushes another match to life.

'Sophie.' As if it's been so all her life. 'Sophie Destivelle.'

'Jean-Jacques Crotteau. They call me JJ.' His accent is from somewhere north of the Seine, but not by much. They shake hands. His grip is hard, his skin like dried cement; he may have a city voice, but he works in the fields, this one. In the flare of the match she sees other things.

She says, 'You've got a parachute.' He is cradling it to his breast. 'We're supposed to bury them.'

He lifts a brow, inviting. 'You haven't buried yours.'

153

'I'm about to.' She brandishes the shovel. 'Where can we put them so the Boche won't see?'

He shrugs, grinning, and she wonders if this is a test, and if so, whether she has passed. Her skin crawls with the uncertainty of it. In Paris, nobody doubted her.

JJ Crotteau grins at her, and death takes a step away. 'The ditch will be fine.' He hands her his cigarette, grasps the shovel and jumps down. 'They don't have time to search every field in France.'

She smokes for two while he digs, then they swap places.

The ditch is a swamp of thick, treacly mud. JJ and Sophie dig down to real earth, and then stone. When they can dig no more, they inter the parachutes.

Together, they shovel-kick the earth back into the ditch and pat it down, standing back to admire the vanishing trick they have achieved. JJ takes a last drag on his cigarette and spins it away into the dark. 'Welcome to France.'

At last, someone has said it. She laughs, loosely. 'The Patron—' she shakes her hand, as if shaking off water. 'Is he always like this?'

JJ regards her thoughtfully for longer than is comfortable. 'Hélène was a mouse; she could tap out Morse well enough, but nothing special. Still, the Boche killed her and it does not sit well with a man like the Patron when a woman dies in pain on his account, even one not so beautiful as you. In every message to the English, he has asked for a Frenchman to replace her as his courier and an army man to replace Albert as his deputy. London promised him both.' He claps her arm with one big, muddy hand. 'At least you are French.' He walks away from her, up the hill. 'We should help to bury the rest of the chutes.'

Twelve parachutes. Twelve vast swathes of silk, enough to make a bedspread, half a dozen shirts, two dozen camisoles. There are, therefore, twelve holes to be dug by men who are variously surly, garrulous, exhausted, scared – and every one of them thinks this is a criminal waste of good fabric.

Georges, Léon, Raymond, Vincent . . . they all glance at her in much the same way the Patron had, with a wary horror. She knows their names from the briefings; now she attaches faces. If I need to, will I give you to Kramme? Or you? Not JJ. Already she thinks she will try not to give JJ to anyone, but she knows that her discretion may not stretch that far.

There are youngsters here, which she didn't expect, and they are both more respectful and friendlier. The oldest introduces himself as Daniel Fayette. He's lean, wiry, dark and looks about nineteen, so when he cadges a cigarette from her, she gives it. His younger brothers try the same and pull faces at her when she tells them that ten and eleven are too young to smoke. Their neighbour, René, is thirteen, with reddish, straggling hair that blows across his face so that he looks like a wild pony, caught on a hillside. He doesn't smoke.

He introduces himself with a gravitas beyond his years. 'I am René Vivier. My father, Raymond Vivier, is Mayor of Saint-Cybard.' It sounds as if he has said this all his life, but he reverts swiftly to a child's gap-toothed, broad-cheeked grin, and joins the other two to dance along beside her, throwing questions in the fast patois of the mountains.

'Is it true that in England, they have a machine to plant the potatoes and another to harvest the corn?'

'Is it true that in England, they have engines that pull the ploughs, and that all the horses have been turned into glue to hold the RAF planes together?'

'Is it true that in England, they make powder that smells nice to spread on the fields instead of dung?'

'Is it true that the English are going to let Russia win the war for them, that they won't come across the sea until the Boche are all dead?'

By local standards, René must be almost old enough to

hold a gun. The last question is his. She answers it as if he were a man.

'The armies are growing day by day; they'll come as soon as they can. And look, to show what they can do, they sent me, and I have chocolate.' Real, French chocolate, or rather, English chocolate, wrapped to look French. The younger boys clamour, as she expects them to. René is not so easily distracted. When he frowns, his brows almost meet across the bridge of his nose in a way that adds to his age.

'Did you bring guns for us to learn to shoot? Bren guns? Stens? Automatic pistols from the Americans?'

'Not Brens, but I brought all the rest. And *plastique*, and timers, and grenades.' She remembers something of her instruction an age ago, in Scotland: *Don't let the children eat the PE.* 'The *plastique* looks like cheese and smells nice, but it will kill you. You must never eat it.'

They know this already, clearly. René's look would shrivel grapes on the vine. He is not diverted from his track. 'Can you teach me to use them, the guns? Can you help me kill the Boche?' When she doesn't answer, his face hardens. 'I'm not too young.'

'You're the same age I was when I started killing the Boche.'

He is not as impressed with this as she had imagined. 'Why, then, won't you teach me?'

'Because the Patron will be in charge of the guns. He will give the lessons.'

So she is not interesting, really. His attention drifts past her to the men carrying in the last precious cylinder, which was lost in the woods beyond the ditch.

She shoulders her pack and follows them up to the road, where they load it into the back of the truck. Three others are already inside; the rest have gone on the horse-drawn carts, to be stowed in barns in places she neither knows, nor wants to know.

'Get in.' The Patron is behind her, speaking to the children, or to her; they are grouped together now. They hand each other up into the back of the truck and sit on benches on either side with the tarpaulin flapping behind and overhead.

Petrol is impossible to get: the Boche have it all. The Gazo, therefore, runs on a mix of charcoal and dried cow dung that burns in the cylinder, giving off a gas that is pumped to the carburettor. The smell is beyond imagining.

The Patron sits in the front with Georges, an elderly, balding blacksmith who is the driver. In the rear, the men doze and smoke and pass a hip flask of coarse brandy back and forth.

Sophie sits between JJ Crotteau and Daniel Fayette. It may be that only they are prepared to sit with her, that everyone already knows she is a traitor. She is too tired to care.

She dozes, her head on JJ's shoulder. Time slips through her fingers like parachute silk. At some point the roar of the Gazo becomes a murmuring, and the ground becomes a soft, enfolding warmth. She drinks hot milk, and realizes she has been shivering when she ceases to do so. And she sleeps.

CHAPTER TWELVE

THE FAYETTE FARMHOUSE
9 April 1944

CAUTIOUS FOOTSTEPS WAKE HER, and the creak of a door, swiftly silenced. She lies still with her eyes almost, but not quite, closed, keeps her breathing even, listens, learns.

It is morning. The day is already warm. Warm and golden, with splashes of cornflower blue, and it smells of warm, soft cattle. Crows call, and doves, the light and the dark of sound playing over the blue and gold world.

She is dressed only in her underwear. She is lying on a soft, well-made bed with sheets that smell of soap and sun and wind. Very faint, somewhere, is the scent of lavender flowers.

All this she absorbs in the time it takes a large man with a long stride to make four paces across a bare wooden floor. He is big, but light on his feet. He is alone.

She rolls a little, so her left arm is underneath her, and her right free of the bedclothes. Straight arm to the throat if she needs to. Elbow in the eye. If he has a gun, then she's—

'Get up. It's late.'

Merde. François Duval is taller than she remembers from the night. In daylight, his eyes are a clear, savage grey. His hair is the colour of new rust. He is thin, and has not had nearly enough sleep.

She swings up to sitting, which at least makes him take a step back. Her underwear is not so substantial as to leave much to the imagination and the Patron is the kind of uptight Englishman who does not relish seeing a woman's part-clothed body in daylight. He hisses an oath and looks the other way. Idiot. She glances past him to study the surroundings.

The room is not vast, but bigger, lighter, than those at the Firm's manors in England. Sun floods in through half-shuttered windows that slice it, so that bands of liquid light pattern the wall.

On a nightstand is a ewer of water in thick, solid-lipped pottery the colour of a June sky, and under her bed is a chamber pot of the same ware, in the bottom of which is a teaspoon of lavender oil. Someone here is kind, then.

She tilts her head at him. What now?

'Get dressed.' And he is gone, out of the door, lightly down wooden steps, hailing someone with a leap of joy in his voice; not her.

Her suitcase is by her bed, retrieved from the first of the canisters to drop. She has the clothes that were made for her in London, and worn for two months, so that they no longer look new. She has washed and rewashed them, put them through the mangle, scrubbed them on the board, until they look as old as did the dress she was wearing when she got onto the boat in Normandy.

Today she chooses one with tiny, dark rosebuds on a pale green background that goes well with her scarf. The cut falls modestly below her knee, flaring out from the belt. Her coat is dusty and has a mended tear on one elbow. Her shoes are leather, not clogs, but they, too, have been distressed to the point of destruction; she will need new ones soon.

Thus she dresses, and, dressing, hears movement beneath

her feet. Bending, she puts her eye to a crack in the boards and sees down onto the back of a brown cow. The smell of hot breath, hot flesh, hot milk, is soft and thick as dough. Quite urgently, she needs to relieve herself, and to eat.

She heads outside, not wanting to soil the perfumed pot, and finds that she was right: the farmhouse is a big one, prosperous. From the top of the wooden steps, she can see out over tended fields, hedges, a cherry orchard in bloom. In the home fields a dozen cows queue to get into the dairy and easily as many graze their way across the release field on the other side. A single field near the road is devoted to lavender, an astonishing extravagance when it could be growing food. Beyond, forested mountains rise in a solid wall, blocking the route east. If she is where she is supposed to be – and it seems she is – then Switzerland is fifty kilometres east. She can walk that in a day if she has to, given good weather and better shoes. I could be free of this, free of choices, free of fear. It won't happen, but she can dream.

The stairs leading down from her room are oak and in good repair while across the yard, a barn is still half stacked with last year's hay, and she is prepared to bet that no arms are hidden under it, bulking out the mass; if this is one of his safe houses, the Patron is not going to risk its being destroyed in reprisals.

Down the stairs, she heads round a corner and finds the Fayette brothers kicking a wooden ball around a yard, waiting for her without seeming to.

The two youngest run from her, screaming.

'*Maman! Maman!*'

'The English is awake!'

Daniel Fayette stands his ground, one foot up on the ball. In daylight, he looks several years older, and more tired than he did last night in the dark. She revises his age upwards to perhaps twenty-five, the age Alexandre would have been had he lived. He lights her a cigarette, passes it over, nods at the door from beyond which the high voices of his brothers are audible. 'They wouldn't speak of you if there was danger, I swear.'

This one, too, I will not give if I can help it: him and JJ Crotteau, who was kind to me when I landed. Nor the children. Definitely not the children.

She says, 'Where is the Patron?'

All Daniel's signals are made with his head. The flop of hair across his brow adds emphasis now, as he nods to the north, in the direction of the barn and the road beyond. 'Gone to fetch the car. You're to go to the house. My mother is waiting. She will like you, but she is also afraid that you will cause the Boche to come.'

'I will leave soon. I don't want to be a danger to anyone else.'

From behind, a new voice says, 'You can't help being that, Mademoiselle Sophie. But you are welcome in any case.' She turns and finds that the door has swung silently on its hinges and Madame Fayette is standing in the opening.

Daniel's mother is a more handsome version of her sons, a big-boned, well-built woman with greying hair and practical hands. Her skin is fresh and clear and youthful.

She steps back, draws them in with a gesture, takes Sophie by the arm and ushers her through to a back door.

'You will need to attend to your ablutions, yes? There's an outhouse beyond the back door. A towel awaits you, and a washbasin. The water is not too cold. After, we have bread for you, and cheese and milk.'

This is heaven. The water is bracing, but after last night, and her waking, it is what she needs. The soap is home-made, and scented with lavender again. It is the smell of this place, beneath everything, the sharp-sweet glory of a summer evening. She washes her face and wets her hair back from her brow. It has a natural curl and she had it cut in London into the kind of head-framing bob that her mother used to favour in the decades between the wars. There is no mirror, but Madame Fayette nods at her as she returns, and Sophie trusts her enough to take it that she looks presentable.

At the table, the bread is soft, white and smells of honey, sweeter than chocolate, richer. She closes her eyes and chews in a kind of pained ecstasy.

'You don't like it?'

'I love it. I am just sorry that it has taken a war to bring me to this.'

Madame Fayette continues to empty her pantry and soon there is not only cheese; there is also butter, more on one plate than she has seen in her whole time in Britain, and a kind of quince jelly, which is sharp, not sweet, and an endless supply of unrationed milk.

A farm dog lies at her feet, sleek and well fed. Sophie is wary of dogs, but this one rests its chin on her foot and she finds herself sneaking it a thumb-sized piece of cheese. In itself, this is remarkable.

After a while, when she can eat no more, Madame Fayette comes to stand at the table.

'You are Parisian?' And at her nod: 'Is it bad there, in the city?'

How can I tell you how bad it is? 'Dead crows sell for ten francs on the black market and women claw each other's eyes to get them. I haven't seen a dog on the streets for three years. For a while, people who had kept them wouldn't eat the sausages. Now, anyone will eat anything and not care whose friend it was. And sugar . . .' She lifts the knife from the honeycomb, watches the bubbles of liquid gold run off. 'We carry sugar in matchboxes and it tastes of cardboard. I have seen a man killed because he had found half a kilo in the back of his cupboard, and made the mistake of telling his neighbour.'

Madame Fayette has produced a bowl and begun to bake. She wipes her hands on her pinafore. 'We shame ourselves.'

'And when we have the chance to overturn that shame, we will blame it all on the Boche.'

She could stay here for days, talking quietly of things that matter, but she hears a car – an actual car, not a Gazo – and her heart is an axe in her chest. In Paris, only the Boche have petrol. If Kramme comes here . . . Rising, she says, 'I could go out the back . . . ?'

'Be calm. He is safe. Physicians are allowed to use petrol. Also the veterinarians, the engineers – some of them – the blacksmiths.'

He. Madame Fayette gives the word a little emphasis, as one might to the president, or a bishop. She might say more but the car brakes hard and its door is flung open and the rust-haired Englishman-pretending-to-be-Belgian is there, giving Madame Fayette a kiss on the cheek, throwing something small and rich to Philippe, who has followed him in, or perhaps Simon – she can't tell them apart yet – and then he is leaning on the table, staring at the remains of her breakfast as if her inadequacies are laid out in the crumbs on her plate.

'What speed's your Morse?'

It's like walking into a brick wall, the assault of his words. She says, 'Fifteen.' Today, because it's easier, she looks past him as he looked past her in the night.

'Words? Or characters?'

'Fifteen words per minute.' Actually, she can do more than this, but fifteen was the threshold above which people seemed to be pulled out of training and sent off to be W/T operators and that was never part of her plan.

If asked, she would have said that spending all day alone in a room tapping out messages that the Boche read as 'I am here, come and get me' never struck her as a useful way to spend her war.

She doesn't plan to do it now, either. He bites his lip, thinks, nods.

'We need to get you proper papers, which means we need to take your picture. You can send to London while they're developing it.'

She remembers the soft young man in Scotland, all his careful work. 'What's wrong with the ones I brought from England?'

'They're out of date. They're printed on the blue paper when it should be green and you're looking forwards when they want you looking sideways. Also, it uses rivets instead of staples. They've all changed since the start of the month. I told London. I tell them everything.' He nods at the door and the car beyond. 'Get in.'

By local standards, the commune of Saint-Cybard is a good-sized metropolis, perhaps half the size of Dijon. The Jura mountains hug it close, blocking the route to the Swiss border, but on a clear day, if Daniel is to be believed, you can see Geneva to the south east, Mâcon to the south west and Dijon to the north, all from the forested heights above the town; certainly, you can see south to the Alps.

On this less-than-clear day, all Sophie can see as the Patron drives her down the main street is the smoke from the chimneys of the Peugeot factory at one end of town and the steam from the station at the other.

The mayor's office has been obliterated in one of the RAF's three unsuccessful attempts to destroy the factory. The town and surrounding area are served now from what may once have been a prosecutor's office, in a plain, whitewashed building with permanently shuttered windows.

In here, on the second of the three floors, she meets Raymond Vivier, father to René of the wild, straggling hair. Here, in an office that smells of printer's ink and stale sweat, he labours to create the permits, passes and letters of introduction that keep civic life flowing, even in war. He also makes the identity papers required by the occupying forces: he is photographer, typesetter and printer, all in one.

'Look to your left, Mademoiselle, if you please?' She looks left. The wall is in need of paint, and perhaps some decoration other than a framed image of the Führer.

Snap-click. The sound is the same as it was in Scotland, two months and half a lifetime ago. A stab of nostalgia surprises her, catching at her breath. 'And to the front? Thank you.' *Snap-click.* 'You are beautiful. The Boche will be dazzled by your eyes.'

'Thank you.' Raymond Vivier is charming, but she knows she is not beautiful, only that men who cannot see into her soul may sometimes think so.

The same could not be said for Raymond. He is unfortunately made, with narrow shoulders and wide hips in a way that reminds Sophie of an inverted parsnip. After a winter in England, the only vegetable she can bring to mind is the parsnip. She tries to think of something more appealing. He has blondish hair, cut short and smooth so that he looks vaguely Aryan.

This, too, is an insult of magnificent proportions. If she is not careful, she will think of Kramme and that would be a disaster. She has a superstition that says if she does not think of him, he will not find her; she will not be required to give up anything or anyone.

Here is the truth. I am Sophie Destivelle. I am here because the English sent me. I do not have the date of the invasion, but I can get it if you let me live, and these men and women who think I am here to help them.

I am Sophie Destivelle. I am a nurse. I will act like a nurse. If revealed to be something else, I will act like a *Résistante*. Nobody will know I am not. Perhaps not even you.

Raymond is wearing clogs. They scuff-click on the floor as he hauls his camera through a rear door into the guts of the building. 'If you can wait ten minutes, I shall have everything in order.' He says it like a question, when really, what else can she do but wait? The Patron didn't even come down the street with her, but dropped her on the outskirts of the town with directions to the office and instructions not to bother him until or unless he sent for her. She knows nobody in this place and without a valid identity card, she's a walking invitation to arrest. Even sitting here, she is a danger to them. It's churlish to complain.

There are two desks in this room, set at right angles along adjacent walls, and four chairs, two against each of the remaining walls. She sits in one. There is nothing to read, nothing to do. When she hears the tread of leather shoes on the stairs outside, a part of her welcomes the distraction while the rest wants to run and hide.

There is nowhere to go. She smoothes her dress, picks at a fray on the cuff of her coat as if it matters more than passing visitors. She has nothing incriminating on her person: no maps, no knife; her scarf is perfectly plain; it does not have worked-out codes printed on it. She is unarmed, but her shoes have steel in the toecaps and she has practised many times the kick that will disable a man. If she is fast enough, she can hit perhaps two before they reach her. She is as sure as she can be that there is only one. She examines her nails, bites at one, languidly, as the door opens.

'JJ!'

All to waste, her dissimulation. The man who stands in the doorway, his bull head cocked to one side, is her new friend, perhaps her only friend in this place: Jean-Jacques Crotteau. There is nothing of the parsnip about JJ, or the Aryan. Seen in daylight, he is built like an ox, with forearms broad as hams. His nose is vast, a crag worthy of a mountain name, and his eyes are sad.

For all that, he grins at her, much as he did in the night. 'Raymond here?'

166

'Developing a film.' The darkroom is through the door to the back. She saw it when he went out, and in any case, she recognizes the smell of developer.

'And the Patron?'

She shrugs. 'Working?'

'Shit.' He bites on his lip. 'Madame Andreu is having her babies. The wife of the Milice.'

'The Milice?' she says. And then: 'Babies? More than one?'

'Twins. The Patron listened to her three days ago.' JJ mimes the stethoscope, the careful patterning across a gravid abdomen. He has remarkable delicacy for one so big. 'He told her there were two and it is true. She is stuck.' He says it as if she were a foaling mare, or a cow; faintly soiled and biologically redundant.

She says, 'The Patron dropped me at the head of the main street and went on. He is a doctor. I assumed he was going on his rounds.'

'He was meant to call in on her.' JJ says this as if the miraculous Madame Andreu had held her two infants inside, especially to await the Patron's arrival.

Sophie is still digesting the start of this conversation. 'The Milice,' she says. 'You mean her husband is chief of the Milice?'

There are the Boche, who are filth, but have some reason for being so: they lost a war and now a madman is telling them they are the master race. There is no excuse for the Milice: Frenchmen who collaborate out of choice, with enthusiasm. They deserve to die in great numbers, like rats in a barn.

JJ's grimace says all that, and more. 'Andreu was the prison governor and now he is captain of sixty armed men, half of whom used to be his inmates. The other half were the guards. The thing they all have in common is that they love the Boche.'

'And the Patron is his doctor?' Truly, of all the madness she has met since she dropped from the sky . . .

'Who else? They think he is as much of a collaborator as they are; this is why he is safe. We have to find him.'

Past the roped muscles, JJ is not altogether easy to read, but Sophie knows the scent of dread, the flexing fingers. In her experience, grown men who would face torture unbowed fall to pieces at the sight of a woman's broken waters.

She says, 'I am trained as a nurse. I have delivered babies. Not twins' – the surging hope on his face crashes – 'but unless she is bleeding, I will keep mother and children alive while you find the Patron, I swear it.'

'What will we tell Andreu? He's never seen you before.'

'Tell him that I am Sophie Destivelle, second cousin to the Patron, and that I have come recently from Paris. My parents are dead. I have my full certificates. See?' She has them with her, and if not wholly genuine, they are perfect facsimiles of the papers she brought when she ran; only her name has changed. They are not out of date. Before she left, Captain Vaughan-Thomas told her that there was now a Sophie Destivelle on the records in Paris, should the Boche choose to check. In this moment, she chooses to believe that he can manage this much magic.

In this moment also, Raymond Vivier returns with her papers. By a miracle, they do not smell of developer, nor do they look newly printed. He has some means of ageing them, even before he has handed them over.

He says, 'Keep them in your shoe for a while, when nobody is about. You will walk with a limp, but it's the fastest way to make them look old.' He notices JJ. 'What?'

'Andreu's wife is in labour.'

'*Merde.*' A hiss, more than a word. 'The Patron?'

'Not here.' JJ looks around, out of the window, through the open door to Vivier's office. 'We need someone to—'

Sophie is standing with her hands on her hips, and if these two men don't recognize this look, they haven't lived around

168

enough women. 'I am a nurse. I have delivered six infants alone, two boys and four girls, the last of whom was the daughter of the second favourite mistress of Hauptsturmführer Dunst of eighty-four Avenue Foch in Paris. You will have heard of it?'

Everyone has heard of Avenue Foch. Whatever Kramme does to his victims in Saint-Cybard, he did more carefully, over longer periods, in Foch, and with spectacular results. The entirety of the Prosper network went down in '43, thanks to Avenue Foch. The Firm will never be the same again.

The two men of the Troubadour network regard her, considering. In silence, they make their decision.

'Come.' JJ flings back the door with a force that makes the hinges shake. 'I'll take you there, and then go and find the Patron.'

Raymond wrestles into an overcoat that is at least two sizes too big. 'René is running errands for the priest. He has a bicycle. I'll send him to you. Anything you need, he'll get it.'

The house of Captain Andreu, formerly of the local gaol, now of the Saint-Cybard Milice, is less than five hundred metres from the office of Raymond Vivier. It is a large place, of classical proportions, with shockingly tall windows that seem, so far, to have escaped bomb damage.

The garden is pretty in an overly tended way, weeded clear of any possible growth. Pearl-blossomed peach trees are trained along walls in perfectly parallel lines. A black-and-white cat – an actual, live, uneaten cat; quite sleek, actually – strolls down the central path, pausing to stare at Sophie as she is ushered past.

Madame Andreu is installed in a downstairs drawing room from which the furniture has been cleared or dust-sheeted. Her eyes are visible over the sheets: nothing else. Her bed is a lumpen monstrosity hand-carved from dark, tropical wood. The lighting is poor, except near the window.

'Bring the bed over here. We need daylight.' Like statues, they glare at her, the big, armed men who cluster here, but, together, four of them pick up the bed and bring it to lie alongside the south-facing window.

Afterwards, one by one, they trot off into the depths of the house and retrieve hot water and newly laundered linen sheets to order. One of them opens a window to let out the stuffy air. Another turns up the heating. Sophie hasn't been in a heated house with hot water on tap since 1940. It is a revelation.

And so to Madame Andreu, visible now in the soft, southern light. She is younger than her husband's reputation might suggest, a brown field mouse with translucent skin and blue-veined hands, closer to twenty than thirty. The mound of her pregnancy is barely visible above the bedclothes. If she has twins, she has hidden them in the hollows of her bones, in the nooks and crannies of her little, angular pelvis. Her labours have ceased for now: she is sweating profusely, but not straining. The only real testament to childbirth is the pile of red, stinking linens and towels screwed up at the foot of the bed.

There are no women in attendance. Sophie sends the men for their wives, sisters, mothers; anyone who will come and be useful. While she's waiting, she washes her hands and brings a wrung-damp flannel to the wife of the captain of the Milice. The girl turns her head away.

Palm to cheek, Sophie turns her back. 'Let me wash your face. You will feel better.'

Madame Andreu submits to the cleansing with the soundless, wordless incomprehension of a foreigner. Sophie lays down the flannel and drags a chair to the bedside. 'Do you speak French?'

'Of course!'

There. See? That wasn't hard. Amazing what a little pride can do. Sophie says, 'I am a nurse. The doctor is on his way, but he may be delayed. It may be that I can help in the meantime. Will you permit me to examine you?'

'Do I have a choice?'

She is the wife of the Milice chief. She probably has almost as much power in this place as anyone but Kramme. Red points of anger tinge the sharp angles of her cheeks and angry women are dangerous.

Sophie chews her lower lip. 'Not if you want to be sure you and your children will live through what is happening.'

Nature has its own comment to make; at that moment, Madame Andreu's contractions recommence with a single, violent heave. The girl's scream is long and hoarse, like the distant braking of a train. There is no need to ask for permission a second time.

Time becomes bloody, cramped and slippery with birthing fluid. Sophie forgets, always, the way her forearm aches, and her fingers become numb, how the first feel of a limb is a mystery, how she has to let go of the part that knows things, and let instinct tell her whether what she has found is an elbow, a heel, a foot. Here, there are not two elbows, but four, four heels, four feet, two heads, or rather one head, almost crowned, but she thinks the foot near it belongs to its twin.

She says things, useful things, perhaps: I am going to have to push him back in, please, if you can, don't push against me for a moment. Never mind. You can't help it, and we made some progress. Again, try again. Good. So now the first one is ready. Send him to me.

It is a girl. She comes out puce, shimmering, cone-headed . . . and whole. Another little Milice. Still, Sophie loves her. Towels are here, and hot water, and all the things she asked for and did not notice when they arrived. A taller, more striking version of the woman on the bed steps forward to take the child. 'I am her aunt. I will hold her now. Until this is done.' Madame Andreu does not demur. She is lost in a world of pain and stretched flesh. She is tired now, and the contractions are weaker.

'She needs calcium. Where is the doc—? Oh.' How long has he been there? He does not have the fresh-skinned look he has when he has been outside. His hair is flat from his hat. He regards her for a long-held breath and then turns to René Vivier, who is standing by the door.

'Get my calcium gluconate bottles, a needle and some rubber tubing.'

He is a good phlebotomist; there is no pain as he slips the needle into Madame Andreu's vein. Everyone watches as the fluid drips in, hypnotically slow. They look from bottle to bed and back again, waiting for the miracle of the calcium to expel the second child.

'Your hands are smaller than mine. Deliver the second one, if you please.'

And so she finds herself once again kneeling, blood stained, reaching, not thinking, hoping.

The second child is delivered whole and alive: a boy. Now that the screaming has stopped, more people are here to observe the outcome, and several of the assembled cross themselves and mutter. With calves, if twins are of opposite sex, they are sterile. They will not believe that this is not the case when a woman has twins.

Sophie does not care. She sits back on her heels, drained, dizzy, hungry beyond anything she can remember. Even waiting for the boat across the Channel, two days without food (or was it three?), she was not this ravenous.

The Patron catches her eye. In the angle of his brow, or perhaps the flat, undemonstrative smile, is a warning. His voice says, 'Monsieur Andreu is outside. You will wash and present yourself to him and then we must go. We have to pay a visit to Madame Labrèche. Already we are late.'

She is too tired to be afraid, whoever is here. Monsieur

Andreu is smaller than her imagination had cast him, but then in her mind, he was bigger than JJ Crotteau, which would be impossible. He is of mid-height, with middling to balding hair that shines with brilliantine. In a world without war, you would think him a bank clerk.

He is not ungrateful, but it is clear he holds with the majority view that his children are freemartins, that his son will be sterile. And so she finds she must talk to him.

'You have names for your children, Monsieur?'

'My son will be Arnaud, after my father. The daughter . . .' His gaze slides past her to someone of more interest in the antechamber. 'My wife will name her. Excuse me.'

It feels like being dropped from a height, this sudden transfer of attention. In one moment, Sophie is the focus of their thoughts; the next, she is stranded, alone in a half-empty room, and everyone is very still, as if a gun has been pulled and the first to move will be shot. She doesn't have to turn to find out why – she is a tuning fork, finding its note.

Kramme is here.

Kramme.

He the stoat and she the rabbit. She cannot look away. He is no bigger or more imposing than Captain Andreu of the Milice. He is a slim man of unassuming proportions. Set somewhere in the decade between thirty-five and forty-five, his remaining hair is a mousy blond, cut to military neatness. He has an open, boyish face, unlined by age or the weight of responsibility. If you didn't know him, you would think he had a keen sense of humour.

He reeks of Boche: that faint almost-ozone of power and expensive unguents, of red wine and good food and the knowledge of superiority. She has seen the way men shrink around him, but she is surprised to see the Patron shrinking with the rest.

He catches her eye. He must not be seen to know her, or she

him, but he smiles, nods, takes off his hat as if they were old friends. His eyes flicker to the Patron, to the others in the room. Her heart is a cascade of terror. She wants to look down. It would be proper to look down. She cannot. The Patron. You must preserve him at all cost. And she wants to. Really, she does. Whatever she may have thought on the night of the drop, here, now, today, she wants to prove to the red-headed Englishman that she is better than any man they could have sent. This is her truth and it is not the right one.

I don't know who this man is. He's the doctor. He's not the Patron. I have not yet met the Patron.

You'll have to do better than that.

I am a nurse. My name is . . .

The Patron catches her elbow, ushers her forward. 'Sophie, let me introduce you to Sturmbannführer Kramme. He keeps the peace in Saint-Cybard.' She is set in front of the monster. 'Herr Kramme, this is Mademoiselle Destivelle, my new nurse, come lately from Paris to fill the gap left when our beloved Madame Florant retired. Sophie will transform the medical capacity of our town.'

'Transform it? That I doubt after all that you have done, but certainly, she will make it more beautiful. She is not only competent beyond her years, she also has eyes in which a man could drown and die happy. Mademoiselle, *enchanté*.'

His French is slightly archaic. Halfway through speaking, he sweeps off his glasses. His eyes are blue-grey and suddenly, startlingly vast. Smiling, bowing, he kisses her hand. His lips are dry. His grip firm. In a world without war, perhaps he, too, would be a bank clerk. He gives her fingers a slight squeeze. She smiles at him. I am your agent, pretending to be in the Maquis, pretending to be Sophie Destivelle, a nurse.

Sophie, who hates you, but will not show it.

Sophie, who will smile and try to make it look real, although she is afraid of you.

She has no idea whether anything she does looks real. 'A delight, Sturmbannführer Kramme. Are you a patient of Monsieur Duval's?'

'Everyone in this town who cares to keep his health is a patient of the good doctor. And today, we have seen why we shall also be overjoyed to be ministered to by you. But you are fainting with hunger, I can see it. François, take her to Monsieur Jacquot's and tell him that I will settle the bill. I will send an officer to Madame Labrèche to explain why you will call on her tomorrow, instead. Her fluttering heart, I am sure, will continue to beat strongly enough for another twenty-four hours, even lacking your ministrations. And sometime in the near future, you must bring Mademoiselle Destivelle hunting. You can handle a gun, Mademoiselle? No? Not even a small one? But then we shall teach you. A lady should always be able to shoot to defend her virtue. Go!' He claps his hands. '*Allez! Vite!* We shall speak again presently. For now, I must congratulate the new father in proper style.'

The meal is astonishing; she hasn't eaten like this ever, not before the war, not in England, not anywhere. She had no idea that it was possible. Which isn't to say the meat doesn't taste like sawdust in her mouth, but she can at least appreciate the work that has gone into making it. Two new men have come with them – two who know the Patron very well, but were not part of the pick-up last night. They are introduced to her as Latimer Bressard and Thibaud Navarre, businessmen of Saint-Cybard.

Bressard is a civic lawyer of some sort; his exact profession is not made clear, but he talks in legal language for the entirety of the meal. Navarre runs the Peugeot factory at the east side of the town, which is no longer making civilian vehicles, but has been retooled to furnish tank tracks for the Wehrmacht.

175

Sophie stitches these facts together from fragments of conversation, all of them innocuous. What is less innocuous is the tap of Navarre's finger on the tabletop. Twice, he spells 'equinox' in Morse. The Patron is talking to Bressard at the time. He nods, says yes, nods again, but it might be entirely unconnected.

The men eat as if it were their first meal, or their last. Sophie picks at her steak flambé and the caramelized peaches that follow it until the Patron stands and makes his goodbyes and leads her out.

Not once in the entire meal has he spoken to her. Still not speaking, he drives out of town, heading east, with the setting sun blazing on the mirrors from behind. Sophie dozes in the passenger seat, lulled by the rocking of the car. It is older than she had thought, and one of the cylinders is not quite firing cleanly. Her father would have had the engine out and stripped it down.

She talks to him in her head, her father, muzzily, as if he were still alive. Did you see me deliver the son of a Milice? I am sorry, but the child is not responsible for the actions of the father. And I shall do things that will balance it out. There will be an assault on the tank factory tonight, I am sure of it. I will make the Patron take me along. He will see what I can—

'Get out.'

Her head is slumped on the window. Her mouth is open, her tongue dry and rough. The Patron is standing at the window on her side, his fists jammed in his pockets, glaring at her.

She is awake, sharply. 'Why?'

One brow flashes up. 'Because I tell you to do so.'

She gets out, keeping the car between them. He does not appear to be armed. If she has to kill him, she'll have to go back to Kramme and give him everything. JJ, Daniel, Madame Fayette, René, Raymond . . . all will be dead.

Nothing happens. He draws no gun, but nods forwards and

she has time to look around. They are in the country, in the mountains, in fact, so soon after the town. A forested slope rises steeply to the south and east, big enough to blot out the horizon and the blue-distant peaks that bite so savagely into the sky. Here, where the car is parked, is a small lane with tall hedges on either side and a river running to the south. To the north are two brick-built barns, their vast doors shuttered. They are lacking, as far as she can tell, any farmhouse.

'Inside.' He jabs his elbow toward the left-hand barn, the one with the tiled roof intact and fewer rat holes along the ground line. 'Quickly.'

He is in a hurry now. He runs ahead of her, in through a small door in the nearest barn's end. She follows him into darkness, dust and streaks of lacerated sunlight struggling through the gaps in the doors. Hay fills one end, dry as spun gold. The Patron throws himself to his knees, where the stack meets the wall.

'In here.'

In here is a space beneath a plank which itself is hidden beneath the hay and then some sacking. It is so well fitted into place that it would not have occurred to her to lift it. Nevertheless, in the space revealed as the Patron tilts it back is a wireless set of the kind she was trained to use: bulky, heavy, difficult to move around and hell to set up the aerial and get a signal. It is also an invitation to arrest and interrogation if she is found anywhere near it by the man she has so recently met.

'We have a send time in three quarters of an hour. The plain text is here.' The Patron pulls a sheet from his pocket. 'You have your own poem, I imagine? And true check? On the assumption that you can encipher, I will return one hour and ten minutes from now. You will open the left-hand door to the other barn just before that as a signal that you are safe. If I don't see the door open, I won't even turn into the lane. Is that clear?'

She nods. She wants to say, 'I am not a wireless operator. Tap out your own codes,' but he's gone, striding, and in any case, she is not certain she has the guts to say that, yet; not to his face. She turns and begins to thread out the aerial. By the time it is done, he has gone.

Cipher Message from KERES of
TROUBADOUR network on behalf of AJAX

9.4.44 1549 GMT

CELERY ARRIVED INTACT STOP INSUFFICIENT
TURNIPS STOP REQUESTED ONE TO OPERATE,
ONE TO RUN STOP WHICH HAVE I GOT QUERY
PARTY MIDNIGHT PLUS CONFIRMED STOP BBC
CONFIRM MSG LE CIEL DU SOIR EST PLUS
SOMBRE MAINTENANT STOP LETTER P STOP A
BIENTOT A

He collects her seventy minutes from the moment he left her. They do not speak in the car, until he draws up outside a row of cottages on the margins of Saint-Cybard.

'You will stay with the Aillardes. They are collaborators. If, at any point, you make them suspicious, they will denounce you. You will not listen to the radio. You will not tap Morse on the breakfast table to keep it fresh in your mind. You will not endeavour to make contact with Raymond, or JJ, or any of the other men. Are these things clear?'

'What about Madame Fayette? She was making dinner for us.'

'That was by way of her humour. She knows you cannot go back there.'

'In case I endanger her?'

'Or her sons. Her family has lost enough to this network already.'

'What am I doing here?' Am I the turnip? In which case do I operate or do I run? She asks this in her head and he ignores her.

'You are my assistant, who is a nurse. You will accompany me by day and you will assist with my work. If there are other things you can do, I will tell you. In the meantime, I expect you will hear more from Sturmbannführer Kramme. He likes you.'

Two days later, a package arrives, c/o François Duval, for his cousin, the nurse, from Sturmbannführer Maximilian Kramme. In it is a dress of flowing burgundy silk, the exact colour of her scarf, cut in a fashion she has never seen and would never dare wear. The note says, 'A gem should have the best of settings.' Shoes and stockings follow a day later, and the day after that, a summer coat with a mink collar.

She opens each in the Patron's presence, increasingly aghast. 'I can't wear these.'

'Unless you want both of us to lose our eyeballs, you will wear whatever he sends you, whenever he asks you to do so.' He turns to walk out of the room. She thinks he is not going to speak to her ever again.

At the door, tight-lipped, he says in English, 'If the bloody idiots had to send a woman you'd have thought they'd have had the basic common sense to send an ugly one.'

CHAPTER THIRTEEN

ORLÉANS
Sunday, 18 March 2018
13.00

A T THE RADICAL MIND studio, Clinton McKinney fields phone calls, most of them from the other side of the Atlantic.

Picaut catches him between dial tones and lays her phone on the table with the Maquisard image on the screen. 'The original of this came from ciné footage shot in 1944. I need to see it.'

'Captain, if we had it, I would show you. Paul Rey had the only copy and Elodie went to collect it. When she arrives, you can add this to the list of your questions.' His fingers hover over the speed dial. 'Did you find anything that might help your investigation?'

'Sophie Destivelle was an assassin in the war, did you know?'

'A member of the *équipes de tueurs*. We had heard rumours to that effect, yes.'

'Did she talk of it on the record to Elodie?'

'If she did, today's events would make it worth its own

weight in platinum. Sadly, she didn't. At least—' He pauses to think. 'Not that I know of. Elodie shot four hours of interviews and I've only seen the rough cuts. It's not impossible. I refer you to Martha, who may be able to tell you more.'

Martha Lakoff is there, as if she has never been away. 'I really can't, but I can—'

Picaut's phone buzzes, an angry-hornet noise that means Rollo is using his spare phone, which means it's urgent, so she answers. 'Yes?'

'How was Pierre Fayette when you left him?'

'Stooped. Quiet. Not as clueless as he wanted me to think. Why?'

'He had a gun, right? You got Petit-Evard to check the registration. Did you take it?'

'His father's M1911 was locked in a box in his shed and no, I didn't take it. There was no reason to. Rollo, *why*?'

'A neighbour rang in. She heard a gunshot and went round to look. She found him in the kitchen. He'd put an old wartime gun to his head and pulled the trigger.'

Oh, dear God. Picaut hits the stairs, running. 'Get someone there, whoever's closest.'

'I'm already here. I was crossing the river when it was called in to the station. I'm in the kitchen, looking at the body.'

'Pierre Fayette shot himself in the kitchen?'

'That's what I'm saying.'

'Can you send me a picture? Give me the widest angle you can get of the body and the area around.'

'Sec . . .'

A click, an electronic bi-tone and an image arrives on her phone. Pierre Fayette's perfect kitchen is a ruin of blood and brains.

'No.' Someone holds a door open for her. She's through and her car is a dozen paces away, in Elodie's space. 'He would never do that. This isn't suicide. We have a second murder.' In her mind's eye is her list, and one name, flashing bold. She spins. Martha is holding the door. 'Where's Martin Gillard?'

'At his desk, last thing I saw.'

'Tell him if he leaves the building, I'll have him arrested on suspicion of double murder.'

'Ah, OK.'

And to Rollo: 'Is there still a maroon silk scarf on the back of the door?'

'Yep.'

'Get it in a bag and send it to forensics. I want to know if Sophie Destivelle ever wore it. Get Petit-Evard there. Leave Sylvie at the airport. Talking to Elodie is still a priority. I'm on my way.'

Pierre Fayette's driveway has been sealed off, and his neighbours have been persuaded to leave the scene.

Fayette's body lies as it did in the photograph that Rollo sent: half slumped in the corner between the oven and the fridge, suit jacket flopped open, tie askew. Picaut wants to straighten it, to return him to the order of his life.

The kettle is still warm. She asks, 'Where's the coffee?'

Rollo shakes his head. 'There isn't any.'

A single blue mug stands on the counter. She pulls on latex gloves and eases open the cupboard immediately beneath. Inside, five mugs stand in a row on the top shelf in careful order: red, blue, blue, red, red. To the right of the last red is space for one mug.

'So we're looking for someone who's either colour blind, or careless. Get fingerprints done on all the mugs. Our shooter will have worn gloves after the event, but he might not have worn them when he first came in. Rollo—' He's there, in the doorway. She points back over her shoulder. Above the oven is a crazy paving of cracks round a circular hole. 'That's the round that killed him?'

'Looks like it.'

'Does it seem like it came from his gun?'

'Hard to tell. Ballistics can get us an answer inside an hour once we let them take it. You're thinking it didn't?'

'I'm thinking that Sophie Destivelle was shot with a silenced weapon. It would be surprising if Pierre wasn't, but the neighbour heard a shot.'

Picaut looks out of the window. To left and right are the neighbouring houses. 'There.' She points to the corner diagonally opposite the shed. 'You can't see that spot from either side. Get someone out there with a metal detector. See if the Colt was shot into the ground, and then brought back and put in his hand. There are blood smears at the edge of the spatter zone. Get someone with UV to see if we can find a bloody footprint. If nothing else, we'll get the size of a shoe. Check the bell on the front door and the knocker at the back for fingerprints. I want hard data from this one. There has to be something.'

It takes perhaps twenty minutes for the first flush of evidence gathering to pass. At the end of it, with the metal detector team just starting on the garden, Picaut finds Petit-Evard standing in the kitchen.

He asks, 'What are we looking for?'

'I have no idea.' Picaut leads the way through to the living room. 'Something that links Pierre Fayette and Sophie Destivelle that made someone think it was necessary to kill both of them now.'

'You think it was the same person?'

'Not necessarily, but we're going to work on the basis that they're linked. Coincidences don't happen in police work. Whatever it is, we'll know it when we see it.' She stops in front of the television. 'What do you smell?'

'Nothing.'

'No lavender?'

He tests the air. 'Maybe a little, under the blood.'

'It was there.' On top of the sideboard is a rectangle of paler veneer. 'A music box, an old one, with a bowl of dried lavender inside, forty centimetres by thirty by fifteen, made of rosewood or something like it, with paler wood inlaid on top, in the shape of the initials *DF MdM*. I saw it earlier this morning. We need to find it.'

They are grasping at smoke. The kitchen is a particular oasis of chaos, but once it's behind them, the rest of the house is as sterile as before. Slipping on a fresh pair of blue latex gloves, Picaut leads the way upstairs where the straight lines and right angles, white paint and dust-free veneer, continue.

In the spare bedroom, Petit-Evard stops her. 'It feels bad, doesn't it?'

'That he's dead, or that we're here?'

'Both. We're intruders. This isn't a place where other people come.'

'And yet,' Picaut says, 'someone else has stayed here recently.'

He looks as she has looked – at the perfectly made bed: flat sheets, ironed and folded at forty-five degree angles on the creases, duvet cover square on the bed. 'How do you know that?'

'The wardrobe.'

The furniture is flat-pack and uninspiring. The wardrobe door hangs ajar. Petit-Evard frowns into the white interior. No clothes hang ready. It could have been empty since it was first taken out of the box. 'I don't see anything.'

'The coat hangers.'

'Right.' And then: 'Right!' And then: 'What does it mean?'

'I have absolutely no idea.' In a row of twelve hangers, the third along is facing the wrong way on the rail. Or the ninth, depending on whether you count from the right end or the left.

Picaut assumes Pierre Fayette would count from left to

right. What Sophie Destivelle might do is anyone's guess. Aloud, she says, 'Three out of twelve or nine out of twelve.'

'Or it points to something.' Petit-Evard pokes around in the base of the wardrobe.

'Or it's one quarter or three quarters.'

'Or it's out in the room.'

'Or it's time. Fifteen minutes or forty-five out of an hour.' And so, finally, Picaut looks at the alarm clock on the bedside table. It's old fashioned, almost fifties retro, might conceivably be an original; big, round-faced with bells on either side of a central ring on the top. The hands are fixed at twelve forty-five. It sits in the centre of the bedside table, facing the wardrobe, and thus is not quite square.

She wants to smash it open on the floor, but propriety will not allow such chaos in Pierre Fayette's house. She has to take it down to the shed to find a screwdriver in his toolbox. Which means she has to go through the kitchen to get the key. Which means she has to pass first through the living room, where Rollo is back from the garden and is studying the magazine rack. 'Find anything?'

'Point four five Colt shell in the far corner of the garden.' He grins. 'I told them you were the best.'

She nods, looks past him to the rack. 'Who reads *National Geographic* any more? Either Pierre Fayette was the most boring man on the planet, or we're being fed a line.'

Rollo raises a brow, waits until she looks at him. 'You're good,' he says. 'It doesn't hurt to hear it.'

She walks past him to the kitchen, where the shed key is not on its hook. 'Who opened the shed?' A uniformed police team has control of the site. Two of them guard the door, one on either side, checking their Twitter feeds. The one on the left, an Asian woman with a pleasing smile, says, 'Nobody. It was already open.'

'Show me.'

The shed door hangs ajar by the width of one hand. The padlock hangs on the hasp, open. The key hangs from the lock and inside, the toolbox is open and the chisel has been used to prise up the floorboard. The cash box is still there, but the gun, of course, is gone.

'Rollo—' He has come in behind her. 'The lump hammer . . .' She nods to the row of tools.

'The one that's out of line?'

The only tool besides the chisel that's out of line. 'Have it checked for prints. And the chisel, the toolbox and the padlock. Whoever did this knows the combination.'

'Consider it done.' He taps her elbow. For Rollo, this is an astonishing intimacy. 'Were you planning to stab the clock to death?'

She had forgotten the alarm clock. She finds a smaller chisel from the set and – yes, sacrilege – uses it as a screwdriver to open the back plate. And is rewarded: inside is a slip of paper folded in half and taped shut. Fragments of dried lavender fall as she eases it out.

Written on the outside is a single word: *Martin*.

She stares at it, long and hard. To Rollo, thoughtfully: 'Does Martin Gillard work for the CIA?'

Before he answers, he checks over both shoulders in a way that would have been funny yesterday. 'I think we shouldn't talk about this in a place we can be overheard.'

'Rollo? We're in a *shed*. You think it's bugged?'

'It doesn't have to be. We're each carrying a phone and by now they're both probably feeding a continuous sound stream into the NSA databases. If we want to go offline, we have to take the batteries out and put them in a safe container. Refrigerators work well, I'm told.'

Picaut shakes her head. 'If Conrad Lakoff wants to listen to us, he'll do it whether we like it or not. And I'm sure he already

186

knows more about Martin Gillard than the best of your contacts. So am I right that he's a CIA hit man?'

'Nothing so clean and neat, although some of his funding may come down their back channels. Gillard's beyond black, which is to say, nobody will ever find actual details, but there's a kind of ghost-media, rumours of rumours of unsubstantiated action: deniable things that happen when he's definitely not nearby.'

'But he is the kind of guy who could put two to the chest and one to the head through a nearly closed car window.'

'He could do that without pausing to think. But here's the thing: it isn't his style. Apart from anything else, there's usually a tonne of unassailable proof that he wasn't in the country when it happened.'

'Great. So why is Sophie Destivelle, a former DB assassin, leaving him messages?'

'Read it and see?'

It's tempting, but the tape would be hard to remove without it being obvious that she'd done so. 'We'll let him open it.' Picaut folds the note into an evidence bag and slides it into her pocket. 'But I want to be there when he does.'

As she turns to leave, Rollo catches her arm. 'I know you think I'm paranoid, but there are some dots to be joined. Elodie Duval was in the US meeting an ex-CIA exec. Martin Gillard's handlers take their orders from Langley, and Conrad Lakoff, grandson of Sophie Destivelle's former employer, is on track to be the next head of the NSA.'

'Your point would be?'

'If the dots join up, this stops being local and becomes international very quickly. Ducat needs to know.'

'I'm going there now. I'll tell him. I'll meet you back at the incident room in twenty minutes.'

Her phone squawks as she is reversing out of the parking space: a text from Eric.

– Appointment. Ingrid's waiting. If you need, I'll come and collect you!

She deletes it.

A second text arrives. She is about to delete that, too, but it's from Conrad Lakoff.

– Where are you? We need to talk.

She writes back.

– Heading to Prosecutor Ducat. Where are you?

– Already there.

14.10

Ducat's famously discreet office is not currently discreet. Two of Conrad Lakoff's big, athletic men stand one on either side of the door.

They recognize Picaut and let her through. Inside, dominating the prosecutor's office – an experience as interesting as it is unusual – is Conrad Lakoff, leaning forward with both hands on the desk. He feels bigger here: the Château d'Alençon warped the sense of scale. His nose is more like a beak, its awkward angle more aggressive.

Ducat is as angry as she has ever seen him. In frosted English, he says, 'Captain Picaut, this is Strategic Operations Director Conrad Lakoff of the Joint Tactical Analysis Research Group. He's here to—'

Lakoff has already taken her hand in his own. 'Captain Picaut, thank God.'

Her guts lurch. 'What's happened?'

'He's gone.'

'Who's gone?'

'My grandfather. JJ. He's vanished.'

'Vanished, as in left home? Walked out? Gone to visit friends? Or are we talking abduction?'

'The latter.' Lakoff lets go of her hand. 'My father left not long after you did to take Martha back to the studio, then came on to the conference to go over my speech with me. Last seen, JJ was sitting in his chair smoking a cigar, reading the paper. Then we heard the news about Pierre Fayette—' He pulls a face. 'I'm sorry if it was supposed to be secret, but members of your Internal Affairs department are at the conference.'

Great. Picaut watches the last colour leach out of Ducat's cheeks.

'Your grandfather,' she says, 'when did you realize he wasn't there?'

Lakoff checks his watch. 'Seventeen minutes ago. That's when we were sure.'

Which was around the time Picaut was standing in Pierre Fayette's shed, looking at a lump hammer. 'You've been to the apartment?'

'I have. When we called him and got no answer, I sent someone round. When they couldn't find him, my father and I went to look. His car is in his parking space on the road outside. His computer is switched on. His coat is on the hook by the door. It's conceivable that he might have walked, hatless, coatless, to see either René Vivier or Laurence Vaughan-Thomas, but he hasn't; I rang them both from my grandfather's apartment and they deny having seen him. I don't know where he is. You have to understand, this is entirely outside our experience of him.'

Picaut asks, 'Does he carry a mobile phone?'

'He has an iPhone. We are endeavouring to track the signal. If he's still carrying it, I'll be relieved, but also surprised. Whoever we're up against knows what they're doing.'

We are endeavouring to track the signal. On French sovereign territory.

Ducat is staring at his shoes. Picaut takes care not to catch his eye. To Lakoff, she says, 'Let us know what you get. We'll put our best team onto this.'

'I thought you would lead it yourself?'

'I'm flattered, but as of half an hour ago, I have two murders to investigate. I can't deal with a missing person as well.'

He frowns at her. 'I thought . . . that is, I heard that Pierre Fayette had killed himself.'

'You heard wrong. I'll keep oversight on the search for your grandfather, but other people need to take this on. Trust us. We have good people.'

'As long as he doesn't end up like Sophie Destivelle.'

'Is that likely to happen?'

He clasps her shoulders, firmly. 'We'll make sure it doesn't, eh?'

The door shuts. After a short time, during which Picaut stares out of the window and Ducat stares silently at the floor, Ducat says, 'We have to find his grandfather.'

'Good luck with that,' Picaut says. 'JJ Crotteau was DB and then External Affairs. He headed up their black ops unit when they blew the *Rainbow Warrior* out of the water in New Zealand. He's as hard as they come, and his experience goes back to the war. If he doesn't want to be found, we won't find him.'

Ducat's face is a study. It's not that he doesn't know all this, it's that he doesn't expect her to know it.

By way of explanation, she says, 'I met him once,' and then, because he is still frowning at her, 'I took a close protection course years ago: rolling over car bonnets, crouching shots, that kind of thing. He was one of the tutors. He'd left the Department by then, but his notoriety sailed ahead of him. Really, anyone who knows anything knows what he's done. Even Rollo. Particularly Rollo.'

'Rollo spends his life surfing hidden espionage blogs: he's supposed to know things like this. You, however . . . Did you pass the course?'

'I am offended that you even have to ask. The point is, if JJ Crotteau is still in possession of any faculties at all, he can drop off the map at will. One of his wartime comrades and the son of another have been shot dead in the space of less than twelve hours. If I were him, I'd be running for the hills.'

'If he's absconded, I don't care. He can hide in dustbins and live off road-kill for the rest of his life if he feels like it. What I don't want is for someone to find him dead on the floor with two to the chest and one to the head. I like my job. Given how hard you fought to get yours back, I believe you like yours, too. SOD Lakoff may be all smiles now, but he's not a man to cross lightly. If you make phone calls, he can monitor them. If you write emails, he can delete them before they ever hit the networks. He can erase your entire existence and rebuild you as someone entirely different. You do not want him to decide you're worth the effort. So I'll harass the search team, and you'll find the shootist and between us, we'll make sure bad things don't happen. Agreed?'

Conrad Lakoff is waiting for her as she leaves Ducat's office, leaning against the bonnet of her car, arms folded across his chest. Seeing her, he spreads his hands, palms out. 'I'm sorry. I thought perhaps I ought to leave before Prosecutor Ducat blew a cerebral aneurysm.'

'We'll do everything we can to look for your grandfather, I guarantee it.' *If he's absconded, I don't care . . .* She wonders if this man was listening to that conversation, to any of her conversations, and what difference it would make if he were.

He says, 'I trust you. Genuinely. But if you're right that Pierre Fayette's death wasn't suicide, we have two people connected to the Maquis de Morez who are dead and one who is missing. In my world, three is a series and we take those seriously.'

'As do we.'

He wants something more of her and she does not know what. He chews his lip. She waits. She has no problem with long silences.

In the end, he says, 'We were wondering if we could see the bodies.'

'We?'

'My father and I.'

'May I ask why?'

'You can, but I'm not sure we'd have a good answer. Instinct, maybe? The hope that we might see something that would crack this open and bring my grandfather back? I realize it's not likely and we're grasping at straws, but sometimes straws turn out to be just what we need.'

His gaze skates off hers, shyly, and he is not a shy man. How can she refuse? 'Of course,' she says. 'I need to call in at the IR. I'll meet you at the pathology suite in half an hour.'

Rollo is waiting for her at the incident room. He hands her coffee and a cheese baguette as she walks in and, through mouthfuls, she says, 'I want you to pick up Laurence Vaughan-Thomas and René Vivier. We're getting a safe house near the river where we can keep tabs on them. Ducat's covering the cost. I'll text you the address when I have it.'

'Right.' He picks up his keys, his phone, his gun. Picaut still hasn't checked her own gun out of central holding. He says, 'If it's urgent, I'll go for Laurence. Send Petit-Evard for René Vivier.'

'No, René has a Colt automatic in a drawer by the front door. Evard doesn't know how to handle a gun. You need to take that one. It's not urgent. You can take both.'

'OK. How was Ducat?'

'Surprisingly calm given that Lakoff just took a piss all over his territory. I seem to be flavour of the month but I can't imagine it'll last. I'm going to ask Ducat to put a tap on his phone. It's time we had a handle on how much he knows.'

There's a pause. She glances up and finds him looking back, shaking his head.

She says, 'Rollo? You think we can't tap his phone?'

He shrugs. 'You can't.' The emphasis is on the pronoun.

'Who then?'

By way of an answer, he lifts her phone from her jacket pocket, and carries it, with his own, out into the corridor. Back inside, with the door shut, he says, 'We need your ex.' And then, in case she hasn't got the point: 'Patrice.'

Patrice. Hardly even an ex, more of a holiday romance except that they weren't on holiday. Anyway, nobody *needs* Patrice, except presumably the team he's working for in Brussels. She says, 'Why?'

'Because if you or I put a trace on Conrad Lakoff, he'll hear about it in exactly the time it takes us to dial the number. Patrice walks the Dark Net the way the rest of us walk up stairs. He can do it under the radar without setting off warning bells – and if someone does notice, he can cover his tracks so the fallout doesn't feed back to him. So if you really want to take a good look at Lakoff without bringing the entire weight of US spookdom down on your head, you need to see if you can entice Patrice back from wherever it is he's hiding.' He checks his gun, slips it into a shoulder holster; a man in his element. At the door, he turns. 'And before that, you need to call Eric. Apparently you missed an appointment with Ingrid. He is not happy.'

14.50

Eric is not at all happy. More accurately, Eric is furious, but because he's Eric, and because Picaut arrives accompanied by

Strategic Operations Director Conrad Lakoff, and his father Edward, the former senator from Illinois, it would be hard for an outsider to tell.

Picaut knows, because he doesn't make eye contact from the moment she walks in. He shakes hands with the Americans and puts himself at their service. You want to see the bodies? Certainly. Sophie Destivelle first. Of course, that's not her real name. I don't suppose we're any closer to knowing who she is? If not, then we'll call her Sophie. Her details are on the wall-file. Her body is here, in the cold cabinet.

And now she is here, lying on the trolley under the cold white lights with the smell of death and Hibitane and surgical spirit tainting the air. Her hair shines like spun starlight. Her eyes are closed. Her mouth is a thin, violet line, closed and stiff now, so that the loss of her tongue is not as evident. The cut to her throat, though, is fully open; Eric has cleaned away the blood and death has retracted the skin and muscle so that, when they tip her head back, both ends of her severed trachea show as a pair of oval pipes and the pale shimmer of her vertebrae is visible deep down in the back of her neck. Whoever made this cut put some power into it.

Beyond the knife wounds, she is whole. Eric has the neatest suture pattern in pathological history. You wouldn't know he'd opened her up to look at her internal organs and closed her again.

They are looking, though, closely, and there is something deeply unwholesome about two strange men studying her naked body with such intensity.

The whole thing makes Picaut's face ache and the sensation doesn't abate when Pierre Fayette's corpse is wheeled across to lie at Sophie Destivelle's side.

'I've only just made a start on Pierre,' Eric says. 'It's a simpler death, obviously, in a much younger man.'

'Definitely not suicide?' asks the older Lakoff, bending

down to get a better look. 'There's some powder tattooing around the wound?'

Speaking for the first time, Picaut says, 'It wasn't suicide.'

'You're sure?'

'I met Pierre while he was alive. I'm sure.'

Conrad Lakoff leaves his father studying the body and goes to look at the images of Pierre's kitchen that are projected on the wall. 'Tidy man?' he asks, eventually.

'Very.'

'And a messy death.'

'Very.'

He steps back. Picaut asks, 'Did we miss anything?'

His smile is a counterpoint to Eric's frigid politesse. 'Nothing that I can see. Good call. Sorry to have wasted your time.'

'Not at all. Glad to have your input.' They shake hands. Conrad Lakoff is charming on the surface, and working like fury underneath. He smooths the sleeves of his suit. 'I ought to get back. Flesh to press, egos to stroke. And I have to go over my speech one more time. I hate speaking in public. If you hear anything of JJ, you will let me know?'

'Of course.'

They leave, gathering their security men at the door. She watches them go and turns, slowly.

'Eric, I—'

'You blew her off. You blew me off. It's fine. Forget it. You're fine. Two failed surgeries that fell apart at round about this date but you don't need a check after the third. It's no problem.'

'I'm—' She runs her forefinger delicately along the scar on her jaw. When she thinks about it, it feels as if someone has slid needles under the skin and wired them up to the mains. 'Am I too late to go up now?'

'She's a professional woman. What do you think?'

'I think I'm fine. I don't need to be seen. But I would like to apologize.'

He turns away. 'She's upstairs. You know how to get there.'

The clinic is on the fourth floor of eight. The lifts have a particular smell that leaves Picaut queasy. The waiting area is lit in a way that smoothes over skin tones. Even after the first surgery, if she waited until she was here to look in the mirror, it looked . . . acceptable.

Dr Sorensen is not immediately available. Picaut glances at her watch – it is nearly three o'clock. She checks her phone and finds no texts she must attend to, nothing in her time-table that needs her urgent attention . . . nothing, in fact, to offer a ready distraction.

She leans back and closes her eyes, which does little to help. It's the smell of this place that undoes her; some part of her reptilian brain drinks in the unique cocktail of surgical anti-septic and hot-house roses and with no control at all, she's back in a bed in a darkened room with a drip in one arm and a pulse oximeter hovering just above the level where the alarms scream in her ear and it hurts to breathe, to move, to open her eyes.

From here, it is too easy to step back through the gates of memory, to heat and smoke and blazing flame and the sense of breathing in death, of her lungs falling in on themselves, of the world narrowing to her hand in front of her face, and then not even that.

'Inès?'

Picaut can stand next to a discharging firearm without flinching, but Ingrid Sorensen makes her twitch. She blinks open her eyes and here is Eric's lover, dark-haired and solemn. If anyone can derail Picaut's return to work, it is Dr Sorensen. Picaut says, 'I'm sorry I'm late.'

'Eric thought you weren't planning to come.'

Well, yes. Is that surprising? 'I have a case—'

'I heard. Congratulations. So we'll be quick, shall we?'

The smell in the air is fear, of course, not roses, and while there may be some catharsis in daydreaming while she's alone, in company it's altogether different. Picaut lies down on the inspection couch under a too-bright light, and all she can see is fire, and all she can taste is smoke, and her jaw is locked and her fingers are crushing each other, knuckle to knuckle, bone to bone, and—

'Does it itch?' A white light etches the edge of her jaw. She doesn't flinch.

'Not much.'

'On a scale of one to ten?'

'Three, maybe? Not all the time.'

'Is that different from the last times?'

'It was much worse last time.' Either that, or her ability to ignore it is greater. She may have said this last time, too.

Ingrid makes notes. Over the scratch of the pen: 'Do you ever see redness at the edges of the scar?'

'No.' This is entirely true: she has seen nothing, because she hasn't looked in a mirror since the first surgery fell apart. Not until today, when Ducat lured her into it. There was no redness then. She would have noticed.

Ingrid writes something that is longer than 'No'. Really, why bother asking questions when Eric is providing all the information? Lean, cool fingers probe at the places Picaut is not allowed to scratch, setting off a fire of prickles.

'I can give you something to take the heat out of it when it gets bad.'

'Honestly, it's fine.'

'If you scratch it and break the skin, we're back to square one and another round of surgery is not going to be easy.'

'I haven't scratched it yet. I won't scratch it now.' Picaut sits up on the couch and swings her legs over. The idea of rubbing cream into the scar makes her want to gag. 'I'm fine. I'm really, really grateful. And I'm fine. Honestly.'

Ingrid Sorensen sits on the chair beside the couch and takes

Picaut's hands. Her thumbs soothe over the white-green knuckles in a way that makes Picaut want to weep. 'You're on the way to being fine. You're not there yet. I would like you to keep heading forward and not back. So I'm going to give you the cream and you don't have to use it. But if you do, rub it carefully from the back to the front in small circular motions. I've put it in your coat pocket. If you never use it, that's fine by me. I'll see you again in a month. OK?'

1942: Baedeker Blitz on English provincial towns underway in revenge for RAF assault on Lübeck. Targets picked from the popular European guidebook.

Home Front, July: 87 British civilians killed, 471 injured. Civilian petrol ration abolished. Widows' and pensioners' allowances increased by two shillings and sixpence per week. Labour MPs say it is not enough.

SOE, F-Section: Of eight agents so far parachuted into France, five are thought still to be at liberty. Of those taken captive, at least one is dead.

CHAPTER FOURTEEN

'*ALORS, MES INFANTS.* HAVE we had an exciting night?'
It is high summer. Laurence's office is busier these days.
He shares it now with his cousin Theodora and her astonishingly attractive raven-haired lover, Julie Hetherington.

Theo was always going to be a valuable addition to the team, but Julie is a revelation. She is, Laurence has discovered, the kind of woman who renders ordinary men dumb, with that glazed look that means they have forgotten, temporarily, about the difficulties in Yugoslavia, where the partisans are fighting each other rather than the Germans; or the failure to destroy the heavy water plant in Norway (so far; that will come, he is sure), or the distressingly short life span of W/T operatives behind the lines in France.

A constant stream of nervous young captains find reasons to visit his office and, on leaving, extend invitations to dinner. Julie rebuffs them with a generosity of spirit that leaves them eternally hopeful and hopeful men work harder, with the result that there is a sparkle to F-Section and to Signals in particular that was lacking before.

Beyond her obvious effect on the Firm's morale, Julie has proved to be a brilliant mathematician. If anyone can squeeze meaning out of a mangled cipher, it is Julie; Laurence has almost begun to look forward to the morning's cache of mis-spellings, fuzzed reception and failed transpositions all neatly realigned.

Just now, a copy of *Le Grand Meaulnes* lies open on her desk and a night's worth of squared paper lies piled, edge perfect, in her out-tray.

He pulls a face. 'Paul Mignon sending us rubbish again?'

'Don't fret, I'm nearly there.'

Whoever is operating the set, Mignon's scheduled time is near midnight. If Julie's near to cracking it, then it's a record: the garbled ciphers from Saint-Cybard are a breed apart. It is to be supposed that men under pressure will make mistakes. The obverse of this is that one might imagine – Laurence certainly does – that German wireless telegraphers are man-machines of immense discipline who can rattle out Morse at over thirty words a minute with never a missed *dit*.

It would be immensely suspicious, therefore, if every missive from an operative supposedly in the field were to be perfect, but the fact that in the past six weeks not a single one of Paul Mignon's twenty messages has come through without an error, is a statistical improbability verging on the impossible. It is this, above all else, that has led Laurence to conclude that the Frenchman is certainly dead, and that a more than usually clever German wireless operator is striving for verisimilitude by inserting errors.

A copy of the mutilated code lies on his desk:

Cipher Message from PAUL MIGNON

1.4.42 0004 GMT

MIDAS QRI3 0004 1.4.42 P28L6W3 P45L9W1
P101L2W4 JIORT FJPEE LMKSA QOCCV FRGPO

And on . . . He has his own copy of Alain-Fournier's novel in his drawer. Mignon never used the poem code: he trained in Paris and then London using the MI6 book-based system, which is infinitely more secure than the poem codes of the Firm. For one thing, the enemy cryptographers are unlikely to know the words off by heart. Furthermore, if they have the wrong edition, the page, line and word numbers set out in plain text at the start of each message will be worthless. The only reason the Firm doesn't use the same system is that Six has forbidden it: their spies are too valuable and they don't want amateurs from the Firm spoiling a perfectly good routine.

Laurence's check on the first indecipherable message was to find out if Mignon had suddenly switched to a new edition of the book, but Julie broke that one after two days' work by finding that he had spelled fiancée with only one 'e' at the end. It's the kind of mistake agents make all the time, but not one you'd expect of a Frenchman who professes to love literature.

That was the simplest of the mistakes. Since then, they have worked hard to crack each one of his messages: the longest attempt took eight thousand permutations before they found the one that worked. On bad nights, Laurence still dreams of it.

'I think I may have got it.' Julie lifts her head. 'He's spelled "Sablonnières" with an "O" instead of an "A" as the first vowel.'

Theo says, 'Are we really supposed to believe that whoever is keying this is not just an idiot, but also functionally illiterate?'

Laurence asks, 'What does it say?'

'Patience, patience, it'll be with you soon enough.'

They work on in silence for twenty minutes while Julie cracks the message, then types it out and passes it across to Theo at the middle desk, who hands it to Laurence on her left.

REPORT INCREASED VICHY ACTIVITY AGAINST
JEWS SOUTH OF DEMRCTN LINE STOP MILICE
RECRUITMENT INCREASING STOP MORALE AMONGST
RESISTANCE FALLING STOP TRANSMISSIONS
NOW V HIGH RISK STOP BOCHE HAS WRIST-
MOUNTED DETECTORS STOP DANGER GREAT
STOP REQUEST NEW CRYSTALS AND SKED STOP

Bluff check: NEGATIVE

True check: GIVEN

Julie lights up a valedictory cigarette, blows an evil-smelling
smoke ring at the ceiling. The cigarettes are not what they
were, even this time last year. Rumours of horse hair being
mixed in with the tobacco may not be true, but it's certainly
been diluted with something unpleasant. Laurence's chest
feels permanently tight and when he coughs in the morning,
his phlegm has a strange dun-coloured tinge.

Theo comes to read over her shoulder. 'Do they really have
wrist detectors? Or is this some kind of Boche bluff to scare
the agents?'

Laurence says, 'Let's hope for Sutherland's sake it's the latter.'

Patrick Sutherland gets on a train every morning and heads
out to one of the research stations in Oxfordshire, helping the
men in brown lab coats to perfect the timing pencils and work
out wireless telegraph techniques that can't be picked up by the
Boche. Some people might be happy to spend their war this
way, but Sutherland has been promised a return to the field and
he is doing a fine impression of a caged tiger while he waits.

'It's not all rubbish,' Theo says. 'Lucas reported the

increasing arrests of Jews in the north when he came home in February. It'll almost certainly be the same in the south. They have deportation quotas to fill, so that's true.'

'Yes, but they'll know that we know that. Lucas's circuit was blown after he left. So they're telling us things that are no longer secret.' Laurence tips his chair back, lifts his heels onto the desk. He thinks better this way and he has a new idea. He passes the sheet back to Julie. 'Take it upstairs. You deserve the credit in any case, and they'll appreciate seeing you more than they will me.'

One has to assume they do because Julie doesn't return to Laurence's den until two o'clock. He hears her long stride and looks up as she bats open the door. 'Good lunch?'

'CD sends his regards.'

'Goodness, you have soared high.' CD is the Firm's new director; the good one, who replaces the utterly abysmal one they had to start with. The new boy is their best, if not their only, hope of fending off the machinations of Claude Dansey and his team of vermin at Six.

Julie pulls a face. 'I did nothing for an hour while you worked on your new problem. I think you have the better deal.' She comes to sit on the edge of Theo's desk and they share a cigarette with the ease of long practice, their blonde and dark heads tilted together.

Briefly, churlishly, he envies them their closeness, and covers it with a laugh. 'What makes you think I have a problem?'

'She means a conundrum,' Theo says. 'A task. Something hard but fun with which to engage your sizeable brain.' His cousin knocks the first tip of ash into the tray. 'I've been watching you for the past hour, but Julie saw it as she walked in through the door. That's because she's cleverer than me. Did you know you only smile when there's something really hard on the table?'

'That's not true. I smile at you all the time.'

'Not like this.' Julie leans over to look at his worksheet and he stifles an urge to cover it up, like a pupil in an exam.

He says, 'I've been back through Paul Mignon's messages. I think there's a pattern to the mis-spellings.'

'A pattern?'

'Theo said it: he only ever mis-spells, he never adds letters in or takes them out. I wondered if there was a pattern to the mistakes and— Why is that funny?'

Julie answers, although they are both laughing at him. 'There are probably six people in the entire country who would think to look for a pattern in that. And you're the one who found it. What is it?'

'Forty-eight messages in total since the Sarpedon raid was blown and the Boche took over the radio. Each of them has two spelling mistakes, giving ninety-six characters. I took the letters they should have been, and the letters they actually were. Added together, you have one hundred and ninety-two characters, and if you interlace those, taking one from each group alternately, you get this—'

```
ERIBMAOQMRTAEMGPVEKLRURMEDAAYNTFOINFK
KFWUIDPCELEZIRGPSVGTEFOSUPAGITXWLYIMES
TPHFHTMNORSSECERGRIHVHDESPHLJIINSMYMRE
ASCJCHEIESFUTPUYYKSEWTQLOBYPOFPEDLPRSE
KIAGNAIFRMOFIRELMCABSLREUITHGDBVWYALLU
EHG
```

'And if you take every third letter of that, you get this—'

```
I AM A GERMAN OFFICER STOP I WISH
TO SERVE HIS MAJESTY STOP PLS INFORM
BRIG VAUG
```

Julie is not laughing now. She stares at the page as if it might burst into flames. 'Is it April the first again and I didn't notice?'

'Definitely not.'

'Are you going to reply?'

Theo says, 'You ought to take it to CD.' This is true. But CD – even the new, more competent CD – is friends with Six, the home of Claude Dansey, who claims personal ownership over anything that smells of espionage and whose deepest desire is to destroy the Firm. So while the rules are straightforward, Laurence has no intention of actually following them. He says, 'I was rather thinking I ought to take it directly to Uncle Jeremy.'

Theo tilts her head. 'You'll have to verify it first. He won't thank you for fairy stories.'

'I know. The question is, how do we do that?'

Julie has been staring at the wall, pretending deafness. Now, she says, 'You need to check two things before you punt it up the line.' She counts them off on her fingers. 'First, is this an artefact of transmission? On statistical terms, we can rule that out: the chances of this happening by accident are millions to one against. So no, not that. Second, we need to be sure that there isn't someone on the listening posts playing some kind of game with us.' She tilts her head. 'You'll need someone to go down to the coast, to check the Y-stations.'

She's right, and she is tilting her head the way Theo does when she's working on her father.

Laurence is happy to oblige. 'Did I just hear you volunteer?'

Her smile is devastating. Were he one of the dry, dusty chaps from upstairs, he'd spend the rest of his life trying to win her hand.

She says, 'I think you did. We need to be there when the next message is due from Paul Mignon, actually standing over the telegrapher and watching the Morse as it comes in. Usually, that would be in a week's time, but if you could reply today in his listening sked, and say that you're sending supplies and need him to nominate a field, he'll send again tomorrow or the next day. We can be there by then. Theo has a cousin down near the coast, I think?'

Laurence thinks not, but Theo says, 'Blythe Chambers lives just west of Plymouth. Mother's cousin, d'you remember? If we go down tonight, we can stay over with her and then go to the Y-station for tomorrow night; we can be there when the next message from Paul Mignon comes in.'

'He needs a new name if he's offering himself as an agent.'

Theo blows a neat smoke ring past Laurence's head and then says, 'Icarus. Call him Icarus. He's already flying too close to the heat.'

And Julie, who is always good on logistics, says, 'Icarus. Perfect. His next sked is two a.m. so we'd need to stay with Blythe again afterwards. We might not be back until Sunday?' There's a hopeful lift to this last remark and Julie is studiously avoiding Theo's eye. Laurence is remembering Cousin Blythe, whose fiancé was widely regarded as a fiction. He is genuinely amazed that Julie knows more of his family than he does, but this doesn't stop him from feeling magnanimous.

'Make it Monday,' he says, expansively. 'There's no big flap on just now. You deserve a holiday by the sea.' He finds a chit for the car pool, scribbles out instructions. 'This should get you the Daimler. Treat it well. I heard a rumour that Uncle Charles is away. If you want to go up to Cambridge for a day or two when you get back, it wouldn't hurt—'

His words remain ever unfinished. Two exceptionally cheerful women kiss him, one on either cheek, and he sits in silence afterwards, feeling the gap of their absence.

27 July 1942

It is Monday morning and Laurence's world is quiet. Outside, the sun is hot and the sky is a pale and delicate blue. Inside, in the quiet of his basement office, Laurence notices the grime, the lack of light, the stale air. Not a single mutilated message has come through for his attention. He has had a telegram from Theo to say that the Y-stations are clear, but he wants to test his theory one more time before he takes it to his uncle. The Brigadier is moving in exalted circles: bothering him with an unproved theory would be unwise.

There are always things Laurence could do to occupy his time, but none of them is pressing. He sends Theo a telegram and, on receiving her answer an hour later, packs up and heads out.

The Daimler being unavailable, the commissar of the car pool gives him an early thirties Hillman Minx with a gear box like a cement mixer and windows that don't quite fit. He heads breezily north and west into Oxfordshire, to another of the Firm's hidden mansions, where he spends a tedious half-hour negotiating his way through a security cordon of middle-aged men, each more desperate than the last to prove that his greatest contribution to the war effort is here, in the English countryside, and not anywhere further afield.

'With respect, sir, you are not on my list.'

'Sergeant, I have no interest in your list. I have clearance from the Director.'

'Sir, I have to confirm his identity.'

'You have to confirm the identity of the *Director*? You do know he employs you?'

'To be honest, sir, if you came with a chit signed by Jesus Christ, I'd have to find the good Lord Himself to confirm that it was authentic.'

'Sergeant, neither the Director nor I claims divine providence.'

'Have to do our best, sir. If you'll wait here?'

'Be my guest.'

Some time later, the good Lord having presumably

vouched for Laurence's credentials, the sergeant returns. Two hundred yards behind him, and gaining fast, strides Patrick Sutherland.

'Thomas! You have no idea how good it is to see you. Are you all right?'

'Perfectly. Just blowing away the cobwebs. Thought I could take you away from all this, for a ride in the country, perhaps?'

Oh, God. The sudden spark in Sutherland's eyes ... Laurence forgets how desperate he is to be gone from here, back to where people are dying. Back to where his chances of living more than a week are too small to contemplate. As if he would be the one to bring the news.

He says nothing and watches while Sutherland regains control; nothing leaks out but a brief, bleak smile and a question. 'What car did you get? Please tell me it's not the Hillman ...'

They drive in silence for the first ten minutes.

Laurence feels uniquely wretched. Maybe he won't go back. Maybe he won't be caught, won't be tortured, won't die slowly, hanging from piano wire with his toes brushing the ground. Maybe none of it matters. He heads east, on quiet lanes.

'Thomas, are you all right?'

'Fine, thank you.' He searches for a safe vein of thought. 'Theo and Julie are taking some R&R. They went up to Cambridge from Plymouth last night. Uncle Charles is away, the house on Devonshire Road is empty: we thought we could stay out of London for a night, just the four of us.'

They've gone out together a dozen times over the past few weeks, two couples in a charming foursome. Bryan at the Queen's Head loves them and the Strand holds their table in one corner on alternate Tuesdays and Thursdays unless they call to say they can't come.

It's as good a way of spending an evening as— Well, no, actually, it isn't. Generally speaking, Laurence spends the evening watching Patrick watching Theodora. And because he knows this is not wise, he inevitably ends up watching his cipher prodigy, Julie Hetherington, who is perfectly delightful and intelligent, and if he were to have a sister, he would like her to be Julie. She, of course, is watching Theodora, so the evening ends in perfect circularity. It's an amicable arrangement, but hardly his preferred choice of an evening's entertainment.

Tonight, therefore, is his gift to Sutherland, who is not showing quite the requisite enthusiasm. Tetchily, Laurence says, 'Do you want to go, or not?'

Sutherland sighs. 'Laurence, the girls come out with us because you ask them to. I come out because you ask me to. Has it occurred to you that we'd all be just as happy sitting at home with a hot mug of something that pretends to be cocoa?'

'Are you telling me you're not in love with Theodora?'

By every measure, this is entirely the wrong thing to say. Sutherland twists round in the Hillman's passenger seat to stare at him. 'Would you prefer it if I were?'

'Don't be ridiculous. I thought—' He has no clear idea what he thinks except that the world should not be as it is. He rubs his eyes with the heel of one hand. 'If you don't want to go, we don't have to. I just thought that Cambridge would be a good change from London. We might enjoy ourselves.' He looks ahead for somewhere to turn. 'If you want to go back home—'

Patrick's hand is on his arm. He's smiling, after a fashion; not like he used to, but like the new, taut, strung-out Patrick. He says, 'Laurence, let it be. We'll have a night out and enjoy ourselves. Such things are not impossible.'

The girls are waiting for them in Uncle Charles's double-fronted Georgian town house on Devonshire Road. Both look younger, fresher, happier, by far. Theo has splashed out on a silk coat in a shimmering green that spills from emerald through to deep jade as it bends and flows with her movement. Julie, he thinks, has a new necklace of pearls, and a new camera, which she insists on using: 'Look, we can all line up and then I can join you and the flash will come in five ... four ... three ... two ... smile!'

They can't take women into college to eat, obviously, and so default to the Eagle on Bene't Street, where the food seems to be a dozen different variants on swede, but the claret is of college standard, and the whisky is perfect. Patrick Sutherland has reverted almost to his former self. He is funny, charming, erudite – and mildly drunk. They all are. Theo smiles at Laurence, who says, 'Let's walk, shall we? I want to hear all about the trip south and we can't talk in here.'

Laurence pays the bill. Patrick doesn't try to share it. Outside, the late evening air smells of mown grass and river water. A gibbous moon casts crisp, hard shadows. Theo says, 'Let's go the long way,' and they walk north along the backs of the colleges, with the river a silver slug to their right and Queens', King's, Clare, Trinity in dusky sequence on its far side. They cross at Trinity Bridge and stroll the cobbled lanes between the colleges.

Patrick hangs back. 'You need to talk about things I need not to hear. If you can get through the business now, we can get the keys to the boatshed and take a punt out on the river. I've always wanted to fish for the moon on the Cam.' And so they head left towards Bridge Street and, finding nobody there who could conceivably hear them, Laurence says, 'So: the Y-stations. Anything else I should know?'

'Nothing.' Julie turns and walks backwards away from him. Her raven hair shines under the moon. The new pearls lie like frozen tears along her neck. 'Whoever your secret sender might be, he isn't an artefact of some addled clerkette's poor fist-work. Or a deliberate plant.'

Theo is watching him. 'What have you got?'

He laughs. Wine thins his blood and leaves his head light. He has never been so easily read. 'In the last transmission after you left, I changed Paul Mignon's sked to something less antisocial than midnight. And then I sent a message via the BBC: "*Icare vole haut.*" He sent back this morning: "Beware Baedeker cities: attacks not over yet."'

'Baedeker?' Theo asks.

'The travel guides,' Julie says. '"Visit Cambridge for the almost-dreaming spires and feed the ducks."'

'Seems so. The Boche would appear to be picking the four-star targets. We bombed Lübeck, they bombed Exeter. We bombed Rostock, they bombed Bath, Norwich, Canterbury; a few nights ago, Hull. Each of these has three stars or more.'

'Dear God: we can destroy more of your ancient architecture than you can ours. That's insane.'

'At least it's taken the focus off London.'

They are evidently no longer talking of secrets. Patrick catches up with them. 'What has?'

'The new Luftwaffe tactic of destroying architecture rather than actual military or industrial sites.'

'Saves them for when you invade: you don't want to have to rebuild all the factories.'

'Then why did we bomb Lübeck?'

'To get to the submarine ports?'

'We did it because it was small enough,' Theo says. 'It was easy to get to, and there wasn't much by way of defence, and the structures were mostly wood so the incendiaries made a big impact. The high-ups wanted to destroy an entire town. To show they could. So they did.' She's angry, and the wine is letting it show. 'It's amazing what the uncles will discuss when they think there's nobody important listening. Harris came to dinner last time I was home. I think they forgot we were there.'

'It's war,' Laurence says, and feels he has just taken

responsibility for the entire bloody mess. 'We have to do something. We'd be speaking German by now if it wasn't for Harris and men like him.'

'Larry, don't be so affronted. We're not cross with you.' Julie catches his arm and kisses his cheek. 'Your cousin Blythe is a pacifist and we picked up her thinking. We'll be back to normal by tomorrow, all gung ho and ready to man the battlements.'

'In the meantime,' Theo says, neatly trapping his other arm, 'we made a new poem for your hapless agents.'

'You mean you wrote doggerel.' Theo and Julie's poetry is famously scurrilous. It's also particularly memorable for those heading into the field and has the advantage that the German cryptographers won't already know it.

'Doggerel, doggerel, my favourite mong-er-el!' Stripped of her inhibitions, Theo can sing remarkably well. She and Julie abandon him, clasp arms and twirl across Midsummer Common. 'It's unbreakable. It's majestic. It's—'

'Gloriouuuuus!' sings Julie.

'Then we must hear it,' Patrick says, grinning, and Laurence lets go of the last vestiges of sobriety and stands with his back to the river, raises both hands, conductor style, and says, 'Sing! I command you, *sing*!' in his best and deepest baritone.

The tune is a music hall stalwart, easy on the ear and unforgettable. The words are . . . highly memorable.

Oh! Did your granny
Use her fanny
Ere your granddad came along?
Did she drop it
On the dance floor
Did she sell it for a song?
Did she share it with her girlfriends?

213

Did they —— the whole night long?
Oh! Did your granny use her fanny ere your granddad came
along?!

They sing it twice through, choking with laughter on the last line. Patrick joins them, spins them round. 'Again! Again! It needs a baritone, though. Laurence, come on!'

He can. He does. He can sing a bass line that works. Julie takes risks on a descant and pulls it off and by the second run through, they can do it all while dancing an eightsome reel, and Laurence throws his head back, howling the words in an abandon of joy and alcohol—

> *Did she drop it*
> *On the dance floor*
> *Did she sell it for a song?*
> *Did she share it with her girlfriends?*
> *Did they —— the whole night—*

'Dear God, is that a Heinkel?'

It's high and fast and it's only one, but yes, it's an He 111.

Patrick says, 'Why are there no sirens?'

'Maybe it's not an enemy. Maybe some enterprising chap has stolen it, and they're nursing it back in so the clever chaps with engineering degrees can take it apart and—' In the clear night, Laurence sees the shadow slide across the moon's face, a duck for the shooting, and in the sly space after, the dribble that falls behind it. 'No, it's not. Run! Bloody *run*!'

Where?

Air raid shelters? There must be some. Don't know where, no time to ask.

The bridge! 'Back under the bridge!' Julie is next to him. He grabs her arm, pulls, hauls her along. Footsteps behind: Patrick and Theo – they are made for each other. 'Sutherland! Run!'

Too late. The first blast rips somewhere over by Sidney Street. 'Julie!' She trips; falls. He skids. The bridge is close, within reach. *Julie!*

Down. He is flung. Or he flings himself. He has lost the ability to tell one from the other, but there is nowhere else to go, and the gutter here is not like the great guttered ditches of Hobson Street that a man could hide in and be safe; here are vague indentations in the roadway, smattered with horse manure, and he is breathing in hot-summer-dry horse shit and here is the whistle-glide and he is braced and braced and dear God, don't let us die. Dear God, don't let us die. Dear God . . .

'Laurence?' So much light. He is blind. A great hoofing kick to his gut and he cannot breathe. He is dying.

'Laurence?' A punch on his shoulder. Punching a bruise. Hurts. Go away. 'Laurence. Get up, man. She's hit.'

Jesus.

He can rise. He does rise. He was lying and now he is standing, swaying. 'Theo?' Dear God, please not Theo too.

'Not Theo. Julie.'

There is fire. A great deal of fire. By its light, he sees that Patrick is in front of him, wild haired, and red down the side of his face. 'Patrick, you're hit. Sutherland – sorry.' Not to call him Patrick. Too familiar.

'A scratch. I'm fine. It's Julie. And Theo.'

'Theo?'

She is by the river, a huddled shape in torn green silk, shimmering in the flame-light. Her blonde hair is short, as if the ends have been severed with a blowtorch. Her face has a red welt down it bigger than Patrick's. Her clothes are filthy.

'Larry?' Her voice . . . she sounds five again, just fallen from the elm in the park at Ridgemount on an August afternoon. He runs to her, as he did then, reaches her, wraps his arms around her shoulders.

'Theo, don't look.' Above all else, it matters now that Theo

215

must never see the mess that is Julie Hetherington. She did not take a direct hit: they would all be dead were it so, but a fluke, a piece of flying masonry, has stripped the skin from her face, crushed her skull, stolen her life. He could pretend it isn't her, but for the sheen of raven hair and the pearls that lie blood-red in the firelight. And Theo, who will not let go. Too late, then. She has seen it.

He stands up. 'Theo, we're taking you home.'

She's on her knees again, picking up Julie's hand. It's warm, still soft, almost alive. 'Make her better, Larry. Wake her up.'

He glances at Patrick, who is weeping, a thing he never thought to see. Patrick's the doctor, he's supposed to be good with blood and death. He mouths, *What do we do*?

Patrick takes her other arm. 'Theo, you have to come home.'

'I won't leave her. I can't.'

'You must. There might be another plane. We have to get to safety. We'll pass the college. I'll talk to the Master. We'll have her taken care of, but we have to go home now. Right now.'

He levers her fingers off Julie's hand and they clamp on to his arms, claw-sharp and white.

'She can't. Larry, she can't leave me now. We were going to . . .'

'I know. I'm so sorry. Come on.' He picks her up, bodily, cradles her like a child. 'Let me take you home.'

Uncle Charles's house on Devonshire Road is unscathed. Just one plane, just one stick, but the fires are big and the fire engines are out, and the police are everywhere, running. Nobody stops Laurence. He carries Theo all the way home, as if she weighs nothing.

Patrick, the trained medic, clears the way, and at the house he puts up the blackout, lights a fire in the grate, finds and pours the brandy, and an unopened bottle of phenobarbitone tablets that he got after France and carries with him, but doesn't use, all while Laurence holds Theo.

He sets her on her feet but he can't make her sit. She won't drink. She is, as far as he can tell, blind, although he thinks she is seeing things, which is different and, tonight, not unusual.

Patrick takes her hand and presses it round the brandy. 'Theo, drink this.'

Her gaze comes back to Laurence, and she is not blind. She says, 'Julie?'

'She's dead, Theo. Julie's dead.'

'Oh, God.' She stands for a moment, her gaze unfocused, and then topples forward out of his grasp.

Neither of them is quite ready. They catch her between them, awkwardly. Her hands trail on the floor, bounce over the threshold as they carry her out of the living room and up the stairs. 'Left. Here. This is her room.'

It smells musty now, and damp. There is only one, pitiful bulb. By its light, her skin is the colour of putty. Her eyes are fixed open, staring. The bed is cold.

Laurence feels uniquely helpless. 'You're the medic – what do we do?'

Patrick is taking her pulse, all his attention inward. Laying her hand back on the bed, he says, 'Keep her warm, give her company, don't expect her to be the same ever again. I'll make us some tea and fill some hot water bottles.'

He leaves, and presently returns with four hot water bottles wrapped in blankets. When he returns a second time, he brings a tray of tea and biscuits. Laurence slides down the wall to sit with his legs straight out in front of him. After another check on Theodora's pulse, a feel of her brow, a lift of her eyelid, Patrick comes to sit against the adjacent wall. Their feet meet, making a perfect perpendicular.

Laurence hugs his mug to his breastbone. In his mind is an indelible sequence of blonde head and brunette; the smiles and the grief; the dancing, the laughter; the love.

As if he had spoken aloud, Patrick says, 'Theo's strong, she'll manage. And I imagine there'll be enough of those present who will understand if she's more than usually upset.'

'How long have you known?'

'About Theo and Julie? Until tonight I wasn't sure. I just knew your cousin wasn't interested in me, however much I might want her to be – and I did, rather more than I was prepared to admit earlier today. One is used, of course, to pangs of unrequited . . . what have you, although I can't remember an occasion when it was quite so inconvenient. I imagine you know the feeling?'

A half-glance in the dark, a half-smile to go with it that slips straight into Laurence's heart and out again. He feels dizzy, but not necessarily badly so. 'One grows used to it.'

'I'll take your word on that.' Sutherland hooks his fingers together, turns his palms out so that all the knuckles crack in a teeth-aching ripple of sound. 'So now there will be two Vaughan-Thomases who have had their hearts ripped out by this bloody war. Do you suppose your uncle, the Brigadier, will want to use this to his advantage, too?'

'He'd better not.'

'I'm not sure you or I have the power to stop him. But we can do whatever's possible to help her when she wakes.'

'If she'll let us.'

'Some things, a man can do without asking permission.'

There's an edge in his voice that causes Laurence to turn, slowly. 'Did you persuade my uncle not to send me into the field? Was that your idea?'

'Emphatically not. But when it was obvious where things were going, I took the liberty of suggesting that you could be usefully employed in the cipher department. Selfishly, I wanted a known face in the boiler room. You've no idea how much safer it feels when you're in the field and you know that there's someone at home who cares that what you send is going to get through even if you make the occasional mistake.'

Laurence shuts his eyes, presses his fingers to the closed lids, watches the bursts of pale violet that result. All things considered, he feels remarkably mellow.

'Do you hate me?' Patrick asks.

'Hardly. I'd rather be in the field, but if I can't do that, I'll stay where I am. And I do, I swear, care that what you send gets through.'

'Thank you.'

They sit a while, drink their tea, say nothing. A threshold is passed, some indefinable boundary and, Julie and the bomb notwithstanding, he feels peace such as he has not known since the flames engulfed him and he fell from the sky.

'Laurence?' Another threshold passed tonight. They've never been on first name terms before.

'Mmmm?'

'There's something I need to tell you.'

It hits him low and hard. 'You're going to France?'

A shrug in the dark: that is all the answer he needs. 'I got word this morning. I'll leave at the full moon a week from now. I didn't know how to tell you sooner. I'm sorry, truly.'

So the spark this morning was knowledge hidden, not hope destroyed. One day, he'll read this man better. He says, 'It's what you've wanted.'

'I know. I also know that it would be so much safer to stay here, telling other people what to do.'

'You'd go mad.'

'I think I should.'

He dares to look then, at the coppery hair, at the face turned towards him in the yellowing light. There is no pain yet, just a kind of numbness that wraps his soul. It was like this in the Hurricane. One's mind puts together the pieces, but one's body takes time to catch up. He has a sense of grasping at smoke, of holding on to what was never there.

Sutherland says, 'I'll still need an ally in the boiler room.'

'You shall always have one. You must know that.'

'And I thought I might use Julie and Theo's poem, if that's not going to upset everyone too much.'

'I think it's a perfect, fitting and honourable epitaph.'

'Your cousin might want it if she goes into the field.'

'If you ever suggest that in her hearing—'

'I won't. I won't. Nothing aloud. Just . . . she'd be good. And after this . . .'

'The Brigadier won't let it happen. The women in my family would kill him by slow inches if he did.'

'I can imagine.' They lapse to silence and, presently, amiably, they retire to the spare rooms. The next morning, they make a series of telephone calls to various aunts so that, by lunchtime, Theo is being cared for with a degree of sympathy that is entirely novel within Laurence's experience of the family.

Soon after, they drive back to London.

No more bombs fall on Cambridge.

The week passes thick and slow as poured treacle, and yet, too soon, Laurence is standing on a dark airfield, a bright moon sneering at him, and Patrick Sutherland, swathed in grey, hunched over with a pack on his back and the parachute harness hobbling his knees, is shaking his hand.

'I want to thank—'

'Don't. It's fine. Just come back in one piece.'

'I intend to. The poem code—'

'Use it. I asked Theo. She says you are the best man to use it.'

'Thank you. And her. I thought we could use it backwards as a bluff check. Just between you and me, if I'm in trouble, I'll tell Jerry we use it backwards every second time. They'll believe that kind of thing.'

'Don't. Patrick, just—'

'And if you get that, I want you to find out where I am and drop a bloody big bomb on it. No heroics, are we clear? Promise me, Laurence.'

'I promise.' He hadn't meant to move, but can't stay still. They grip, arm to arm. '*Merde alors*, Sutherland.'

'I'll be back. You still owe me a bottle of Talisker.' He turns at the tail. 'Whatever Theo and Julie were doing down south, make sure it was worth it. For all our sakes.'

CHAPTER FIFTEEN

ORLÉANS
Sunday, 18 March 2018
16.00

THE RAIN HAS RESUMED, with greater determination.

Picaut runs from the car to the studio and shelters from the downpour under the overhang outside the glass doors. Inside the big open-plan office, the conversation is all in minor keys. The dull-striped fish drift and sink. Nobody looks at her; she is the bringer of pain, but also, she belongs here now.

She wants to go upstairs, but she is not ready to face McKinney and his endless questions. If she smoked, this would be the time and place to do it. She leans back on the glass and stares at the old-fleece sky and makes a list of priorities.

Rollo thinks she should call Patrice. He is probably right. She hasn't thought about him for days and now, just when she should be moving forward, this gate has opened, too, so that memories leak out when she is not expecting them.

They were lovers, once, twice, maybe three times; the exact details are lost in the fire. They parted kindly, she remembers that: there was no rancour. If he were someone else, they could have kept things going on Facebook, but he knows too much of how attention is mined and data harvested ever to go near social media, except to hack someone else's account.

And now she needs him. And he might not be free.

Her face itches fiercely. She has Ingrid Sorensen's ointment in her car, but cannot imagine using it.

Behind her, the door hisses open. She spins. Martin Gillard stands in the open space. He's found a pale blue fleece to pull over his polo shirt that makes his hair look even blonder and takes ten years off his age. Sharply, she says, 'Can I help you?'

'I don't know.' He has a way of measuring her, head to foot and back again, that feels less dangerous than it probably is. 'I was wondering the converse. Can I help you? You looked as if perhaps help would be welcome.'

Attack has always been Picaut's preferred form of defence. She slides her hands in her pockets. 'Why would Sophie Destivelle leave you a note?'

'I have no idea.'

'Did you know her?'

'We met on the day of the filming in Saint-Cybard. I went down to help out.'

'To provide protection?'

Unsmiling, he says, 'Maybe we could say I was there to make sure protection wasn't needed.' He looks around, glances back into the studio. 'Which would have been laughable until we heard about Pierre Fayette. And JJ Crotteau. McKinney is . . .' He makes a wobbling motion with his hands. 'Maybe we could go upstairs?'

On the upper floor, Martha is making more coffee. Picaut takes the office she used earlier. Clinton McKinney follows her in, the very picture of agitation. 'We heard about Pierre. And now JJ Crotteau is missing. This is growing out of hand.'

From Gillard, that would have been a condemnation. From McKinney, it sounds peevish. Picaut says, 'We are working on it. And we have a lead. Sophie Destivelle left a note for Martin hidden inside an alarm clock in Pierre's spare bedroom. So we know he was lying at least this far: she had been to his house and he must have known it.'

She lays the evidence bag on the desk so that the writing is uppermost. She is watching Martin, not the note, and so she sees the moment when his pupils flare, when the lines about his mouth grow tight.

'That's . . .' He chews his lip. 'It's not from Sophie.' His voice is tight. He raises his head, looks at Picaut. 'May I open it?'

She carries spare blue gloves in her car. She passes him a pair. 'Go ahead.'

He has a pocket knife that looks long enough to cut throats with. The scent of lavender rises thinly as he opens the bag and then slits open the tape to lay the note flat. They gather round to read the neat, bold hand:

> *Sunday, 04.27*
> *MARTIN: CHECK YR EMAIL*
> *ED*

McKinney says, 'That's Elodie!'

'It can't be,' says Martin. 'She was still in the air at four this morning.'

They speak in unison, even as Picaut is pulling out her phone and thumbing a speed dial. 'Sylvie? Did you get Elodie off the flight from the US?'

'She wasn't on it.'

'How could she not be? She texted Clinton McKinney to say she was leaving.'

'I know. That's why we didn't bother to check the passenger manifest. I'm sorry. She wasn't on board.'

Fuck. Fuck, fuck, *fuck*. 'McKinney, I'll need her address. Sylvie, drop whatever you're doing and get to 531C Rue de

Bourgogne. It's not likely she's gone home, but we have to check. Go now. Do nothing else.'

'On my way.'

She hangs up. Gillard catches her hand. 'I can help.'

She pulls free. 'BlueSkies and the Foreign Legion? I think not. We'll do this legally.'

'But—'

'Mr Gillard, you will not get in the way of this investigation. In fact, if you so much as leave this building without my written permission, I will issue a pan-European arrest warrant on your name and I don't care who you're really working for. Do I make myself clear?'

He takes a step back. Under his five o'clock shadow, he is pale. Hoarsely, he says, 'I didn't kill her.'

'Who, Elodie?'

'Sophie. Elodie isn't dead. She can't be.'

And now he sounds like McKinney. 'We don't even know if she's in the country. She might have missed her plane.' She takes his shoulders, turns him round, presses him into a chair. 'Sit.' She calls Petit-Evard, who is back manning the incident room. 'Get details of her hotel from Martha. Get onto the US, find out if she's still there.'

'On it.'

Gillard says, 'You don't believe she's still there.'

'I don't believe anything until I have proof. We are looking for the proof. In the meantime, why don't you do what her note says and check your email?'

'Because she hasn't sent anything.' He throws his iPhone on the table, thumbs it open at Mail. 'You can check the servers if you like. The last thing she sent was the text to McKinney last night. I got a copy.'

'The one that said she was on the plane?'

'It said she was about to board, yes.'

'But this is Elodie's handwriting?'

'Definitely. And it's timed at four twenty-seven this morning. At a point when she should have been halfway across the Atlantic.'

'It's not proof of anything. She could have written that days ago.' Picaut looks down at her feet. 'So, think it through. We don't know when, we don't know why, but we know that Elodie wrote this and someone planted it so we could find it and the bad guys couldn't, which means—'

She looks up. 'Check her drafts folder.'

McKinney heads across the corridor to Elodie's office. He stalks back as the printer in his own office coughs to life and spits out a page. 'Well done.' He picks it up on the way past. 'Only one. It's for Gillard.' He lays it on the table in front of Martin Gillard: personal, and yet private.

From: Elodie Duval <ecd1@radicalmind.com>
To: Martin Gillard <mg@radicalmind.com>
Subject: I'm sorry

My love,

Things are running out of control and I must leave. There is too much at stake and too many questions that remain unanswered. Martha has all the data to finish the film. Tell Clinton I'm sorry I can't be there.

I never expected when we started the project that things would move so fast, or in such dark, dangerous directions. If you are reading this, then this evening's gamble has failed. Or perhaps it has succeeded beyond my wildest dreams, but I have failed to take enough care. You have to believe me when I say that I am trying to be safe. To do this right, without endangering anyone – without endangering you. Because I know you would be here if you could, and I grieve that I have been distant these last few days. That's not an indictment of you, or of what is growing between us, but only of my inability to make the world as I want it.

I want it safe. I want it whole. Above all, I want the truth of our past to be laid open for all to see.

Tonight, I hope to find that truth. I may have done so. If you are reading this, I suspect I will have done. What I will not have been able to do is to let you know. Keep watch on JJ and the rest of the MdM. They are active again, and hunting, and may need your help.

Know that, for all the ambiguities of my childhood, I love you, and do not wish you harm.

Take care. Above all else, take care.

'No.' Gillard's face is lost behind his hands. He may be a paid assassin, but if this is acting, it's good.

When he looks up, he meets Picaut's gaze. His voice is thick. 'This doesn't mean what you think it means. "For all the ambiguities of my childhood . . ." – I don't even know what that means. This isn't meant for me.'

'Perhaps not all of it.' Picaut is careful. 'You think she doesn't love you?'

'I really don't.'

'Maybe she just hasn't said so. Women often don't until it's too late.'

'Not Elodie. She wasn't shy at making her feelings known, and I guarantee you, whatever she felt for me, it was not what you would think reading this. And no' – he is recovered enough that he can hold Picaut's gaze squarely now – 'I have not killed her out of some warped sense of rejection. Or for any other reason. I swear to you, whatever else you might think of me, I have not harmed, nor will I ever harm, Elodie Duval. If she is dead, it is not my doing.'

'Is she dead?'

'I don't *know*!' He slams his hand on the table. The noise shocks everyone.

She believes him. She doesn't need to ask if he loves her; it's obvious.

Picaut says, 'If you're right, then this is another layer of a cipher, and we need to find the key.' To McKinney: 'I'm going to need full access to her office, her computer and anything else we can—' Her phone buzzes: Rollo again. 'What?'

'Laurence has gone. I'm at the apartment in Rue Parisie. Door's open, teapot is warm, radio is on; nobody home.'

'Signs of violence?'

'Nothing.'

'Music box gone?'

'No. It's still here. There's a note underneath it. Hang on.' She hears the slide of wood on marble. Good, heavy paper unfolds. 'It's in English.' Rollo's voice becomes formal.

' "Please pass our apologies to Captain Picaut. We will be safer if our whereabouts are not known and we have the skills to ensure this is so. Neither René nor I killed Sophie and Pierre; indeed, we cherished both of them, but we have no doubt that our actions in the past have led to their deaths in the present. We will endeavour to find the proof of who did this. If we succeed, we shall communicate it to you. Once again, our apologies. Please do not waste time or effort in looking for us: we shall keep ourselves safe. In the meantime, I suggest you find Elodie's music box and search within it. If you find Elodie herself, tell her that Céline's poem remains extant. Blythe spirit, LVT." '

'What about René?'

'I'm on my way, but he's not answering his phone.'

Ducat is going to go wild. Picaut says, ' "Céline's poem remains extant." What does that mean?'

Gillard says, 'Céline was one of the original Maquis de Morez. She was English.'

'And Laurence Vaughan-Thomas was SOE and MI6.' A string of facts knits together. To McKinney and Martin Gillard: 'The SOE used poem codes. They were famous, remember? "The love that I have is all that I have . . ." That kind of thing?'

'Life,' Gillard says. 'It was "life", not "love".'

Very clever. 'But we're on the same page. Does Elodie know it too?' McKinney looks blank. Gillard shrugs. It is Martha Lakoff, the intern, who says, 'Sophie and Laurence are her godparents. When she was a child, they taught her ciphers, invisible ink, all the old wartime strategies: they said it was a life skill every child should have. She told me on the way down to interview Sophie.'

'So Elodie's note could be the key to a cipher embedded in the email? That would make more sense.' To Rollo, who is still on the end of the phone: 'Does Laurence's note smell of anything?'

'Besides lavender? Not that I can tell. What am I looking for?'

'Lemon juice.'

'Don't think so.'

'Never mind, bring them in: the note and the music box both. We're going to check out Elodie's apartment. I'll call you if we find anything.'

16.45

'This is just like Sophie Destivelle's place was,' Sylvie says. 'Nobody has lived here for years.'

Elodie Duval is missing. She is not in the US, nor on any transatlantic flight, at least under her own name. In a flurry of activity, McKinney has provided several contemporary images and Picaut has sent them out to the Europe-wide mispers database. Her car is a powder-blue MX-5. The search for this is given the highest possible priority Ducat can command.

Picaut herself, meanwhile, is presently at Elodie's second-floor apartment on the Rue de Bourgogne and, yes, if it has been inhabited at all, it was a long time ago. Walking through the door, the smell is of new paint left to age with no windows open, of light dust and of carpets.

Picaut sets the forensic technicians to check it out in case there are things hidden beneath the surface, but she doesn't hold out much hope. The only good thing is that it's a fast drive back to the studio, where she can work on Elodie's note.

If Elodie's disappearance is bad news, the good news is that nobody has yet found a body and the first thing that greets Picaut at the studio is the CCTV footage from the Charles de Gaulle airport car park, which caught a frame or two of her car pulling out around 21.30 on Saturday – not long, in fact, after she called McKinney to tell him she was still in the US. It is definitely her car, but she might not be the occupant. The MX-5 hangs very low to the road and the cameras were not set for that kind of angle. The images are blurry, dark and of poor quality.

Sylvie leans over and zooms in on the faces behind the windscreen. 'If someone can lend me some software, I can try to make these sharper.'

'This is a film studio,' says Picaut. 'They'll have software better than anything we've ever seen. Ask Martha.'

Petit-Evard calls in from the incident room with news of his own. 'The red scarf you found on the back of Pierre Fayette's kitchen door hasn't got any of Sophie Destivelle's DNA on it, but it has been worn by a red-headed woman.'

'Elodie?'

'Could be. Which means that Pierre Fayette was comprehensively lying: his sister has been there, and probably Sophie, too.'

Which means, in turn, that working out what Elodie Duval was trying to say in her note is at the very top of Picaut's to-do list. In the context of which, she has yet to find an iron.

'A smoothing iron,' she says, for the third or fourth time. 'You know, for making clothes flat.'

'What do you want it for?' McKinney asks.

'To iron Elodie's note.'

'Yes, but why? It's two lines long.'

'Smell.' Picaut thrusts the slip of paper at McKinney, who takes a sniff, shrugs and passes it round. Martin Gillard, predictably, is sharper. 'Lemon juice?'

Once they have been told, they can all smell it: a delicate under-note, overlaid by the lavender. 'She used the lavender flowers to cover the scent,' Picaut says, 'like in the old days. We need to iron this and see what it says.'

'They didn't do things like this in the old days.' Martin Gillard is still angry with her for not letting him take part in the search for Elodie. Half the forces of Europe are on this, but he thinks he can do it better. 'Even in the war, nobody used a child's trick like this. Kramme would have been onto it in moments.'

'Elodie was in a hurry. And Kramme isn't hunting her.'

'Are you sure about that?' McKinney is pacing the room, twitching.

Picaut says, 'If he was a German officer in the war, he'd be over a hundred, so let's assume for the sake of argument he isn't.'

'But somebody . . .' He feels the threat in the air, stops and restarts. 'So, just send an intern out for an iron? Not Martha, obviously, but one of the others?' He reaches for a button on his phone.

Gillard says, 'No, wait. Let me try something else.' In the smart little kitchen beside Elodie's office, he boils a kettle and wraps the paper round the belly as the steam churns out. His hands are red raw when he takes them away, but Elodie's message is clear. The time on the note is ringed thickly in brown: 04.27.

'Is that it?' McKinney lifts it to the light, as if there might be something else hidden within the weave of the paper. 'A number we already had?'

Martin Gillard snatches it back. 'Fuck's sake, Clinton. She's a clever woman and she's left it to us and we found it. What more do you want?'

'To have it make sense, perhaps?' This is the first time Picaut's seen a hint of steel in Clinton McKinney. Perhaps Martin Gillard wasn't the only one in love with Elodie. At least both men are speaking of her in the present tense.

'If this is a key to the email' – Picaut lifts the note – 'which would seem the most likely, we need a cryptologist to work out how to use it.' To Sylvie, she says, 'Can you do that?'

'Sorry.' Sylvie bites her lip. 'You're going to need outside help.'

Rollo isn't back yet, but all the same she can hear him say, I told you so.

Fine. 'I'll be in Elodie's office.'

Elodie Duval's office is a mirror image of McKinney's, except that her long picture window looks south over what was once a derelict brownfield site and has become, in the past eight months, a replica of Saint-Cybard's town centre, down to the dry fountain in the town square. A factory is set off to one side, and a railway station with its many sidings to the other.

Inside, the colours are different. McKinney's office is an exercise in minimalism, all blonde wood, steel and glass; the paint is white. Elodie's walls are painted robin's egg blue and the rest is pleasantly cluttered with books, scripts, pieces of technology. An oak bookcase lines the wall from door to window: eight metres or more. Six shelves reach from floor to ceiling. Picaut walks their length. The books are precisely the same, in the same order, as the ones on the bookshelf in Laurence's living room: English literature and poetry: Auden, Rilke, Emerson, Hilda Doolittle, Stevie Smith, Mary Oliver, Jean Atkin. If the cipher's a book code, they'll never work it out.

She draws out her mobile phone as she looks at the shelves. Her thumb hits keys. Somewhere in Belgium a number rings.

'Hey!' Patrice sounds upbeat, exhilarated, surprised to hear her. 'Sup?' He speaks fluent cyber-English: the lingua franca of international hacking. It may be he's forgotten how to speak French.

She says, 'I'm working again.'

'Cool! Anything exciting?'

'We have two murders, a missing film maker and three old-age pensioners missing, all linked to the Maquis de Morez. I think that qualifies.'

'They don't let you in gently, do they? Wasn't someone making a TV series about the Maquis? Elodie Duval?'

She forgets how closely he follows media culture. 'She's the one that's missing. Her twin brother is one of the murder victims: shot with an old wartime gun and made to look like suicide. The other's a woman who was in the Maquis: professional hit – two to the chest, one to the head, and then some knife work, the detail of which you don't want to know.'

'Who'd she upset enough that they'd pay for a hit on a woman in her nineties?'

'They may not have had to pay anything if it was ordered by a state security service. What can you tell me about Conrad Lakoff?'

The silence on the line has a dead quality, a lack of echo, as if he's put his hand over the mouthpiece. 'Patrice?'

'Don't mess with him, Inès.' The laughter has gone from his voice.

'That's what Rollo said. And Ducat, more or less. He's been thoroughly decent to me.'

'Don't depend on it lasting. Lakoff could erase your existence and still make you wish you'd never been born.'

That, too, is an echo of Rollo. She says, 'I can't ignore him. His grandfather's gone missing.'

'From a graveyard? Seriously?'

'*Patrice!*'

'Sorry, but Lakoff's grandfather died a year ago last August. The Russians held a celebration party that went on for a week. You could smell the vodka halfway round the globe.'

'That'll have to be on his father's side.' Picaut grabs a piece of paper and starts to sketch out a family tree. 'Name?'

'John Lakoff. If he had other names I don't know them. He was old-time CIA. He pretty much ran the Soviet desk through the worst years of the Cold War. The Russians hated him.'

She says, 'OK, so spookery runs in the family, which may be scary, but just now, it's the other one that matters, the mother's father. He was definitely alive this morning because I spoke to him. JJ Crotteau.'

'DGSE? Organized the hit on the *Rainbow Warrior* in New Zealand?'

God, why did he leave? 'That's the one. He was here in Orléans. And now he isn't.'

There's another pause, the click of a keyboard, as if Patrice's attention has wandered, or perhaps focused for the first time. 'Inès, why are you telling me this?'

'Elodie Duval hid a cipher in her brother's house before she went missing. Or at least, we think she did. A set of numbers and an—'

'No!' Harsh. Retracted as soon as it's out. 'Sorry. Not on this line.' A pause, and then, 'Can you find the IP address of the computer nearest you?'

'Yes, it's—'

'Don't say it yet. Your father had a favourite date, d'you remember it?'

The sixth of May 1429: the day Jeanne d'Arc relieved the siege of Orléans. This is the advantage of their having been close. She says, 'How could I forget?'

'Express it as eight digits and add it to the IP number.'

'European or American date format?'

'Ours.'

'OK.' She's standing in front of Elodie's iMac. Brushing the trackpad, she brings the screen to life. 'Hang on.' She puts a hand over the mouthpiece and shouts across the corridor. 'What's the password for Elodie's computer?'

Martin appears at the doorway. 'Carpe Diem. It means—'

'I know. Thanks.'

She does the arithmetic and reads the adjusted IP address to Patrice.

'Well done.' He's laughing at her again. Or with her, maybe. 'Don't go away.'

A click and she is left hanging on an empty line. She drums her fingers on the desk, picks up a pen, puts it down again.

'Inès?' The screen flares to white and then colour and Patrice is there. Alive. Real. He looks tired. 'Can you hear me?'

'Yes.' She reaches for the screen – he is that close, and that far away.

'Cool.' His smile is just as she remembers it. 'First rule of mobile phones says that you don't say anything you don't want the Americans to hear. Particularly not if Conrad Lakoff's involved. This isn't totally secure, but it's better. We've got about three minutes before someone starts to get curious and a minute after that before they work out how to find us. Write the cipher and key on a sheet of paper; hold them up to the screen so I can grab them.'

She already has both the email and the initial note in front of her. She holds them to the screen and hears the crisp crunch of a screenshot, twice.

'We think the numbers are the key,' she says, 'but we don't know how they're used. It'll most probably be some ancient coding system from the war. It might involve a poem, or a book. Probably one of these.' She angles the screen so the webcam takes in Elodie's bookshelves.

'Inès?' His laugh is ragged at the edges; how long has he been awake? In the old days, he could do three days without sleep and you'd never be able to tell. The wild look in his eyes now, the way he drags his fingers through his hair . . . this is like a week without enough Red Bull. 'You know this is impossible, right?'

'Yes, except that Elodie Duval was trained by the old Maquis: she did nothing by accident. She left the note, and the numbers. She meant us to find them and she wouldn't have left us something completely impossible. There's something called "Céline's Poem" which might help if we could find it. I've drawn a blank on Google, but not looked much deeper than that.'

'God . . . OK. I'll work on it. If you turn up anything that might be useful, let me know.'

'Thanks.' Three minutes must be nearly up. Patrice is reaching forward to cut the link. She says, 'Give me a ring sometime when you're not too busy.'

He looks surprised. 'I thought . . . Never mind. I'll call when I can. Soon. Bye.'

The screen flashes briefly, and he is gone. Picaut's chest is hollow, but she feels more solid than she had expected, and more hopeful than is probably reasonable. 'Elodie Duval. Whatever you're playing at, we're going to find what this means, and work out what's happening. And we're going to do it while you're still alive.'

SOE, F-Section, April 1944: General Charles de Gaulle takes command of all Free French Forces. SOE remains under the command of the Ministry of Economic Warfare and thus, ultimately, of Churchill. British officers in command of French networks continue to take orders from London.

Maquis in the northern Jura request arms to defend against increasing Milice and German assaults. Fourteen canisters are sent – half to the Lornier network, half to Troubadour, which lies to the south, but is considered more reliable.

CHAPTER SIXTEEN

SAINT-CYBARD
15 April 1944

A MÉLIE FABRON, AGENT OF the Allied forces, would have
been – is – an exceptional hunter. Sophie Destivelle,
recently qualified nurse and unwelcome assistant to François
Duval, is not.

She fires, and misses a target a six-year-old could hit. The
men of Kramme's hunting party contrive not to notice. The
only other woman present, Luce Moreau – Madame Andreu's
striking younger sister – laughs aloud.

Earlier in the afternoon, as they swept with dogs across the
fields, Mademoiselle Moreau took two hares with two shots,
effortlessly. She is loathsome. Already, Sophie is planning
how to kill her. She would denounce her as a *Résistante*, but
nobody would believe her: the Moreau family are the very
epitome of collaborators. Mind you, the same could be said of
Sophie. And the Patron.

A week has passed since she landed. It is six days since she
delivered the Milice chief's twins, and four since Kramme sent
her a dress of burgundy silk that matches her scarf. The invitation to join him for a day's hunting arrived a day after that.

Sophie wanted to turn it down, but the Patron would not let her. So she is here, under the tall, broad trees with the last of the morning's rain drizzling from the leaves and the sky above blue and the scent of moss and forest so strong you could weave ropes from it, or shackles, or *plastique* . . .

Her weapon is a Mauser K98 and she loves it. All those weeks on the firing ranges in Scotland and Surrey trained her body to become as one with the stock, the barrel, the beautiful action of the bolt. The effort of not-merging has left her with a crippling headache. Her fingers twitch with the urge to strip it down, build it up again, turn, and fire, fire, fire until all the smiling Boche are dead.

Instead, she takes another shot that clips the edge of the oak that is her target, and wrestles badly with the bolt. Kramme takes it gently from her, chambers the next round and reloads her magazine. He is charm personified.

'Do not be downhearted. Mademoiselle Moreau herself was not so good a shot when first we brought her here. We shall make of you the best markswoman in France, I swear it. You are discomfited by the stares of the others. You will do better if we step away from them. Here, let me show you.'

He takes her elbow and steers her away from the group towards a notional gap between two grandfather trees, where the undergrowth parts slowly and has to be swept aside, to crash back in place when they have passed. On the other side, they are still in earshot, at least if she were to shout. He lets go of her arm. They walk together along a narrow path between the trees.

Kramme is different here: still perfectly pleasant, but blunter, while the knife-edge on which she walks could not be sharper. Here, even lies have to taste like the truth. 'Have you the invasion date?'

'No. I would have told you already.'

'And yet you came back.'

'You killed two of their people. They sent me to replace them. I couldn't refuse.'

'Did you know I was here?'

'Of course. In London, they are terrified of you. They use your name to scare the trainees. Learn this, or Kramme will skin you alive. They think every other Frenchman in England is your agent.'

He laughs at this, and allows himself to preen a little, but not so much that his eyes ever leave her face. He reads others for a living and his ambition is dwarfed only by his suspicion. She stares at him, and does not smile. He laughs again and pats her arm. 'Well done. I am proud of you.'

She hears Laurence Vaughan-Thomas in her head so loudly that she thinks the whole wood must hear it echo from her ears.

He will believe in you because he wants to.

He will. He does. He must, must, must.

Tilting his head, Kramme asks, 'What are we to do?'

'You are asking me? I'm a nurse. I will do what I am told to do, but nobody has told me to do anything yet. They don't trust me yet: not here, not in London. There is a radio I use to send messages. I can tell you where it is.'

'I know where all the radios are. We monitor their transmissions. Can you really not fire that thing? There's a pigeon on the oak at the bend in the path. It's a good hundred paces but if the English taught you anyth— Ah. We will have to pretend I did that.'

Thoughtful, he walks through the trees to gather up the bounty, leaving her with the rifle. When he turns back, she is aiming at his heart. Alexandre died with eight shots to the chest. When they walked into the wood, she had only five in the magazine and she has just used one of these to kill the pigeon, so just four left, but even one would be enough, and so very easy.

Laurence again: *There may be times when you have the perfect opportunity to kill him.*

240

'Sophie?' Kramme stands very still. He has ceased to smile. She thinks this may be the one moment in their joint existence when he is more afraid of her than she is of him.

But she has seen what happens to a town where an officer is shot, particularly one who is a favourite of the Führer. The Boche know no restraint. The Patron would die slowly, simply for being here, and Daniel, René, JJ, Raymond, Madame Fayette and her beautiful boys . . . all those who had ever been associated with Nurse Sophie Destivelle.

Besides, there will come a time when this man's death might change the course of the war and that time is not yet.

I am the Wild Card.

I can wait.

This is my truth.

With a dry, almost English, smile, she salutes, reverses the stock and offers it to him. For one fractional moment he remains frozen and she thinks he might order her arrest. Then, relaxing, he laughs and salutes her. 'Ah, little fierce cat, it is good that you have come back. We shall enjoy each other, I think.' He removes the magazine and the rounds in the chamber before he hands the gun back. He is a careful, careful man.

She says, 'They picked me up at the drop point, eight of them. I don't know all of the names, but Raymond Viv—'

'Stop.'

His hand is across her mouth, lightly. 'You cannot do this. If I know their names, I will act differently around them.'

'I don't understand.'

'You walk on thin ice, *ma belle*. As you said, they are suspicious, these people, and they will do things to you that are beyond thinking if they believe you a traitor. Do not tell me names; I don't want any of the small mice. I want the one who leads. Give him to me, and we shall take them all. I shall protect you then.'

'I don't know him. He does it by the book, as they say.'

'The book . . . ?'

'The instruction book. Sleep in a different place each night. Only talk to those whom you absolutely trust. Use dead drops and signals, no personal connections. Take no risks that cannot be avoided.' Most of this is true. Kramme drinks it in as if she has offered him the keys to Churchill's heart.

'It is true, then: others have said this but I did not wholly believe them, even . . .' He lets it drift. Amongst civilized company, he does not speak of the pain he inflicts on others. His gaze grows distant. 'He is a fox, this one. But with your help, we shall take him. Until then, you will be everything they want of you.'

'But that's what I'm telling you. They have asked nothing of me. *Nothing!* They had me tap out one message, but I think it was just a test. I'm not even sure they do much, here. They watch the trains and send details of what travelled where back to London. It's pathetic.'

'It's the kind of detail that wins wars, *ma belle*. Many routes go through Saint-Cybard, east and west.' He is laughing at her, and not, at the same time. 'Is that really all they have asked you to do?'

She flings out her hands. 'I listen to the BBC. I give out pills for sick old women who want to fawn all over the doctor and I wrap bandages round young men's hands so they are not sent to the east. The only true bit of nursing I did was delivering Madame Andreu's children.'

'Who thrive. For which they thank you.' He pushes away from the tree. 'You are bored. I can see that. But you must win their trust and if boredom is the price, it will pay for itself in the end.'

Is that it? Does he not want more? Tentatively, she says, 'I will have to do things – listen on the radio, call in drops, maybe even go on a jaunt.'

'A jaunt? Is that what they call it when they kill men doing their duty?' He smacks his balled fist against the tree trunk. In so many ways, he is the mirror of Laurence Vaughan-Thomas; only, his hair is less blond. Turning back, he says, 'This is war. Do what you must. I want their Patron and I want you in place when they have news of the invasion. Nothing else matters. In the meantime, you will watch and listen and tell me what you can, when you can. Nobody will think it strange that we speak: you are, after all, acting out your role as a nurse.'

'The doctor is jealous of you.'

'And so he should be.' Kramme is pleased about that. 'But we should return to him before he feels the need to call me out for threatening your honour. The Führer doesn't approve of duels, certainly not with Frenchmen.' Cheered by his own humour, he leads her back to the main body. There, handing the pigeon to the hound-keeper, he says, 'I think we have hunted enough for one day. Let us return to the hotel. The ladies, I'm sure, will wish to make use of the facilities before dinner.'

'Have you a beau, Mademoiselle Sophie? It is hard to imagine one so beautiful must languish in solitude.'

They are in the Hôtel Cinqfeuilles, Kramme's base in Saint-Cybard. For good reason was this place fêted throughout the Franche-Comté before the Boche took it over. The private dining room is oak panelled, ostentatious without being tasteless, roomy without being too big to heat. The fire in the grate is big and bright. The wine is warm and sweet and strong. The chandeliers catch handfuls of mellow firelight and shower them across the room, sparkling off buttons and medals, rings, necklaces, the bright shine of an eye.

It is nearly nine o'clock. The officers have changed from hunting grey to SS dress uniform and you have to hand it to the Boche, they know how to make a man look good. As he was at the hunt, Kramme is friendly, attentive, charming. He monopolizes Sophie Destivelle, which annoys both the

Patron and Luce Moreau, a state of events that, as the wine flows, Sophie finds increasingly congenial.

She relaxes more in his presence, and he, likewise, opens up to her, telling her of his life. He was a lawyer once, not particularly fashionable, but young, hungry, sharply competent. His successful prosecution of a prominent Jewish journalist won the eye of the Führer and his star rose ever after in the party's firmament.

As they progress from the first course to the second, she finds that he has a greatly loved daughter of three years (named Eva, naturally), and an infant son, whose arrival six months ago coincided with the death of his dearly missed wife. For this reason, he is in awe of all women who take the risk of bearing children, and deeply grateful to those who help new mothers to live through the ordeal.

He is seeking a replacement to share his life, his success, his children, but will not sully Clara's memory with anyone substandard. All this, Sophie has learned as they eat.

And now for his question, to which he already knows at least one answer: he was present when Alexandre was shot. He is supposed to be on her side. But then again, he is supposed not to be. She has had three glasses of wine, which is two and a half more than she has drunk at one sitting any time in the past twelve months. She is mellow. She is probably going to die. She hates everyone else equally: all of them.

She looks up. 'In Paris, there was someone, yes.'

If the Patron could wrest her from her seat and throw her from the room, he would do so; this she reads in the angles of his back.

'Was?' Kramme asks. His eyes signal caution. He, too, thinks they are on dangerous territory.

She answers, 'He was killed – assassinated, really.' The whole table is listening. To left and right conversation has stalled.

'Assassinated?' asks the SD officer who sits beside the Patron. 'By whom?'

'You have heard of the *équipes de tueurs*? They hunt down men – and women – who are too friendly with those they hate.'

All eyes are on her. The Patron's larynx is in spasm: up and down. Softly, Kramme says, 'They hunt, in fact, those who are friends of the Reich.'

'Yes.'

'They killed him, your beau?'

'His name was Eduard. Eduard Dourant. They cut his throat.'

Rudi Schäfer, the albino SD, leans across. 'But it could have been bandits, robbers, thieves. They operate in every city at any time, not just in war.'

'I wish it were so, but they left their mark.'

Obersturmbannführer Schäfer is an intelligence officer. Even had he not been introduced as such, it would be obvious. His pale gaze is like a searchlight, but finer, more intense. Twice, he has cornered Sophie. Twice, she has stepped aside from his probing.

Now, he asks, 'And what was this mark that they left, Mademoiselle Sophie?'

'Before they killed him, they cut out his tongue.'

'*Dieu!* Do not say such a thing!' This from Madame Andreu's raven-haired sister. 'Say at least that he was dead first.'

'Their note said not, but I like to think maybe he was. It would be hard, I think, to cut out the tongue of a living man without causing a great deal of disturbance.'

'Is this the reason you left Paris?' Kramme asks.

She nods. 'I did not go immediately; my life was there, my work, my training as a nurse. But yes, in the end that was the reason. My uncle said that in Saint-Cybard, life was much more civilized and I have found it so.'

Kramme's laugh is more thoughtful than reassuring. 'We have no teams of killers roaming the streets, I promise you. But then we are, shall we say, perhaps more humane than our colleagues at the Avenue Foch. We support those who support us, and in turn, we have more supporters. Thus everyone wins. No man – or woman,' – he raises his glass to Sophie – 'need ever lose her pride or her honour. We do not come here to undermine your nation's self-respect, but to sustain it. And so I propose a toast: to Saint-Cybard and the future of France.'

They toast. She drinks. The Patron raises a toast to the Führer, Monsieur Andreu to Germany, Schäfer to the defence of liberty that is taking place on the Eastern Front; the eradication of the Slavic races, who, really, have been genetically proven to be less than human.

Nobody mentions Jules Cloutier, a guard at the Peugeot factory who was denounced as a Maquis by his cousin's husband three days ago and whose body was dumped on the steps of the town hall last night.

Sophie made herself walk past. Her medical training listed the injuries, and their order: fingernails and then toenails ripped out; short bones and then long bones shattered; skin flayed from ribs; gelded. This last was what upset the men most, as it was meant to. She was surprised at how deeply it affected her.

She lay awake all through the night, fearing sleep, and the dreams it might bring, wondering if Cloutier had been sacrificed to divert attention from her: a victim who knew nothing, and could say nothing, whose only crime was being on guard duty at a factory on the night of a recent Maquis raid. She thinks of Raymond Vivier, whose name Kramme now has, and has to drink, or she will be sick.

Kramme catches her eye and raises his glass in a private toast. Dessert comes, and then coffee – real coffee – and

Cognac is served, and cigars, and long black cigarettes, and there is a moment's hilarity while a photographer is summoned and photographs taken – they will be in colour. Really, have you never seen a colour photograph? But you must see this, the prints will be here in less than a week, you will adore them – and even now, the women are not banished, but invited to the side of the blisteringly hot fire. When was she last truly warm?

They discuss the early parts of the war as if it were a day or two ago, and the obstacles to German victory minor irritations. They consider the ways by which Kramme may make the life of all in Saint-Cybard easier in the time they have left before peace is restored. Top of his list is the eradication – he uses Schäfer's word – of the minor inconvenience of the Resistance. He is working on it. He has high hopes for his success. In the meantime, they should turn the talk to better things, to the afternoon's hunt, to the improvement in Mademoiselle Sophie's shooting, to how he will make of her the best shot in France. He raises his glass to her. She laughs, and drinks in his name and it is not forced, and everyone knows it.

And here's the reality: in Kramme's company she is warm, when everywhere else, winter still chills the air, and she is fed better than she has ever been in her life, drinks wine she could never aspire to, travels in cars she might in other circumstances have seen passing on the street.

In the past hours, she has discussed world politics, the science of antibiotics and where it might go, art, theatre – and music. Kramme himself prefers Beethoven to jazz, but he does not consider the latter to be dissolute and would be happy to dance to it had the Führer not banned all such things.

No man, in England or in France, has treated her with such respect. And while Kramme plainly pays her court, he has not

247

yet touched her except to lift her hand and kiss it. Tonight, tentatively he helps her to fasten her coat as they leave.

'*Au revoir*, beautiful woman. I shall look forward to our reunion.'

'And I, Sturmbannführer Kramme.'

'Max, please. We are beyond formality.'

'Max.' Drink fuels her smile. 'Then I must be Sophie. Sleep well.'

The drive back is uncomfortable. The Patron throws his Peugeot around corners at speeds it was not designed for. Sophie hangs on to the strap and fights waves of nausea. They stop at a junction and she throws open the door and begins to step out.

The Patron grabs her arm. 'What are you doing?'

'I'll walk. It's safer.'

'It's another two kilometres. It's raining.'

Each of these is obvious. She ignores him. He drives alongside.

'Sophie, get in the car.'

'No, thank you.'

'Get in!' He's agitated now. 'If Kramme comes along, we can't be seen to be arguing.'

'I'm not arguing. I'm walking.'

'Sophie!' He's out now, walking round to stand in front of her. 'Get in the car.'

It's odd, now, how easy it is to defy him. With anger comes a different kind of clarity. It's in the tilt of his head, in the way he holds himself, in the way he says Kramme's name. Either he knows she's working for Kramme, or—

'You *are* jealous!' She had told Kramme he was, but she thought it an act.

'Don't be ridiculous.'

'You are.' Her truth for Kramme has become a reality. She starts to laugh, thinly, with too little control. She really does feel sick. He takes a step closer. She thinks he might slap her, but he takes her by the wrist, carefully, and guides her back to the car. In English, he says, 'Get in. Please.'

Please. Only the English . . . There is a moment when she might vomit all over his suit, but it passes. She does as he asks, because he has asked it. They drive a while in silence. She says, 'I am going to kill him.'

'Sophie . . . you don't have to—'

'I'm telling you so you know why this happens. I have to get close to him and when London gives the word, I am allowed to kill him. This is their promise to me.'

He is not stupid, far from it. She watches the veins at the side of his neck, the creases by his eyes. He has hypnotic eyes; they change so fast. She sees the moment when he begins to ask what her deal is with London, what leverage they have over her, and then realizes he cannot risk knowing. He says, 'I see.' She does not trust herself to answer.

They do not speak again until they are outside the door of her lodgings. He steps out of the car and comes round to hold her door. 'They will check,' he says. 'By tomorrow, they will have full details of the autopsy on Eduard Dourant.'

'And they will find he had his tongue cut out and his throat slit and they will have the typed note left by the member of the *équipe de tueurs* that killed him.'

'If you were his lover, they will find that. They will find your real name.'

'Then it is lucky I was not.'

He stares at her. He is not entirely sober. She is really quite drunk. Her headache is spectacularly bad. She says, 'I killed him. And yes, I took his tongue out before he died. And no, nobody knows but me. And now you.'

She steps close, and places the flat of her palm on his sternum. It is the first time she has touched him. The shock on his face is laughable. 'So if Kramme finds out, I will know who

249

told him.' She leans up – in these heels, it is not so far – and presses a full, hot kiss to his cheek. 'Goodnight, Patron.'

19 May 1944

'*Ici Londres. Veuillez escorter tout d'abord quelques messages personnels. Ecouter bien . . . Le cheval noir se promène sur l'eau. Merci Icare; vous nous encourager très bien. Le chat a dix vies. Il fait froid en l'hiver. Le ciel du soir est plus sombre maintenant. Sur le soleil . . .*'

That's it. Weeks of listening and at last, the evening sky is darker on the BBC's French transmissions; the party is on: the Maquis de Morez will have air cover for a major action.

It is a fine, clear night with the gibbous moon not yet risen. Sophie is in a part-full hay barn half an hour's walk from the Fayette farm.

All through the occupied territories, it is forbidden to listen to the BBC, but all through the occupied territories, everyone listens. There is a joke she heard in Paris that goes like this: It is said that a Jew meets a Boche officer on a bridge at 9.10 p.m. one night, cuts out his heart and eats it. But this cannot be true, says the joke, on three counts: First, a Boche officer has no heart, so one cannot be cut out. Second, even if he did, a Jew would not eat the flesh of a swine, so again it cannot be true. Third, if he did and he did, it still cannot be true because at 9.10 p.m. everyone – Jew and Boche alike – is inside listening to the BBC on the radio.

Everywhere else, this joke works, but not in Saint-Cybard. Here, in a forgotten corner of the Jura within spitting distance of Switzerland, Patrick Sutherland's Troubadour network is staffed with men and women so pristine that Kramme could take their homes apart brick by mortared brick and find not one single incriminating item that might warrant their arrest.

Only Sophie Destivelle is allowed to – ordered to – take the risks. In the dark of the night, when her fears come to taunt her, she wonders if the Patron knows that Kramme will not touch her. The thought is almost as terrifying as the fear of being caught, because while she is not at all sure that Kramme would hesitate to make an example of her if she was found with a radio, she is certain the Patron would shoot her with his own gun if he found she was Kramme's agent. She dreams, sometimes, of the look of reproach in his eye as he does so.

Just now, she is on her own, which is how she likes it. A heap of last year's hay lies at the barn's southern end. Holding her torch in her mouth, she pulls back an armful from the wall, lifts the board lying there and slides the radio into the dark space beneath. Lumpen shadows scuttle in the dark. She shoves the cover back over, piles hay back on top, and five minutes later, she is cycling back to the chilly, comfortless house of the chilly, comfortless collaborator couple with whom the Patron has lodged her.

There, in her upstairs room, she sits on the sagging bed, eats tepid cabbage soup and chews at gritty bread the colour and texture of mortar. This is more like it was in Paris: Madame Fayette's farmhouse was an oasis of plenty, soon forgotten, except in her dreams. She listens to the Aillardes take themselves to bed, waits half an hour, then tucks the ends of her scarf under her sweater, and climbs down from her window to the ground. From there, she walks into town. It is midnight.

The Hôtel Cinqfeuilles is in blackout, but inside, chandeliers shatter light and spread it, crystalline, over oak and maple, jet and onyx, silk and pure, perfect wool. This is not Paris, but it is older, and in its own way, grander. The guards on the door ignore her as she walks past and turns right at the corner, but on the second circuit a back door opens and Kramme slips out. 'You have a date?'

251

'For the invasion, no. For a raid, yes.'

'In Saint-Cybard?'

'The Peugeot factory.'

A slow smile spreads across his face. He gives a small salute. 'Will the leader be on it?'

'I don't think so. He is cautious and this is not considered a major target. It will be led by—'

His finger to her lips. 'Don't.' He leans back on the wall, takes out a cigar and thinks better of it: if she is caught with the scent of good tobacco on her clothes, she may as well paint 'collaborator' on her forehead. 'When?'

'Tomorrow night, under cover of an RAF raid.'

'They would raid a town? Butchers!' He is genuinely angry.

'No. They'll pretend to raid the factory, but they'll miss, so they don't risk hitting the *Résistantes*.'

'I see.' He stares into the distance a while, until her presence brings him back. 'Will you take part?'

'Yes.' And then: 'I took the message. This may be a test.'

'Obviously. He is smart, your Vaughan-Thomas, but we are smarter.' He takes her hand and kisses it. 'You shall be safe, *ma chérie*, never doubt it. Go now. We shall mitigate what damage we can.'

The Aillardes are still asleep when she returns. She lies awake, counting her untruths. Sleep steals them from her, and gives them back at dawn, but if she is crabby all day, the Patron thinks it is because he was rude to her, and does not enquire further.

~

SS-Stubaf Kramme, personnel file Diem
Message # B8/C3.1.7-
19/5/44 2215 Hrs

To: SS-Ostubaf Klaus Weissmann

SOURCE 'DIEM': RAID ON PEUGEOT FACTORY
TONIGHT. WILL BE DISGUISED AS RAF RAID,
PROSECUTED ON THE GROUND BY LOCAL
REBELS. LEADER NOT INVOLVED. WILL
ENSURE NO SERIOUS DAMAGE BUT TAKE NO
OTHER ACTION. HH CARPE.

CHAPTER SEVENTEEN

Picaut is spending her free moments in the spare office at the studio: it's considerably more comfortable than the over-air-conditioned incident room, has technology every bit as good, and most importantly, it lets her keep an eye on Martin Gillard.

Conference or no conference, there's an international call out for Elodie Duval, although so far nobody has turned up sightings of her or her car. Ducat has a team manning the phones and another out on the streets of Orléans. Every station, airport, car hire and taxi company has her image on a screen and her name on their search systems.

So far, there has been nothing, nor has anybody cracked Elodie Duval's cipher. On the positive side, forensics have turned up a partial footprint highlighted by the UV scan of Pierre Fayette's back garden. It's small and could be a woman's. It's probably the next-door neighbour's but if it's Sophie's or Elodie's, it would tell them . . . something. The technicians are checking the neighbours on both sides.

Picaut writes herself another list on her phone:

1. Maquis de Morez: three left alive – Laurence, René, JJ. <u>Anyone else?</u>
2. Next generation: Pierre Fayette, Elodie Duval (Was Fayette. <u>Why did she change her name?</u>)
3. Two ageing Maquisards on the run. Possibly dead. Why?
4. JJ, ditto.
5. JJ —> Edward —> Conrad —> Martha. All in Orléans when JJ's old comrade is murdered.
6. Common to all: image from the war & music box & lavender.
7. Two ciphers: one from Laurence, one from Elodie. <u>What's the key?</u>

Shortly after five, Rollo slams in through the door, bringing Laurence Vaughan-Thomas's breathtakingly beautiful music box, and the note that came with it. He sets both on Picaut's desk.

He says, 'The garden footprint is not from any of the neighbours. But it's definitely a woman.'

'Elodie, then,' Picaut says.

'Or Sophie. We need to find their shoes for a size match. Also, there's a partial fingerprint on the red mug at the wrong end of the line in the cupboard at Pierre Fayette's house that isn't Pierre's or Sophie's or, if the prints on her computer, doorknob and mouse are accurate, Elodie's. We don't have a match on that yet, either.'

Picaut says, 'Did you get Conrad Lakoff and his security team?'

'Not yet. Acronym people don't like having their prints on file, but I'll get on to it. And ballistics have confirmed that Sophie Destivelle and Pierre Fayette were killed with the same weapon. Their current best guess is a Glock 19, current issue, which is, and I quote, "The concealed-carry favourite of

Americans who like to think they can carry guns the rest of the world can't see." '

Rollo chews his lip. 'Just because a gun is fired twice, doesn't mean the same person fired it both times.'

'Exactly. And if you're right that faking an airtight alibi is Gillard's modus operandi then . . .'

'He needs to be top of the list for Pierre Fayette.'

'Done.' On her phone, she adds to her list:

8. Two deaths, one gun.

Guns . . . *Guns!* 'Rollo!'

He's halfway out of the door. 'Yep?'

'The wartime Colts, the M1911s – you said they were registered in sequence. Did you get the names?'

From memory, he recites, 'Laurence, René, JJ, Daniel Fayette, Amélie Fabron and . . . Wait—' He pulls up the list of names, and reads it, frowning. 'Céline Vaughan-Thomas.' He looks up. 'I'm sorry, I should have seen this sooner. A relative of Laurence's?'

'We'll ask him if we ever see him again. Certainly there was a Céline in the Maquis. I'm not sure where this takes us, though. I was sure it was going to be Paul Rey.'

'This list was from the fifties and at least one of the people on it is dead. He might have had one by now.'

'True. Don't go away.' She is up and out of the seat, across the hallway to McKinney's office. 'Clinton, where was Paul Rey living when he died?'

'Virginia.' Martin Gillard answers her before McKinney can. 'About thirty miles outside Langley there's a "rest home" for former intelligence officers. Just because they're in a wheelchair, doesn't mean they're at any less risk.'

'Risk of being compromised?' Rollo has followed her through.

'Of being shot,' Gillard answers, crisply. They're like dogs, these two, bristling.

'Back off, both of you.' Picaut steps between them. To Gillard, she says, 'Martin, I'll need the address, phone, email, website: anything and everything you've got, starting with the name of someone I can call. Can you do that?'

'Of course.'

To Rollo: 'See if you can get me lists of the other inhabitants going back at least five years. If you find anyone with the surname Lakoff, tell me ASAP.'

'Done.' Rollo's happy with that. He and Gillard compete to see who can get the information fastest and both sets of data arrive on her desk more or less simultaneously.

Thus she learns that the manager of Paul Rey's 'retirement home' is one Kathryn Kochanek, fifty-four.

From Rollo, she learns that Kochanek was CIA station chief in Jakarta around the turn of the millennium and 'nobody will tell me why she's not there any more'. Whatever she did, it must have been bad for her to get shunted to running a home for geriatric field agents.

Sometimes, not often, but sometimes, a dead end suddenly becomes live. Picaut checks her watch, subtracts six, and tries the home number. The line purrs and is answered. A soft American voice says, 'Kochanek.'

Picaut sits up straighter in her chair and glares at Gillard until he backs out of the room and shuts the door. Rollo, grinning, hitches a hip on the edge of the desk.

'Ms Kochanek, this is Captain Inès Picaut of the Orléans police . . .'

'Wait.' This voice is a steel door, slammed. 'You understand I will need to call your superiors and confirm your identity. Whom should I call?'

Whom? Wow. 'You can call Prosecutor Ducat, but I have to tell you that time is not on our side.'

'Everyone says that, Captain Picaut.'

'In this case, it's true. Conrad Lakoff's grandfather is missing.'

'*What?*'

'Lakoff is here in France with his father.' Picaut pulls his business card from her pocket. 'I can give you his contact details. It might be more useful if you were to call him rather than my superior. He is working on the case.'

'I don't think so. Strategic Operations Director Lakoff's grandfather was shot dead in my facility eighteen months ago. The date is not in question. I was posted here three days later.'

'I'm sorry?' Picaut's pulse makes a strange rolling leap. Rollo seems to have stopped breathing. He lays down the lists he was examining. 'John Lakoff was shot?'

'You just told me he was missing. I am about to—'

'No! Don't hang up! Not *that* grandfather. The missing one is on the maternal side. JJ Crotteau. He's French, formerly Maquis, then of the DB, which is the old name for our External—'

'I know what the DB was, thank you.'

Of course you do. You were a station chief. I really do want to know why you're not one now. 'I understand that you have to call to check my credentials, but before we hang up, if I told you the signature victim in this case was shot in the early hours of this morning with two rounds to the chest and one to the head, would that ring a bell with you?'

Warily: 'It might do.'

This is what it sounds like to talk to someone who can think eight moves ahead. Picaut says, 'We believe it was a professional hit. Was John Lakoff's death in any way the same?'

There's a brief pause in which options are considered and one chosen, then Kathryn Kochanek says, 'You understand there are limits to what I can say.'

'I do.' She takes a moment to formulate a question that can be answered. 'Did you find the weapon used in the attack?'

258

'No. It was a Browning Hi-Power. Is that pertinent to your case?'

'Not that we are aware of. I'll let you know if it becomes so.' She writes Hi-Power on her phone. 'We heard that Colonel Rey died this morning. Is there any chance his death might have been unnatural?'

'There is no sign at present, but I've asked for an autopsy report. When we finish this call, I will make it a priority.'

And no longer any talk of hanging up to check identity. Picaut says, 'I believe he may have had a visitor sometime earlier this week – his goddaughter, Elodie?'

'Yes. And Theodora. They usually came together.'

'Theodora?'

'Theodora Sutherland. Her aunt, I think. I suspect she may have been an . . . intimate friend of Colonel Rey's. She was his most frequent visitor.'

Eight moves ahead. Perhaps more than that. Picaut feels her jaw tingle, as if someone has injected lava along the scars. She says, 'I'll need CCTV if you have it.'

'I'll get someone to cut the relevant sections.' A keyboard ripples, softly. Everything former station chief Kathryn Kochanek does is soft, but sure. 'If you give me an email address, you'll have everything I can give you inside half an hour.' Picaut gives her address and hears Kochanek type it in. 'Is there anything else I can help you with?'

Yes. Maybe. 'Was John Lakoff's body mutilated after his death?'

'Go on.'

'It was common in wartime France for collaborators to have their throats cut and their tongues cut out. My victim displayed exactly these injuries.'

'The wounds were post-mortem?'

'We believe so. The interim report says she was shot first. If Lakoff was killed the same way, then you will understand how it changes the profile of our case.'

'I understand completely.' There is a pause, another decision weighed and made. 'Regrettably, my predecessor chose to have the details classified and so, on this, too, I am not at liberty to divulge the precise nature of Lakoff's injuries. Were I to do so, however, you might widen the scope of your case.'

Oh, clever woman. 'Thank you. You've been more than helpful. I may be in touch later.'

'Surely. Anything, anytime. We're here to serve.'

Theodora Sutherland visits Paul Rey . . . And Sophie Destivelle is not the first one to have her throat cut and her tongue taken out. Clarions are sounding in Picaut's mind. Throwing herself back in the chair, she makes two calls.

To Petit-Evard, she says: 'Check the passenger manifests of all inbound flights from the US: you're looking for Elodie Duval and Sophie Destivelle in any of her aliases. Include Theodora Sutherland and all variations thereof.'

To Sylvie: 'We need to find where she lived because it clearly wasn't that apartment. Look particularly for a cabin near Saint-Cybard.'

To Rollo, who is no longer sitting on the edge of her desk: 'You can stop looking for Lakoff's name in the facility records. John Lakoff was there until just over eighteen months ago. Instead, see if you can get me the name and the phone number of whoever was in charge of the Bide-A-Wee rest home for Ageing Spooks before Kochanek took over. Sophie Destivelle was not the first in this series of killings. I want Pierre Fayette to be the last.'

17.45

Half an hour after her phone calls, Picaut gathers her team together and with them come answers to some of her questions.

Petit-Evard hits pay dirt first with news that 'Theodora and Amélie Sutherland' flew into Charles de Gaulle airport last night, arriving shortly before nine o'clock. The passport photographs show a mother and daughter, both dark haired, active, cheerful. Assuming that they both know how to put on a wig, they could easily be the two in Elodie's Mazda MX-5.

'Bingo. Give that man a week's leave. Not till the case is over, mind you.' Petit-Evard glows.

The rest of the debrief is put on hold when Kathryn Kochanek sends the CCTV from Paul Rey's room through to Picaut's laptop. The team huddles round her desk to watch.

From the start, it's clear the CIA rest-home has a good, high-resolution camera which is filming continuously. This is not the jerky stop-start of intermittent CCTV shots generated in most of the world's larger municipal areas. This footage is well funded and shot with a view to archiving the result.

And so here is a room: clean and homely, with a view from a high window over a meadow with woodland beyond. The weather is good. Trees sway with airy decorum.

The camera makes a lazy swing and here is a bed, a white cabinet laden with flowers, cards stacked in military lines: Pierre Fayette would approve. A uniformed nurse swabs the mouth of the man on the bed and, as she rises to answer a call out of shot, Picaut and her team are given their first clear view of Paul Rey.

Some people look relatively well as they near death. Paul Rey does not. Toothless, bald, with skin that is more liver spot than clear, he has the fallen cheeks and yellowing complexion of end-stage metabolic failure. His eye sockets are sunken pools, barely alive. Still, he brightens as a door opens and, yes, here is a slim, slight, elfin-faced woman, with rust-red hair that shines in the sanitized light: here is Elodie Duval. It is good to see her alive.

She moves fast, with a self-assurance that speaks of many

previous visits, and she is weeping as she reaches the bed. She speaks a word, a syllable: his name. Paul Rey lifts a skeletal hand and they embrace, carefully, as if she might break him. She sits at his side and they turn together to watch a woman hesitate in the doorway.

Alive, Sophie Destivelle has a translucent quality, as if light might pass through her undimmed. Her hair is crystalline white. Her eyes are black, still a-spark with a fire of surprising strength in one her age.

Smiling, Paul Rey calls her in. As Kochanek noted, they are at ease in each other's company in a way that speaks of old, old intimacies. Watching them, though, Picaut sees something else, deeper: an ancient electricity that lights them up.

René Vivier said that they had all loved her, yet none of them had trusted her. In Paul Rey's case, at least, the former is certainly true and his love, it seems, is matched. On the CCTV feed, Sophie Destivelle speaks his name and the tenderness, the sharp edge of grief, the rage at a life ending, are all in the shape of that one unheard word.

She sits at the bedside opposite Elodie and says something Picaut cannot see, and, because there is no sound, cannot hear. As the segment ends, the camera pans slowly back to the view of the window.

'That's her,' says Martin Gillard, who seems to have attached himself to the group. 'That's Sophie Destivelle.'

'Obviously.' Picaut leans back in her chair. 'Why, though?'

'Why what?'

'Why is she there? Why is she calling herself Theodora Sutherland? And why has she been doing so for nearly two years?'

An email from Kathryn Kochanek says that Mrs Sutherland has been a frequent visitor for the past eighteen months. Her first visit was on the day that Assistant Director John Lakoff died.

Picaut says, 'Rollo, any luck with finding the earlier manager of the care home?'

'He's dead.' He sways back from her look. 'I don't think you can blame this on anyone else. He had laryngeal carcinoma. Secondaries got him six months ago.'

'For real?'

'He's CIA. They have proper pathologists and they will have checked. So yes, I think we can say it's for real.'

'OK. So Sophie and Elodie knew Paul Rey – and each other – well enough to be at his bedside when he died. Look at the way they are with each other. These relationships go beyond one day spent filming.' Picaut chews on her knuckle. 'I need to know more about John Lakoff. Rollo, can you get anything?'

'I can try.'

'The rest of you, whatever you were doing, put finding Elodie Duval at the top of your list.'

They filter out, all except Martin Gillard, who is not hers to command. He fiddles with objects on her borrowed desk; straightens the phone, puts a pen into line, the music box and the note that came with it. He picks up the paper and holds it so Picaut can read the lower half.

> *Once again, our apologies. Please do not waste time or effort in looking for us: we shall keep ourselves safe. In the meantime, I suggest you find Elodie's music box and search within it. If you find Elodie herself, tell her that Céline's poem remains extant.*
>
> *Blythe spirit,*
> *LVT*

In quiet moments over the past hour, Picaut has sniffed the paper and pressed it to the kettle, but there is no evidence that it contains any wartime ciphers. She says, 'I've never heard anyone say "blythe spirit" before.'

'I was thinking that. Amongst other things.' Gillard is silent a while. He raps a knuckle on the music box. 'Elodie had one just like this. I don't know where it is, though.'

Laurence Vaughan-Thomas's music box is the single most beautiful object on which Picaut has ever laid hands. The walnut is so dark as to be virtually black; the inlaid initials are silver-pale ash scrolling across the lid: *LVT MdM*. She smoothes her palm across the surface, feels the wood silky soft, resonant, almost. Whoever made this had a level of skill beyond ordinary mortals, and a great deal of time. She lifts the lid and listens to the first few bars of 'God Save the Queen' play in slurred, unwound dissonance.

'Did Elodie's box play the "Marseillaise"?'

'It did not. For reasons I never understood, it played "Scotland the Brave".'

He's not about to go away. Picaut sets the box down. 'You went to Saint-Cybard when Elodie filmed Sophie. Were you in the room when she filmed her?'

'No, but Elodie talked about Sophie on the way down. I was listening.' He doesn't say he was in the car, which is interesting. Picaut wants to ask more about the box, but she's getting to know this man, and there's something he's trying to tell her.

She waits. After a while, he says, 'Sophie Destivelle was a double agent, run by both Max Kramme and the British. She was infiltrated into the Maquis de Morez and each side thought they owned her.'

'Which one was right?'

'That's the thing. Elodie didn't know. She interviewed René and JJ and they were adamant that she did not betray any of their inner circle in the months leading up to D-Day, or at least, if she did, Kramme didn't act on it. But that's the thing, we're dealing with very subtle men.'

'René told me she killed Boche with alacrity.'

'That's true, too. JJ said the same thing, that she hated the Germans. She went on four raids with them altogether and she was their expert for opening locks, a demon with the explosives and the best shot they'd got. They didn't question her at first. But then . . . she grew very close to Kramme, like, seriously close. Nobody knew if she was doing it so she could destroy him, or if she really did fall in love with him.'

'She hated Germans – is it likely she'd fall in love with one of them?'

'He was charming, intelligent and capable of great generosity. It's not impossible.'

'What did Elodie think?'

'She said there was no reason both couldn't be true: that she was intent on destroying him, and she nonetheless fell in love with him.' He gives a small, defensive smile. 'She's a woman. I am not going to argue with her assessment of this situation.'

'Would Elodie's knowing this be enough to put her life in danger, do you think?'

'Only if something new came up.' He spreads his hands in a way that opens a world of possibility. 'That's what you need to understand; it's why Clinton is so nervous and keeps thinking you're going to shut him down. It's why Elodie hired me in the first place. In making the movie, we're turning over stones that have been left where they fell at the end of the war. We could have triggered all sorts of things without knowing it and some of them, frankly, would have been better left undisturbed.'

'Laurence said as much earlier today.' Picaut is growing a faint, but threatening, headache. 'You think I should watch the movie McKinney is making?' she asks.

Martin Gillard shrugs. 'There's nothing to watch yet, just hours of raw video. In any case, we're not the right people to recognize the things that might trigger old wounds. We need

Laurence or René or JJ, or someone else from the old days. If they're alive when we find them, we need to start asking those kinds of questions.'

She is growing to like this man. He feels honest but there is, of course, no reason why he, too, can't be playing both sides against the middle.

She turns her attention back to Laurence's box. Opened, the lid hinges widely: she lays it back flat and lifts out the lavender basket, revealing the brass mechanism inside, winding down on the last of its notes.

'The key's underneath, clipped into place. There's a slot for the rewind.' Gillard hasn't taken the hint and left yet. Turning the whole thing over, Picaut feels the metal shift slightly. In a lesser box, this might be an accident or an artefact, but nothing in this is a hair's breadth out of place. Turning it upright again, she takes hold of the sides, shifts them left and right, and yes, the entire mechanism lifts out, and underneath it—

'My God.'

AND THUS BY ACCIDENT WE BECAME AS GODS
BLYTHE CHILDREN OF THE MOUNTAIN
WARRIORS OF VENGEANCE
UNFORGIVING, UNFORGIVEN
UNFORGOTTEN

'Christ . . .' Gillard takes a step back. His eyes flare wide, showing white at the margins. He lifts his hands, as if warding her off. 'I had no idea. I've never been allowed to touch it. I swear to you I did not know this was here.'

'But you led me to it.'

'I was reading the note. I'm not pushing you somewhere I know. I'm following. You have to believe me.'

. . . find Elodie's music box and search within it. Blythe spirit, LVT

266

Picaut says, 'You're sure the box you saw was Elodie's?'

'It was here, on her desk.' He lays his hand flat, by the phone, showing the place. 'It was the inverse of this: pale wood with an ebony inlay.'

'When did you last see it?'

'A week ago? Ten days?' He closes his eyes the better to think. 'It was definitely here right before she left for the US.'

'Right.' Picaut writes herself a three-line note and when she looks up Martin Gillard is leaning over so he can read it. She says, 'Thank you. I'll let you know if we get anywhere.'

He plants his thumbs on the desk and doesn't budge. 'The poem code,' he says. 'The one they used in the war. The first line of any message listed which line numbers and words they were using. As long as London knew the poem, they could decode it.'

'Yes. Thank you.'

'Elodie's note – the one in the alarm clock – the bit she highlighted was a sequence of numbers. We just have to work out what poem she was using.'

'I have a cryptologist working on it, but if it's "Céline's Poem" and that was made up, we stand no chance at all of working it out. Unless you know about Céline and her poem?'

'Nobody ever mentioned anything like that to me.'

'Then we're stuck. I'll let you know if anything moves. Thank you.'

The note flips in the breeze as he throws the door shut. *Blythe spirit.*

Her fingers smooth over the lettering inside the music box. *Blythe children of the mountain.* So beautiful, so raw, so much time taken to shape each letter, and yet . . . as she smoothes her fingers over, again and again, there's a step here: a hairline indentation along one of the letters.

Her left hand senses it, the burned one, where the skin still feels sandpapered in places and her sense of touch is either too fine or too dull, with no mellow ground between. Like she did with her face, she nags at it, presses, pushes.

Her mind is on her list. Unthinking, she continues to press, running her finger up and down the indentation . . . which becomes, in time, a groove.

And so she looks. The 'I' of CHILDREN is a channel in the wood, and try though she might, she cannot undo what she has done. She hunts for other letters she can press but does not find them, until she closes her eyes and lets the fingers of her left hand stray as they did before, and yes, here is another hairline anomaly – not even a crack, just an unsmoothness in the otherwise silken surface of the wood – that, as she nags at it, becomes an indentation. And then another, and another. Ten letters have become indented by the time she has finished: IOUASCOTCH.

As she presses the last H, wood slides on wood, a hiss of silken surfaces. A drawer opens that covers the entire base of the box, three centimetres high, by forty across, by thirty deep.

Inside is an envelope, and inside the envelope are three prints, two in black and white, the third in early, unsubtle colour. Written on the outside in a strong, bold hand:

For Laurence – Carpe Diem

2 June 1944: Two Royal Navy mini-submarines set sail for Normandy to guide Allied landing at Juno and Sword beaches. Warships depart Scapa Flow, Belfast and the Clyde.

SOE, F-Section: All networks given notice that the invasion will begin within the next few days.

CHAPTER EIGHTEEN

SAINT-CYBARD
2 June 1944

'*ICI LONDRES. ECOUTER BIEN: La grand-mère dit aux cousins qu'ils sont forts. Chocolat meilleur goûte consommé sous les pins, Jean a un . . .*'

Sophie and Max Kramme are in the private dining room of the Hôtel Cinqfeuilles with Luce Moreau, Rudi Schäfer and François Duval. This one night, everyone is inside listening to the BBC and nobody is pretending otherwise.

Kramme makes sharp remarks about Churchill, but when the French notices come on, he is silent. Halfway through the first sentence, he reaches out for Sophie's hand.

His touch is familiar now. She reaches to meet him, hand to hand, eye to eye. He says, 'Chocolate tastes better eaten beneath the pines. This is it. This is their first notice of the invasion.' He is certain. He has contacts in Paris who are running at least two radio sets as if their agents were still alive, whole, unbroken. And he has broken enough men here in Saint-Cybard to know the code.

And so the chocolate tastes better and there is no doubt that the Allies are coming. Not today, probably not tomorrow, but sometime in the next week, the landing craft will power across the Channel and pour their many thousands of men onto French soil. Sophie bites her lip. A part of her cheers. A part of her – the one she shows to Kramme – does not.

He says, 'It's a feint: we know this. But it will be big, because they want us to believe it.'

'Are you going to go to Berlin?' Even to herself, she sounds strained.

'No. Don't worry.' He pats her shoulder. 'We are asked to keep the supply lines open. Later, maybe, when they launch the real assault on Holland, we may have to go to help with the mopping up.' His thumb runs down the back of her hand, tracing the hollows between the tendons, and then the length of her finger. 'It is nearly over and you have been all I could ask. Nearly all.'

He smiles. Behind him, Luce Moreau's eyes shine with pure loathing. Kramme was hers until the *kleine Krankenschwester* came along. Now, Luce is left with Rudi Schäfer, the albino SD officer, who is considerably less alluring. The Patron is, as ever, bereft of female company, but he's laughing with Schäfer as if the prospect of an Allied landing is a good joke, with the punchline worth the waiting.

Sophie does not meet his eyes. This is the way it is, the way it has been, the way it has to be: she is Kramme's; everyone knows it. They have not slept together yet, but she is no longer entirely clear why not. She has made her pursuit of him so true, so utterly compelling, that her body has come to believe it. He is diffident, which in its own way is frustrating. He has only ever kissed her hand.

He draws her in now, her hand entwined with his. He strokes her hair, runs the length of it between thumb and finger, then her scarf, so that the back of his hand brushes lightly over her breast. 'When is the raid on the train station?' He asks his question softly, fondly, so that the others, if they choose to look on, will think they speak of love, perhaps of a future together. She has met his infant son, has commented on how he has his father's eyes. She has told him about the raid, because she could not do otherwise. Smiling, she answers, 'Tomorrow night.'

He lifts the ends of her scarf and slides them between his fingers, makes them flow, silk made water. 'And still no Patron?'

She gives a little huff of frustration. 'They don't tell me these things. I still don't know who the Patron is. I don't even know if it is a man. It could be Luce Moreau and I wouldn't know it.'

He laughs, softly. His gaze drifts to Luce and back. 'Do you think she could be the Patron?'

'I want you to think so.'

His laugh this time is loud enough to make everyone turn. Luce Moreau, in all her careful lipsticked glory, glares at Sophie as if at any moment she might walk across the room and stab her in the eye with a hatpin.

Calming a little, Kramme says, quietly, 'If she is, you are in terrible trouble. I should give you a car of your own, so you can escape.'

'You'd have to teach me to drive.'

'JJ will do that with great pleasure, I'm sure.' JJ has recently become the administration's driver, a position that is intended to demonstrate the amity between Germany and France, and is already proving useful to the Maquis.

Kramme takes her hands in his and leans forward. 'What about the raid? Will the Patron be there, whoever he – or she – may be?'

'I don't think so. If he comes, it will be the first time, and I think he would not take such a risk this close to the invasion. He will want to save himself for bigger things. So no, I think no Patron.'

'No. Of course. He will not take risks when he thinks the end is in sight.' Kramme's gaze loses focus. By this time, she can tell whether he's thinking of her or something else, and just now he is planning. He says, 'I have to go to Lyon tomorrow: the mayors of the local towns have convened a conference on the future of the Jura and I must regale them with all the potential of Saint-Cybard for the Reich in the years to come. It will be good to be out of the way. I will, perhaps, have to reprimand someone when I return, but that is no bad thing. There are one or two who will benefit from strong discipline.'

Sophie has a moment's pity for JJ who, as Kramme's driver, will miss the jaunt, but then there is no room for thought because Kramme shakes his head and brings all his focus back to her, his gaze on her face. Surprisingly, he strips off his glasses. His eyes look naked.

And then he kisses her. She has no time to prepare, no defence – not even any proper response, except that of her body, which has wanted this for longer than perhaps she has known.

Wine and warmth and the press of him, close, and he is a man who knows women, but he is not hard, as Schäfer would be, or scared, as Alexandre was during their first kiss. He is more tentative than she had imagined, though; more vulnerable. She is given space to be herself, to respond, to lift to the fierce ache of—

'. . . *dans les culottes. Joker, joue le sept de pique. Joker, joue le sept—*'

The seven of spades. Seven. Seven. Wild Card, play the seven. Jesus, Mary and Joseph, on the BBC: *Seven!*

'*Ma coeur?*'

She has barely moved, yet her body is ice now, not fire.

You have to make it true. Whatever you are doing, whoever you are being, every part of you must believe it.

She lets out the breath she was holding. 'Max . . .' She picks up his hand. Five days. Five. No more. No less. She traces a finger along the lines of his palm. She is shaking, only a little, but enough to be seen. It is not feigned. Hoarsely, she says, 'I will not be your mistress. I have more dignity than that.' How does she say this? Her voice has a script of its own, uncoupled from her mind.

'My dear . . .' His finger down the side of her cheek and she can feel the burn of Luce Moreau's hate, and the extra weight of the Patron's disapproval. He doesn't trust her. He thinks she is too close to Kramme. He is not wrong.

And Max? He is struggling. 'I do not want a mistress and even if I did, I would never ask that of you. How could you think I would do such a thing?'

'Then what?'

'Is it not obvious?' He is hurried now. He leans forward, lays his hands on her shoulders. 'I want you to be my wife. Please, Sophie. Please. I know it's war. I know we're the occupying force. I know there is horror all around, but in spite of these facts, perhaps because of them . . . Will you marry me?'

'Oh, Max . . .'

'Is that a yes?' He is a boy, shy, eager, trying to be suave.

'Of course. I think . . . Yes. But must we rush? Even in war? Please. Let me write to my uncle. Let me get his permission. It's proper. A week, maybe ten days, and then yes. Oh, my dear, yes!'

Driving back, the Patron won't speak to her, which is no bad thing, because she would have trouble answering him.

He drives too fast from the Hôtel Cinqfeuilles and she can taste the layers of his rage.

Outside her lodgings, he parks, stone-faced. Someone has to speak and so she says, 'I'm not going to marry him,' and watches the lines of his mouth grow tighter.

'You will have to. You cannot avoid it now.'

'It's a war. Anything could happen.'

'Not here. Not this far back from the lines. The invasion won't touch us for months.'

'We have the raid tomorrow night. He might die. I might die.'

'He won't be there, and you can't come now. You have to—'

'No! I'm coming! You can't stop me.'

He can, obviously. What she means is, Please let me do

something to restore my honour amongst my countrymen because otherwise they will think I'm a worse collaborator than Luce Moreau and her sister who married the Milice, and I am afraid of what they will do to me if the Boche do not win.

She says this, maybe, with her eyes, with the tightening of her own lips, with the air that grows fragile between them. She takes a breath.

He says, 'If you accuse me of jealousy, I shall send you back to Paris and deal with Kramme's wrath on my own.'

They are beyond such trivia as jealousy; she had no intention of mentioning it. What she was going to do, what she does, is to lean across the frigid space between them and kiss him full on the lips. All the savagery of her burning heart is here, right at the surface, searing them both.

It doesn't take long. She lets go before he can jerk back. Bright-eyed, she says, 'See? A kiss means nothing.' If she says so, they may both believe it. 'I killed my last lover. I cut his throat and took out his tongue. On the seventh of this month, five days from now – four if we are already after midnight – I am to do the same to Kramme.'

'*What?*'

His eyes are wide and dark, like an owl's. She could get used to the giddiness of this, the sense of pushing him off balance, except for the sharp, insistent ache in her loins at the feel of him, close. First Kramme, and now the Patron: both. But then again, neither. She is stronger than the treacherous fires of her body.

She leans back against the door, out of his reach. 'I told you this was their promise to me: if I wait for the signal, I can kill him. Tonight, there was a message on the radio. *Joker, joue le sept de pique.* That was for me. I heard it and he felt the change in me and if I hadn't done something, he'd have pushed until he got the truth. You are a man. You, obviously, would have stolen his dress pistol and shot your way to safety. As a mere woman, I must use the skills at my disposal. Do not read into it anything more than that.'

With what dignity she can find, she steps out of the car. 'Kramme is going to Lyon tomorrow. I will meet you at midnight, at the place appointed. If you give me a good partner, I can plant the explosives.'

~

```
SS-Stubaf Kramme, personnel file Diem

Message # J4/F19/Gb-

3/6/44 2317 Hrs

To: SS-Ostubaf Klaus Weissmann

SOURCE 'DIEM': RAID ON RAILWAY EXPECTED
TONIGHT UNDER COVER OF RAF BOMBING.
LEADER WILL BE PRESENT. REPEAT PATRON
OF SAINT-CYBARD MAQUIS WILL BE PRESENT.
REQUEST ORDERS. HH CARPE.
```

~

3 June 1944

Four days to go. Four.

Kramme's time has come. His death will change the course of the war. Sophie does not know how, or by what means this decision has been reached, but she knows that on the seventh of June, she can kill Max Kramme. All she has to do between now and then is stay alive, and not give anything away.

The day goes very much too slowly. She is slow in the dispensary, slow in applying dressings. She has a headache. The Patron sends her home early and a boy she doesn't know spits on her as she walks down the street.

Back at the house, the Aillardes are solicitous. This is their way now: she is favoured. Beatrice makes pea soup with real milk in it and sends her to bed. She sleeps, which is surprising, but not for long.

The night is clear and still. At the point of midnight, she rises, dresses in her dark clothes, and slides out of the window and down to where Daniel is waiting to bring her to the raid. She would rather it was JJ. She misses his bulk, and his trust in her, but Daniel is the next best thing: in the two months since she landed they have become a partnership, adept at the placing of explosives, the insertion of timers, the quiet, safe retreat.

He has his own bicycle, too, an oversized brute made of cast iron that weighs almost as much as Sophie herself but is, so he says, much less attractive. He is charming as he holds the handlebars for her to mount. She smiles and blows him a kiss. He, too, is her friend.

Through the dark night, they ride towards the railway bridge. In preparation for the Allied landings, London has asked specifically that the vast, complex, sprawling rail yard at Saint-Cybard be disabled and the Patron, a conscientious man, has dedicated his entire group to the mission. He has not excluded Sophie.

Together, Sophie and Daniel join the rest of the Patron's inner circle half an hour after midnight at the southern edge of town, three hundred metres from the railway station. Léon is here, and Raymond, Vincent and René, who has been allowed to accompany his father for the first time and has gone about all day with a grin on his face that would alert Kramme to everything were he not in Lyon.

René has a Sten with half a magazine; the Patron has been giving him personal tuition. He knows how to kneel and shoot in single fire, as well as how to lie flat on the ground and rake a line between two trees. He is a boy transported. They

277

sneak forward, keeping to the edges of the road, until they come to a dip just beyond the northern railway bridge.

It's three weeks to midsummer; the night is warm enough that they have abandoned their coats – all they need are their dark trousers, shirts and caps. Each has a haversack and this time, along with the *plastique* and the detonators, the Patron has taken delivery of a special device that can be laid on the track in a certain way, and will judge the number of trains that go over it before it explodes.

The Patron is already in place, lying in his shirtsleeves in the grass.

Sophie drops down beside him. 'I have red pencils,' she says. 'Set for half an hour.'

'Good. Thank you.' There is something light about him, too, a fierce aliveness that lights his eyes. Sophie has never seen him like this, but then, he has never been on any of the jaunts she has taken part in. In this, she did not lie to Kramme.

They are too close to Saint-Cybard to risk using their torches properly; tonight they are slid into socks with tiny holes clipped in the toes, to keep the beam as narrow as possible. There was a time in Paris when Sophie believed she could see like a cat. Now, she really can. Her ears are sharper as well. From the rail yard, she can hear the quiet clank of an engine uncoupling, and the voices – German, not French – of the men working on it. And far, far away, so far that she can only imagine them, the heavy bombers of the RAF.

'Sophie? Are you coming?'

The Patron is ready to leave and she has been listening to the song of the stars. She hitches her haversack on one shoulder, her weapon on the other, and runs after his shadow. The Patron has made maps of the whole yard, nearly a hectare in all – of the lines coming in and going out, the sidings, the parked engines and goods carriages, the points that must be jammed; everyone knows where to go and what to do. They are quiet now, when they have to be, all the noise of the dropping zone gone. The Patron was right about this, as about so much else.

Sophie and Daniel have their pouch of explosives and the timing pencils. They crouch almost to crawling and slide down a bank onto the railway track where the sleepers are smooth, slippery with the day's rain. Step by step, pace by slow pace with their Stens on single shot and their fingers on the guards, they pass to the left of a signalling box, to the right of the stationary engine of the Lyon train, and left, down to the turntable that is their target.

Working by touch, Sophie places the charges as she was taught: five at seventy-degree angles, each to the other, wedged down deep into the mechanism. Daniel keeps close to her shoulder, his hand on her hand, feeling the charge, stamping on the ends of the detonator pencils and passing them over. They go faster in the heat of the night. A clock ticks in her head, counting down the bare thirty minutes they have to get clear; all of them, including the Patron, who has to set his magical device that will (if it works) count five trains over in the morning, all of them full of French citizens coming into or going out of Saint-Cybard, and then will destroy the sixth, which is coming from Italy with munitions destined for the imminent war front on the Atlantic coast. Thirty minutes. Or less, because really, the timers have never yet been reliable. Move!

'Wait!' Daniel's hand is on her arm, his voice almost soundless in her ear. And on the far side of the turntable, a tin-headed Boche with his Mauser a black stick in the starlight and his cigarette a single red dot. She could aim for that. It's so very tempting.

'Wie spät ist es?'

He is young, the Boche, and nearly he dies, just for calling out to a friend. Daniel's knife is in his hand. The enemy is four long paces away. He'd be hosing blood across the gravel before he knew what was happening. Sophie clamps her hand on the boy's shoulder, her fingers digging into his collarbone. Not yet. Not yet. Not yet. He quivers under her touch.

An older, deeper voice in the guard hut near the signal box answers the Boche's question. *'Fünf vor zwei.'*

Really? Time moves too swiftly. The planes are due between half past two and three o'clock.

The Boche moves on past. Working slowly, as if through liquid gelatine, Sophie and Daniel place the remaining two charges. They finish at nineteen minutes past two and she has put red-banded pencils in the last. The guard has walked by half a dozen times. He is on the long reach to their left when a telephone rings in the guard hut to the right and is answered. The older guard comes out, calls over to the younger. They confer, looking up at the sky. Somewhere to the north, a searchlight blinks on and pokes at the lacewing cloud. Sophie fancies she can hear the pulse-thunder of heavy bombers, but it's a sound she hears in her dreams now and it may be her imagination.

She catches Daniel's arm, puts her mouth to his ear. 'We must leave.'

Moving is even harder now, because telephones have rung in other guard boxes and a klaxon sounds and there are men, running; many, many men. With torches. And searchlights: bright, *bright* beams that do not turn up at the sky to tease out the incoming planes, but turn in and down, to rake across the rails, the engines, the turntable.

And behind them, a wall of grey-clad men.

Merde!

No point in silence now. As loud as she can, she shouts, 'Daniel, *run!*'

Her Sten is an extension of her forearm. Running, she spins and fires. Her hands judder. Such a good feeling. She has wanted to do this for so long and has never been allowed to. Rifle fire whistles back, but the lights have not found her yet.

She wrestles the spare magazine from her haversack, tucks it in her belt and throws the sack away: there is nothing in it to incriminate Sophie Destivelle, collaborator nurse.

The others? Where are the others? She cups one hand to her mouth, yells, '*Troubadour!*'

'Here!' The Patron is two hundred metres to the south, at the far end of the yard, where the line from Lyon joins it. Between them are three sets of tracks.

'Troubadour to me! All of you. *This way!*' The Patron, too, turns as he runs, Sten at hip level. So many hours of training, and here they prove their worth. She sees the muzzle flash a moment before she hears the rip of rounds, the scream of falling men. Eight shots in that burst. You have twenty-eight rounds and only one spare magazine. Be careful.

The rumble in her bones is not from heavy bombers; it's from trucks coming down the road from the town.

Sophie changes direction and angles down towards him, shouting, 'South! There are truckloads of Boche in the north! We have to go south!' South, where the fields are, and the possibility of reaching the woods where Kramme has three times taken her hunting. She shot nothing, but she learned the layout of the woods – the ways in, the places nobody goes – she can hide all of them in there if she has to, and worry about escape in the morning. 'Go for the woods. *Go!*'

Run. Run. Run. And hear footsteps behind, to the right and running, turn and running, fire a long, sweeping burst. Ten rounds? Twelve? At most half her magazine gone. Keep running. There are so *many* Boche. Why so many? Kramme did not say he was going to do this, and he would have told her, surely? The British should be here. Where are the planes? If they'd come over now, they could— 'Daniel! Don't stop!'

He hasn't had their training; he can't fire while he's running, and his need to kill the Boche is greater than his need to get away. He's kneeling, firing at them as they come.

Sophie catches his shoulder, pulls him towards her. Rounds spray off the ground, chattering. She knocks the gun's barrel down with the stock of her own. 'Daniel. You'll kill one of us and none of them. We have to leave!'

He can run as fast as she can, because two months here has slowed her, when all the training had left her fast. Over tracks, under a carriage, slide in, slither. This is what the obstacle courses in Scotland were for. Go over the ones marked A, under B, to the left of C . . . and then we'll change them as you approach and you can curse all you like but you'll be glad when you're heading for something and there's a Boche machine gunner on the other side that you didn't see and you have to change direction, and—

'Left! Daniel, go left *here*!' Not a machine gun, but a row of men and two of them with dogs; big, leashed Alsatians, white teeth ghostly in the unreal light. 'Go under the carriage!' Good that Daniel's lithe and used to scrambling. They're under and up again and running on the other side, but there's someone behind the massed men, calling orders through the ranks upon ranks of grey uniforms.

'Nicht töten! Ich will sie lebend!'

Merde! But Kramme's in Lyon! She spins, running, and can see nothing in the dark, but there's no doubt it's him. Jesus, Mary and Joseph, *Kramme* is out in the middle of the night, directing the troops. How is he here when he's supposed to be in Lyon? Dear God. God. God. I didn't tell him. I did *not*.

Somewhere too near, the dogs are screaming. The sound breaks open her terror.

'This way!' She makes herself move, jinks right, down a siding, and where's the Patron? She can hear shooting up ahead, but there's shooting everywhere now; if the Boche don't start killing each other, it'll be a miracle. Where is the Patron?

A commotion to her left, and there is René, racing down the side of the Dijon line, waving the Sten he doesn't really know how to use, shouting abuse in his high, boy's voice. 'Bastards! Sons of whores! You don't scare me!' He is heading towards the dogs.

She shouts, 'René! Not that way!' He ignores her. He is going to be a hero. And dead. She angles down towards him. There's another bridge ahead that takes the rail over the road. They were supposed to blow that. Too late now.

Talking of charges, they're well within the time when they—

God, it's a long time since she was this close to *plastique* when it erupted. It's like being hit by a train, the blast hurtling into her spine, slamming into her, surging her forward, stunned, dizzy, staggering. She doesn't fall, though. She slaps her own face and, turning, slaps Daniel, once, a crack on the left cheek. 'Come on! This is our chance.' Because the Boche didn't have Captain Vaughan-Thomas teaching them and they are still recovering from the shock and any minute now, the next charge will—

'Hands over your ears!'

Sten on its sling, swinging, banging her ribs, her hands are over her ears when the second blast comes, and she doesn't so much as trip this time, isn't dizzy, and René is ahead and the Patron is a dozen strides away, dancing, windmilling his arms. 'Troubadour! Come on! Come on! Come *on*!'

He fires a long burst into the light-crazed night, stopping the rifle fire for the moment. She slews to a halt beside him. His ginger hair is a blaze of joy. He is laughing. Laughing! He is a god in his element and she so badly wants to join him. This is what they were trained for. This.

He catches her arm, pushes her past him. 'Go on. Get Daniel clear. I'll cover you.'

'Patron . . . back there, it's *Kramme*. He shouldn't be here.'

'I know. Someone sold us.' His eyes pierce hers, sharp as knives. She wants to weep. I didn't tell him. I *didn't*. He grins at her and there is no rancour in it. 'Go. Don't stop. I'll follow.'

'René's there.' The child – not a youth now – has seen the

dogs and is stranded in the middle of the railway line, bracketed left and right by searchlights. 'We can't leave him.'

'I'll get him. You take Daniel.' He grabs her elbow, wheels her round, pushes her towards the road, the bridge, the shape in the distance that is JJ. Kramme is back, so JJ is back, that much is good.

'That's an order, Sophie. Go!'

The Patron shoves her away. She stumbles and when she turns, he's flying down the track towards René, firing short bursts at the searchlights, at the men and their dogs.

He trusts her to follow an order. She feels sick. 'Daniel?'

'I'm here.' A small voice, off to her right.

He's crouching on the line, trying to hide between the rails. She grabs his hand and, together, they run along the road, out of range of the gunshots from the yard.

Halfway along, a single body lies black in the dark. The smell of blood is a wall. Sophie does not stop to see if it is friend or foe, but hurdles it and carries on. A hundred strides and they are under the bridge into the dark, damp stuffiness where neither searchlights nor stars can reach and here is JJ, who has never yet missed a jaunt, standing on his backpack, reaching high up into the mouldering brickwork of the bridge, placing a charge. He's mad. Insane. 'JJ, you can't . . .'

'Have you got a timing pencil?'

Of course: she was trained well. She pulls it out, stamps on the glass, hands him the closed end. Without any order from her, Daniel kneels at the tunnel's mouth, looking out, providing cover.

She says, 'The Patron . . .'

'He knows.' JJ jumps down, dusts his hands, says, 'That's a red. He'll be under and through long before it blows.'

'It's not that.' She shakes her head. 'He's gone back to get René.'

JJ frowns at her. 'Raymond went back to get René. You must have passed him on the road?'

'We didn't pass—' Her guts, already clenched, tie in a knot.

In her memory, the lumpen shape is of a parsnip. And herself, careless, jumping over.

She opens her mouth to speak but JJ reaches out to stop her. His face frozen, he says, 'So the Patron is the only one going for René.'

'He should be here by now.'

'Which means—'

Understanding reaches them together. Sophie sees JJ's move before it comes and grabs for his arm. 'JJ, stop!' He's a big man, and she only has a hold on the back of his shirt; her dead weight against his urgency. 'Listen!' Oh, God. Oh, God. Oh, God. *'Listen . . .'*

They do. Amidst the shouting and firing, the dogs are no longer baying. Over all the hysteria is the slavering relish of hounds that have brought down their quarry.

'Bastards. Bastards. Bastards!'

Sophie hauls the big man round. In the part light, his face is a streaming mess of tears. She is dry-eyed. She neither swears nor weeps. She thinks she will never do either again. I didn't tell him. *I didn't.* This is her truth and she believes it. She believes it because it is true. And she will avenge him. This, she swears to herself and the distant watcher, Laurence Vaughan-Thomas, who is unlikely to forgive her. He will not forgive her, either, if she fails now to follow orders.

JJ is fighting her, but not really. Her nails are claws sunk into his shoulder and she will not let him go. He'd have to kill her to go after René now, and he won't do that. She has control of him and Daniel – just these three, the survivors. If anybody else were coming, they'd be here by now.

Distinctly, she says, 'We can't go back for the Patron, for any of them. We can't save them. We can't give them a clean death. We have our orders. In case of emergency, we are to make our way to the mountains. No hesitations. No turning back. It's what we are trained for. So we fucking *go!*'

CHAPTER NINETEEN

THE MOUNTAINS OF MOREZ
4 June 1944

THESE WERE THE INSTRUCTIONS: if you have to run, go to the Maquis de Morez. There was never any indication of how, but half the training in Scotland, in Hampshire, in the other small country houses out of the way of the war, taught them how to move fast in enemy territory, to navigate where there are no road signs, to take what you need without remorse or regret.

First they run, through fields and copses, over walls and along ditches; if you're running fast you can't think. Conversely, if you start thinking, you can't run fast. So don't think. They lose the dogs running through a river and on the other side, turning left and down a part-metalled road, they hear a car; just one, coming into town, not out of it. It's big and it's running on gasoline, which means it's the Boche.

Sophie says, 'We need a car,' and JJ and Daniel nod at her and duck down in the ditches on either side and she watches the almost-not-there beams of the headlights until she can see the Mercedes, its driver, the two officers in the back. Neither one is Kramme. Neither of them is anyone Sophie knows; just

286

random Boche, in the wrong place at the wrong time. She stands up and empties the remains of her magazine into the rear windscreen.

They have to sweep the broken glass off the seats after they have hauled out the bloodied bodies, but she didn't hit the engine or the fuel tank and the car runs as well as it did before. JJ drives. He knows where the caches are along the route – of fuel, of *plastique*, of guns. They stop at the first and load everything into the trunk, and now if they are stopped, they will go out in a blaze of arms and explosives.

They go fast, with no care. They are not stopped.

Sophie does not know the route to the Maquis de Morez, but JJ has been often. He drives east and north, up out of the farmland to the foothills, where the forest shrouds the road.

The car is overladen and struggles as the hills grow into mountains and the road must switch back and forth up the side. Tall trees grow on either side, hiding the coming dawn. JJ flashes the headlamps, *dit dah dah dah, dit dah dah dah,* over and over – his own initials, JJ, JJ – on and on until it is too light for them to be seen, and he turns them off for another kilometre and then has to turn them back on again as he swings the car off the road and onto a forest track that ends in a clearing with tyre tracks crusted into the mud.

'We get out here.'

The silence bludgeons her ears. All around, big, black pines thrust up, rank upon disordered rank, old and wild and full of primal terror, so close together that they crowd out the sky.

The scent of resin makes the air viscous. Underfoot, centuries of leaf mould soak up the sound as she walks. Her breath shimmers in the morning light. Nobody steps out from between the many trunks to greet her, only the shadows of her fears. Don't think. Don't think. How in God's name did Kramme know the Patron would be there? She didn't tell him. She *didn't*. JJ is there, unloading the car, picking the best weapons. He has a Bren gun over his shoulder, which it would take two normal men to carry. Already sweat beads his upper lip.

Sophie says, 'What now?'

Harshly: 'We walk.'

Birds sing around them, and then don't. Sophie feels a dozen men take aim at her and decide not to fire. Her guts are water. At any moment, she may disgrace herself. She follows JJ along narrow deer tracks that show little signs of human use, winding uphill much as the road did, with hairpin bends curving round the trees.

They stop near the upper tree line. Here, the great pines are smaller, the trunks further apart, and Sophie can see grass and blue sky, can smell the smoke of a fire, and the scent of sweat and cigarette smoke and charred meat that makes her gag. She needs to piss and heads off behind a tree.

'Stop!' JJ's voice, urgent behind her. She freezes, fearing trip wires or land mines. There are none of these, but three men step out from the darkness of the forest, Stens held level.

The youngest of them, a youth barely out of his teens, steps forward. JJ salutes and a heartbeat later, Sophie does likewise. So this is Fabien, Patron of the Maquis de Morez. Back in the early days, she recalls the Patron – her Patron – saying, *He looks young, Fabien, but he leads his men with the skill of a sage. Don't underestimate him.*

Round-faced, smooth-skinned, lean, no taller than Sophie . . . Fabien doesn't just look young; he also looks innocent, but his gaze is hard and when it meets hers Sophie is first to glance down.

'He is dead, or captured?' His voice, too, is deeper and harder than she expects.

JJ says, 'Not dead.' He cannot make himself say more.

Sophie can. She steps forward. 'He was taken four hours ago in the raid on the trains. We need to get him back. I can go—'

288

'Wait.' The voice is a woman's, from their left.

JJ spins, sweeping off his hat. 'Mademoiselle Céline. I am so very sorry.'

The woman who stands on the far side of the clearing has the most startling eyes: like looking into polished platinum that promises riches and hardness both. She is as tall as the Patron, and as slender, as straight-up-and-down. Her bright blonde hair is cut in a twenties bob. It would not be hard to imagine her at the old nightclubs of the Montmartre; Le Cabaret des Truands, or even Le Monocle.

She would be as much at home there in a flapper dress with a cigarette in an impossibly long holder as here, where she is in men's boots and trousers and shirt, just as Sophie is, but on her, they are elegance embodied. She carries her Sten over her shoulder with the ease of long familiarity, and just now it is pointing at JJ.

Sophie has known of women like this, but never met one. It is like encountering a creature from another world. More importantly, she has never seen JJ at a loss for words. She sees it now.

Whey-faced, he says, 'We tried to get him. I swear to you, we tried. There was nothing we could do.'

So much information in so few words and most of it in the cracks of his voice. The woman, Céline, stares at him, nodding slowly.

'Then now that we are all together, we shall find something that will work.' Céline speaks French with the accent of blood and money, of Chinon and Blois and old, old royalty. Her ice-flat gaze rakes them, and comes to rest on Sophie. She thrusts out a hand. 'Céline. You are Sophie Destivelle, his deputy?'

'I am.' I did not betray him to Kramme. I did *not*.

Céline favours her with a long look.

'Do I gather you have a plan to get him back?'

Yes! She has spent the whole drive thinking this, every

289

frozen kilometre. 'I can go back. I am a nurse. They'll let me in. Kramme trusts me. At the very least, I could take him an L-pill.' He would want that. She, Sophie, would want it; therefore he must want it.

'Really? If he was going to use one of those, I imagine he'll have done it by now.'

'No, he won't. He didn't carry one in case they searched him and it was found.'

'Because a capsule of cyanide smaller than the size of your little fingernail is a dead giveaway, while hurling Mills bombs around a railway yard is obviously going to be overlooked. Dear God in heaven, why do they leave their brains behind when they pick up a gun?'

Céline lights a cigarette and then offers the packet round. Whatever the deprivations of wartime, this Maquis is well stocked. 'You can't get in. Kramme would have you arrested. They'd shoot you on the spot if you were lucky.'

'Two nights ago, Kramme asked for my hand in marriage.'

'Did he? I imagine your handlers were exceptionally proud of that.' Céline breathes smoke through her nose. 'Sadly, all that effort for naught. Word is that the Aillardes were taken in for questioning this morning. From what I understand, it couldn't happen to a better couple. But you're on Kramme's wanted list now. You can't walk back in.'

The Aillardes will be dead by now if they are lucky. Sophie digests this news and wonders how it got here so soon. Someone else must have a faster route from Saint-Cybard to here than JJ. Either that, or there's a telephone line to somewhere close, and someone in Kramme's close circle who is able to use it.

There's something interesting in that, but she hasn't time to consider it. Thinking aloud, she says, 'Then I won't go in as Sophie Destivelle. I'll use a wig, padding, new clothes. If you did the same training as I did, you know how we can look like other people. If I can get onto the Paris train somewhere west of here, I can come in as a refugee.' I can kill Kramme, too, and then perhaps Laurence Vaughan-Thomas will not have me hanged.

'I did exactly the same training as you, but you have to believe me, they won't let you near the prison. Kramme's been trying to get your Patron for a year now. He won't take risks with his prize. The guards will have had all leave rescinded. The Hôtel Cinqfeuilles will be in lockdown. Nobody they don't know by sight will be allowed within half a kilometre of the walls.'

'We can't do *nothing*.'

'It's what we were told to do. It's the standing order. To go against that is a court martial offence.'

'What does London say?' Because her experience is that standing orders are malleable, particularly if certain people in London want them to be.

Céline bites at her thumbnail for so long that Sophie thinks she will never answer. Her nails are ragged. On closer inspection, she looks tired, as if she has not recently slept. Her hair is unwashed, and her battle shirt has seen better days.

At length, she says, 'I have a sked in an hour that might shed some light. If you'd care to join me, you'd be welcome. It's a fair distance, though. We have to leave now.'

Thus is Sophie introduced to the Maquisards' camp, which is, in fact, three camps, spread out. She, JJ and Daniel arrived in the most southerly one and she is led along the chain, along tracks that show more signs of use, with the trees marked, occasionally, at head height. They go north and uphill all the while.

Each camp is laid out to a similar plan: the latrine trench lies downhill and downwind, with cooking fires thirty metres uphill. Here, logs are laid around the fires, and around them are sleeping areas for the men, bedded down with pine needles, sheltered with pine boughs: everything here is pine. Above the trees are shepherds' huts and a couple of pine-built log cabins in which the commanders sleep, these being more comfortable, but also more likely to be seen – and so bombed – by the Boche.

From the last, most northerly camp, the route to the radio hideout heads almost straight up the mountain, out beyond the last of the pines, into rocks and rough grass and scrubby, stunted birch trees that grow out of the scree. It is not a difficult trek, but it's steep and there are places where they are climbing up near-vertical mountainside, grabbing young, whippy tree roots and unstable rocks as handholds, hauling up with their faces buried in soft, sweet moss and lichen in their hair.

'This is like Arisaig,' Sophie says, pushing herself onto a ledge halfway up the latest ascent.

'Fewer midges, though, or we'd have gone mad long ago.' Céline offers her a hand, pulls her to her feet. 'The mosquitoes can be a bugger at dusk if you haven't got a great big smoking fire to keep them off, mind you. When you get to the top, veer to the right and follow the deer track. We're looking for a cave on the left hidden behind some scrubby pines.'

They climb on. Sophie is first up the final stretch and so she turns right, follows a path through heavy undergrowth and finds that the 'cave' is a jagged horizontal rift in the mountainside, less than a metre high, with a patch of soft earth about two metres wide at the front.

Kneeling, Céline studies this for a minute or two. 'We're clear. Nobody's been. Come on in.'

'How?'

'Like this.' The Englishwoman slides her Sten onto her back, lies down and wriggles on fingertips and toes, like a rather lengthy crab, in through the letterbox gap. A grunt, a stamp or two, and: 'Come on. You can stand up in here. It's not as small as it looks, and it's not as dark inside as you'd expect. There's a hole in the roof somewhere that lets in the light.'

Sophie goes down on her belly into the flat, hard mud and crawls sideways under an arm's span of solid rock into a grey-green opacity of dusty light and the sharp, peppery scent of crushed lichen.

'Welcome. *Welcome. Welcome.*' Bat-like, the echo swoops over their heads. Sophie presses on her palms and stands up. The roof is high, high over her head and its central part is a vein of greenish light. Céline is sitting on a natural shelf in the rock with one of the new, lightweight wireless sets at her side. Her hair is ghostly in the grey light. Her smile is richly warm.

'The only problem with this place,' she says, holding out the aerial, 'is that we need to string this up outside or we don't get a signal. Would you mind terribly taking it out again and hanging it off a tree or two?'

So Sophie wriggles out and wriggles in again, and in between she loops the length of wire across some branches and, at twelve minutes past four, the signal comes in, clear and clean.

They have played scissors/paper/stone for the right to take it and Sophie has won. She transcribes the Morse and Céline has the harder task of deciphering it. The result is shorter than any message she's worked on since she came to France.

To: JUNO from HERMES

CHRIS STOP JULIE STOP NOW P STOP WHAT
CAN WE DO QUERY AIR RAID QUERY
ANYTHING QUERY SOMETHING, SURELY QUERY
HE HAS NOT TALKED YET STOP WE HAVE
BLUFF CODE THAT WORKS STOP SLAINTE L

'Slainte?' Sophie runs her finger under the word. 'Is that right?'

'It's Scottish. It's what the boys say when they're drinking whisky.'

'I never heard them.'

'I didn't either. But my cousin evidently did.'

'The Patron is your *cousin*?'

'No. My cousin is the one sending the cipher. Laurence Vaughan-Thomas. I thought he'd gone to train with the Jeds, but evidently he's wormed his way back into the Firm for this one. I suspect our uncle is involved. It's amazing how previously rigid rules bend like India rubber in his presence.' Céline leans back against the wall, her face bisected by the strange, slanting light from the ceiling. She catches sight of Sophie's expression. 'What?'

'Laurence Vaughan-Thomas is your cousin?'

Céline sets down the ciphered script. She explores one tooth with her tongue, then: 'Either the echo in here is slow and selective or my French is worse than I thought. Shall we start again in English?'

'Not unless you want to.'

'I don't. So, yes, Larry is my cousin. Do I gather you know him?'

'If he's the Boche-blond RAF officer with the crippled hand, he trained me.'

'Did he, by Jove? I expect that was an excoriating experience. So we've established that you now know more about me than you should and it would be useful if you were not to mention this to the Boche if caught. That apart, we are also agreed that all three of us want to free your Patron from Kramme's attentions as a matter of urgency, and we can explore our individual motives later. Would an air raid work, do you think?'

'To kill him? I think the cellars are too deep.'

294

'You are desperate to see him dead, aren't you? I was think-ing more whether it might lure the Boche away from the prison, and break down a wall or two so we could get in.'

'We?'

'Really, this constant echo is particularly tiresome. You didn't think I was going to let you go in there alone? They might be looking for one dark-haired nurse. They won't be looking for sisters, particularly not if we both look suitably Aryan. How good is your German?'

'It's not.'

'Pity. How good is your coding?'

'Average.'

'Well, it's your turn. I did the incoming. My silk's there, under the box. I'll write the plain text, you turn it into some-thing we can safely send.'

Céline writes swiftly, neatly. Her handwriting is like her face, all angles and lines, perfectly symmetrical.

Sophie says, 'Don't we have to wait for your sending sked?'

'In theory, yes. In practice, if we send it fast enough, they'll still be listening. Trust me, I used to work there. We always stayed on the wavelength for ten minutes, just in case.'

'Nobody ever told us that.'

'They don't want anyone to abuse it. But it's true. If you can do the cipher in time—'

'If it's more than about six words, I can't. Nor can you and you're a lot faster than I am. But if you're his cousin, we don't have to cipher it. You can write something only he will understand.'

Silence, and a long look, softening at the end. 'You know, I could. I really think I could. What's today's date?'

'The fourth of June.' Three days to go, and how is she going to kill Kramme now?

'Right.' Céline does some calculations involving fingers and silent counting. The old message is crossed out. The new message is this:

295

JUNO to HERMES

C AND P MORE THAN ENOUGH STOP WITH
SUFFICIENT GIFTS CAN MAKE MERRY AS PER
THREE LITTLE PIGS ON J'S DAY MINUS LUNA
MINUS C'S DAY STOP WILL DO WHATEVER WE
CAN STOP SANTE C

Sophie reads it once, twice, a third time, looks up. 'Well, I don't understand a word of this and the Boche certainly won't. We can send it in plain text and I swear Kramme won't be any the wiser.'

Céline clasps her shoulder. 'You send it – they'll know your fist and that way they'll know we're together without us having to say so. Larry's there, obviously. We should get a reply.'

And they do.

H TO J

GIFTS NOT AVAILABLE IN GREAT NUMBERS
BUT IF HUMANLY POSSIBLE J'S DAY MINUS
LUNA MINUS C'S DAY SHALL GO WITH A BANG
AS PER GRANTCHESTER 28 STOP LOVE YOU
STOP REGARDS TO YOUR TAME SHREW STOP
TELL HER WE KNOW SHE BURNED HER HAND
STOP NOT TO WORRY STOP WE ARE PROUD OF
HER STOP MERDE ALORS L

Proud. I am the Wild Card and I have failed. Kramme is alive. The Patron, whom you loved, is held captive. There is nothing of which to be proud. Sophie sits in the mellow light and watches her hands shake. Céline sits behind her, out of sight.

In the end, because she can't bear the silence, Sophie says, 'I never thought of myself as a shrew.'

'You're quite the opposite, that's why he said it.' Is that a smile? She turns. It is. Céline says, 'It's an English thing, peculiar to the upper classes.'

'Like J's day?'

'No, that's the date a mutual friend was killed in a bombing raid in Cambridge: the twenty-seventh of July. C's day refers to a second cousin of ours, who was killed on the twenty-first of the month. One month before Julie died is the twenty-seventh of June; and minus Chris's day is the sixth, which means we're on two nights from now, basically.'

God. Two more days in which the Patron's every hour is a living hell. Sophie closes her eyes and cannot bear what she sees. Opening them, she asks, 'And three little pigs?'

A dry smile. 'I'll huff and I'll puff and I'll blow your house down. And before you ask, nineteen twenty-eight was my uncle's fiftieth. Laurence's father. He hosted a bonfire party at their house in Grantchester, near Cambridge. It went down in the annals of our relatives as The Biggest Family Bonfire ever seen. God help Patrick in the meantime, but this is the best we can do.'

Patrick. The Patron's real name is Patrick. She isn't supposed to know these things, but it helps, in the next few days, to have heard it.

CHAPTER TWENTY

5 June 1944

'*LES SANGLOTS LONGS, DES violons, de l'automne . . .*'
On the radio, the message all of France has been waiting for. The violins sob, and thus is it known that within twenty-four hours, somewhere on the coast of France, men by their thousands, their tens of thousands, will race for the sand, the turf, the embankments, the gun emplacements and the bloody, desperate towns and villages, against gunfire and rocket fire and tank fire and everything the Luftwaffe can bring to bear. They may succeed.

At the end of the longest set of BBC announcements ever made comes this: '*A Hermès de Juno – trois petit cochons vont danser dans le salon des cousines.*'

Outside the cave in the mountains of Morez, Céline blows smoke rings at the sky. This, Sophie is realizing, is her equivalent of dancing a jig. 'God knows how they managed it: planes must be worth their own weight in gold tonight, but we're on. Couldn't ask for a better cover than an invasion.' She spins, arms outstretched.

Sophie is not in the mood to dance any jigs. Losing herself in business, she winds up the aerial, slithers back into the cave and hides the radio on its shelf at the back.

Céline helps her to her feet as she emerges. 'You're not happy?'

'Kramme's had him two days now. And René.'

'We're doing what we can. It might be enough. We have to hope so. Come on. Let's go and break the good news to the boys.'

According to Céline, the 'boys' are twice the number they were even a month ago. The promise of victory has brought men out of hiding, youths out of school, priests from their prayers. The encampment has swollen to an unmanageable size; the latrines alone span thirty metres.

Fabien may look like a beardless youth, but in the time she has been here, Sophie has recalibrated her opinion of him several times, and always upwards. He fights like a rattlesnake, the men adore him and, very clearly, organization is his forte. He has split his group into five and sent men off to build, to guard, to hunt the forest for boar, deer, rabbit, to forage for food and haul water. The weather has been kind and the newcomers think this is how it has always been, a sylvan idyll.

To rein in their hubris, Fabien has picked his best storytellers and they spent the entire first evening telling stories – folk tales, almost – of the early days, when a dozen boys from one of the outlying villages lived for eight days in the forest on raw onions and nothing else, and had to go back into the town on the ninth day, shitting through the eye of a needle and too sick to resist when the Boche bundled them onto a train bound for the east.

They spoke of snow and men losing their vital organs to frostbite, of what it's like not to sleep for the cold, to have nothing to eat for five days in a row, so that sucking on a lump of ice feels like a feast.

They talked at length and in detail of collaborators who bring the Boche to the mountain and how hard it is to stay awake all night on watch, but you have to, knowing that men will die in their sleep if you don't; and it is this, Sophie thinks, sitting in the fire's rich light – the threat of death and cut throats and blood – that makes Daniel draw in his shoulders and shudder.

He brightens, though, when Céline appears: everyone does. She is wearing a pair of khaki trousers and a man's linen shirt. She has wound a strip of someone else's shirt round her head as a bandana and her Sten is an extension of her arm. She is beautiful and unobtainable, but they have seen her fight, those who have been here longest, and the storytellers speak of this, too, telling of the many raids in which La Fille Anglaise has played a starring role, but none so heroic as the time when Fabien's gun jammed and the Boche were about to pick him up – until Céline wrenched a rifle from the man beside her and, standing with her arm braced on a tree, shot every Boche officer who tried to give an order.

One after another, they raise a hand, commence a command and – *pouf!* – this, the storyteller's mime: a slap to the forehead shows a bullet between the eyes and they stagger, arms flailing, for death. The magazine was empty by the time the enemy ran, but they did run, and Fabien was saved to lead them still.

And so the men roll over now, and sit up when she appears. And when she climbs onto the remains of a wine barrel and unhitches her gun and fires three single shots up and out into the night sky, they are on their feet before the echo of the third has rattled off the trees.

JJ is in the front row, with Daniel and Vincent, who appeared yesterday, footsore and hungry, having walked from Saint-Cybard. They are quiet, these three, more so than the others, and they are accorded the respect of the newly bereaved. Daniel, particularly, is treated with something approaching awe: his father, evidently, was a Maquis legend – Kramme's first victim – and the fame devolves to the son.

'The planes?' JJ asks, as the last shot fades to silence. 'Are they coming soon?'

'They are, but before that is the invasion. It's happening! The English and the Americans land tomorrow. And tomorrow also, we need twenty volunteers to come with us into Saint-Cybard to open the prison and get everyone out: JJ's Patron, the boy René, and anyone else alive we can find in there. The planes will be over at eleven o'clock in the evening. We will be in place before then.'

SAINT-CYBARD
6 June 1944

It is dusk. Moths and bats sift through the last shadows. Sophie lies in a musty, dried-out ditch at the side of the road into Saint-Cybard. She is hungry and thirsty and desperate to smoke, and she is hardly alone. Céline, lying to her left, is the same; and JJ, Vincent and Daniel to her right. On the far side of the road, and spread over several hundred metres, Fabien and twenty volunteers from the Maquis de Morez lie similarly hidden.

Ahead and to her left, half a kilometre away, are the remains of the bridge that JJ demolished in their retreat three nights ago. Ruined brickwork stands starkly naked, lacking even a shroud of rubble. The road has been swept clear and German trucks run along it, in and out of the town.

The invasion is old news now: the first day's fighting is over and, if the rumours are right, it all took place on the Normandy coast, which is half a week's drive away, even under the best of circumstances. The Boche still think this is a feint and the main thrust will come to Holland, but, even so, the German garrison on the edge of town is buzzing like a kicked hive and the rest of Saint-Cybard is curfew-quiet.

The planes of the RAF are due over within the next half-hour. There is no guarantee they will come.

Patrick. Her Patron. She will see him today. If he's still alive. If he's whole enough to walk. If the kindest thing, the only thing, is not to put a bullet between his eyes.

Sophie mouths promises to an unheeding god: I will be good; I will kill Kramme. Or if you prefer, I will not kill Kramme. I *will* be good.

'Here.' Céline, at her elbow, pointing. 'Or rather, there.'

It's not even fully dark. The planes are a denseness on the horizon, a thrumming, distant gut-churn that grows louder, deeper, angrier. They could be returning Luftwaffe, come to bomb the whole of Saint-Cybard to a bloody pulp in revenge for the Allied attacks on the north coast.

They are RAF. The first flare drops over the fields behind the Peugeot factory. Fabien has not been able to send a man to warn the owner, but at least the guards will have time to get clear.

'Not yet.' Céline catches her arm when Sophie didn't know she had moved. 'Wait until they hit the prison.'

'What if they don't?'

'Trust, *ma petite*. Others amongst us have as much to lose as you do.'

She doesn't want to think about that. She shelves her elbows on the road and peers out into the fire-lit night. Three of the planes turn north and head back the way they have come. Three others veer south, over the city. The searchlights are a net, sweeping the sky. Each plane is caught, lost, caught again.

'God, they're coming in low.' Céline stands up, her hands over her mouth. 'Take care. Take care. Take care. Strewth. How can they fly so *low*?'

So low the navigators could read the writing on the newsprint plastering the windows of Raymond's former office. So low they could shave the grass. So low they can drop their bombs – one, two, three – onto the Hôtel Cinqfeuilles, the delight of fin-de-siècle architecture that may shortly cease to exist.

There is a hiatus, a moment of breath-held astonishment in which all sound drops away. Caught in this bubble, Sophie can hear neither the planes, nor the guns.

There has been no explosion. Hands clamped over her ears, she is counting: one thousand and one. One thousand and two. One thousand and three . . . One thousand and eight. Eight seconds and they haven't gone off. Nine. Ten. Dear God, they all misfired. Surely, they can't all have—

God.

If he was above ground, he's dead. She thinks this so quietly, the words barely sound in her head. Outwardly, she's standing on the road, shouting.

Move! Let's go! Move!

It's her own voice, but she can't hear it. Her hands over her ears were as much use as gossamer against a train. She signals Céline, JJ, Vincent, Daniel. Across the road, Fabien raises his so-young head. She screams at him, voicelessly. He nods, turns, gestures. A mass of men rises from the ground, each one armed. Laden with her own two guns, magazines, torch, other essentials, Sophie runs towards the fires. As hounds, hell-bound, they follow.

In the outskirts of Saint-Cybard, tall, shuttered houses lean in across the streets, whispering one to another of impending doom. Shadows shift in the light of the burning factory, but nobody hides in the dark places; nobody is outdoors at all. Every house is boarded and still. The trucks on the southern road grind through gears and there's a hubbub of German voices, but they are heading for the fires, not into town. She runs on, left, and then takes the second right at the crossroads by the fountain; into the heart of town.

'Wait here.' Sophie holds up an arm. They are at another crossroads, two blocks from the Hôtel Cinqfeuilles.

The streets are clear, except at the hotel. Here, a dozen men play fire hoses onto the flames. They may be Frenchmen and she has promised herself and the nameless god that she will not kill Frenchmen unless they are actively collaborating. Dousing a fire isn't that, but it's hard to tell the French from the un-French and there's no doubt that the latter will shoot without compunction.

The Firm gave them a half-day of training in propaganda: its uses and effects. They advised the use of a megaphone. She puts her hands around her mouth.

'Men of Saint-Cybard.' The echo slams in off the high, close walls. *Cybard. Cybaaaaard.* 'We are the Maquis de Saint-Cybard. We are here for France. If you stand against us, you will die. Go back now. Go *back*!' *Back. Back. Baaaaccck.*

The hoses wilt. The men retreat, step by slow step, until one breaks and runs, and the rest follow. Behind them they leave a knot of men by the open door: collaborators who will not run. The fire lights them in silhouette. The echo has confused them. They don't know where she is, where the danger is coming from. Like sheep in a pen, they mill and gather.

Sophie lifts her arm again. 'Get them!'

This is like shooting crows on a church roof: impossible to miss. Twenty-four men and two women fire a single short burst each.

The noise! It chatters down from the walls and in its stutter, the eight men at the doorway are reaped as summer corn.

'Come on!' No going back now. Her heart is a piston, driving. She leaps over the bodies and in through the door.

What now? Smoke. Fire. In the lobby, the chandelier is a scatter of needled light. To the right, the reception desk has been abandoned. To the left is the chaise longue on which she has lately sat with Kramme, a low table, turned on its side, the fire still vast in the grate, blazing. Ahead is the big curving sweep of stairs leading ever upward.

A second look: Cinqfeuilles was expensive, once: the wallpaper in the hallway is thickly textured with silver embossed over a once-pure white; the reception desk is gilded mahogany; the chaise is stuffed with horse hair and covered in a heavy burgundy velvet.

All is ruin now: the chaise, the desk, the walls, the floor are coated in a melange of dust and smoke and the air is dense with the scent of boiling blood and burned hair.

'Look out!' Beyond the chaise, a doorway, and in it, a shape that sees them through the smoke and recoils. She huddles down behind the desk, fires a short four-shot burst, hears someone die and someone else scream a warning. Céline is somewhere close behind, firing up the stairs. Someone dies there, too. Not Kramme. She would know the sound of his voice.

The Maquisards press in from the street. Some of them she knows. 'JJ!' He's big, easy to see. 'The cellars are on the right past the desk. The door will be locked.'

'Not for long.' He is a bull. This is his china shop. He carries a crowbar, long as a rifle, and thicker. He elbows past her and kicks open a door on the far side of the reception desk. Silver-grey smoke billows out. Sophie can smell burning Bakelite. She fires back into the corridor opposite and follows him. 'Daniel! This way!'

The hotel has a telephone exchange. It's only a small one, but she rakes a burst of bullets across it in passing. It isn't on fire; the smoke is coming from somewhere further in and deeper down. JJ kicks through another door and beyond, stairs spiral down. He fires down the first curve, just in case. They are coughing now, choking into their sleeves.

'Cover your faces with your scarves.' Céline, calling from behind. They all have scarves; she insisted on it. They don't make the breathing any easier, just less hot. Going down, though, they pass through gradients until, at the foot of the stairs, the air is cool, almost cold, and free of smoke.

The cellars are a well of black: no light is here, but men are shouting in French, beating on solid wood. 'Here! Here, for the love of God! Open the doors!'

The beam of her torch is a knife, paring slivers of dark. 'Left!' This voice is heavier, more authoritative. 'Come to me. Left at the foot of the stairs and ten paces along. The first cell is on your left there. The boy is in the second.'

She reaches the door, presses her hand to it, as if he might feel her. 'The boy? You mean René?'

'Vivier's son. Yes. If there are more of you, turn right, take the cells there. Hurry, there is water coming in and some are on the floor, unable to stand.'

On the stairs, their feet were dry. On the floor, frigid water sloshes thickly around their ankles. Things bump and swirl, and are caught underfoot, softly. The stench of raw sewage rises in gagging waves, smothering the aftertaste of smoke.

'JJ!' He is there, at her side. 'Let me hold your torch. You need both hands on the crowbar.' Now she wishes for proper light. The torch barely illuminates the splintering wood, the buckle of steel. 'Look out!'

The lock breaks with a retort like a gunshot. Along the corridor, men flinch and duck. Sophie stabs the dark with her torch. 'Are you there?'

'Here.' He is medium height, dark-haired, unshaven, the man in the cell. He has been beaten, but not recently. She doesn't know this man but JJ rushes past her to embrace him. 'Verne Bedard! We thought you were dead!'

'I should be, but Kramme caught your Patron and decided he had better things to do than hang me from the ceiling.'

Her guts coil and clench. 'Where is he? The Patron, *where is he?*'

306

'I don't know.' Verne unpeels her fingers from his shirt-front. 'He was here. I spoke to him two, maybe three days ago, when he first came in. In the dark, one cannot tell the passage of time and they bring food only once every three days. I haven't seen him since the last meal. Before you look for him, you need to release the child. He has been badly used.'

Gunshots ring out behind her. She spins, trigger finger already flexing. 'Don't shoot! Sophie, it's us!' Céline flashes her torch at the ceiling to show where she is. 'Fabien is shooting the locks. The stairs are safe, but we have to get everyone out fast. Get the boy and the others in the adjacent cells. We'll do the rest.'

JJ is already muscling René's door but this is too slow. To Verne, she says, 'Where are the keys?'

'Upstairs in Kramme's office. He never leaves them down here. Look, the boy . . .'

The door has broken open. JJ is in, and crouching in the filth. 'René. René. René. Oh! Your father would be proud of you . . .' The big man comes out, carrying his new burden. René looks small, frail, fragile, so young, so broken; feverish. His head lolls on JJ's elbow. One arm is a mess of blood. His hand is bandaged, badly. His fingers . . . it may be he has lost some of his fingers, perhaps the whole hand.

JJ is going to extract blood price for this; his face says so. Sophie asks, 'What have they done to you?'

Verne is still at her side. 'They crushed his joints with a hammer, one each day, and sent him back here. If the wounds are infected now, he'll die.'

'I didn't tell him anything.' René's voice has been shredded, all the life dragged from it. His smile is flat. His eyes will not focus on her face. Doggedly: 'I told him nothing.'

What was there left to tell? She wants to be sick, only her body will not let her. First, she has to get everyone else out. She says, 'Give René to Verne. We need to keep opening doors.

JJ, listen to me. There are men in there who have had worse than this. We need to free them.'

And so it is done. René is passed to Verne and JJ becomes a door-breaking automaton. Wedge-lean-snap. Wedge-lean-snap. Wedge-lean—

At the end of the row, one last door resists JJ's weight: lean again.

Lean some more.

He gives up and shoots out the lock, and finds that even then, the door won't open.

'Is there anyone in there?' she shouts, banging on the wood. She has never been down here; she doesn't know where the door leads. She calls out, 'Where does this go?' and, from along the corridor, a voice says, 'That's the way out. There are stairs from there up to the kitchens and outside. The Boche went that way and barred it behind them.'

'Stand back.' She has some *plastique* in her haversack and she knows how to shape a charge. 'Back! Right back!'

The door splinters. An iron bar has been slid into iron hasps. She hauls it out, kicks open the wood, and yes, her torch finds another door, half open, and beyond a flight of wooden stairs, coiling up. Kramme has been here – she can feel his nearness as a prickle on the skin of her forearms, but it is old, by an hour or more.

'Don't.' She catches JJ's arm before he can charge on up the stairs. 'They might have laid charges. Besides, it matters more to get everyone out of here.'

'What do we do?'

'Blow the kitchen stairs so they can't come down at us.' Another shaped charge. Another retreat around the corner. Another satisfying explosion and the stairs are splintered matchwood, burning.

The men of the Maquis are carrying those from the cellars who cannot walk, which is perhaps half of them. Some are too thin, some too badly injured. Nobody, as far as she can see, has lost a limb. They head back up the stairs.

On the ground floor, Fabien is maintaining order: the fire burns less fiercely, the smoke drifts in patched clouds and there is clear air between. The Boche are not much in evidence, except on the floor, dead.

Outside, groups of men guard the roads with mortars, but nobody has faced them down yet. A line of Maquisards moves wounded men from the stair-head out onto the street where Fabien has commandeered three petrol-driven trucks. 'Sophie! We have Kramme's car.'

'Where's Kramme?'

'Gone. One of the Milice said a message came, warning him to leave before the planes arrived.'

She doesn't want to see the Milice who gave this information. If he's dead, he's lucky, but it won't have been clean. 'Someone needs to show us how to get to Kramme's office.' She should know, but Kramme never mixed business with pleasure, so she doesn't.

Beside Fabien is a big man with a beer paunch who smells of the cellars. He grins, showing a row of rotting teeth. 'I can find another one to question,' he says.

Ignoring him, Sophie says to Fabien, 'Where's the Patron?'

'Not here.'

Verne is back. He has found a Luger and looks as if he knows how to use it. 'Kramme's office is on the second floor.'

Thank God someone knows. She asks, 'Do you know the way?'

'Follow me.'

They run up the long, shallow, spiral stairs, slipping on blood-slicked marble, past punctured bodies all clad in grey. JJ stoops to put a bullet through the skull of one that might not be dead.

Verne turns right at the top of the stairs and they all follow. 'Third along.'

Third along looks like any other hotel suite: big double doors with much glass, curtained. Brass handles the length of an arm stand proud, stained now with smoke and fire-scorch. The carpets smoulder. The smoke here is thin and acrid. Sophie can smell burning flesh and will not think whose.

'Céline. Verne.' At her nod, they take up positions either side of the double doors. JJ kicks them open, ducks to the side and waits. When nobody shoots, they push through, all four together, weapons to the front.

Into an empty salon that smells of burned flesh and fear and death.

It's a big room, well appointed. The stabbing lace of their torches lights a dress uniform on a hanger in an open wardrobe; a desk, neatly ordered; a bar, well stocked. But nobody is here: not Kramme, not the Patron. Nobody.

'Patron?' Sophie sets her voice above the general melee.

She is answered, after a fashion. A grunt, a swift scuffling, soon suppressed, and these from behind a door on the room's far side.

Kicking it open, she enters what was once a bedroom, and now has been stripped of all amenities. The floor is solid wood, painted black. The walls are white. There are no curtains and the windows are barred. Yet another door leads off into a bathroom, and in that sits a full bath with old blood on the curved edge.

She sees these peripherally and only because she has been taught to observe all that is out of the ordinary, and everything in this room is extraordinary, from the raw stink of blood to the pile of telephone directories with the scuff marks of men's shoes on them to . . . the thing she does not want to see: the man hanging from the ceiling.

'Patron!'

His eyes are whole. They have not taken his eyes. This is what she sees first, ahead of all the rest: he is not blinded. That was her first fear.

But the rest is as grim as her nightmares. He is hanging by his wrists from a meat hook bolted onto the ceiling joist. A bloody cloth gags his mouth wide open. His teeth are bared in a white-lipped grimace of pain. Ligatured by the handcuffs, his fingers are red-blue swollen sausages, and below them his wrists are green-white dead. Dark, crusted blood tracks down his forearms. His chest is a burned and bloody mess. His bare feet are pulped and he has no toenails.

All this as she crosses the room. She is a nurse. Her mind is clean and clear. 'Verne – there'll be a doctor's room somewhere nearby: next door, probably. Find it. We need morphine, penicillin and iodine. Get them. And mop handles to make a stretcher. Use Kramme's greatcoat, it's on the hanger in the outer room.'

She is in front of him. He's still alive, breathing, however shallowly. She shifts across the pile of directories and stands on it, grasps his hips, takes his weight to release his arms, feels the gasp as the pain is lifted. 'JJ!'

JJ is tall enough to stand on tiptoe and flip the chain of the handcuffs over the hook with the crowbar.

The Patron's weight is all hers. She holds him, staggering. Céline helps her. Between them, they lay him down on the matt-black floor. Verne is somewhere, blundering. He has morphine, a syringe, a needle that may be clean. She cracks open a vial, draws in, taps out the bubbles, injects into his arm.

'Patron. Patron. Patron.' Her mind is not clear now; the word is the only one she can find while, of its own accord, her body goes through the mechanics of her trade. He has a pulse. It is hard and shocked and rigid under her fingers, but he has a pulse.

Céline leans over him, ragged. 'Patrick. Oh God, Patrick.'

His eyes float open, green-grey with vast, black pupils.

He is alive.

He is not dead.

Sophie says, 'We have you. You're safe. Safe. I swear it.'

Weeping, Céline reaches for the gag.

They do not sleep: it is not that kind of night. In the early light of next morning's dawn, Céline leans against the pine log wall of the infirmary, gripping a bottle of the local Calvados by the neck.

Sophie sits with her back to the closed door. Patrick is inside, with enough morphine to give him sleep. She has washed every part of him, sponged off the blood, catalogued the injuries. A part of her knows all that was done, can list the broken bones, the torn tissue, the joints wrenched out of alignment, the burns, the contusions, the lacerations. This knowledge is sealed in the growing part of her mind that hides what she does not want to see.

She takes the bottle, swallows, holds her breath against the burn. To Céline, she says, 'Did the invasion succeed?'

'Not yet. I radioed London. They said, "progress is smooth" which means, I think, we haven't lost yet. It won't be swift.'

Nobody thought it would be. Nobody who knew anything about war, anyway. 'How's René?' Céline took him on: Sophie had no compassion to spare.

'He's eaten. He's drunk a lot. Everyone is praising his courage. The pain will hit him later, in the night.'

'We have enough morphine.'

'He says he doesn't want it.'

'Still.'

'Still.'

They drink, quietly, beyond speaking. Except that Céline

312

keeps looking down through the trees to the fires and the camp. 'Sophie?'

'Mmm?'

'Did you ever think you were betrayed? That Kramme knew more than he should?'

Merde. She sets the bottle down. 'What have you found, Céline?'

'This.' She has them tucked into her shirt, warm from her skin: three slips of paper, thin, lined in pencil, with typed messages that look very like the Firm's ciphers except they're in German. The top one makes her eyes dance.

```
SS-Stubaf Kramme: Akte: DIEM

# F3/A1.9.4-

1/6/44 2217 Std

An: SS-Ostubaf Klaus Weissmann

V-MANN 'DIEM': INVASION FINDET STATT 6
JUNI. INFORMATION GILT ALS 100 PROZENT
ZUVERLAESSIGKEIT. ERBITTE BEFEHL FUER
WEITERES VORGEHEN. HH CARPE
```

She says, 'I can't read German,' which is not wholly true, but it buys her time to think. She has not brought a weapon here. She has the bottle, which is weapon enough, but she is not sure she has the heart to use it. The yammering in her head – I did not, I did not, I did *not!* – fell silent for the duration of the raid and there is a void where it was, a space, on the edge of which she sways. Now the voice of her guilt asks, Did I? and if the interrogative ever becomes a statement, she is finished.

She looks up and finds that Céline is watching her. Céline, of course, reads German without effort.

'They were all sent to Berlin. This one –' an elegant finger runs across the top – 'says that Kramme has a new informant who goes by the name of Diem. The others detail information this Diem has provided about jaunts and so forth, and ask for permission from the highest authority not to act on it, for fear of endangering the life of his source.'

The highest authority. Christ. 'Was he given that permission?'

'Signed by the Führer himself. The corporal is most impressed with Sturmbannführer Kramme.'

Something hard and ugly jabs at Sophie's heart. 'Where did you find these?'

'In a drawer in Kramme's desk, tucked under a diary.'

'He's a Boche,' Sophie says. Her voice is holding up remarkably well under the circumstances. 'He does nothing by accident. He wants us to destroy each other.'

'Quite so. And Larry said he was proud of you, which, translated from family-speak, means you are to be kept safe, come what may. Some things may invalidate that, were he to find out about them.' Her finger is under another line. 'You can read this, I imagine?'

SS-Stubaf Kramme: Akte: DIEM

J4/F19/Gb-

3/6/44 2317 Std

An: SS-Ostubaf Klaus Weissmann

V-MANN 'DIEM': ANGRIFF AUF EISENBAHN
ERWARTET HEUTE ABEND UNTER DECKUNG VON
RAF BOMBARDIERUNG. ANFUEHRER WIRD VOR
ORT SEIN. WIEDERHOLE PATRON VON SAINT-
CYBARD MAQUIS WIRD VOR ORT SEIN.
ERBITTEN BEFEHL. HH CARPE

She cannot breathe. Did I? Did Kramme play me when I thought I was playing him? How? Aloud, because she might die here: 'Céline, I swear I did not give Kramme the Patron. I would never do that.'

'Did you give the date of the invasion? Because that might actually be worse.'

'*No!*' How can language be shaped to do what it must? She is on her knees. Her hands hold the neck of the Calvados bottle as if it were some holy book, or a Boche neck. 'How could I? I was here when you found out and I didn't leave until we went down into town tonight.'

'So what, then, did you give?'

How has it come so fast to this? But it has, and Sophie has not the will to evade it. She says, 'As much as I had to, as little as I could: the false cards in the index files, details of our training, the code words for operations that happened months ago. I did not give anything I was not told I could give. Ask your cousin, this was his idea.'

'My uncle's, I think, rather than my cousin's. This has his touch. Did they say you could give up any people?'

'Some. The small ones who knew nothing. I tried, but Kramme didn't want them. He said if he knew someone was a *Résistante*, he wouldn't be able to hide it and then they'd know it was me who had told him. He was trying to protect me.'

'He valued you.'

'Of course he did! That was the point. Céline, I was to get close enough to kill him. That was the order. I don't know whether it came from your cousin or your uncle or someone else, but I have orders to kill him on the seventh: today. And now I can't. I am guilty of failure, but not treachery. I did *not* give him the Patron, you have to believe that.'

'It's not up to me.' Céline folds the slips of paper back into their hidden place. She crouches down opposite Sophie. Her face is a short arm's length away. Her hair is gold, her eyes a blistering grey-blue ice. Her voice is soft. 'You are either an exceptional asset or an exceptional liar and I have no idea which. Fortunately for us both, I don't need to. The cavalry is on its way, which is to say, my cousin will be here on the next available transport.'

'Laurence Vaughan-Thomas is coming *here*?'

Céline laughs, mirthlessly. 'Don't get your hopes up too soon. Under current circumstances, the next available transport is unlikely to be today, or even next week.' Her smile is bright and clear and deadly. 'Until he arrives, I am the agent on the ground and if you do anything at all to endanger the Maquis de Morez, if I so much as suspect that you are sending messages to Kramme, or aiding him in any way, you will have a fatal accident while cleaning your gun and I will deal with whatever repercussions may fall on my head as a result.' She reaches out both hands, takes Sophie by the wrists and raises them both to standing. They are close now, face to face, warmth to warmth, brow to brow. 'Are we clear?'

Céline the stoat and she the rabbit. She nods. She doesn't say, I could cut your throat in your sleep. It may no longer be true.

'Good.' Leaning forward, Céline presses a dry, cool kiss to her brow. 'We both care about Patrick Sutherland, I believe that much. However he was ruined, let's do what we can to get him better, shall we? Seeing him on his feet and walking would make up for a lot.'

CHAPTER TWENTY-ONE

ORLÉANS
Sunday, 18 March 2018
18.20

PICAUT HAS IDENTIFIED THOSE pictured in the three images that emerged from the base of Laurence Vaughan-Thomas's music box.

The woman in the static black-and-white shot is Sophie Destivelle, circa 1944. The photograph was taken in Scotland when she was partway through her training, and was for her fake ID, to be carried behind enemy lines.

The livelier image – still in black-and-white; four young people standing in a staid-looking living room – shows Laurence and Céline Vaughan-Thomas with a stunning dark-haired woman who nobody can name, and a tall, possibly red-headed man who Martin Gillard thinks is Patrick Sutherland. Nobody knows where the shot was taken but the furniture in the background is darkly, solidly English.

The dinner party shot in overdone colour was apparently taken in Saint-Cybard: similar images were used to help set up a recent shoot for the film. In the centre of a group of five stands Sophie Destivelle, utterly compelling in a dress of dark red moire silk. To her right are Maximilian Kramme and maybe-Patrick-Sutherland, the former in SS dress uniform. The brunette on her left is thought to be Mademoiselle Luce Moreau. To her left is a white-blond SS officer, Rudi Schäfer.

It is not, however, immediately obvious what use these images are to her current investigation. She goes in search of someone to talk to and finds McKinney alone in his office. Hands flat on his desk, Picaut leans into his space. 'Where does Elodie Duval live when she is in Orléans?'

His mind is somewhere on the far side of the Atlantic. 'She has an apartment on the Rue de Bourgogne, near Laurence Vaughan—'

'It's uninhabited. Nobody has lived there for months, probably years. There must be somewhere else. Does she have a lover? Is there someone else we need to be looking at?'

'A lover?' His gaze snaps to her face. 'I thought Martin . . .'

'Is she living with Martin?'

'No! That is, not that I know of. He'd have said something, surely?'

'Then where—'

'Yes, I'm with you.' McKinney pulls a face that is intended to show how hard he is thinking. It may be true. At length, he says, 'She inherited another apartment, I think. From one of the old Maquisards. Céline, I think?'

That matches what René said about her having inherited everything of Céline's when she passed twenty-one. Picaut asks, 'Where?'

'In the same block as the other one, but one floor up.'

Dear God. Picaut leans so far across the desk that McKinney pushes his chair away. It's a big desk. 'Why did nobody tell me about this before?'

'You didn't ask?'

'Mr McKinney, I am this close' – thumb and forefinger millimetres apart – 'to arresting you. We are in France, where

318

our anti-terrorism laws give me powers of detention you would not believe. So think very carefully. What else might I need to know that I haven't asked you about yet?'

Nervously: 'Do you know about her other car?'

'*What?*'

'Besides the MX-5, Elodie had an electric Golf, a silver one. She was given it in the US and had it brought over here? It's in the garage in the basement under her apartment?'

Sweet sliding Jesus . . . 'Rollo! Petit-Evard! Sylvie!'

She is expecting another death. Watching Rollo prise open the garage door, every part of her is braced for the sweet-sick smell of decay, with its underlay of blood and urine. Even as the door groans up and the ceiling lights flicker on the hood of the silver e-Golf, Picaut holds her breath.

And then not, because this place is clean and smells of nothing, not even the fuel-oil smells of a normal garage. It's not quite as clean as Pierre Fayette would have left it, but in all respects this is an ordinary garage with an ordinary car inside, and nobody has died in it or on it or under it any time in the recent past.

The forensic team has come along just in case. The white-haired car-breaking tech does his work but there is nothing in particular inside this vehicle, either.

He looks at Picaut. They have developed something of a rapport in the past hours. 'We could take it away?' he offers. 'Just in case?'

'Do. I want to know if an elderly woman wearing a wig sat in the passenger seat in the recent past. Anything else you find is a bonus.'

'Do we break into the flat?' asks Petit-Evard. He's enjoying the breaking-in part.

'Bet there's a key,' Sylvie says.

And she's right. In a locked toolbox on a bench – Rollo opens it without effort – is a Yale key which, twenty minutes later, unlocks the front door to the third-floor apartment on the Rue de Bourgogne, and yes – *yes!* – this one has been lived in. This one is eclectic, intriguing. This has Elodie written all over it. Elodie, in fact, has been here since her flight from the US landed.

On the surface, she shares some common habits with her brother. They both have on display the now-ubiquitous image of the Maquis de Morez jumping a wall, but everywhere else, where Pierre was OCD-tidy, Elodie is charmingly chaotic. On this wall is a hand-woven rug in cerulean blue and gold that smells faintly of raw wool; on that, a patchwork of old prints, maps from forgotten centuries of lands long renamed: Persia, Siam, Rhodesia. Half-read books lie open on the sofa. Mugs stand on three surfaces. The scent of incense lies, peppery, over a sweeter smell that is a meal, made and not eaten: two plates of spaghetti with a rich wine sauce.

Two. Picaut says, 'Sophie was here with her. They must have come after they got off the flight.'

'They left in a hurry,' adds Sylvie.

Picaut says, 'Check the numbers on the landline: who has called her, who did she call? Check her mobile again. I want to know every single call that came in from the moment her plane landed. Actually, from before that. Get me everyone who called her in the past week.'

'On it.'

'But it might not have been a call. Someone might have turned up in person. The killer, maybe?' To Petit-Evard: 'Call in the forensic team. Make sure we fingerprint everything.' And then, because she is thinking of it: 'Rollo, where are we with the prints from Pierre Fayette's?'

'The partial print on the mug wasn't Martin Gillard's or McKinney's. We're still trying to get prints from Conrad Lakoff and his men. It's not trivial. As we are all too aware, they take very badly to having their prints on anyone's files. Even their own.'

'Ask Ducat if one of the techs can dust his desk. Lakoff was leaning on it at lunchtime. And see if his heavies touched anything: a door handle, a toilet lever: anything. What about the footprint?'

'It's definitely a woman's. I'll take one of Elodie's shoes and see if we can rule her out.'

'Or in. Take her hairbrush, too. I want to know if she was wearing the scarf that was hanging on the back of Pierre Fayette's door.'

'Right.' Rollo heads off to hunt down shoes, leaving Picaut to search the apartment. The bookcase contains, yet again, English classics and the now-familiar selection of poetry. Unlike those in Elodie's office and Laurence Vaughan-Thomas's living room, they are ordered alphabetically. Except for one – Mary Oliver's *Dream Work* is lodged at the wrong end, between Jean Atkin and W. H. Auden.

That's enough of an anomaly for Picaut to pick it out and flick forward to the fourth poem, 'Trilliums':

> *Every spring*
> *among*
> *the ambiguities*
> *of childhood*

In Elodie's note: . . . *for all the ambiguities of my childhood, I love you.*

Her heart turns a cartwheel. She spreads the book flat, photographs the poem and sends it to Patrice.

– Holiday snaps. Thought you'd enjoy . . .

She is about to set the book back in its place when she sees, in the faintest of pencil marks on the preceding page, a mobile phone number with the initials LVT beside it.

Rollo, looking over her shoulder, whistles. 'Solid gold.'

Three digits in, Picaut stops dialling. *First rule of mobile phones* ... She writes the number on the heel of her hand instead and, clenching it shut, heads into the bedroom.

The bedstead is wrought iron in modern lines, the sheets cotton, printed with patterns of tigers. The drawers are tidy, but not obsessively so. A laptop is inside the pillow-case, on the underside of the pillow, where a casual visitor would miss it, but a professional would find it in seconds. Picaut is a professional. She also finds the missing music box hidden in the base of the wardrobe under a pile of old laundry.

She carries her trophies out to the table in the living room. The laptop, of course, is password protected and Carpe Diem does not work; nor does Wild Card, Accidental Gods, Maquis de Morez or any of the names she can think of. Not if she changes the case, not if she runs the words together. She calls Martin Gillard and he has no better ideas, so she leaves it on the coffee table and moves on to the music box.

As Gillard said, this box is the exact inverse of Laurence's. Where his has a dark-wood base with silver-grey inlay, this one is made of ash, with walnut or ebony inlaid in the same cursive script: *CVT MdM*. Picaut lifts the lid but all is silence: this mechanism has not been recently wound.

Rollo comes to join her. 'Techs say they've found a spare set of prints on Ducat's desk. Looks like we've got Conrad Lakoff and at least one of his grunts.' And then: 'Neat box. Can you open that one, too?'

'I can try.' Picaut clears a place on the coffee table and lifts out the lavender bowl, and – with some effort – the brass mechanism beneath. Underneath is the same script: *AND THUS BY ACCIDENT WE BECAME AS GODS*...

She tries pressing the same letters as she did before: IOUAS-COTCH. Nothing. She presses each letter of the verse in turn.

Still nothing. She has to let her gaze drift to the books, the CDs, the black-and-white prints on the wall, until her mind has slipped free of the need to succeed.

Now, unthinking, the fingers of her burned hand slide across and across and pick up the fractional hair's breadth indentation in the silken finish. This one, and then when it is fully down, this one . . . and this.

The letters lay themselves out in her mind: BE STRONG BRAVE HEART. The drawer opens freely, smoothly. Inside is another envelope, with the same handwriting on the front as in Laurence's box.

For Céline – Carpe Diem

In the envelope are three thin slips of paper, old, yellowed, thinly lined.

Picaut unfolds the first:

`SS-Stubaf Kramme: Akte: DIEM`

`# F3/A1.9.4-`

`1/6/44 2217 Std`

`An: SS-Ostubaf Klaus Weissmann`

`V-MANN 'DIEM': INVASION FINDET STATT 6 JUNI. INFORMATION GILT ALS 100 PROZENT ZUVERLAESSIGKEIT. ERBITTE BEFEHL FUER WEITERES VORGEHEN. HH CARPE`

Underneath, in a neat hand, is written:

Source 'DIEM': Invasion takes place 6th June. Information accorded 100 per cent reliability. Request orders for action. HH 'Carpe' (assume code name for Kramme?) CVT

Underneath, in another, blunter, bolder hand:

Who is Diem?

19.00

Three slips of aged paper. One question.

Picaut takes it back from the glorious chaos of Elodie Duval's apartment to the studio. The interns have been sent home. The lower floor is a graveyard of unlit computers and dimmed fish tanks.

Upstairs on the first floor, Clinton McKinney and Martin Gillard are still holding calls with backers, or, by now, with the backers' legal representatives, as previously enthusiastic money scents panic and a herd mentality sets in. The air smells of mass-produced coffee. McKinney has given up on the green tea. Picaut walks over to his desk and leans her hands on it.

'Who is Diem?'

His gaze skates left and right. 'It's been a long day, Captain. I literally have no idea what that question means.'

Literally? Dear God. The ghost of her father scrapes its fingernails down a blackboard. She had almost forgotten him, her father; one more way in which today is unique. He used to be the bedrock of her life.

From her left, Martin Gillard says, 'Carpe Diem. Seize the day. Just before she got on the plane, Elodie said she wanted to change the name of the film.' To McKinney: 'You did know that.'

'Sorry. Yes. I'd forgotten?' McKinney is becoming fractious. His smile is thin and tight. 'That's not a name, though, it's a Latin aphorism, and there's nothing like that in the shooting script. You can do a word search on the hard drives if you want. It's got nothing to do with us.'

'It became a name.' She spreads the three slips across the big, pale table. 'Kramme had an informer inside the Maquis.'

'An informer? A Nazi agent? In the Maquis de Morez? You're sure?' Four questions in one breath. How does Martha handle this without killing him?

'Yes,' says Picaut. 'I am sure.'

'Right.' With exaggerated care, McKinney lifts his iPhone from his desk. 'May I?' He takes three pictures, one of each cipher slip. After the last, he leans across, grasps Picaut's shoulders with both hands and plants a kiss on the better side of her face. 'You may just have saved the project. I'll put you in the credits. Fuck, I'll give you the top line.'

He picks up his landline handset and swivels his chair to face the wall. The dial tone ripples past and becomes the purr of a ring and the click of an answer. Then: 'Frank? I know what time it is in every single fucking time zone. Listen, I have something new . . .'

Picaut catches Martin Gillard's eye and, together, they walk across the hallway to Elodie's office. She settles into the thousand-euro chair behind the desk. 'Carpe Diem. Tell me all you know.'

'There's nothing to tell beyond what you just heard.' Gillard hitches one hip onto the corner of the desk again. He's becoming altogether too comfortable there. 'Elodie came to me after her interview with Sophie Destivelle and said she thought we should change the name. I said good luck getting that past Clinton – he's sold *Wild Card* to the Americans and they won't budge. She left it at that, but I knew she'd come back at some point. She was like a terrier: once she had hold of an idea, she wouldn't let it go.'

'Had she found these?' Picaut indicates the slips of paper.

'She didn't say.' He lifts one, sniffs it, reads it half a dozen times. 'You found her music box?'

'Yes.'

He catches her eye and there's an offer somewhere in the drift of his gaze. 'At a time like this, it would be very useful, wouldn't it, to be able to talk to Laurence Vaughan-Thomas?'

The number from Elodie's apartment is still written on Picaut's hand. She folds her fist closed over it. 'Exceptionally so.'

Gillard reaches into his pocket and produces his own slip of paper. 'The old Maquisards . . . they lived in a world of semi-paranoia where it was always safer to stay off the grid, but we wanted to talk to them. Elodie bought them each a pay-as-you-go mobile phone. They were registered to the studio, so in theory, nobody else knows about them.'

Four phone numbers, each marked with the relevant initials: LVT. SD. RV. JJC. The first is identical to the one written on her hand.

A fuse blows behind Picaut's eyes. 'You didn't think to give me these sooner?'

'I didn't know they existed. Martha had them. She's—' He waves his hand, tugs at his ear lobe.

'Pregnant?' Picaut offers, archly.

'Well, obviously, but I don't think I'm allowed to comment on that. I'm probably not allowed to say this, either – but what the fuck, eh?' He shrugs, thinks, dives. 'She's lovely, charming, effusive, beautiful, and quite competent, but she's not the sharpest knife in the block; just the one who can handle Clinton without wanting to stab him between the eyes. Elodie told her not to share the numbers, and so she didn't.'

'Why has she changed her mind now?'

'She heard you threaten McKinney with French counter-terrorism laws if he held anything back. I think you frightened her.' With a small, tight smile, Martin Gillard slides off the desk and heads for the door. 'Good luck finding the oldsters. They were trained in a far more brutal era than ours.'

18–20 June 1944: Allied forces take Elba, Assisi and Perugia.

SOE, F-Section, 9–20 June: Jedburgh triads – Ammonia, Frederick, Gilbert, Hamish, Ian, Marmalade, Quinine and Veganin – parachute behind enemy lines. Though in uniform, under Hitler's Commando Order of October 1942 they were liable to be tortured and executed if caught.

CHAPTER TWENTY-TWO

NORTH AND EAST OF SAINT-CYBARD
25 June 1944

RED TO GREEN: THE light above his head.

A confusion of scuffles, a tight grin, thumbs up, a man's hand on his back – *don't think* – and he is falling again, into the endless night.

One, don't think. Two, don't think. Three, don't think. Four, don't—

Jesus Christ.

The harness grabs at his groin and shoulders. The canopy unfurls to a taut shape blotting out the stars. Impact comes sooner than Laurence expects. He rolls with it well enough and rises to haul in the lines. A dark mass targets him from the sky and he skips swiftly left.

The earth judders under his feet. A big, muscled body careens past his head, slams into the ground six feet away and, grunting, rises: white teeth, grinning; red-gold hair above; a square jaw, pale, almost luminous grey eyes and a profusion of broad freckles laid over a southern-suntan that nine months in Britain hasn't washed away.

'So this is France?' Hands on hips, Paul Rey surveys his new domain. Princeton-educated, born with a mouthful of silver dollars, he has the same effect on women that the late Julie Hetherington used to have on men. Laurence has seen entire bars fall silent at his entry, giggling coteries who skin men alive with a glance reduced in a handful of seconds to slack-jawed, glaze-eyed putty in his hands. He is waiting, with some interest, to see the impact this paragon will have on Sophie and Céline.

Rey looks around. 'Where's Gaspari?' he says. 'He jumped first.'

'Over here, where there's a proper view.' Toni Gaspari speaks English like a Valleys Welshman and French like a Marseillaise. His Italian, one assumes, is equally ripe. His Morse averages twenty-two per minute and he can put out the eye of a seagull at four hundred paces with a rifle. Whippet-thin and wiry, he has shaggy black hair that falls to his shoulders in contravention of every regulation of every one of the world's military institutions.

He grins at Laurence and then, to Paul Rey, says, 'I thought your Yank flyers were supposed to get us to the right place?'

'We're in France, what more do you want?' Paul Rey joins them on the higher ground. They are on a long, low slope with trees at the far end, but there are no flares, no torches, no fires. He pulls a face. 'So where's the reception committee? I can't wait to meet the legendary boy-chief.'

Nor can Laurence. Two nights ago the Brigadier plied him with wine, venison and coffee in that order and, amidst a cloud of relatively innocuous gossip, let slip that Fabien, the code name of the Patron of the Maquis de Morez, is, in fact, the fresh-faced, almost-certainly-underage Alain Devereaux from Laurence's group at Arisaig.

'He's doing well for himself politically. There's word that he'll be in the French cabinet when the dust settles.'

'He's a communist.'

'Yes, well, I'm sure that can be smoothed over when the

time comes. The point is that he's good. He's got a grip on his men and he knows how to use them strategically.'

'And Theodora is with him.'

There was the briefest of pauses at this juncture. There is a family fiction which maintains that Theodora is still on English soil. The same brand of mythology swears that Laurence, too, will never leave. The women of the family may not wholly believe it, but they will disembowel any man who sends their loved ones into harm. The Brigadier has the grace to look discomfited. Then: 'Indeed. Theodora is with him. I gather they make rather a good team.'

And so here they are, three officers of differing nations, come to offer the advanced services of the Allied Expeditionary Force to this legendary team. Except they have missed on the drop.

'We're not too far off.' Gaspari has a compass in one hand and a silk handkerchief-map in the other. 'If that mountain is the one I hope it is, they're somewhere between three and five miles that way as the crow flies.' He points one thin arm south and east. 'By road, it's probably twice as far.'

Rey shrugs. 'That's what comes of jumping in the middle of an invasion. We got the navigators from the bottom of the barrel.'

Mildly, Laurence says, 'We got the USAF, which isn't even in the barrel. The RAF never misses.' And before Rey can respond: 'Hands on belts, children. Best foot forward. People are waiting for us, at great risk to their lives. It would be a pity to let them down. Shall we go?'

They have trained for this. Ten miles is barely a warm-up. By starlight, they march, each man holding the belt of the one in front, except Laurence, who is in the lead and so has nobody's belt to hold, but the night is clear and warm and the roads are small, winding and empty, and he can see well enough.

Periodically during the second hour, Laurence puts his

cupped hands to his mouth and makes the noise of a hunting tawny owl, three times over. One hundred and two minutes after they leave the landing ground, with the sky one shade darker than night and the first dunghill cockerels rustily rehearsing, he hears a response. 'That's them.'

Gaspari says, 'Sure it's not an actual owl?'

'I'm sure. Actual owls either *to-wit* or *to-woo*. They don't do both in the same sentence.'

'Not even French ones?'

'Particularly not French ones.' A new call comes, long and high, almost a yodel. His heart leaps strangely in his chest. 'That's *definitely* not an owl.' He angles his torch. He hasn't seen her since Julie died. He has no idea— 'Céline! My God, you look like an Amazon warrior. Let me see . . .'

'Larry. Charming to see you, too.' She's stronger now, and not only physically. Her face is Mediterranean brown. Her pale hair shines silver in the narrowed light. She carries her weapon effortlessly. And she is smiling. It's a tight, dry smile, with the same old grief at its core, but it lifts his heart in ways little else has done these past months.

They embrace, closely. He asks, 'Are you well?'

'Under the circumstances.' Her grasp is brisk and firm. 'You got my last message?'

It was arcane, even by her standards, but yes, he did, and yes, it has shadowed his last hours. 'You have a mole. We'll find who it is.' Unless it's Sophie Destivelle, in which case, she may well have been doing her job. She is alive too, if the cables are right.

Now is not the time to share secrets. His cousin's gaze sweeps over Rey and Gaspari as only an upper-class English-woman's can do. 'Were you going to introduce us?'

'Captain Paul Rey, Lieutenant Antonio Gaspari, please meet my cousin. For ease and security, we shall call her Céline. When the war is over, we'll introduce you properly. Céline, meet Jedburgh team Marmalade.'

'Please tell me you didn't choose that name.'

'It was that or Marcel, so yes, I did.'

'Heaven help us all.'

There is a shaking of hands that tests mettle and balance. Rey and Gaspari step back from it, uncharacteristically quiet. Laurence says, 'We'll need a fuller briefing than the cable.'

Céline says, 'And I'll give it, but we had an order from SHAEF this afternoon sending us on a jaunt that seems rather urgent. Fabien's been dragged off to some post-war political preparation committee, so this is mine, which means if you come, you're under my orders. If you'd rather not join in, you will be escorted back to camp.'

Patrick is at the camp.

Patrick. Alive. Injured. Céline's ciphers refused to say how badly. At the last analysis, the frantic pulling of strings these past twenty-four hours were designed so that Laurence could take over from Patrick, but now that he is here, it is clear that he is redundant: Céline can do anything he could do, and better.

One hour more, maybe two at the most, with a chance to watch Céline leading. Laurence says, 'What's the jaunt?'

'Tank trapping. Or rather, engineering with a view to tank trapping. A Panzergrenadier division from the Eastern Front is due to pass north of here sometime soon after dawn, heading for Normandy. We need to blow a bridge before it gets there.'

The sky is more grey than black. The dunghill cocks are more musical. 'Are we not too late? If the Luftwaffe see you in daylight . . .' He has read the reports of what happens when the Maquis work without cover of night.

She shrugs. 'We'll make the time. The question is whether you three are with us or not.' She directs her question this time to Paul Rey, who is standing an arm's length away, holding his helmet as if it were a cap. Laurence has never seen him look subdued by rank or anything else. He salutes, crisply. 'At your service, ma'am. Jaunts always welcome.'

Céline rolls her eyes. 'And your other friend?'

Gaspari is standing some distance off, feigning inattention. Laurence says, 'Toni will kill anyone who tries to get in the way of his killing Germans. They slaughtered his entire village after the Italian surrender, last year. The women were raped while they lay dying, the men were gutted and shot in the knees and elbows and left to scream. He was away, which is why he is the sole surviving member of a four-generation family that once boasted twenty-seven members within a two-mile radius. You will have to shoot him if you want to stop him going with you.'

'And you can wait?'

Always, she knows what matters. 'Unless you think it's unwise.'

'Quite the reverse: I think it's the best decision you've made for months.' She is already turning. 'JJ, we're all going together.'

Céline has two trucks under her command, both petrol-driven.

Laurence rides in the back of the second, sitting on a rough bench with Paul Rey and Toni Gaspari on one side and Céline and JJ on the other. Opposite, seven men cradle guns. None makes any effort at conversation.

Laurence says, 'I thought your motive power was dried cattle dung?'

'Not these days. Patrick stole . . .' She stops, stares at the floor. He sees her blink. 'He led a jaunt in the last week before he was captured. They took a stonemason who knew how to break through the wall of a barn in a way the Boche couldn't see afterwards. They tapped off an entire tank of fuel, then bricked up the hole and rolled off down the hill. We have enough gasoline for the rest of the summer.'

'Well done, Patrick.'

'You can tell him when you see him.' And thus, the conversation dies.

They wind along lanes for a bone-jarring eternity, at the end of which the driver cuts the engine and they coast down a long, gentle slope, pull off to the left at the foot, and sigh to a halt.

The dawn rustles to the movement of silent men disembarking, and now they have no need of torches. The horizon is a layering of apricot and peach. Beads of dew dangle from the tall grasses. Céline raises both hands and combs her fingers through her hair. 'That was the easy part. Now we find out if the Boche have put a guard on the bridge.'

'Is it likely?' Laurence asks.

'They'd be stupid not to, and they haven't been stupid up to now. Desperate, maybe; angry, definitely; but never stupid.'

They are not stupid. The bridge is two hundred and fifty yards long. In one elegant concrete and iron arch, it spans a fast-flowing, mountainous river from east to west. It is just wide enough to take a tank, providing the driver can keep to a straight line. On both sides of the river are German officers and men in generous numbers.

Laurence lies on his belly amongst the pines, two hundred yards up the western slope, looking down through his field glasses, relaying all that he sees in a quiet murmur. 'Two platoons at least. Estimated number of men – one hundred, maybe more. Motorcycles, trucks and one Horch sedan staff car with an MG40 mounted on the back. They're rare as hen's teeth these days: only the corporal's favourite friends get one, so they're taking this seriously. The officer's just beyond the staff car. There's an Oberstleutnant in there; they really *are* taking this seriously. His guards have Schmeissers. Everyone else has Karabiners. No heavy artillery. Most are on the far side. On this side, one Rittmeister and a dozen men with motorcycles and a radio. They're brewing coffee.'

The morning air is crisp with pine resin, loam and the light, heady scent of gun oil. Sitting up, he says to Céline, 'If they've

334

sent this many, they either know you're coming or the tanks are close. Or both.'

'Never let it be said we don't offer sterling entertainment.' She has her own glasses, big as pint jugs. She stands with one shoulder pressed to a tree for support. Like Laurence, she speaks quietly, under the rustle of the pine needles. 'If we could hit the lieutenant-colonel, they'll be headless until someone else takes charge.' She bites her lip. 'Thierry's not bad with a rifle, but it's a long way to be accurate.'

Thierry is middle-aged, balding and lame in his left leg. He has a shy smile and the internal stillness of a shepherd. Laurence has no doubt he is accurate at reasonable ranges, but this is not a reasonable range. He says, 'I brought you a sniper who can kill at four hundred yards.'

'The Yank?' She rolls her eyes. 'He's pretty, but is he any good?'

'He's the best I've ever seen, but not at this.' Laurence points over his shoulder. 'Gaspari's good for twice this distance and he brought his own rifle. If your man Thierry can take out the captain, they'll be paralysed for long enough for you to even out the numbers. Otherwise twenty to one hundred is a massacre in the making.'

'It won't be a massacre.' She gives orders in a patois French too thick and fast for him to follow.

Left alone, he works his way down through the trees to the forest's edge until he can stand behind one broad trunk and listen to the dozen men of the Wehrmacht section, who smoke, talk, stamp their feet a bare twenty yards away. A call comes in on the radio. The reception is exceptional, the sound quality high. A while later, he worms back uphill to Céline.

'The tanks are due within the next forty-five minutes. The captain on this side is named Hauser. If I call him, bring him this way a bit, give Thierry a clear shot at him first, and Toni

335

takes the colonel at the same time, then you can get on with your mortars.'

'You don't have to—'

'Theo, I sat on my backside in an office, listening to you having all the fun. Let me do this.'

It's the use of her name that makes the difference. She gives a short, one-shoulder shrug that he remembers from somebody else, and turns back to Gaspari. 'Can you get the colonel while Thierry takes the captain? And if I give you a spotter each can you go on to take out everyone who looks as if he's taking over command once they have gone?'

The little Italian is sitting with his back to a tree cleaning his rifle with the care of a mother for her newborn. His smile is angelic. 'Hunting Boche is what I do. If I miss, I'll parachute back up to the plane and go home again.'

Céline laughs for him, with him, then turns back to her men. 'D'accord, mes amis . . .'

Laurence is alive, truly alive, for the first time in . . . too long. Possibly since he last flew a plane on his own. He has borrowed a grey coat from a Maquisard named Guillaume, who took it from the body of a German officer one week ago. There's blood on the back, but they're not going to see his back, so it doesn't matter. He has no hat, but then the shine of his hair is half his disguise, so he doesn't want one. He steps one pace out from the shelter of the last tree, raises his hands.

'Schiessen Sie nicht! Ich bin Deutsch. Deutsch! Hauptmann Hauser! Eine moment! Ich muss mit Ihnen sprechen.'

The men by the bridge turn. They lift their rifles. His chest is a target. Every muscle braces. They do not shoot.

The radio hisses. A voice comes through the static. 'Wer ist das?'

The captain signals his men to hold fire and takes three swift paces forward. 'Wer sind Sie?'

And dies, neatly. Well done, Thierry.

'Down! Laurence, *down*!'

His instincts are faster than he knows. He's already down, crouching in the shelter of an oak before Céline's shout reaches him. A mortar howls over his head. A dozen Stens clatter in counterpoint. He gets up, runs sideways and back into the shadows of the trees, finds new shelter, pulls his own Colt and fires two-handed at the three remaining Boche left standing on this side of the river. His shots are lost in the overwhelming fire of the Maquis de Morez. The three men drop. He has no idea if he killed them.

From high in the trees, he hears Toni Gaspari, clear in the chaos, shout, '*Yes!*'

So the lieutenant-colonel is down. Maquisards are running across the bridge, keeping up a smothering, lethal wall of fire. Céline is in the centre, her short hair loose in the wind, shouting orders.

He needs something better than a handgun. Dodging forward again, he wrests the Schmeisser from the dead German captain. Three times, maybe four, he has fired one of these, and each time has found it sits nicely in his hands. He joins the running ranks and ducks into the feeble shelter of a concrete pillar along the bridge, firing.

A round or two cracks past his head, but not many. The Maquis are well trained. There isn't much cover, but they use what they have and the Boche have nothing to aim at. Céline is kneeling behind another concrete pillar one third of the way along. Laurence comes up beside her. 'Where's your *plastique*?'

'Here.' She has a pack on her back, bulging.

'Give it to me.'

'Larry, you don't have to—'

'Let's not go through this again, shall we? This is your show. You direct the men. I am wholly superfluous, but I do know how to place charges to blow a bridge. I may as well make myself useful.'

Wordless, she hands him the bag. 'It needs to break—'

'Either side of the centre. I do know this.'

'I can take one side.' Paul Rey is beside him. Laurence wants to say no, we can't both take on a suicide stunt, but Céline nods, as if this has sealed it. 'Do it. We'll hold them off. Call me when you're done.'

She is gone, a wisp in the morning mist, easing up the bridge, pausing, firing, moving on again.

Paul Rey watches her go, thoughtfully. 'Is she spoken for?'

Laurence says, 'She was.'

Rey is smarter than he looks. He gives a rueful shrug. 'Reckon she'll get over it?'

'Not so that you'd notice.'

'Pity.'

'You should meet Sophie. I think she may be less one-hearted. If we live through the next half-hour, I'll make the introduction.' And then, swiftly, because this is altogether too much like the real thing: 'Shall we go?'

This is the real thing. Every bridge is built to be repaired, and if it can be repaired, then you can demolish it. This is what they were taught in lectures, and in Cambridge, in Slough, in Shrewsbury, it proved to be true: always there was a way of gaining access to the underside – handholds or foot-plates, or something to give the maintenance engineers an easier life.

And so it is in France. Laurence goes back to the head of the bridge and squirms down the embankment, next to the con-crete footings that tie bridge to bank. Here is an iron ladder leading up to a set of rusting handholds, set into the fabric of the bridge, so that he can remain upright, with his head almost meeting the concrete and his feet braced against the edges. 'Found them.'

'Here too,' Rey says, from the other side.

'See you at the middle.'

His injured hand is functional. It is not fully fit. He does what he can to spread the weight to his feet and crabs sideways, hand over hand, shuffling, listening to the chatter of machine guns up above, to the intermittent *crump* of a mortar. He isn't hearing much by way of German guns, but perhaps he is not in the right place.

He moves on and is out, over the river far, far below. In practice, they were always roped on.

Hand over hand and don't look down. Hand over hand, feet shuffle sideways. Breathe in the dust, the old concrete, the rust, the meaty, fresh-iron scent of gunshots and blood. His shoulders ache. His hand is cramping, badly.

There's a notch in the concrete on the underside of the bridge: a mark deliberately made. Here is a place where he can sit and breathe a bit. He says, 'Here.'

And now the difficult part. Bracing his feet apart, holding on with his good hand, he brings the sack of explosive round to lie on his belly. From there, he pulls out the doughy balls of *plastique*. It's the 808, the one that gives everyone vomiting headaches. His cousin has wrapped each grenade-sized mass in rags. He lifts them out, precious as Fabergé eggs, and jams them deep into the heart of the superstructure, an arm's length either side of the midpoint.

Rey asks, 'Black or red?'

Black is ten minutes. It's taken them six to get here and the pencils are notoriously unstable in warm weather. Laurence says, 'It has to be red. And we have to hold them off long enough.'

'Let's do it.'

And so to the detonators: crushed, inserted.

'Time to go,' Rey says.

'Fastest one wins!'

339

It feels a lot further back to land. The bridge has lengthened and he is clambering for ever, making no progress. He swears in his head, every blue word he has ever heard or even imagined. His legs judder. He thinks of Patrick, and what has been done to him. He has no idea of the detail, only that he was left hanging by the wrists when Kramme left. Three days of torture and he told them nothing. And so it is possible, after all, to go on.

And on.

And—

'OK. You're here. Larry, it's OK. Let go.' Paul Rey made it to dry land ahead of him. His hard, competent hands reach for his shoulders, lift him bodily from the bridge and set his feet on the bank.

He can't stand. He kneels at the bridge-end, cups his hands to his mouth and gives the same high call he gave in the dark, the one her mother used to use when they were children at Ridgemount, playing too far from the house. For good measure, he fires his Colt into the air three times, aiming down the valley.

He doesn't know if he has been heard. He stands, shaking the tension out of his limbs. 'I swear my arms are two inches longer.'

From higher up among the trees comes a boy's voice. 'Tanks. I can see tanks.'

So he can stand after all, and run. A boy with a bandaged hand is sitting on the branches of a tree with Céline's field glasses making red circles around his eyes. 'Over there.' He points with his good hand.

Laurence hoists himself up beside him. 'Let me see.'

'Alongside the river. At the notch where it goes between the hills.'

And yes, on the road, too far away to be heard, are the child's toys, weaving among matchstick-trees, a long, unending line, all in grey.

'Will the bridge blow up in time?'

'That's the question, isn't it? We have twenty minutes, give or take five.' Laurence squints through shaded eyes. 'We need to call Céline back.'

'You won't get her,' the boy says, with evident pride. 'When she's like this, the only thing that will stop her is a rifle.'

Paul Rey winces. 'So let's go give a helping hand. The sooner finished, the sooner they'll come back.'

They run. They fight. Here, more than ever in training, the Jedburghs are free of all constraint. They are apart from time, from care, from fear. Death walks amongst them, whistling. They are invincible, invulnerable: gods of devastation and vengeance.

Ten minutes into the most vicious fire fight he can imagine, they find Céline crouching behind the smouldering-hot wreck of the Horch sedan. She's firing a Schmeisser. Her Sten is empty, discarded. A welt of red, wet blood stretches from her nose to her temple. Laurence is fairly certain it isn't hers.

'If the timer holds, you have five minutes to get your men back to the bank.' He is laughing, breathless. She stares at him a moment, as if he's spoken Greek. Or rather, some language she doesn't know. He thinks he may have to slap her, but she shakes herself, dog-like, and smiles at him distantly, and then, in a moment, more warmly.

'We'd better go.' She takes a whistle from her pocket and gives three ear-rending blasts.

Five minutes later, all but two of her men are back on the right side of the bridge, crouched behind the poor cover, killing anyone in a grey uniform who strays into view. The two left behind are dead. Two out of two dozen: a miracle.

The tanks are audible now. The bridge reverberates to the throaty rhythm of the treads. Amongst the trees, grey uniforms come and go.

Paul Rey crosses himself. Beneath his sandy thatch of hair,

his freckles make islands in the whey of his face. 'We're not going to make it.'

Céline shakes her head. 'We already made it. They won't get over now.'

Her words cause the world to end. A blinding explosion, a brilliance of sound. Everything stops: hearts, breath, thought, sight and sound. And when each of these returns and is assembled in its rightful place, the bridge is gone, and on the other side, tanks round the elbow of the hill and judder into line. Their turrets turn and waver, blindly. Men jump out, men with machine guns. Viewed through the field glasses, it is clear that one or two have rifles. At least one has a sniper's scope.

Laurence says, 'We should leave now.' And they do.

CHAPTER TWENTY-THREE

SOPHIE WAKES TO THE distant grind of the trucks and, by this, knows she has been asleep.

She lies a moment, steeling herself, then rolls off the straw palette, shrugs on a shirt and men's trousers, pulls on socks and boots.

Here, under the trees, there's a fire to build up – small, so that it does not light the forest – and a kettle to hang on the cast iron hoop that stands over it, 'coffee' to pour in from the tin in the box that's kept in the small shed next to her sleeping hut. She does these things automatically now, and swiftly, with her attention divided between the trucks grinding their way up the hill and the shepherd's hut set away from the rest: their infirmary.

She has lived within reach of this hut for nearly three weeks, during which the others have been out on nightly raids. She has always been invited, but each time, the need to be here has outweighed the need to kill and she has turned them down.

The Patron is her priority. Céline didn't need to push: since the moment they cut him down from the hook in Kramme's office, his welfare has been Sophie's sole concern. Her guilt drives her, and the uncertainty of her culpability, but even without that, she is a nurse; it was her vocation long before she discovered a penchant for killing.

Thus, day by day, hour by hour, she has sat with the man she now knows as Patrick, helping him to drink at first, and then, later, to eat. Eating is still not easy. Speaking is almost impossible. He doesn't try except *in extremis* and they both regret it after. Céline's wish to see him up and walking is a fantasy of impossible proportions.

To the south, a small stream skips down the mountain. Sophie kneels and washes her face in the snow-cold water, straightens her collar, pulls fingers through her hair. Small things matter. She learned this long ago in Paris: an injured man sees himself reflected in the woman who tends him. Today matters more than most.

She pushes open the door to release the first gust of not-quite-healing flesh. Her stock of penicillin is running low. Kramme told her once that when he was with the armies of the Eastern Front, he saw the nurses set up condensing stills to boil the men's urine and reclaim the penicillin so they could use it again.

She isn't sure she believes this will work, and certainly doesn't want to test it, so she is using smaller doses, further apart, and keeps asking for more. When Laurence Vaughan-Thomas comes, he will bring it. All night, she has thought this: he will come. He will bring what the Patron needs. What else he may say or do is beyond her ken. He would be well within his rights to shoot her. Pick your crime: I was ordered to kill Kramme and I failed. I was ordered to protect Patrick Sutherland at all costs and at that, too, I failed.

Céline, she thinks, would be happy to see her dead, but Céline is very hard to read. Since the confrontation over Kramme's ciphers, she has been affable, almost friendly, except last night, when she was on edge, smoking too much, counting the minutes until she could round up the men and drive out.

They have not spoken of Diem, of who betrayed the Patron to Kramme. If it was not Sophie – and she holds a corner of her heart where it was not – there are only a handful of other options: JJ, René, Daniel – each unthinkable. Maybe it was Raymond. Maybe he isn't dead, after all, but living a good life under Kramme's protection. He can't be, though: they would never have done what they did to René if Raymond was still alive. It could have been him, though, and he died by a stray shot gone wide from the main battle. Maybe.

The trucks are back again, grinding up the hill from the valley.

Sophie crosses the three paces to the bed. 'He's coming.'

A nod. The Patron is not sleeping. She is not sure he has slept at all in the past three weeks, certainly not since she first let him surface from the morphia dreams. 'Do you want to sit up?'

He doesn't respond. She thinks this means no, that he doesn't want to sit up, that he very much wants to lie in the dark, possibly that he wants to be dead. He could have killed himself by now if he really needed to: his hands, remarkably, have returned almost to their ordinary size and the tendons have healed enough that they have at least enough function to use a knife. She has left one within reach: she is not without mercy, or understanding.

He has never used it, but she has seen his gaze follow the guns slung on the backs of those who have come to pay their respects: Vincent, Daniel, René of the ruined fingers.

She says, 'I can give you morphine now, or later, after they've gone. It's your choice.'

He stares at the ceiling. There are new lines at the margins of his eyes. She thinks he may be afraid, which is both new

345

and terrifying. A stray flare of sunlight catches his hair and turns it from rust to liquid fire. She has come to see him as a Greek god, a thing of tragic destruction.

'You should drink.' She brings an enamelled tin mug full of stream water. He lets her lift him to sitting, with care for the still unhealed wounds on his chest that let the bones of his ribs show through, and the obvious damage to his arms and shoulders from hanging.

These last few days, he has held the mug almost on his own. Today, when it matters that he feel more whole, she lets him take the full weight of it and watches as he drinks, slowly.

Swallowing is still hard. It may be that for the rest of his life, it will pain him to eat and to drink. For this alone, she will hunt Kramme and kill him, inch by slow and unremitting inch. The Maquis have men out tracking him, but Céline, so Sophie has discovered, has contacts in town: nameless women with courage beyond measure, who are pretending still to be loyal to the Reich. She salutes their bravery and waits each day for their reports because she, Sophie, will kill Kramme, even if she dies in the attempt. For days, she has promised herself this.

She catches the mug as his fingers lose their grip, and blots the spillage with the hem of her shirt.

'I have some soup from last night?'

He isn't listening. His attention is all on the door, and the world beyond, in which the trucks are almost here.

Her mouth is dry, her hands wet. She wipes them on her sleeves. 'Do you want me here? I can go if you want, and leave you alone with him? You'll have a lot to catch up on.'

Ro.

She spins. Things fall from her plank-shelf and she does not heed them. 'Patron?' She wants to kiss him, to hold his hands and dance. She wants, actually, to scream. She won't do any of these, of course.

346

He is smiling a little, though his gaze is hot, and full of a pain she hasn't seen before. He says, *Stay. Please.*

It doesn't sound like that, not remotely so – it's a mangled, garbled bastard of the words, but she understands what he means and each of these things is remarkable.

She holds his hand. She lets it go again, not wanting to disgrace them both. She says, 'Wait, I have something,' and runs back to her own pallet, to the collection of bottles and the hairbrush that she keeps as a last grasp on normality. A moment's frantic search and she finds what she needs, runs back to show him. 'From Marianne Fayette,' she says. She doesn't have to explain what it is for.

Thank you.

She does embrace him, then, and she does weep, and dries her eyes before the footsteps sound on the hill below the camp. Together, they wait for what is coming – who is coming – as they might await a death sentence.

~

Patrick is alive. Laurence has killed a man: many men, actually.

Until today, Laurence knew the number of men he had killed because it was exactly equal to the number of planes he had shot down: five. And now, he has no idea, except that it is many. Many, many, many, and so few lost. The bodies of two Frenchmen are in the lead truck, honoured war-dead, to be buried in the forest and their names remembered for ever. He doesn't know their names, but he will find out.

The camp is ahead: he can smell the latrines and the cooking, in that order. He passes the first armed guards and there's still half a mile to walk uphill, through a damply verdant landscape, carrying machine guns, ammunition, Mills bombs, cigarettes, food: all the supplies that were dropped in the right place and collected by Céline and her men.

Laurence is impressed with his cousin, and has said so. There was a time when his approval would have meant something. This morning, she was more concerned that nobody else was wounded, that the Boche did not call in an air strike before her men could leave, that the ammunition was packed in the same truck as the vast giant, JJ, who carried the mortar under his arm, so that if they were attacked they could defend themselves.

These are small things, and obvious, but she was the one thinking of them at a time when all Laurence could think of was the blood rushing in his ears and the flashing memories of the rounds that hissed close. He imagines that she has seen action so often that she is immune to the after-burn of danger.

Her Patron is not back yet. This is a matter of some concern. She issues orders, men run to her bidding. She walks up the hill, carrying a German rifle, her own side arm, two boxes of ammunition, and still she is walking on sprung feet, almost at a trot. They pass upwind of the latrines, and he smells something meaty.

'Is that pork?'

'Wild boar. In your honour.'

Strewth.

Céline strides on, well ahead of the rest of her men. It occurs to him that this may not be an accident. He hurries to catch her up.

'Do we need to talk?'

'You'll want to see him. Best if your flash Yank and the little Italian sniper aren't with you.'

There's an edge to her voice that kills the morning's joy. He snatches at her sleeve. 'Céline . . .'

She is hard now. He hadn't seen it before, but there's a layer of armour that even Julie's death didn't create.

'What is it?'

348

She pauses a moment, sifting through things he can't read and doesn't want to. 'Don't stare. That's the main thing. Treat him as normal.'

A vacuum opens in his solar plexus. His courage plunges through. 'He still has his eyes?' In the back and forth of ciphered wires, he has not dared to ask that. Now he doesn't dare not to.

There's a thatched hut ahead, set apart from the rest, and a door half open and—

'Theo, *please.*'

She turns, planting her feet. 'He still has his eyes. Both of them. He isn't blind, Larry. Remember that as you go in. He is *not* blind.'

In the gloom, he sees Sophie first; slim, slight, dark-haired, knife-like features etched deep with lack of sleep and a desperate vulnerability that leaves her achingly fragile.

By any means, she is not his first priority, but there's an odd gravitational force that keeps his gaze fixed on her, so that pulling away feels like pulling out of a tight turn did in the old days, when his eyes became gimbals, floating through glycerine.

Slowly, therefore, against the pull of the moon and the earth, he hauls his gaze from Sophie to the man on the bed. To Patrick.

As if appraising a stranger, he notes that he has copper-red hair, cut short. That he is undressed. His arms are a mess of healing bruises in greens and pale lilacs, like tattoos on an ageing mariner. His chest is a lacework of unhealed savagery.

His face . . .

'Patrick?' There's something not right about the way his jaw sits, the pressure of his lips. This is not a man to say 'Sláinte' and swallow half a tumbler of Glenmorangie without pausing for breath, to tell a joke after, and then run up a mountain for the sheer hell of it.

Sophie holds his hand. Or he holds hers. Their knuckles are green-white tense. He can taste fear or loathing on the air, sharp, like old cheese.

Laurence says, 'Patrick, it's Laurence. I heard—'

Tho!

It's a dull noise, but desperate. Thick. Uneven.

'I'm sorry?'

Tho! A hand, pointing. Shaking. *Veeve. Ow.*

'Patrick . . . I don't . . .' He wrenches his attention back to Sophie. 'I don't understand.'

Tears make shining trails down the sides of her nose, crawl to the corners of her mouth. She has to try twice before she can speak. 'He's asking you to go. To leave. To go. Now.' She lets go of the hand she is holding, and stands up. 'But I don't think he means it. I'll go. You should stay.'

O!

That one is clear enough. But not clear. Not clear at all.

'I don't . . . why is he speaking like this? What's happened?'

'He can't speak. He can't eat. He can't drink.'

'Why?'

'Is it not obvious? Kramme cut out his tongue.'

5 July 1944

The three Jedburgh incomers wear uniform; that's the first and biggest difference. The flash of buttons, of rank badges, gives a new air of purpose to the camp, but little else changes: between them, Fabien and Céline run a tightly disciplined unit and there is little that can be added. The Jedburghs are useful on the firing ranges, training the incomers to shoot, and they are three more sets of hands bringing in the materiel after a drop; but they are also three more mouths to feed, three more fillers of latrines, and no more inclined to dig new ones than anyone else.

They can call more supplies from the sky: in this, Sophie's imaginings were right. She was wrong in her fears, at least so far: Laurence Vaughan-Thomas has not yet shot her for treachery. He is quiet around her, and won't come near the infirmary. He talks a lot with Céline, who is less edgy, friendlier. Neither of them mentions Sophie's role as the Wild Card, or Kramme's telegrams, and it's not as if there is a lack of opportunity.

In the first days after his arrival, she lies awake, braced for a voice in the dark, for his pistol by her head. When it doesn't come, she thinks he is too shocked by Patrick. Then she thinks he has forgotten. By the day of Daniel's news, she has begun to think he just doesn't care.

And Daniel's news is big. 'Kramme's back!' He is the go-between with one of Céline's contacts amongst the wives of the Milice. 'Kramme ate dinner at Jacquot's last night!'

So Kramme, who has not been seen since the raid on the Hôtel Cinqfeuilles, has returned. Nobody knows why, but then nobody really cares. Daniel tells Céline, who passes the news to Paul Rey, who careens up the hill on a 'borrowed' Boche motorbike and tells it, mouth to ear, to Laurence, who shouts it to Toni Gaspari, who is on his way back from training the latest recruits and tells it to Sophie, who brings it, precious, warm, to the Patron as he lies in his bed in the infirmary.

'Kramme's back in Saint-Cybard. We can get him now.'

The Patron neither smiles nor cheers. He stares through her, as he has since Laurence Vaughan-Thomas pushed his way into her infirmary and broke apart all the good she had done.

She has no idea what was said in the ten minutes when she left them together, but the Patron is a dead man breathing. He will eat what he is given, he will drink – he is, in many ways, a perfect patient, better than he was before – but he will not speak to her, or to anybody. It is like nursing a corpse, and it is killing her.

She is not, evidently, alone in this. 'Did you hear the news?' Laurence Vaughan-Thomas runs up the hill towards her. She thought she'd never see him here again.

'Just now.' She is back outside the infirmary, drinking something hot that she will not dignify with a name. The morning is cool, flavoured with smoke, bright and beautiful.

'Did you tell him, the Patron?'

'Of course.'

'No response?'

'What do you think?'

'I think this has gone on long enough. I'm sorry he took badly to my coming, but I'm here now, and it's time someone spoke to him in a language he understands.' He strides past her, and she hasn't got the speed to stop him. In all honesty, she's too bone weary to fight either of them just now.

The door closes with a finality that sets her teeth on edge. She wanders fifty metres down the slope and sits on a pine stump, listening, but Laurence speaks in his native tongue when her ear is attuned to French and she can't make out the words. The tone is clear, though, sharply clipped, military in its inflexibility and lack of compassion. She thinks, that won't work, but then she's tried everything she knows, so maybe it will.

A gap comes, when she hears the Patron try to speak, and then a question from Vaughan-Thomas, harsh. She turns to push her way back in, and finds the route blocked by Céline.

'Trust him.'

'Why?'

'If that isn't obvious, I'm not going to spell it out for you, but you do not own that man. At some point, you have to let Patrick Sutherland make his own decisions.'

'I did that. Look what happened.'

'It's not a single event, Sophie. Let him breathe, or you'll lose him. We all will, and you won't be the only one left grieving. He may love you, but others love him and they matter. Come away with me. Step beyond the mountain. We're going on a jaunt. You'll enjoy it.'

'Kramme?'

That earns her a laugh. 'Not yet, we need to plan for him and we won't get a second try. But even so, you need to come away from here. Killing's in your blood as much as it is mine. Paul Rey's coming, the Yank who makes eyes at you when he thinks you're not looking. He may be an oaf, but he's an artist with a Sten. You'll enjoy it.'

It is frightening, how readily she abandons the Patron, but Laurence is there, and she needs to get away.

She faces death and deals it and finds joy in the killing and in the not-dying, and Paul Rey is far from being an oaf, and he is definitely an artist with a Sten. He is, in fact, a man in whose company it is easy to remember that life is for living.

She comes back flushed and ebullient with her blood streaming thick as lava and her heart awake again. She drinks Calvados, gives Daniel, René and JJ a lesson in unarmed combat, and lets Céline trim her hair back to the short twenties bob that is their Maquis fashion.

Her neck feels cool afterwards, an oddly liberating feeling. And it is with this new sense of the summer air pressing on her neck that she lifts a bottle of Calvados and a mug of the not-quite-coffee and steps away from the big fire to one of its smaller satellites, where Paul Rey sits alone on an oak log.

'Hello.' The fire is behind her. She has some idea of how it lights her hair.

'Hello.' He lays down his bowl, empty. 'The Patron needs help?' He is so different from the English men. Their politesse is centuries old. His feels as if it is learned, and not yet quite polished. He is older, she thinks, than either the Patron or Laurence Vaughan-Thomas, but youth holds him, his language, his way of being.

'Captain Vaughan-Thomas is with the Patron.'

'Ah.'

'So I came to you.'

'I see. I think.' He stands, slowly. She holds up the bottle she has brought. Wordless, he holds out his mug. When she pours, the light of two fires joins in the thin stream of spirit. Briefly, liquid gold flows between them.

He stands, as if glued to the ground. She takes both mugs and sets them on the planed flat surface of the log. This close, he smells of fire smoke and sweat, of fake coffee and gun oil; of life and hope. She lifts his hand, slides her fingers through his. 'I'm not Céline. I know that. If you'd rather I left, I will do so.'

'What? No! No, no, no, *no*.' The spell that held him drops away. He steps in to close the last space between them. The fabric of his battle shirt presses on hers. In wonder, his fingers thread her hair. 'I thought you and your Patron . . . ?'

She and her Patron are not his business. She puts a hand on his chest and pushes him gently back. 'Don't think. Really. We may die tonight, tomorrow, the next day. Thinking is for staying alive. We don't need it for this.' She kisses him, and if neither savage nor white hot, it is full of the day and the killing and the pain of waiting, and it is true that they don't need to think at all, except briefly, with urgency, of where they might go.

She has not seen where the men go when the town girls come, but he has. He takes her hand, leads her, then lifts her and when he sets her down, the bed is of mosses on pine needles, and the stars light the sweat on his naked back, and he has ginger hair all down his chest, like the Patron's, except that it is paler, and not ruined, and there are no bruises – well, not many, and none of them is likely to kill him.

It may be that he has a wife. She doesn't ask.

354

Later, walking back up to the infirmary, she counts the bats patching the starry sky, and the owls summoning their young to feed.

A shadow waits for her, sitting on the infirmary porch, and she thinks it is the Patron and is surprised at how tetchy she is, how the anger of weeks rushes in and is not readily laid aside, how much she hates Laurence Vaughan-Thomas for finding success where she has failed. How she hates Céline more, for being right.

The shadow gains form, and she stops. 'You?' Her throat cramps. Not the Patron. It is Vaughan-Thomas himself, holding an empty bottle of brandy. She is not ready for this. Not now.

'Me.' He tilts it at her in a kind of salute. 'Not him. Never again him. I'm sorry.'

He is exceptionally drunk. She is not sober. She's not sure what she is. She doesn't want to have to think about it. Her heart folds in on its own chaos. 'Is he dead?'

'You may wish he was. Certainly he does.' He pushes himself to standing, sways, belches. 'I thought . . . I was arrogant. And stupid. He is all yours. I have done all I— All he will let me do. Ever.'

He walks away.

'Laurence!' She catches him within a dozen paces, spins him, ungainly, to face her. 'What have you done? What did you say?'

'I told him to stop wallowing in self-pity. That he's alive and he should be grateful for it and he can't keep on hiding behind the damage of the past.'

Wallowing? The tubes of her guts twist, awkwardly. 'Was that this time, or last time?'

'Clever girl. I always underestimate you. Must remember not to do that.' He salutes her again, loosely. 'Céline likes you, you know. She's trying hard not to be jealous of you and Paul Rey, and not *quite* succeeding.'

Does she smell of him? Is it written on her face? She snaps, 'And you are changing the subject. Was it this time, or last time, that you told him he was wallowing in self-pity?'

'This time. Last time, I tried to appeal to his sense of compassion, for himself, for the rest of us who care for him.'

'What did he say? This time, not last time.'

'He told me to leave and never to return. He was really quite vehement. And loud. Unambiguous. I am, therefore, leaving.'

'You can't leave. We need you. *Céline* needs you. Anyway, where will you go?'

'Not the Maquis. Him. I have said I shall not inflict myself on him ever again.'

He sits down, suddenly, a marionette cut off without warning. Rocking forward, he presses his brow to his knees, then turns his head sideways, laying his cheek flat, pushing his mouth out of line.

She folds her arms and takes a step back: this man, she has no intention of nursing.

He sets the bottle on the summer-hard earth, draws a ring around it with his forefinger, thinking. She begins to walk away. He calls her back, softly.

'I am going to regret all of this rather a lot in the morning, but for now, while I am able to speak without self-censure, I will say that I give him to you without any of the usual half-cocked, mealy-hearted platitudes. He is yours. He always has been. I was never in the running. I have always known that. It is important that you know it, too. I didn't intend for our parting to be so . . . acrimonious, but it may be that it was necessary. Certainly it was unambiguous. I will stay until we have found Kramme and carved him into particularly tiny pieces, and then I shall leave.'

He looks up, blinks her into focus. She thinks he is going to be very sick, very soon.

She has to say something, and doesn't know what. 'I care for him.'

356

'I know.'

'I don't love him.' It may be that she pities him, which would destroy him, so she doesn't let herself think it. Beyond that, her heart is a bruised mosaic, a lump of coal with too many facets to count, so that she has no idea what she feels, except that all of it is too much, and threatens to overwhelm her.

Of only one thing is she sure: she loved in Paris, and she is not planning to do so again. The hurt is too great. She said these exact words less than an hour ago to Paul Rey, who didn't believe her.

Laurence Vaughan-Thomas doesn't believe her, either. 'I think you feel more than you let yourself know, and it is not all guilt. Did you love Kramme?'

'No!' Lust, she will allow. Never love. 'I hated him then. I hate him now.'

'But you made it your truth and he, by all accounts, loved you.'

'He wanted a mother for his children.'

'I gather he proposed to you on the night the invasion was announced. And you accepted.'

Oh, God. 'I . . .'

'You did what you had to do.'

'You don't know what I did.'

'I do, actually. We have a man on the inside who has told us quite a lot of what was going on. Not all of it, but enough to paint a picture. Name of Icarus. Might mean something?'

'Of course.'

'Good. Because at some point, you and I shall have to get him out. Or her. It might always be a woman, but I believe not. There can't be two like you in the whole of France, I think.' He pushes himself to his feet, makes a full, unsteady bow. 'You are really rather wonderful. Céline's loss is Patrick's gain. Now go to him, and see if you can undo the damage I have wrought. I *am* truly sorry.'

357

CHAPTER TWENTY-FOUR

ORLÉANS
Sunday, 18 March 2018
19.30

ELODIE DUVAL IS STILL missing. So are Laurence Vaughan-Thomas, René Vivier and JJ Crotteau. The difference is that Picaut has phone numbers for these three, and not for Elodie. They are burning a hole in her phone, but Eric sent her a text asking her to drop by and she's not inclined to blow him off, so she has come down to the pathology suite, where Pierre Fayette is lying naked on the table, opened and stitched up again, neatly.

Now that she can look at him without the Lakoffs on either side, it occurs to her that he is fitter than she might have thought: less flab, more muscle. More tanned, too: he didn't look the kind of man who would lie on a sun bed.

Eric is talking to her again as if nothing untoward had happened. He hands her a mug of coffee. She says, 'Thank you. I'm sorry. Thank you.'

He says, 'It's fine. Don't worry.'

Which is enough, really. She leans back on the wall. 'What did you want me to look at?'

'The red silk scarf you found at the site of the second

358

murder.' He sends an image of it onto the big wall screen. Laid flat on a white surface, it looks less exotic than it did hanging on Pierre Fayette's back door. A second image joins the first: the scarf under UV light, where it becomes strikingly piebald. 'Blood stains?' asks Picaut.

'Washed-out blood stains.' Eric's pointer circles them one after another. 'Many, many washed-out blood stains, and some of them very old. We're struggling to get useful DNA from any of them, but either this was worn by a lot of very unlucky people or someone used it to scrub up after a whole bunch of killings.'

'Sophie Destivelle was in an assassination squad in Paris in the war. She killed a lot of people, apparently.'

'But we have Elodie Duval's hairs on here, not hers. Were they close, Sophie and Elodie?'

'At Paul Rey's bedside, they looked it.' A thought strikes her. 'Can I get an international line from here?'

'Be my guest.'

She dials. The connection is slow, but it is picked up at the second ring. 'Kochanek.'

'This is Captain Picaut of—'

'Captain! I was about to call you. You go first, and then I'll share what I have.'

'How often did Elodie Duval come in to visit Paul Rey in the company of the woman you knew as Theodora Sutherland?'

'She never came alone. That is to say, over the past eighteen months, the two visited a total of thirteen times, and on each occasion, they came together. Madame Sutherland came a further twenty-one times unaccompanied. Do I gather that was an alias?'

'You do. We don't yet have a complete fix on a real name, but the most common one seems to have been Sophie Destivelle.'

'Who was shot this morning. In the context of which, I am sending you an email with the pathology report from the post-mortem of John Lakoff, Conrad's grandfather. The photographs may be of use. They're coming through to you now. I'll wait while you take a look.'

Her phone sings to incoming mail. She sends the images straight to the wall screen where she can look at them full size. John Lakoff is a small, shrunken prune of a man, with fish-belly skin tinged yellow in the places where the skin creases fold over each other. The gunshot pattern is striking. The cut to his throat might also have been, but it has been stitched shut, and his mouth is closed, so the post-mortem mutilation is all but invisible.

Picaut wants to ask if Kochanek got clearance to send this, but can't, and she suspects not. This is the kind of thing that lands you running a retirement home, but once you're there, what else can they do?

She hits the button to put the phone call onto speaker so that Eric can listen in. 'We have a match,' she says. 'Whoever shot Sophie used the same pattern. Did you check out Paul Rey's gun?'

'We did, and that, too, is a match. The interesting thing is that Colonel Rey was lying in an MRI machine at the time of the murder. Any number of security-cleared medical staff will attest to his having been in their facility between noon and eighteen hundred hours, when he returned here. Lakoff's nurse served him lunch at noon and he was most certainly not dead then. His body was discovered at fifteen thirty. The pathologist put the time of death approximately half an hour before that.'

'That's convenient.'

'Isn't it? I am endeavouring to gain access to further records of the time. You'll understand these are of a sensitive nature.'

'I certainly do.' Picaut is still staring at the screen. 'Lakoff has muscular atrophy in his lower limbs, but good definition in his shoulders. Was he in a wheelchair?'

Kochanek says, 'He was ninety-six, Captain Picaut. He was infirm, with faecal and urinary incontinence, and virtually blind. Paul Rey was, to all intents and purposes, his eyes and limbs. He wheeled him everywhere, described the world to him, helped him remember his past. They talked of the war, mostly.'

'Lakoff was a veteran?'

'He was a paratrooper who was dropped behind enemy lines. He was captured three weeks after D-Day and released from a living hell in Sachsenhausen concentration camp by the Soviets nearly nine months later. We got him back three months after that. He was something of a hero to our predecessors in the Agency, I believe, but quietly. He went on to serve in the Soviet desk when it was formed.'

'And his son and his grandson continued in his footsteps.'

'So it would seem. There's a photograph in the file from his younger days that shows all three. Here.'

And by the wonder of technology, it is here, on Picaut's phone. An autumnal shot, taken on a lawn, with maples in full, red riot behind. Three men stand in line, three generations from right to left. Two, she knows. The third is lean and sharp-eyed and . . .

'Is John Lakoff wearing a scarf?'

'He is.'

'Dark red silk?'

'Yes. It became rather notorious. One of the nurses took it away to wash it and he threatened to have her hanged.'

'Why was it not listed in his personal effects?' She has them in the pathology file: a full list of his clothing. There is no mention of a scarf.

For the first time, Kathryn Kochanek is unbalanced. 'I'll find out.'

'This is a criminal waste of talent, but thank you. If you can find me anything about John Lakoff's wartime past, I'd be enormously grateful.'

'I'll do what I can.'

Picaut cuts the line. Eric is watching her. 'Do we dance?'

'We dance.'

They hook arms and swing round, something they haven't done for years. She laughs, and he laughs with her and, releasing her, gives her shoulder a squeeze. 'I'm sorry.'

'Don't be. I deserved it.'

'So what have we learned?'

'I have no idea, but if it's the same scarf, and it came from there to here, there will be a reason. All we have to do is find it.'

Picaut hums as she extracts her car from the multi-storey car park and heads back through the evening traffic. She continues to hum as she drives and is onto the third iteration before she realizes the tune is 'Yankee Doodle Dandy'.

Paul Rey. Did they come for you and hit John Lakoff instead? Or was he their target all along? And how – really, *how* – did he come to be wearing a red silk scarf?

Picaut takes the images of the scarf with her on her phone. She is on the road back to the studio when a thought makes her indicate left and she drives instead south and east to the Château d'Alençon, where the door guards recognize her.

'Is Strategic Operations Director Lakoff available?'

'He's giving his speech, Ma'am. If it's urgent, I may be able to get him a message?'

The guard is one of those who was standing outside Ducat's office. 'No, thank you, I had a question that only— Senator? You're not attending your son's talk?'

'He hates me listening.' Edward Lakoff is paler than she remembers, with blue patches under his eyes. 'Have you news of my father-in-law?'

'I'm sorry, I don't. I came to look at the images again, the ones in your museum. I thought . . .'

It's not a concrete idea and even now, she isn't sure it is worth it, but the senator brightens and sweeps her past the door guards as if this is the answer to his worries. 'Please, let me show you. I set up the exhibition. It took me two years. Conrad knows nothing about the war, he just pretends he does. If you'll let me take you round it, I'll consider it an honour. You just have to tell me when to stop talking.'

The foyer is all but deserted as they pass through: Conrad Lakoff's speech has drawn in everyone who is anyone. Upstairs in the museum, the air smells of cigar smoke and Scotch. Edward Lakoff stands near the door and views the array of images and short, succinct histories with a paternal air. 'You didn't come to look at all of it, I realize. What can I help you with?'

'We found a silk scarf of uncertain provenance. I wanted to see if Sophie was wearing it in any of the wartime photographs. It's not obvious in any of the pictures of her that I've seen from that era, except possibly under her jacket in the one of the Maquis jumping the wall.'

'You've seen that?' At her nod, he looks wistful. 'The only one I don't have a copy of. Paul Rey sent prints out to the old Maquis, but none of them would relinquish theirs, nor even let me copy them. Just asking, I felt like an anthropologist trying to steal the souls of a primitive tribe with my magic lantern.'

'But you do have images of Sophie. Conrad and I looked at some earlier today with the images of the Maquis, but I think there were others, down the right-hand wall.'

'Be my guest.' He stands back to let her go before him and yes, here are two rows of images mounted on display boards. 'On the top line is a series of Sophie when she was with Kramme. We were very lucky to get those. The Gehlen

363

Organization kept them in their archives. She was beautiful, don't you think?'

She was gamine, wide-eyed, stunning in dark red silk, leaning on the arm of a German in full dress uniform. 'That's Max Kramme, the Gestapo officer?'

'It is. There's a rumour that they were in love; certainly he proposed marriage to her and she accepted. They look good together, I think. If you didn't know the background, they'd make a fine couple.'

They do. There is no scarf, though. Picaut is already looking at the rows beneath, at the grainy black-and-white shots that are less grainy than she thinks they ought to be. 'Did you use image enhancement on these?'

He gives a wry smile. 'A little. I tried not to be too obvious, but the modern eye isn't used to drawing detail from indistinct blobs the way we were in our youth. Or I was, anyway. She's wearing a scarf here. And here. And here.'

And here is a treasure trove of images of Sophie Destivelle. Three of them are taken in a forest in summer. She is scruffy, happy, leaning back against a tree, cleaning a gun. Or sitting on a log raising a glass to the camera. Or lying along a log with one knee up and her head on a man's thigh. He is stroking her hair. On his face is the dreamy look Picaut has seen once or twice in other men lost to love. 'Is that Paul Rey?'

'I believe so. Is this the scarf you're looking for?'

'I don't know . . . it would help if I could see it in colour.'

'We have images of her time in the DB. They're in colour.' Lakoff moves round to the back of the board. And here is Sophie in early-fifties colour, faded but clear. And yes, the scarf is the same.

'That's it.' She shows him the image on her phone. More to herself than to him, she says, 'So the question is, would she have given it to Elodie Duval? Or was she a guest of Pierre Fayette's last night before she took his car?'

364

'Are these two mutually exclusive?'

'Not necessarily. We have DNA that says Elodie wore it. And yet Sophie seems to have kept it through the war and on into the decade after.'

The senator – who, if Rollo is correct, was once a case officer in the CIA – leans back against a wall and folds his arms. 'What do you know of the killing squads of Paris, Captain?'

'The *équipes de tueurs*? Only that they existed. I heard a rumour that Sophie was a member of one.'

'It's more than a rumour. She had a dozen kills or more before the Gestapo ran her out of town. She escaped to England, was trained by the SOE and sent back into the Maquis de Morez, but even after the war, she never lost her taste for assassination. She joined the DB and as far as I know, she did the same in peacetime as she had in the war. Perhaps more subtly, but still . . . We live in an odd world. If she had been a civilian, she'd be hunted by people like you. Because she worked for the government, she was a heroine, if only to a small and select group. It's possible, I imagine, that the scarf was marked with the blood of her kills.'

People like you. Picaut taps her phone against her teeth. 'Such a thing would be cherished. Why would she give it to Elodie?'

'Maybe she knew she was going to die?' Edward Lakoff tilts his head to one side. 'Has it occurred to you that Sophie was not working alone – that perhaps she never had worked alone – and that she was playing a far more complicated game than we, who are not privy to her past, could possibly know?'

From the conference, Picaut heads directly to the studio.

Clinton McKinney has gone, and Martha. Martin Gillard is not in evidence although his Mercedes is still in the car park. Nobody else is around. Sylvie has gone to watch the mechanics take Elodie Duval's silver Golf apart. Petit-Evard has been sent to gain access to, and then read, the mobile phone transcripts of all those involved, insofar as he can. Rollo has gone off to tap 'a source'. He hasn't said who or for what. It will be clandestine and may well involve the institution once known as the DB and now more properly called the Department for External Affairs. By any analysis, Picaut is better off not asking.

She could go home. Probably she should, but Elodie's office is open and alluring. The windows look down over the unlit expanse of the shooting lot with its mock-ups of wartime Saint-Cybard, the dry fountain, the train station, the Hôtel Cinqfeuilles. The outlines are familiar from old documentaries, but today, there is a sense of things stirring under the surface that she has not felt before.

Her phone has synchronized with the white board in the office. She writes a new list on it:

– Sophie Destivelle: 2nd victim?
– John Lakoff: 1st victim? (Were they going for him? Or for Paul Rey?)
– Paul Rey: Are we sure he died of natural causes?
– Sophie gave her scarf to Elodie? Why?? (And how did John Lakoff get it in the first place? How did it get back to France?)
– Sophie and Elodie visited Paul Rey, took a flight back to France, ate together then . . . ? Went to Pierre Fayette's? Why?
– Where is Elodie?
– Why did Sophie Destivelle die *now*?
– If Sophie is not working alone, who is she working with – and to what end?
– Did she know she was going to die?

Too many questions and too few answers. The phone numbers of the runaway Maquisards lie on the desk in front of her, waiting. She watches a stray shard of starlight pierce a cloud and, still watching it, picks up her phone and dials Patrice.

'Hey, sup?'

'When did you forget how to speak human?'

'It's the world I live in. Everyone talks like this.' Patrice is smiling, she can feel it. 'You OK?'

'I have two fresh murders and one eighteen months old in a different jurisdiction that bears the same hallmarks. I have a list of suspects that starts with a CIA assassin of impeccable deniability and moves swiftly on to someone you think I shouldn't touch. Other than that, I'm fine. How are you getting on with the cipher Elodie left us in her hidden note?'

'Making progress. The poem helped, but I've still got a section in the middle that doesn't make sense.'

'Does it mention Diem, as in Carpe?'

'Ah.' She hears him click his fingers. 'Why didn't I think of that? I thought Die, then M and couldn't decide if it was German or English. OK . . .' Keys rattle. 'So the text is "Paul Rey's son stop Diem's legacy query".'

'Is that it?' She sounds like Clinton McKinney.

'Inès! Getting to this has taken me the best part of—'

'Sorry. Sorry. Really. But there were a lot more words than that in the email. I thought it would be telling us something more . . . substantial.'

'The cipher was based on numbered letters inside each sentence. To be honest, it's fantastically clever that she managed it at all. Your missing woman is a brilliant cryptographer. Anyway, the question is, who is Paul Rey's son?'

'I have no idea. Paul Rey was a wartime Jedburgh who went on to be one of the founding members of the CIA. He died this morning, a fact which is increasingly ringing alarm bells, although, in the absence of any actual evidence to the contrary, we're still treating it as a natural death. He leaves behind five wives. He could have a dozen sons, or none. He was almost certainly Sophie Destivelle's lover. One of them.'

'Want me to look into it?'

'If you can. I'll see what I can do to find Diem. In the meantime, can you patch me through to a mobile number in a way that can't be traced?'

'Anything can be traced. First rule of mobiles. I can buy you three minutes max. That's the magic number.'

'OK.' She does a swift piece of mental arithmetic. 'Subtract my father's date from this.' She rattles off the number.

He says, 'Stay on the line. I'll patch you across.'

She stays on the line. A pause, a dial tone, three rings and a click later, and Laurence Vaughan-Thomas says, cautiously, 'To whom am I speaking?'

'Picaut.'

'Captain!' It might be relief – his exhalation – or laughter. He is walking on a pavement somewhere. She can hear the length of his stride, and passing traffic. 'I rather thought we might hear from you. Did you open the music box?'

'I have opened two: yours and Elodie's.'

'Well *done*, Captain.'

'Thank you. We have three minutes in which we may be secure, probably less. In which case, the pertinent question is: Who is Diem and what is his legacy?'

'Or hers. We have been asking ourselves that question for many, many decades – some of us. He, or she, betrayed us to Kramme. That is as much as we know.'

'You must have some ideas. Elodie answered it in her cipher.'

'Did she?' There's a change in the length of his stride, as if the mention of her name has caused him to stumble. A pace or two on, he says, 'Where is she now?'

'Elodie? We don't know.'

'Blast.' The word has more impact than any of the coarser

368

expletives she's heard so far today. He walks half a block. A car horn sounds. He says, 'Two things. First: Elodie's box belonged to my cousin Céline: everything of hers passed to Elodie when she died, including her apartment. That fact may be of use to you at some point. Second – and bearing in mind that this is an open line – can you tell me exactly what Elodie wrote?'

'Henry the Eighth minus one's son stop Diem's legacy query. She used the proper name of the man who was not king, obviously.'

'Yes. I understand. Thank you.'

'Who was his son, do you know?'

'I can't answer that. But I shall work on it. Diem wasn't me. I can tell you that categorically, but you don't have to believe me. I believe it wasn't Sophie, but even now, I am not wholly certain of that and you can't be, either. In fact, what matters more than anything is that you make your own judgements. We must be near the end of our three minutes, Captain.'

'Fifty-eight seconds to go. I have two further questions.'

'Fire away.'

The first is something that has nagged at her all day, without any obvious reason. 'Why did you come to Orléans, all of you? You are English, your war was spent in the Jura mountains. JJ and the others worked for the DB, which is based in Paris. You had nothing to do with Orléans. Why did you all retire here?'

'Exactly because we had nothing to do with it. No residential streets and avenues named in our honour, no men and women whose parents, brothers, sisters, children we saved – or didn't. The war was uglier than you can ever imagine and bad blood festers. Nobody of our generation escaped without losing friends and making enemies. JJ came here first and we all followed him. We wanted to stay together, obviously – some bonds are not made to be broken – and we thought that

369

here, we would be anonymous. Until Elodie started making her film, it was working.'

'Why did she start?'

'You will have to ask her that; I'm sure she had her reasons. And to do so, you must find her. Please do this, Captain, as a matter of urgency. To lose Elodie now would be ... heartbreaking.'

'We are doing our best.'

'You had another question?'

'What happened to Toni Gaspari, the third member of your Jedburgh team?'

There is a pause, and a heaviness that is felt, rather than heard. 'He was shot during the assault on Kramme's wedding. He was our sniper. They had one better. It's not fashionable to say these things, but some of the Boche were exceedingly good at what they did.'

'There's no chance he might have escaped? That he could have made a new life for himself in the US under another name and turned up in a CIA care home for ageing spies?'

'Sadly not. I buried his body with my own hands.'

'Right. I'm sorry. Thank you.' Slowly, she is learning to read him and he is not telling the whole truth about this. She could call him on it, but decides not to. She says, 'You should dispose of this phone.'

'I am in the very process of doing so. Goodbye, Captain. Good luck.'

He is gone, leaving no real trace. Rarely has she been so deftly, delicately obstructed. You are good. Do old spies ever retire?

She dials once more. 'Patrice? It's me again.'

'Hey.' He's walking. Actually, he's running; she can hear the pound of his feet, the judder of it in his breath. Somewhere in the background, a tannoy announces places and times, too fuzzily to make out.

'Hey. Can you locate another phone? I don't want to call it, I just want to know where it is.'

'I can try. Same arithmetic as before.'

She gives him René's number and sits in the dark, listening. 'Are you in an airport?'

'Kind of.'

She laughs. 'Patrice, it's like being pregnant, you either are or you aren't.'

'Yes, but sometimes it's not useful to tell the listening world.'

It's been a long day. She should know this. 'Right. Sorry.'

'No worries. I've got your answer. Do you remember the place that got one star on TripAdvisor where we . . .'

Didn't quite get around to having sex: a museum in the centre of Orléans. She says, 'I remember.'

'Two streets south is a small, rather chic hotel: two floors only, very discreet.'

'I know it.'

'Room number is the first two digits of your father's date added together and then subtract the first digit of my birthday.'

That's nine. Her lips tingle, as if newly kissed. 'You're a magician.'

'I do my best. Take care, eh?'

'You too. Travel safe.' Wherever you are going that I can't know because now you live in the world of spies and secrets and I am only paddling in the shallow water at the edges.

But she has information and she can act on it. She wants to call in support, but the first rule of mobile phones means she can't. She pulls on her jacket, throws back the last of the coffee and heads—

And here is Martin Gillard, standing in the doorway. She springs back from the sight of him. 'How long have you been there?'

'A while. Did Laurence know who Paul Rey's son was?'

'You listened to my phone call?'

'I realize you don't believe this, but we are on the same side.'

'Until you kill someone on my watch. Unless you already have.' She is sharp. His stare is his answer. Defensive, she says, 'I thought you'd gone home?'

'I don't have a home in Orléans, I have a room in a hotel, which is one elevator ride from a well-stocked bar.' He leans back against the doorpost, hands in pockets. 'There's no alcohol here, you may have noticed. McKinney won't have it on the premises. Tonight, that has to be the better choice.'

'I didn't know there were many paid assassins with an alcohol problem. Is that compatible with the job description?'

In the late evening light, Gillard's eyes are more grey than blue. His gaze, meeting hers, is intelligent and calculating, but it is not hiding anything; she would bet quite a lot on that. He says, 'I think you have a particularly skewed opinion of my function. I make things happen. Sometimes I stop things happening.'

'Or not.'

The lines at the sides of his eyes tighten. He runs his tongue round his teeth. 'I was not paid to protect Sophie Destivelle. If we are truthful, I have not been paid to protect Elodie Duval, but whoever I am, whatever I may or may not have done, there is not a man alive who doesn't feel it his duty to protect those he loves. If Elodie is dead, I will live with that failure for the rest of my life. I would appreciate it if you didn't find it necessary to gloat either in prospect or in retrospect.'

Picaut regards him, thoughtfully. 'Do you think she's dead?'

'I am trying very hard to believe she isn't.'

She looks down at her feet and contemplates the beginnings of a plan. In a while, with a nod to the absent Rollo who will hate this, she looks up again. 'Have you ever killed a police officer?'

'No. Nor will I.'

'Are you armed?'

'Not at present.' He chews the edge of his thumb. 'It could be arranged.'

She says, 'Do you trust me?'

'Strange that you should ask. I was just wondering that.'

'And?'

'I think I do.'

'Can I trust you?'

'Absolutely.'

'Then get your gun and come with me. We're going to look for JJ Crotteau and it may be that he doesn't want to be found.'

12 August: US Third Army captures Alençon.

15th: Operation Dragoon: Allies land on the south coast of France.

19th: Resistance uprising begins in Paris.

30th: Allies enter Rouen.

CHAPTER TWENTY-FIVE

SAINT-CYBARD
August–September 1944

S UMMER CREEPS PAST AND the Allied tanks become snarled in the hedgerows of Normandy, fighting over villages whose names they don't know for fractions of inches on a map, back and forth. The Boche should just give up – everyone knows this – but they have been ordered to fight to the last man's last round and those who think this is a foolish notion are hanged in sight of the rest. So they fight, and die, and the fractional inches become actual inches, saturated with the blood of the dead.

In between jaunts of its own, the Maquis de Morez garners this information hazily, from the BBC, from notes in the drops, from the radio contact with Laurence's brigadier, and, rarely, by word of mouth from Saint-Cybard: from the Milice women, and from Véronique, a rather striking young woman who is, it becomes evident, on intimate terms with Céline.

The Frenchmen among the Maquis affect not to notice as the two women sit pale head to dark by the fire, and retire early to Céline's cabin. Paul Rey has no shame: he stares and grins lopsidedly, and, on these nights, Sophie has no trouble persuading him to bed.

Not that she has trouble anyway; just that if he has more than a mouthful of Cognac, or if the killing has been hard that day, and perhaps a man has been lost, he becomes prone to long soliloquies on love and commitment that stray too close, too often, to a proposal she has no intention of accepting. At least when Véronique is visiting Céline, he thinks only of sex, which is fine.

July becomes August and the tanks break free of the bocages. Caen falls, and Montgomery is bogged down in Holland, or so it seems. In the middle of the month, the Americans land in Saint-Tropez and begin to fight their way north. On all sides, the Boche are under assault, and on all sides, the Maquis are let off the leash to join that assault. There are specific actions required at specific times: a rail line destroyed or (less often) mended, telephone exchanges destroyed – or mended. Panzer divisions, infantry divisions, staff cars to blow up.

But in between, they can pick their own targets, and they do. They call guns, food, coffee, tobacco from the sky and it is delivered. Ask and ye shall be given. Seek and ye shall find. Sophie wakes in the morning with her blood on fire and goes to sleep beside Paul Rey the same. This is what they were born for. Life is short and bright and nobody has to think more than half a day ahead.

And yet, they have not found Kramme. This is the cockroach in their wine. Her dreams are all of him: living, smiling, laughing, the touch of his hand, the kiss; or dead, bleeding, with his throat laid bare to the bones of his neck, and his tongue cut out.

She wakes, and neither is true, and it is her fault. All that she told him of the rule book, he has taken to heart: a different bed each night and never let anyone know where it is. Every day, more of the citizens of Saint-Cybard join the Maquis;

winning is contagious and there are few who believe the Allies will not win. And yet none of them knows where Kramme is. Or if they do, they are afraid to tell of it.

Véronique brings their breakthrough. She arrives one morning, which is not her usual time. Sophie is sitting in the sun on the bare grass outside the infirmary, re-rolling newly washed bandages. The Patron lies on a straw-filled pallet in the shade of a canvas awning behind her. René sits on a log, washing three glass syringes ready to be boiled. Everyone else who is fit to work is out foraging; in the mountains, food is plentiful, but you have to know where to find it. Their increasing numbers means more hunting for food. Also, the Boche are no longer sending spotter planes over the hills. It has been possible to light fires in the open for several weeks now.

René is almost always left behind. He is shorter of temper since he was rescued, and she has twice had to treat his ruined hand for infection, but in between he has become a good nurse, and is growing more skilled in the cleaning of wounds. He is first to see Véronique. They knew each other before the war and he is fond of her, so that when she arrives, he scoots along the log to make space for her.

She won't sit. She stands, weaving her fingers through her hands. 'Céline isn't here?'

'She'll be back,' Sophie says. Probably. Nobody adds the conditionals; they are part of the life they lead.

'When?'

'Three o'clock? Five?' It's hard to tell.

'I have to go back.'

'We'll tell her you were here.' It's not that Sophie dislikes Véronique, she just doesn't really have time for her.

The girl takes a breath and bites it back. And then: 'Kramme is getting married.'

'*What?*'

'Luce Moreau: Kramme has asked her to marry him and

she's said yes. They are to wed tomorrow at the church at Arc-sous-Montagne at two o'clock in the afternoon. All the Boche will be there.'

'How do you know?'

'Lisette sent me, her sister.'

Lisette, so Sophie has learned, was Daniel's fiancée until the war came, at which point, such was her dedication to the Resistance that she married into the Milice in order to provide the Maquis with intelligence. She has never yet sent them bad information.

'Hold on, are you telling me Lisette is Madame Andreu? That *Luce Moreau* is a *Résistante*? Seriously?'

'You know them?'

'I delivered Lisette's twins. I . . .' Took dinner many times with Kramme and Luce Moreau, but she is not about to tell them that.

Fuck.

Fuck.

Her mind is a litter of smoking parts. Kramme is to marry Luce Moreau. Luce 'I would die for the Reich' Moreau is one of the so-courageous women who give themselves to the Boche so that they can send word to the mountains. And she is to marry Kramme.

What is there to say, but fuck?

And yet, Kramme will be in public. Out in the open. Visible. A pulse begins to pound behind Sophie's eyes. She says, 'Véronique, thank you. Céline and Fabien will decide what to do. We'll tell them as soon as they get back. In the meantime if you want—'

Ro!

The noise is more like a cough than a word, but it's forcefully said. She turns, slowly, suppressing a sigh. The Patron cannot walk. It is possible he never will, but she has JJ lift him outside every morning so he's not just staring at the ceiling. Beyond that, they barely communicate. She hasn't heard him speak since the day of Laurence Vaughan-Thomas's confrontation and has long since stopped caring, or so she thinks. Now, he is partway off his pallet, struggling to sit.

In a flash of anger, she says, 'I'll be back at two to move you before the sun moves round too far.'

Ro!

Hesitantly, René says, 'I think he means "no", not "go".'

There was a time when she was the one who understood the Patron. She stands square in front of him, her hands on her hips. 'Is it no?'

He shakes his head, and then, somewhat frantically, nods. He works his mouth, and this sound, she almost recognizes. *Ramme.*

He stares at her, full eye contact with an intensity bordering on mania. This is entirely new: whole or broken, he has never held her gaze before.

'Patron?'

He grunts, struggles off the pallet onto his knees and drags the edge of his thumb across the parched ground, making marks that turn out to be letters.

Because she's expecting it, she picks out KRAMME from the strange scrawl, but the rest is a drunk-spider mystery, as opaque as his speech.

To René, she says, 'Go down to the cook-fires. Marcel has a chalkboard he uses for writing out what he needs done. Bring it. And the chalk.'

She and the Patron share an awkward silence while the boy runs down and back again. When the chalkboard is given to him, she finds that his hands may be able to hold a mug, to grasp a spoon and shovel food into his mouth, but the intricacies of writing take him to the border of his own limitations. He holds his right wrist with his left hand, carves out each letter, like a mason with a chisel.

380

Watching him is painful. Sophie gazes up at the mountain until he makes another sound that might be, *Look*.

She does.

KRAMME DESPERATE TO FIND MOTHER FOR HIS SON. BEEN LOOKING FOR WIFE ALL TIME IN FRANCE. WANTED YOU, COULDN'T HAVE YOU. IF PERSUADED LUCE MOREAU NOW, WILL LEAVE ASAP AFTER WEDDING. THIS LAST CHANCE TO KILL HIM. URGENT!

Kramme. Kill Kramme. The pulse behind her eyes hammers harder. Already, the shock of Luce Moreau's part in this is fading into insignificance. 'You really think Kramme will leave Saint-Cybard?'

The Patron nods, once, fiercely, smears out the first message and stabs down, double-fisted, to write again. CA—

The chalk skitters away from his fingers. He grabs it, tries again. And a third time.

Fuck.

She gapes at him.

Sorry.

'No, no, it's fine.' It's not the word, it's just that he can say it, whole, unadulterated. The only word she's heard him say that sounds completely normal. She starts to laugh, and the look on his face does nothing to stop her. Helpless, she slides into a breathless, whooping, gut-cramping hysteria, and is only saved because he joins her, so that when the fit passes and she winds down to sobriety, and the vast, unquenchable grief, he is ready for that, too, and comes to hold her in a rough, hard embrace.

I'm sorry.

'Oh God, Patrick. Don't be sorry. Don't ever be sorry. It's me who needs to say that.'

No.

'For so many things. Yes.' She leans her head on his

381

shoulder, turns her face sideways, says, I'm sorry, I'm sorry, I'm sorry, over and over while he strokes her hair. It is René, standing awkwardly a few paces away, who brings her back to herself.

She takes a steadying breath. 'What were you trying to say? What do we need to do?'

Call him.

She understands him now. How could she have thought 'no' meant 'go'? And by 'him', he means Laurence Vaughan-Thomas. The man from whose presence he has emphatically turned.

'Laurence is with Fabien. They'll be back by mid-afternoon. Do we need him before then?'

Yes. Now. All of them.

In the infirmary, she keeps a Very flare for precisely this purpose. A green star lifts high over the mountain, scaring the crows. She sets the pistol back under the plank that is her only shelf. 'Would you like some coffee while we wait?'

Thank you.

Laurence Vaughan-Thomas returns with a gang of eight Maquisards. He runs ahead of them, and stops. The Patron has been working with his chalk again, working on his sentences so they make proper English.

KRAMME IS TO WED AT THE CHURCH OF ARC-SOUS-MONTAGNE TOMORROW AT FOURTEEN HUNDRED HOURS. THE ENTIRE GERMAN GARRISON OF SAINT-CYBARD WILL BE THERE. HE THINKS HE HAS KEPT IT SECRET. HE WILL NOT BE ON GUARD. IF YOU TAKE ENOUGH MEN, YOU CAN KILL HIM.

If he reads it at all, Vaughan-Thomas does so in a passing glance. The rest of his attention is focused on Sophie, as if the

Patron were not there. She has seen dogs like this, beaten so that they will not look at their masters.

The Patron, astonishingly, impossibly, has commandeered René as a crutch and pulled himself to standing, or at least, something closer to vertical than he has been. *You have to lead them.* He lays a hand on Vaughan-Thomas's arm. And that's enough, really. Relief transfigures him. From the crown of his head to his feet, he is lighter.

There is a possibility he might weep, which would be uncomfortable, not least because Céline has arrived, and JJ, Fabien, Daniel. Paul Rey is there too. His presence makes Sophie's skin tingle. He grins at her, and she returns it, dizzied by the moment.

The men stand around the chalkboard, reading – some of them slowly, because the Patron has written in English.

'What do we do?' Céline asks.

Assault them. The Patron speaks and Sophie translates.

Not everyone can understand him yet. Vaughan-Thomas does, obviously. Before she is done, he says, 'How many men will we need?'

How many have you got?

'One hundred and four.'

Take them all.

'It may well be a trap.'

Of course. But you will be prepared for it.

The sun sets gold and scarlet on their plan. It is not a subtle plan, but it is powerful and they feel powerful now. Beyond those first few, only a small corps of the central command knows the full detail: Fabien, who trained long ago with Laurence, Céline, JJ, Daniel, the Jedburghs, and Thierry, of course. The remaining ninety-six Maquisards think they are at last going to liberate Saint-Cybard.

Céline's hair shines in the late evening light. Véronique is back again and they stand together, arm in arm. The men know something has changed. Even those outside the central corps, who have not yet been told what is happening, pat her on the shoulder and raise toasts in her direction. Céline is their mascot: along with Fabien, she is lucky, and so Véronique, too, now brings them luck.

Sophie sits on an oak log, leaning shoulder to shoulder with Paul Rey. Toni Gaspari is on her other side, talking with Thierry, who was the best sniper in the Maquis until Toni came along. They could have been rivals, but the Frenchman is too old to take umbrage, and instead they share kills – I'll take the left, you take the right. The Boche officers now drive in fully armoured vehicles, if they drive at all.

Watching them, Sophie thinks she might like to become a sniper one day, but knows she has not the patience. Besides, her killing is done up close. Toni Gaspari shoots them; she cuts their throats if they are still breathing. They trust each other and there's a peace between them that she has rarely found with another man. He leans on her and she leans back and thinks this might be what having a brother is like; a very silent brother, who watches her back and doesn't care who she sleeps with.

And now here is Laurence Vaughan-Thomas, who is not like a brother at all, more like . . . she doesn't know what he's like. In some ways, perhaps the ways that count, they are too alike, she and he. In others, he is so distant as to be of a different species.

He has spent the past two hours at the radio cave, which is never a good thing; London gives him orders and he doesn't always agree with them. He catches her eyes now, and she follows him away from the light of the fire, to where they can sit and watch the last light of the sun stitch sky to earth.

'What?'

He hands her the transcript. His handwriting is solid and blocky, so that it's like reading a type-print.

*HERMES TO ZEUS: HIGH FLYER MAY WISH TO WAX
LYRICAL STOP MAY BE FINAL CHANCE QUERY
ZEUS TO HERMES: ODDLY ENOUGH, HE SAID THE SAME
STOP
HERMES TO ZEUS: WE'RE READY STOP JUST GIVE THE
WORD STOP*

Laurence is Hermes, the messenger – also the god of thieves. The Brigadier is Zeus, the Allfather, this much is obvious. Beyond it, their conversations are as cryptic as the messages sent to and from Céline.

*Z TO H: YOUR FATHER'S MOST HATED EVENT TAKES
PLACE TOMORROW STOP FLYBOY WILL BE THERE
STOP COUSINS ARE WITHIN SAME DISTANCE AS
CHARLES TO BOG EASILY DRIVEN STOP HIGHEST PRI-
ORITY STOP TPTB CARE DEEPLY STOP MAKE IT
HAPPEN STOP
H TO Z: WILL DO*

She hands him back the slip of paper. 'Translate for me, please?'

'My father's most hated event was a wedding: any wedding. The Cousins are the American Seventh Army, which is approaching from the south and getting closer to us by the day. They are currently the same distance from us as my uncle Charles – Céline's father, who lives in Cambridge – is to the family's stately home, which is colloquially known as The Bog: essentially a six-hour drive away. Thus, from Saint-Cybard to them is six hours' driving time on good roads. TPTB are The Powers That Be. In my uncle's frame of reference, that equates to either Churchill or Roosevelt. He doesn't deal with underlings.'

'And High Flyer, who is also, I assume, Flyboy?'

'That's our friend Icarus, who flew too near the sun and fell to his death. Or not, in this case. He's been providing us with solid intelligence for years now and we have a duty to help him, besides which, he claims to have a dozen agents embedded deep inside the French Communist party and twice that number highly placed in the Soviet Union, which makes him, frankly, worth any kind of risk.' JJ was with the communists, once, and has contacts there still. And Fabien, of course, is an active member. Sophie makes a note to tell them that there are moles within their ranks. Aloud, she says, 'Your people think there will be war with Russia when this is over?'

'There might be. We have to act as if there will be.'

'And so we are disposable, while Icarus is not?'

He has to think about this. 'I imagine that would be hotly denied were we to say it aloud in the hearing of the high-ups, but yes, essentially that's it. Tomorrow is probably our last chance to get him out before he is either sent east or dies gloriously, but pointlessly, slowing the Americans down for the two whole minutes it takes them to drive their tanks over his body. The wedding is going to give us the ultimate cover to extract him. The question is, will you help?'

'Those are my orders. Even if I have Hitler himself in my sights, I'm to drop everything to get him out.'

'I know, but still . . .'

He understands her too well. 'I will kill Kramme. Whatever else is going on, I will kill Kramme. You can't take that from me. But if I can help your agent escape in the process, I will do it.'

'Thank you.' He pats her on the shoulder, a trait that has begun recently and is, she thinks, friendlier than it seems. 'Call Paul and Toni, then, can you? I have to have a workable plan ready to send back to the Brigadier by eight o'clock tonight.'

CHAPTER TWENTY-SIX

SAINT-CYBARD AND ARC-SOUS-MONTAGNE
4 September 1944

EVEN IN SEPTEMBER, DAWN comes fast to the mountain. Amongst the Maquisards, few words are spoken. They dress, eat, check weapons, swiftly. Céline threads between the fires, checking their checks of their weapons, giving encouragement where it's needed, or caution.

They take six trucks. Those who know the plan spread themselves out, one in each truck, so that when they reach the bottom of the hill, they can say, turn right, not left. We are not going to Saint-Cybard. Look – Céline is already turning. Follow her truck. And when they pull in at a ruined farmstead and alight, it is Céline who lines them up in ranks, as if they were in the army, and issues the orders. We are going to the churchyard. We wait until the bells ring and the congregation walks out of the church – and then we take Kramme.

For the bulk of them, this is news: only a very few were brought into the planning. There are too many semi-strangers here whose ultimate loyalties are unknown.

'Kramme's here?' The question goes around. '*Kramme* is getting married?'

'Is he marrying a Frenchwoman?' Ancil Roche asks. He is a big man with black teeth and halitosis.

He's brash and vulgar and thoroughly dislikeable. In recent weeks, he has been foremost amongst those calling for the summary execution of all collaborator women. Now, he leers at Céline. 'One of the Saint-Cybard whores?'

Laurence would dearly like to strike him. Céline studies him for long, thoughtful moments before she answers. 'Luce Moreau has put herself in the most appalling danger specifically in order to bring about this moment. She is a member of the Maquis as much as any of us, and has been so for far longer than most. If you touch a hair of her head, I will see you shot for murder. I am serious about this.'

Céline is leaner than she was, and grimmer. Ancil Roche does not have what it takes to answer back. He looks down and away and joins the small band of followers these men always attract, the bane of any army.

Céline ignores him. Her orders are crisp. 'Stay silent on the approach. Do not smoke. Do not cough. Do not speak. As we wait behind the wall, do not give us away or we lose our chance to get Kramme. On Fabien's signal, go. If you move before he orders it, I'll shoot you myself.'

Sophie is in the lead truck. Laurence did not – could not – show her the rest of the cipher exchange with the Brigadier:

Z To H: IS OUR SHREW RELIABLE QUERY

*H To Z: SHE PLAYS WITH FULL PASSIONS FOR HERSELF
   FIRST AND THOSE SHE LOVES AFTER STOP*

Z To H: DOES SHE LOVE KRAMME QUERY

*H To Z: PATRICK THINKS SHE DID STOP HE MAY BE RIGHT
   STOP SHE DOESN'T NOW I THINK STOP*

Laurence doesn't want it to be necessary. He wants her to keep killing Boche with the alacrity she has shown heretofore. In battle, she kills with a single-minded dedication, and most of it at close quarters.

In many ways, she carries more luck with her than Céline does, but the men do not view her as their mascot. They laugh with her, and make coarse, affable jokes about her affair with Paul Rey, but there's a grimness to her that causes them to keep well away on the field of battle and nobody was in a hurry to pile into the truck with her.

She follows Fabien out of the truck. Alain Devereaux still looks as much like a teenager as he did when Laurence first met him in Arisaig, but his men adore him, and one day soon he will make a good minister of finance, or perhaps even a president: nothing is impossible. If one hundred and four Maquisards of mixed political affiliation are prepared to follow him through all the vicissitudes of war, hundreds of thousands could easily follow him in the years of peace.

For now, Fabien leads his band over warm grass, ducking low through an orchard to the wall. It is barely four feet high, dry stone, loose in places, with plates of lichen furring the contours. He kneels and places his eye to a gap. Behind wait his dry-mouthed warriors. Keeping so many silent is hard for this length of time, but the forest is a quiet place; they have all taken time to stand beneath the trees and listen to the rush of their own heartbeat, even Ancil Roche.

It occurs to Laurence that he and his fellow Jedburghs are the only ones who don't know what Kramme looks like, and that it would be good to see him before he is shot so full of holes that there's nothing to see. If Sophie wants to be first to kill him, she'll have to run spectacularly fast.

Finding his own gap in the wall, he peers through at the enemy. Fifty yards in front and to his right is a small, stone-built church, with a lean bell tower. To the rear of which is, apparently, a small door. From this, so they have been told, Icarus intends to exit, at the precise moment when Kramme and his new bride emerge from the front and pose for the ciné camera. The bells are their signal: thirty seconds after they start, the action will begin.

The wall that surrounds the church encloses a cemetery that could grace any small – really small – English village. There is a patch of stubby grass that looks as if someone has swung a scythe over it in a hurry, and on this stands an elongated camera atop a tripod. A Boche corporal stands behind it, bored.

Laurence looks away. He has never come to the point where he can stare a man in the face – even at this distance – see the planes of his features, the memories, the hopes . . . and then kill him the way the snipers do.

Snipers are at the heart of the Icarus plan, reckless and desperate as it is. If it has gone well so far, Toni Gaspari and Thierry should by now be in place, rifles steady. When the shooting starts, they are to kill the drivers of all four staff cars and steal the one Thierry estimates to have the greatest speed. They are wearing stolen Boche uniforms and have three American uniforms in the back of the car. When they near the Seventh Army, they will swap and so hope not to be shot.

This is the extent of their strategy. Laurence and Paul Rey – and Sophie if she is remotely willing to follow orders – are to prevent any of the Boche from harming Icarus as he runs from church to car. After that, they can join in with shooting whatever is left of Kramme.

He backs away from the wall and lets out the breath he has been holding. Breathing in again, the air is clear and still, and the smell is of grass and last night's cigarettes, of men's sweat and gun oil. He counts the minutes by the concussion of his heart. His whole body shakes to each beat. He is fitter now than he has ever been, fitter even than he was in Arisaig when he had been carrying logs up hills for weeks. Unexpectedly, he finds himself happier than he has any right to be. Whatever else his life brings, he is grateful to have been a part of this.

A blackbird lets loose a sharp, scolding chuck. Inside the church a hymn rises, of massed male voices in harmony, beautiful in its way. There was a time when he loved German more than English and he hears it now, and knows a passing nostalgia.

And then the bell tolls. By a miracle it is whole, uncracked, and has not been melted down for war munitions.

Still, Fabien doesn't move. Laurence is locked between men: Paul Rey, Daniel, René of the ruined hand, JJ, who is a rock of solid muscle. Céline is at his far side, and Fabien, but it is Sophie who presses against him, a hair trigger ready to fire.

Inside the church, the hymn stops. A priest speaks a last blessing. Amen. Fabien is so still. How can he be still when Laurence can feel a scream rise in his own throat? Over this wall, across the meadow, over the cemetery wall and then death, one way or the other. Sixty German officers, maybe more. Every Boche of any rank from a fifty-mile radius is here, and they're all desperate. The British are close. The Americans are closer. Getting married here, today, is an insane act of defiance. Or it's a trap. This is possible. They know the risk.

Please, God in whom I have never had faith . . . Please let the plans work, both of them.

Please—

'*Go!*'

Up. Up. Up. A hand on the wall, up and over. And run.

God, she's fast, Céline. She's over the wall before Laurence is fully on his feet, but he's always been quick out of the blocks and he's a bare half-stride behind her by the time they pass the nearest yew trees, and JJ, René and Daniel are to his left and Sophie to his right and all he can hear is the rattle-bark of the Stens and the shouts of German officers who have trained for years and do not panic, and the screams of the few who do, and a single shot from his far right that might be – please God, let it be – a rifle, or perhaps two, fired so close together that he can't separate them.

And then again, and it is two. Toni and Thierry, each out-doing the other. Four shots in all.

Kramme! There, on the church steps, a bluster of silver and gold braid on crisp, black wool. And beside Kramme, his bride, ivory to his jet. This must be Luce Moreau, bravest of the brave, standing tall and proud in white satin and lace. She is not screaming. She is shouting, pointing, frantic, directing them out, past the church.

What?

His eyes meet hers, a chance moment, frozen in the bloody chaos. Laurence reads fury on her face and doesn't under-stand it, but he has no time, he has to break the contact, duck and roll. Shots hiss and spit from his left. Out of the side of his eye, he sees the German corporal with the big camera on the tripod. He is panning round, slowly, as if the lens were a machine gun. Laurence lifts his Sten, flips it to single shot and kills him, all without thinking, without even rising to his feet. Not so hard after all, then, to kill a man on whose face he has looked. He turns back to see that, at last, Kramme is running away from the church. Fabien is after him, and Céline, JJ and Daniel, René of the ruined hand . . .

Sophie is not here. Nor Paul Rey.

His orders are redundant. None of the Boche is trying to get to the back of the church. They are all being heroes, sprinting forward to make a wall between the retreating Kramme and the Maquis: grey uniforms and black, sparks of gold, flesh and blood. Why do men do this?

Where is Sophie?

Instinct thrusts Laurence down again. He hears a round smack into the wall of the church above him. He rolls away and comes up with the church to his left, running back towards the Icarus door.

Two hundred yards ahead is a road, at the edge of which is parked a row of German staff cars. Toni and Thierry have done all that was asked of them. Dead drivers lie on the blooded earth and – yes! – a single Mercedes convertible is rolling forward at walking pace with Thierry at the wheel.

A lone Boche is running towards the open passenger door, stripping off his jacket as he does so: Icarus is keeping his side of the bargain.

Toni Gaspari is ahead of him. As Laurence watches, the little Italian leaps into the rear seat facing backwards, and props his rifle on the back of the bench. His head is bare. He, too, has thrown off the German uniform. He never wanted it in the first place. He is shouting at someone.

'Sophie!'

Laurence hears the word faintly, in echo.

Sophie? So she is here, not back at the church, killing Kramme. He is surprised at that. He looks around and she is ahead and to his right, running at an angle towards the road, to the car and – what? – even as he watches, she lifts her Sten and fires an eight-shot burst at Icarus. The range is too far for accuracy; a line of rounds smacks up dirt from the road a good twenty yards short of the running man.

'Sophie!' Toni Gaspari shouts again from the car. 'Stop!'

She doesn't stop. She fires another long, raking burst that empties the gun so that she has to change the magazine, but she can do that on the run, Laurence knows this – he taught her. Jesus Christ and all his little fishes, is she working for bloody Kramme after all?

'Sophie! *Stop!*'

Laurence is as fast as Céline now, faster. But Sophie is thirty yards ahead and she has her new magazine in, and while she may be doing her very best to destroy the car and all its occupants, the thing about Toni is that, whatever she has done, whoever she is working for, he is never going to shoot back. Not at her.

Laurence is gaining ground. A dozen strides and he'll reach her, maybe less. Laurence hasn't fired yet. *Be ready to pull the plug.* He might want to, but his fingers are not willing. If he can kill a Boche corporal, surely he can kill a traitor? He raises his Sten.

Ten more yards.

Icarus, sprinting like a man possessed, reaches the car and throws himself into the back seat, leaving the door swinging. The tyres scream on the road as Thierry puts his foot to the floor and slews it out into the road. Sophie's mouth is open in a silent scream and Laurence, slowing, sees her go down on one knee and flip her Sten to single, take aim and fire one final shot.

There's a foot, maybe less, between the two men in the back seat: the German and the Italian. And the car is moving forwards and sideways with exhaust smoke pluming the air. It cannot be that she was aiming for Toni.

But that is who she hits.

A plash of red and Toni Gaspari, sole survivor of a bloody Boche assault on his village, spins back and round and the swerving car completes a balletic pirouette that jettisons him from the back seat onto the road.

Icarus is gone and Sophie has stopped shooting. Maybe her gun has jammed or is empty or . . . it doesn't matter; Laurence is on her, and he doesn't care. He slings his Sten over his

394

shoulder, draws his Colt and places the muzzle against her skull, at the back, angled down. He is breathing hard as a raced-out horse. His pulse pushes dark flashes across his eyes. 'I should kill you now.'

'You should have done it months ago.' Her voice is free of all inflection. Her gaze rests on Paul Rey, who is here now, his face a chalky grey, his freckles splashed like old blood across his nose. He has seen Toni, but his focus is on Sophie and hers is on him. Laurence is irrelevant. Paul says, slowly, carefully, 'Sophie, we didn't know. We. Did. Not. Know.'

'You didn't, maybe. What about him?' Her chin jerks over her shoulder at Laurence. She really doesn't care about his gun. 'Or his fucking uncle?'

What?

And then: *What?!*

It's Paul he reads, the disgust written raw across his features, and it's not directed at Sophie, but at him, Laurence, and through him, to—

Oh, Christ. He looks at the departing car, at the man in the back seat, who is waving. He never knew what Kramme looked like. He does now: middle height, sandy blond hair, on the lean side; fit as a flea.

Hell. Bloody hell. Three years of bluff and counter-bluff, of ciphers and cryptic half-tells and the long, slow dance of deception. Icarus is Kramme. Kramme is Icarus. There is a terrible symmetry to it and he is not at all sure that the Brigadier does not know.

Laurence turns to look at the church, where men are dying in a blaze of gunfire, and slowly, he turns back to Paul Rey and Sophie.

To Paul: 'You've never seen Kramme. How did you know it was him?'

'I didn't.' He jerks a thumb down towards Sophie. 'She did. And I trust her.'

There speaks love. But love is not always blind.

To both of them, Laurence says, 'I didn't know. I swear to you on Toni Gaspari's life, I had no idea.'

'And the Brigadier?' Sophie asks, flatly.

He remembers a conversation at Montagu Square: a hint of other wars being fought behind the scenes, of priorities beyond the obvious. He says, 'We are family. He wouldn't lie to me.'

'Tell that to Toni Gaspari. And whoever court martials me. Paul, I'm so sorry. I didn't mean . . .'

'I know.' Standing, Sophie lets drop her gun. All the fight has gone out of her, but she is gazing over Laurence's shoulder towards the church, where the firing has stopped. To him, she says, 'You need to tend to your cousin. The Boche have just killed her Patron.'

'Stop. Theo, *stop*. It's over. It's over. It's . . . over.'

The Boche are dead. They are beyond dead. His cousin Theodora has emptied six magazines into the bodies and is still firing. Approaching, Laurence coughs on cordite and his ears sing.

'Theo . . .'

'Céline. I am Céline.' She is a doll, a marionette. She is not weeping any more than Sophie is. He wonders when women stopped weeping and why he didn't notice. The barrel of her gun is giving off a radiant heat, like a furnace. Empty magazines lie at her side. She runs out of rounds, and so has to stop.

He turns her, shoulder and arm. 'Céline, then. Come away.'

'Fabien?'

'I'm sorry.'

Alain Devereaux, known as Fabien, is not dead, but he is not likely to survive the day. Three rounds have hit him: leg, shoulder and gut, and he is losing blood, fast. His life is measured in hours.

396

'Patrick will save him.' Céline stands, looking round the men, counting casualties, and deaths: two others, dead. And Toni Gaspari. How can he tell her this? That he, Laurence, has just helped Sturmbannführer Maximilian Kramme escape. I'm sorry. I'm so sorry. I didn't know. He says it over and over in his head. I did not know. How could I know? Each word, each syllable, sounds hollow. The Brigadier knew: as time passes, he is coming to believe that. He is not sure he can ever forgive him.

Aloud, he says nothing. Sophie says nothing. Paul Rey is carrying Toni's body back to the trucks. Céline does not ask how he died, or whether Icarus made a clean escape. Certainly, she does not know who Icarus is.

Her priorities are elsewhere. 'Patrick's a doctor. He'll make it all right.' Her battle shirt is black with blood. As far as Laurence can tell, when she saw Fabien fall, she ran out into the open and stood there, firing in arcs until every Boche soldier in front of her was dead.

Laurence finds the body with many medals. 'Kramme', who was not Kramme, is a pulped mass of brain and bone. He could be Hitler and nobody would be any the wiser.

So the world will think that Kramme died this day. Christ, it keeps on getting worse.

His bride . . . she knew. She was trying to warn them. 'Luce?' Laurence asks. 'Where's Luce Moreau?'

Nobody will tell him. By looking where they will not glance, he finds that Luce, too, is dead. He is afraid that Céline killed her in a red-mist rage, but when he looks at her body, she has a single shot through the centre of her forehead, fired at close range: the scorch marks are clear. When he asks, nobody will admit to doing it. Nobody particularly seems to care, except Daniel, whose fiancée is her sister.

And so for Daniel's sake, and for his own sanity, Laurence asks everyone, man after man, and thus, by a process of elimination, comes to the conclusion that Ancil Roche shot Luce

Moreau for the crime of sleeping with the enemy. The fact that she sent the message with Véronique that brought them here seems not to have mitigated any actions on her part.

Laurence tells Céline, who is now, by default and by popular acclaim, the Patron of the Maquis de Morez, and it is not his place to usurp her authority.

She steps back from organizing Fabien's transport back to the camp. 'Sophie, go with him. Keep him alive until Patrick can heal him.' To Laurence: 'Where is Roche now?'

'I don't know. Nobody can find him.'

Under Céline's questioning, the men are more forthcoming. Ancil Roche, it transpires, has stolen one of the trucks and gone to 'liberate' Saint-Cybard.

Which is, when they think about it, not such a terribly bad idea.

The battle for Saint-Cybard is short and brutal. Two things are clear: first, that they are expected, and second, that without Kramme (God, how did we not *know*?), there is no real defensive organization.

Very few Boche are here, none of commissioned rank, and those that remain have poor morale: they die easily. With fresh ammunition, and fresh guns where they need them, the fighters of the Maquis storm in the wake of Ancil Roche. Laurence finds himself at one edge of the main square, a place he has never seen except on maps, and in his head, listening to the stories of Sophie and Patrick.

Thus he knows as if by sight the Hôtel Cinqfeuilles to his left; to his right the town hall steps where so many broken bodies lie. A desultory fountain dribbles water ahead. Outside the hotel, a burned-out staff car spews oily smoke to the sky. Inside it, men shout in French. A woman screams, a high knife of sound that ends for lack of air, not an end to the pain.

'That's not right.' Paul Rey is with him. He is quiet, and seems uniquely uninterested in killing Boche.

The scream comes again. Laurence sets his jaw. 'I never liked Ancil Roche.' He shoves a new magazine into his Sten and sets off towards the Hôtel Cinqfeuilles.

'Wait.' Rey catches his arm. 'It's not our place to stop it.'

'Then whose?'

Paul nods to where Céline sprints across the square. 'Look.'

'She'll kill them,' Laurence says, and he, too, begins to run. He shoulders in through the door of the hotel. He won't be in time to cut her off, but he may be in time to—

'Dear God.'

Amidst the debris of ruined opulence, two children – infants, really – lie dead, their throats opened to the backbone, their bodies sheathed in blood. And between them, a young woman, straggled-blonde, thin, dressed in pale-green linen with lilies embroidered on the hem, sprawls against the back wall, unconscious, or nearly so: she might be dead, Laurence can't tell.

Her face is red raw and swollen. Her dress is dragged obscenely high. Dark blood pools beneath it. Off to one side Daniel is being held in a bear hug of iron by JJ. The big man has bruises on his cheeks where Daniel's head has battered him, but he is not letting go.

So this is Lisette Moreau, Daniel's fiancée, sister to the dead girl at the church. Laurence thinks she may still be alive.

Céline, evidently, thinks the same. 'Larry, see to her.' There is a world – the military world – in which Laurence Vaughan-Thomas outranks his cousin, but it exists on another planet. Here, he follows her orders, and Paul Rey with him. They muscle through the ring of a dozen men, one of whom is Ancil Roche. Inside the ring, a raw-faced bank clerk is held at gunpoint.

Laurence reaches the fallen woman, seeks the pulse at

her neck with one hand, while with the other he draws down her dress to cover her modesty. A pulse jumps and threads beneath his fingers. She is alive, but mercifully unconscious.

He lifts her. She has bird-bones that weigh nothing. Her head flops against his shoulder. He carries her out of the circle, lays her on the remains of a chaise, sends René for water and whatever else he can find to clean her up.

'Who did this?' Céline's voice is a knife blade. Anarchy stalks here: already, it pushes at the walls of this shattered, echoing space.

'We did,' Ancil Roche answers. He is bearded, broad with a drinker's belly and a backside like a rhinoceros, even now, after all the deprivations of the war. His teeth are foul.

Céline is taller than he is. She looks down at him, a thoroughbred amongst carthorses. 'We?'

'We, the men of the Maquis de Morez.'

'You slaughtered two children and raped Lisette Moreau because you are of the Maquis? *Fabien's* Maquis?'

'She is Lisette Andreu,' the clerk says, 'my wife. And they do this because you ordered it.'

'I did not.'

'And yet, you did not control them.'

'I am controlling them now.' There is a tone in his family that Laurence has not heard in many years and this is it. Beside him, Paul Rey sucks in a breath. All around, men stand more upright.

Céline's gaze rakes the circle and comes back to Ancil Roche. 'Come here.' She crooks a finger. Roche steps forward. Laurence cannot see his face, but Paul, who has a better angle, murmurs, 'The bastard still thinks it's funny.'

Laurence shakes his head. 'She's got his back to the stairs. Wooden panels all the way up and nobody behind.' He feels faintly ill.

Roche hooks his fingers in his belt, and sets his feet apart. 'I am here.'

'I gave very clear orders that the women were not to be violated. I am anxious to hear why you felt you had the right to ignore me.'

'She was a whore. She married the Milice. That filth' – he spits at the clerk – 'filled the cellars for the Boche. We who suffered there knew him.' Roche was held for questioning earlier in the war. He was released unharmed, but he wears his three days of captivity as a badge of honour. 'It is what she deserved.'

He talks past her, expecting support, but the men who were with him before are not any longer. They stare at the floor and those with stains at their groins stare hardest.

Céline allows the silence to grow. At length, she says, 'The Moreau sisters were the bravest women in Saint-Cybard. Luce kept herself close to Kramme, at enormous personal risk. Lisette slept with a man she despised' – her gaze rests on the clerk, who is not a clerk – 'for four years so she could bring us information directly from the heart of the beast. She bore his children, for God's sake. She has saved your life more often than you will ever know. And now, by your actions, you have thrown it away.'

Roche's smile fades. His eyes shift, left to right and back again. 'You can't seriously—'

Céline doesn't move except to alter the angle of her Sten by a few degrees and slightly flex her index finger. The single shot takes Roche on the brow, centrally, a neat, black hole; exactly the shot that killed Luce Moreau. Roche stumbles backwards onto the stairs where the girl lay. His body spasms in the aftershocks of life.

Céline turns a full circle, taking up the gaze of each man, and dropping it again. 'I will not enquire further as to who took part in this, when Roche so clearly led. But if any one of you touches another woman against her will, I will not take the time to ask you why, I will simply kill you. Anyone who thinks this is unreasonable may make his case now.'

Nobody speaks against her. Nobody is ever again likely to speak against Céline. She nods at the shattered bank clerk. Laurence has heard of Gaston Andreu, prison governor, chief of the Milice, the man whose children Sophie delivered at the start of her tenure as the nurse of Saint-Cybard. The man whose wife was Daniel's fiancée, whose children are dead. To him, Céline says, 'Lisette Moreau will live her life a hero. Your marriage was never real. Everyone will know she made a fool of you.'

The shot that kills him is a mercy. Céline steps back, away from the growing leak of his blood. 'Take these two outside and burn the bodies. I want nobody made into a martyr for later. JJ, take Daniel back to camp. Laurence, Paul, take Lisette. The rest of you, come with me. We have a town to clean up.'

CHAPTER TWENTY-SEVEN

THE MOUNTAINS OF MOREZ
4 September 1944

FABIEN, FORMER PATRON OF the Maquis de Morez, holds
Sophie's hand as he dies.

He takes a long time of it: longer than her first, urgent triage
had suggested. She gives him morphine, although he tries to
order her not to; but Céline is Patron now, and Céline has
ordered him to be given whatever Sophie has. So he survives the
ruts and potholes of the road, and then the ruts and ridges of the
track and the stretcher up to the infirmary, where Patrick,
alerted by their shouts, has lit a fire and put water on to boil.

Arriving, Sophie says, 'Céline says he's to have everything.'

In English, Fabien countermands the order, 'I'm still the
Patron and I say you are not to waste drugs on a dying man.
Patrick, you are my friend. Listen to me.' It takes him a long
time to say this, but Patrick is his friend, and listens to him: he
doesn't waste the drugs.

In the silence that follows as they wait for Fabien to die,
Patrick says to Sophie, *What can you tell me?*

For years afterwards, she wonders at that. Not 'What happened?' but 'What can you tell me?'

She thinks, Nothing, I can tell you nothing, not you, not anyone, but Fabien grips her hand and nods and so she opens her mouth and it all spills out: Kramme was Icarus.

Icarus was Kramme.

The whole wedding was a set-up and I killed Toni Gaspari.

The fire sparks and spits. Flames sigh up by her head. She wants to swap places with Fabien. She looks past him to the pines and pleads with the dark and settled silence: only let him live, and I will die in his place.

She does not die. Nor, yet, does Fabien.

Patrick says, *Sophie, help me.*

It's an order and she doesn't resist. Patrick has poured brandy. The harsh, sweet smell of it mingles with the smoke. He wants to give some to Fabien and so they hoist him, one on either side, and hold the mug to his lips and wait while he fails to swallow and has to spit it out and then tries again and gets some down.

As they lay him back down, the dying man grips her arm. He has no strength. 'It wasn't your fault.'

'I shot a lieutenant of the US army. They'll hang me for it.'

'They might not. But anyway, you don't need to tell them.'

'Someone will.' Laurence. Céline. Paul Rey. Patrick. Laurence, definitely.

Patrick says, *You'd be surprised what will not be said.*

He sits on Fabien's other side. He has taken it remarkably well, this tale of treachery. Kramme has run free when he was promised a death and he sits there, looking at her, and she can't tell what he's thinking. She meets his gaze. He holds it for long enough to show he can, then turns to Fabien. *What can we do for you?* Because it is obvious he is holding on for something.

'Tell me Céline is alive, that Saint-Cybard is liberated. Then I can die at peace.'

They can't tell him that yet, and they can't lie. There's an uncomfortable gap. He grips Sophie's arm again. 'The notebook in my cabin. Can you get it?' And she goes, even though she thinks she is being sent away so the men can talk in her absence. Certainly there is a change in the air between them when she comes back, although she has no time to test its textures because the ground shakes with the throaty thrum of the trucks and all he has to do now is stay alive while they climb the hill.

Something must show on her face because Fabien says, 'They won't hang you.'

And Patrick: *Trust us.*

Still, she tastes bile in her mouth as they come fast up the hill and yes, Céline is alive, and yes, Saint-Cybard is French again, although there are two small bodies carried up to lie beside Toni Gaspari.

A bruised and weeping Daniel carries his fiancée up after them: Lisette Moreau, who was once Lisette Andreu, and whose so-courageous sister is dead. She is unconscious and will need a great deal of help, but she will have to wait a moment longer, because Céline has come to kneel at Fabien's side and Sophie wonders that she did not see this love between them. Like everyone else, she was too busy looking at Véronique.

Céline lifts his hand and kisses it. 'Don't go, Alain. Don't go. Please, don't go.'

'I have to go. You have to stay.' He pats her arm. He is beyond gripping. 'My book?' Sophie brings it. 'Inside the front cover.'

They read together the English lines he has written: for Céline, for Patrick perhaps, for Laurence. For all those who came to liberate the nation of France.

AND THUS BY ACCIDENT WE BECAME AS GODS
BLYTHE CHILDREN OF THE MOUNTAIN

WARRIORS OF VENGEANCE
UNFORGIVING, UNFORGIVEN
UNFORGOTTEN

Fabien kisses the back of Céline's hand. 'Never forget,' he says, and lets go.

Shovels are found enough for one in five people and Sophie joins the others to dig graves in the soft, black loam beneath the trees – for Fabien and Toni and the two small bodies, who are, it transpires, the twins of Lisette Moreau.

The circumstances of their death are obscure to her, but Daniel has two broken ribs, one on either side, where JJ held him, so it can't have been good. They give him morphine, and still he does not sleep, only sits by the fire, staring into the flames, not quite watching while Patrick and Sophie bathe Lisette Moreau, inject morphine and penicillin, wash her wounds with river water, well salted.

Later, alone, Sophie leans back against the wall of the infirmary and tries not to think about the day.

A shadow falls over her.

'Sophie?' It's Laurence. She hasn't seen him since the trucks came back. In a part of her mind, she thought he might have died in Saint-Cybard except that someone would have told her. He comes down now, from the direction of the radio cave. She feels sick again. It may be she will never feel anything else.

Outside, the others are sitting round the infirmary fire: Patrick, Céline, JJ, Paul Rey – who keeps trying to get her alone to speak to her. She is apart from them, as she always has been.

To them all – to Sophie most – Laurence says, 'I told the Brigadier that Toni Gaspari was shot by the Boche. If anyone chooses to tell him anything different . . .'

406

'They'll hang you, too,' says Paul.

Sophie says, 'Then you'd better plan a way out because Thierry will have told them different by now.'

'Thierry is dead. Kramme shot him shortly before he got to the American lines and drove the car in himself. He told his debriefers that he was shot by the Maquis as they escaped.'

'That's not true!'

'I know. And the Brigadier knows it too. He has had someone track down the body and it is clear that he died with a single bullet to the head, fired at close range from the passenger side.'

'So they'll hang Kramme?' The black cloud that envelops her heart parts a little, lets the firelight in.

'I'm afraid not. Kramme is a prize worth any number of Thierrys. I tell you this not because I believe it is right, or reasonable, but to explain that we do ourselves no favours if we tell the world what we know. In fact, the first one that decides to do so is likely to find himself, or' – to Céline as much as to Sophie, which is interesting – 'herself, dead in a ditch. This particular game is played for the highest stakes by men whose priorities are wider than ours and whose sense of morality is weighed on different scales.'

'So your uncle did know all along?'

'About the identity of Icarus? He swears not. He was most emphatic.'

'Do you believe him?'

'I want to.' Laurence stands alone on the far side of the fire, looking uncomfortable. As far as Sophie is concerned, he has good reason.

Céline, who knows him better, says, 'There's something else.'

'Yes. I'm sorry.' From his pocket, he draws a slip of paper and lays it on the log.

They read by firelight.

407

**BY ORDER OF GENERAL DE GAULLE STOP ALL
NON-UNIFORMED BRITISH FORCES PERSONNEL
TO QUIT FRANCE BY 17 SEPTEMBER STOP**

**GENERAL ORDER SOE (F) SECTION STOP
TRAVEL TO PARIS ASAP BY ANY MEANS
NECESSARY STOP**

TRANSPORT LEAVES 1600 17.09

'But you have fed us, armed us, led us . . .' Sophie stares at it, uncomprehending. 'How can he do that?'

'He can't.' Paul Rey grabs the slip and crumples it up. 'The stupid, stupid, jumped-up, pathetic little . . . fascist. He can't do this. He *can't*!'

Not you. You're in uniform. You can stay. Patrick's voice is different, harsher. They all turn to him. He says, *So that we are all clear, I am not going home like . . . this.*

Laurence catches his arm. 'Patrick, you'll be a war hero. You'll get a VC, a pension. It won't be like the last war with boards of retired colonels carving men up on the basis of their injuries: half a pension if you only lost one limb, a third if you lost an eye but the other one still works. It won't be like that. We won't allow it. It'll be done properly this time.'

You think? And then what? How many tongueless doctors do you know?

'Your family will—'

Despise me. My nearest and dearest are entirely like yours. A man comes home with his shield or on it. Half measures are not worthy. Trust me on this.

With his shield . . . ? Sophie has met the Brigadier only briefly and she doesn't pretend to understand Céline, but she sees the glance that Laurence shares with his cousin and the understanding that passes between them. Their family, evidently, is not like hers, or any other that she knows.

With finality, Laurence says, 'We'll get you a uniform and you can stay.'

That raises a smile, at least. *I don't think it works like that.*

Paul Rey has been saving a cigar for an important moment. He lights it now, and blows blue smoke at the sky. 'Who's going to know? I mean, really. The whole damned country's in chaos. Nobody knows from one moment to the next if Patrick Sutherland is alive or dead. Larry's right. We'll get you a uniform and a new identity and then . . .'

And then I go home later? To a court martial for insubordination on top of everything else? I don't think so.

'What do you want, then?' Laurence wrests the slip from Paul Rey's hand and throws the fragments on the fire, where they spin and turn in the heat. The ink becomes white, the paper a silvery grey. They become dust that rises to the dark. 'If you tell me you want to die, after all we have done, I shall strike you, honestly. I'm not listening to that ever again.'

I don't want to die. I will remain here.

Laurence runs his hands through his hair. With deliberate brutality, he says, 'Patrick, you can't. France is liberated. The Maquis will disband by the winter. Everyone will go home and start rebuilding their nation. What will you do then? Is a tongueless doctor more useful in France than in England? I'm sorry, but nobody else is going to say this to you and it always seems to come down to me, but you can't live here on your own.'

'He won't live on his own. I'll be with him.' Sophie finds herself speaking the words without any conscious thought. The sentences pile on after, one atop the other as if they have always been there, somewhere, in the back of her mind: whatever Paul may want; whatever I may want, this is my duty, the contour and shape of my life. I have always been coming here.

Sophie doesn't look at Patrick, and certainly not at Paul Rey, whose gaze is a burning brand in her back. She looks at

Laurence. 'Daniel's family owns half of the Jura. They'll sell us some land near his mother's farmhouse, I'm sure. They'll help us build a house. We can stay here, among friends.'

'Sophie, that's charming, but he's a British army officer. He can't just ignore an order. He has to go back. Maybe later, when the army has let him go, he can return, but—'

'Laurence, think. Paul was right, this whole country's in chaos. Men are being let out of prisons. Others are being shot for collaboration. So Patrick Sutherland died in the fighting today and someone else is here, François Duval, a French national, or maybe Belgian, returned home from the war to settle. We even have the papers to prove it.'

'The Firm knows that name. It's on file.'

'Files can be lost. You can make that happen.'

He doesn't deny this, but, nodding, says, 'You'll need a back history, bigger than the one we made. Both of you will need this.'

'JJ can fix it.' JJ is a fixer. He can make anything happen.

Paul Rey is starting to stand up, and so, to be clear, to show them this is not negotiable, she has to say something more. 'In time, Patrick and I will be married, if he'll have me. I will become Madame Amélie Duval. We will build a life here.' She turns to him. 'If you will have me?'

This is not as it should be. Whatever she has felt for Patrick Sutherland, or feels now, this is not what he has imagined or wanted. He stares at her, flatly. She thinks he will refuse her. It may be that a part of her hopes he will.

In the end, he takes her hand and lifts it to his lips. *That would be very kind*, he says, which is almost enough to finish her.

'You might want this.' Paul Rey from behind her, thickly. He steps forward and lays by their fire a flat cylinder in a dulled, pale metal. Nobody knows what it is. It may explode, but she doesn't believe that of him.

With a fixed-tight smile, he says, 'It's the film from the ciné camera at the church. Kramme wanted to record his wedding. The photographer swung round. It has the detail, I expect, of Kramme's escape.' His pale grey eyes find Sophie's. He is brave, truly. If the world were different . . . it would be different. He gives a small salute. 'There may come a day when you will find it useful.'

It can't end like this. Sophie has to give him something. She kneels, and finds she cannot stand again. From beside the fire, she offers him back his gift. 'It will be safest kept with you,' she says. 'We know then, who we can trust to show it to the world if Kramme comes for us.'

It is not a great gift, but it is better than nothing and he, who understands her best, understands this. He takes it, and salutes a second time, and walks away so that neither of them has to speak again.

CHAPTER TWENTY-EIGHT

I N THE DARK NIGHT, the rain has settled to a steady drizzle that picks up the shine of the headlights and sprays it left and right with the windscreen wipers.

Leaving the studio, Martin Gillard offers to drive and Picaut accepts. On the way to the car, he retrieved a SIG Sauer exactly like her own from a locked drawer in the basement, and he currently wears it openly in a shoulder holster over his shirt. She is not armed and hasn't been since the shootout in the burning cathedral and all that followed it. She has trained again, with Rollo helping, but, thus far, has not carried her gun in a professional context. Tomorrow, she will pick it up again, definitely.

The wipers are hypnotic. Half asleep, Picaut runs through the moment when Laurence Vaughan-Thomas opens the door of his hotel room and realizes how she has found him. She can see the wry smile, the small shrug, the decision to trust her with all that he knows and—

'Here. Pull in here!' Give him credit, Martin's not a bad driver and his Merc handles neatly in the wet. He angles tight across the road and pulls up at the kerb outside the wine mer-chant's, where a big, broad, bald drunk is slumped in the doorway. It was his size that caught her eye, the shine from his head, the style of his shoe as it flopped on the pavement . . . Christ on a bike, Conrad Lakoff is going to go ballistic . . .

Picaut is out, running through the rain, kneeling, careful already not to disturb the crime scene, leaning in to feel the carotid to be sure Jean-Jacques Crotteau is dead; not that there's any doubt when a wartime Colt lies beside him and the neat hole in his right temple is matched by a less neat one on the opposite side of his head.

He is warm. When she nudges his foot with her own, it flicks away and rebounds back, as it would if he were merely unconscious. When she holds a piece of coarse paper edge-on to the blood-and-brain mix on the wall, the liquid fraction soaks into the weave. So death was less than an hour ago, probably less than thirty minutes.

'Fuck. Fuckfuckfuckfuck *fuck*.' The only good thing is that JJ does not have two bullet wounds in his chest and one in his head. Thus far, and thus far only, Ducat has been spared his worst nightmare, but the Americans are going to go mad, par-ticularly Conrad and Edward Lakoff – the future head of the NSA and the former senator with friends who still walk the cor-ridors of power. Countries have gone to war over less than this.

Picaut calls Ducat second, after the ambulance. 'We're in the Rue d'Angleterre. We can hold this, but not for long. You need to call Conrad Lakoff.'

Ducat says, 'He's giving his paper.'

'He'll be finished by now and if he isn't, one of the guards will get him a message. You need to be here before him.'

'On my way.'

Rollo says the same thing, as does Sylvie, who volunteers to pick up Petit-Evard in passing.

Martin Gillard tucks himself into the doorway of the

413

pharmacy next door. There, in the relative dry, he rolls himself a cigarette and lights it. 'Want one?'

'Not yet.' She has never smoked. Tonight might be a first, but she'd rather have coffee. The wine merchant's is closed, which, given Gillard's earlier confession, is probably a good thing.

'We're meant to think it's suicide,' he says.

'Or, given Pierre Fayette's murder-made-to-look-like-suicide earlier today, we're meant to think it isn't.' She presses her hands to her eyes. 'Either way, this is Conrad Lakoff's grandfather. Life is about to get messy.'

'Not if we're clever.' Gillard blows smoke at the sky. 'We could move the body.'

Picaut laughs aloud. 'Martin, we're the police. Just at this moment, you're my assistant. We can't move him.' Interesting thought, though. She tilts her head. 'Anyway, what use would that be?'

'I'm not sure. But this isn't an accident – not the death, not the location, not the way he's died. He was placed here for a reason. If we move him, that reason might show itself.'

'You're speaking from experience?'

'Let's say that I know how these people think, and just now they think they are driving the narrative. If we change it, they might panic, and panicked people make mistakes.'

'They also kill people. Although actually, in terms of our suspects, the field is narrowing fast. The only real question' – Picaut leans back against the wall – 'is whether they are fit, young agents of the special forces, who don't care what we know because they've got the protection of the world's only remaining – and deeply unstable – superpower. Or very, very old agents of long-dead units who don't care because they don't have long to live anyway.'

Martin Gillard says, 'There's always a third option, which is that whoever they are, their motives outweigh any sense of risk.'

'In which case, we need to find the motive.' She stands

upright. 'Stay here. When Rollo turns up, tell him to process as usual and keep it quiet.'

'Where are you going?'

'To find the very, very old agents.'

He catches her arm. 'Not alone, you're not. You're unarmed.'

'Yes, alone. Exactly because I'm unarmed.' She pushes him away. 'If I'm not back by the time the ambulance comes, tell Rollo to call Patrice. He'll let you know where I've gone.'

The hotel is set back from the street, behind spear-topped wrought-iron railings. The concierge is white-haired and charming and yes, it is possible for her to visit room nine, if Madame will wait while he makes a phone call?

Madame reveals herself to be Captain and it transpires that, this being the case, the phone call can be dispensed with.

Room nine is on the second floor. She runs up a curving staircase in pre-Revolutionary style beneath the light of an understated chandelier. Left at the top and third on the right and she doesn't knock.

'Laurence. René. JJ Crotteau has been—' The room is empty, neatly cleared. It smells of cigarette smoke and coffee and action. A footstep falls behind her and the concierge is there, with the whine of an elevator in the background.

'If the Captain would allow me?' He carries a message, left by the elderly gentleman with the white hair and the British accent who said she might call in for it. 'He also left a mobile phone, for your safekeeping.'

The message is written in English on the hotel's headed notepaper.

Captain Picaut: My apologies for brevity, but events are moving faster than we can control. I advise you to look in the oldest book on Elodie's shelf. Read what you find therein concerning certain salient events that

415

*occurred deep in our past. They may help you to fill in
the gaps.*

*We did not kill JJ; on this, I give you my word. It may be
that this death is exactly what it seems. In any case, we
deliver to you his mobile phone. It may be of value in
your investigations.*

Yours truly, LVT.

To the best of her knowledge, the message is plain text
without any kind of code, but she trusts nothing any more,
least of all Laurence Vaughan-Thomas. She photographs the
page, sends it to Patrice and folds it into an inner pocket. *We
did not kill JJ.* She might believe him. She's not sure. What
matters, anyway, is why. Why JJ Crotteau? Why now? Why
Sophie, Pierre – and John Lakoff in Virginia? Why . . . and
then who?

Back at the crime scene, Rollo and Sylvie are struggling to
retain control in the face of gathering crowds, a steaming
Ducat – and Conrad Lakoff, newly arrived. He has not brought
his father, but four of his big, muscled guards stand behind
him. More and more, Orléans is beginning to feel like an
extension of Washington DC.

'I told you he was in danger. I *told* you . . .' Lakoff's grief fills
the street around his grandfather's body. He grasps Picaut by
the shoulders. 'You said you'd put your best people on it.'

Behind, she feels Rollo and Martin Gillard each take half a
step forward and then stop.

'We did put our best on it,' Picaut says. 'And you said you'd
let me know if he used his mobile phone. Did he?' Her face
itches again, which is interesting given the long gap since the
last time she noticed it.

She steps away from his grasp, slides her hands into her
pockets and hitches her heel up a wall. She could not be less of

a threat. In the background, the four guards lift the body of JJ Crotteau into the ambulance. He really was remarkably large. Death has not diminished him.

Conrad Lakoff and his men stand by the doors as the body is hefted in. 'I can't believe . . .'

She says, 'I am genuinely sorry for your loss, but we did everything we possibly could. You know what your grandfather was, and what skills he had. If he didn't want to be found, we stood no chance of finding him. What we need to do now is to find out why he died.'

'You need to find out who killed him.'

She catches his eye. He shifts away first. She says, 'It looks like suicide. It's possible that's exactly what it is.'

'You can't believe that? After Pierre Fayette . . .' The silence stretches thin and tense.

Eventually, she says, 'If you have any new information about Fayette's death that might help our enquiries, now would be a good time to tell me.'

'I don't.' Flushed, he says, 'If you need me, I'll be at the conference—'

'If we find anything, I'll let you know. Give your father my apologies and my condolences for his loss.'

'Thank you, Captain. In spite of everything, you have my full confidence.' He passes his hands over his eyes. 'Please—' That grip on Picaut's shoulder again. 'Let me know the moment you have anything.'

He leaves in a black BMW, flanked by a security detail of men who very nearly match him in size. Ducat stands in a puddle of light beneath a street lamp, watching the tail lights depart. 'Well, that could have gone worse.' He turns to her, hands deep in the pockets of a gabardine coat. 'Does he know who did it?'

'I'm not ruling it out. This is either a murder that we're meant to think is a suicide because this morning's so clearly wasn't – in which case he's in the frame for that one. Or it's a suicide that we're meant to think is a murder, for exactly the same reason. In which case we have to ask ourselves why JJ Crotteau, a man with no scruples, and no conscience that anyone has ever detected, might choose to shoot himself in a public place while his grandson is live on a stage in front of fifty of the world's highest-classified intelligence professionals, if it wasn't to give him a cast-iron alibi?'

'Good luck sorting that one out.' Ducat laughs, dryly. 'Who's next?'

She shrugs. 'Two old Maquisards are still on the loose. They'll be dead if our killer finds them before we do, unless one of them is our killer. Either way, we have to find Elodie Duval before anyone else does.'

'And perhaps find a motive?'

'That would be good. All of this goes back to their war. I just don't understand exactly how.'

'But you will.' He smiles again. Twice in one day. 'Keep me in the loop.'

She watches his tail lights go: red patches, reflected in kaleidoscope patterns on the road.

From behind her, Rollo says, 'And that, too, could have gone worse.'

'I liked it better when it did. There's something wrong with him when he's not angry.'

'Time enough.' He leans against the wall beside her. 'In the meantime, I've been pulling in some favours. According to people who know these things, Sophie Destivelle worked under the direct command of one JJ Crotteau, recently deceased. But she also did work on the side for the CIA and MI6, in which context she was run by Paul Rey and Laurence Vaughan-Thomas, respectively. Nobody really liked this blurring of boundaries, but they were old school, tight as a gnat's arse – I am quoting directly – and they were very, very good.

Between the three of them, they pulled off several high-profile and extremely unattributable assassinations.'

'Extremely unattributable? Is that even a thing?'

He grins. 'It gets better. Laurence Vaughan-Thomas was amongst the luminaries of the British SIS until well into the eighties. His full title is Sir Laurence Vaughan-Thomas, sixth Viscount Sarnforth, DFC, VC. He tried to turn down the VC but they wouldn't let him. I couldn't find out what it was for. Either way, his kindly old buffer image is well honed, but it's a front. His sort never really retires.'

'Does anyone think he shot Sophie?'

'Absolutely not, under any circumstances – unless it was some kind of mercy killing and nobody has mentioned anything about her having terminal cancer. So no, they don't. Nobody is suggesting their relationship was sexual, but that notwithstanding, they were as close as two people can get.'

'What about Paul Rey? It looked to me as if she and he were pretty close.'

'They were, and that definitely *was* sexual. Paul Rey was a Jedburgh in Laurence's team that jumped to join the Maquis de Morez after D-Day. Again, they were pretty close. After the war, Rey and a few others started the CIA. He kept the Europe desk while his new colleagues spent the rest of their professional lives trying to recreate the summer of forty-four in countries where the government was anything other than neoliberal free-market screw-the-people-for-everything-they've-got-and-give-it-to-the-multinationals. Korea, Vietnam, Cuba, Afghanistan: all over the world, they kept dropping money and weapons from the sky and joining up with the local resistance against whatever regime the US wanted to get rid of.'

'Look how well that worked out.'

'Exactly. And someone in that early group was responsible for running Max Kramme.'

'What?'

'Kramme had agents inside the French Communist party and behind what became the Iron Curtain at a time when the British and Americans had nobody at all. Even before the war was over, he remade himself as a Western intelligence asset. MI6 and the CIA ran him jointly until fifty-seven, after which, he dropped off the map.'

'This doesn't get any better, does it? Can you keep on top of things here? I have a book to find that might give us some answers.'

The oldest book in Elodie Duval's office is a first edition of Stevie Smith poetry, *Not Waving but Drowning*. Picaut can find nothing relevant inside it, although clearly that doesn't necessarily mean there is nothing to find. She takes it with her as she leaves.

On the other side of the city, amidst the charming chaos in Elodie's apartment, the oldest book she can find is an edition of the *Encyclopaedia Britannica* published in 1939. The cover is chestnut and gold, the weight pleasingly solid. When she opens it, the first few pages are unremarkable, but the edges of the rest do not move as they should and, opened fully, it is a child's toy: a book made into a box, with the pages glued fast and the centre hollowed out to provide a resting place for two age-ambered cuttings from the London *Times*.

Lifted out and laid on her table they are:

1 – A wedding notice for Mademoiselle Sophie Destivelle and Monsieur François Duval, from 10 May 1945.

2 – An obituary for Brigadier Sir Jeremy Isambard Vaughan-Thomas, fifth Viscount Sarnforth, who died on 20 February 1957.

1946: Gehlen Organization established by agents of the United States Office of Strategic Services. Named for Reinhard Gehlen, head of German Intelligence on the Eastern Front, it employs many former Nazi officials with a remit to continue the clandestine war against the USSR.

1947: The OSS becomes the Central Intelligence Agency. Intelligence from eastern Europe sourced largely from Gehlen.

March 1957: Belgium, France, West Germany, Italy, Luxembourg and the Netherlands sign the Treaty of Rome, giving rise to the European Economic Community and the European Atomic Energy Community.

CHAPTER TWENTY-NINE

HAMPSHIRE
25 February 1957

THE DAY OF BRIGADIER Sir Jeremy Isambard Vaughan-Thomas's funeral starts cold, and then mellows to a surprising, unseasonal warmth, wrong-footing family and mourners alike, so that the suits at the graveside are wool, not linen, and women in winter hats and gloves glow lightly through the formal reception afterwards on the lawns at Ridgemount.

The old house has never seen such a concentration of gold braid and empty language. I'm so sorry. Thank you. He was a wonderful man. Yes, thank you, we'll all miss him terribly. Such a loss to the nation. Thank you, Prime Minister. Uncle Jeremy would be honoured to know you thought so highly of him. Archbishop, so kind of you to come. An inspiration? Was he? And my father? Yes, I'm sure. Together again. Resting in peace. That's so kind. Why, yes, since the death of my cousin Christopher, I would appear to be heir to both. I'll do my best to honour their heritage. I'm sure he did. Thank you. Thank you. Thank you.

Laurence spots Céline at a distance. In his mind and hers,

she ceased to be Theodora on the day Fabien died and she became Patron of the Maquis de Morez. The rest of the family has never quite caught up.

'Shall we escape?' He taps her elbow. Coolly resilient as ever, ravishing in pewter-grey linen with a single band in her hair as a hat, she, alone, was not fooled by the weather. He steers her past the Duke of Plymouth, smiling broadly. So kind. Thank you. Yes, deeply.

She asks, 'Where are we going?'

'To a place where we can drop the terrible rictus grins. You look as if your cheeks are aching. Certainly mine are. Come on. I have something to show you.' He leads her inside, up the stone steps and the big, cascading staircase in the entrance hall, with the spikes on the bannisters to stop the family's generation of youth from sliding down them. As a child, he never wanted to slide down them. Now he has an urge to rip out every spike and try it, just to see if he can.

He runs. It's that kind of day. Up two flights and he's onto the landing on the third floor that was his uncle's domain. On the top step, he hits a wall of memories, but he has been here before. Céline, who hasn't, stops at the top stair. He says, 'Come on. He wanted us here.'

'On the landing? Really?'

'Beyond the landing. The snug.'

She laughs. 'Now I know you're making this up.'

'I'm not and I can prove it. Come *on*.' It is a central tenet of family mythology that nobody but the Brigadier is allowed inside the snug at Ridgemount. In childhood, it was a magical place, the repository of all things hidden, and even now, to enter is to feel the kind of light-headed terror he has only otherwise known just before a parachute jump.

It is his now, and all around it, but even so, coming here feels as if he has stepped into a no-man's-land of otherness. The room itself is both ordinary and astonishing. It smells of tobacco. The curtains have suffered at some point from an excess of moths. The fat, sagging, endlessly comfortable arm-chair is easily as old as the house, the leather cracked and dry and worn here and there so that strands of horse hair poke through.

Nevertheless, in the order and placement of the minutiae of living, there's a balance between control and the clutter of a busy mind. Here are files and folders in alphabetical order, a globe marked with pins, a larger map of Europe the same, and books . . . everywhere books, read, half-read and unread, not one of them fiction, all engaged with the working of the world.

A Remington desk is the room's focal point, set away from the windows to avoid the dual risks of distraction and spies. It has the feel of much action though it is empty today, but for a reel-to-reel tape recorder and a thickly stuffed manila folder.

Céline is more comfortable here than he was when he first came. She scans the room once, then settles in the armchair as if it were her own. She says, 'It's not just Ridgemount you've inherited. You're the heir apparent, aren't you? I thought the old boy would see sense in the end.'

'I didn't want it. I still don't.'

'No, but we don't often get what we want.'

'You'll get a place of your own in time, if you don't upset C too much.'

'Larry, I don't want that any more than you want this. I'm not a desk man. Not even a desk woman. Especially not that. I'm happy in the field for as long as they let me stay there.' She lights up a cigarette, stares out of the window. 'What kind of a bombshell has he left us?'

'The unstable kind. Tell me what you thought of Sophie Destivelle when you were with her in the mountains?'

'We're going that far back?' She drags on the cigarette. 'She was dangerous. She was mixed up and ambivalent about all kinds of things, but she was devoted to Patrick. She was, I

424

think, consumed with guilt at his having been captured. I assume she still is, particularly after the debacle of Kramme's escape.'

'Suppose she had nothing of which to feel guilty?'

'I don't follow. You're telling me she wasn't Kramme's agent?'

'I am telling you she wasn't *only* Kramme's agent. She was ours, too. What she did, she did because we told her to. Specifically, she did what the Brigadier told her to.'

'I know, she told me that, but even so, Kramme captured Patrick and someone gave him the information that let him do so. By accident or design, I think Sophie Destivelle led Kramme to the Patron. More importantly, she thinks so, too. Why else give herself over to a living death in the mountains if she's not waking every morning to the guilt of what she's done?'

'Feeling guilty doesn't make her culpable. Think about this: when you rescued Patrick, Kramme knew you were coming in time to get away – true?'

'True. The Milice said he'd had a message.'

'Who sent that message? For the past thirteen years, I have struggled to see how Sophie could have done so unless you let her near the radio alone. Did you?'

'No. I rigged it so I thought I'd know if she'd been, but as we know, tradecraft is never wholly reliable and she has always been good.' Another long drag on the cigarette, another string of smoke. Céline continues, 'The alternative answer has always been that our esteemed uncle knew that Kramme was Icarus and saved his life twice: first when we went for Patrick and then again at the wedding. Have you proof that he did? Because if you do, I might just dig up his body and parade it naked through the streets.'

Laurence laughs aloud for the first time in days. 'But then we'd become the focus of attention, and as my father always said, attention is an agent's death.'

'But have you proof? Did the Brigadier know from the beginning that Icarus and Kramme were the same person?'

'I don't think so. I've been through his files, I've read every page, every cipher sent and received. There is nothing to suggest he knew before the debacle at the wedding.'

She eyes him, sideways. 'How did you manage to search his files when the Firm's entire records department went up in a blaze in forty-six?'

Now it is Laurence's turn to look out of the window. 'It was forty-five, and you'll be surprised to learn that a substantial portion of the Brigadier's records survived.'

Celine's cigarette smokes, unheeded. 'Not forty-six?'

'That's when word got out. Trust me, the fire started on the twenty-sixth of December 1945. Eleven thirty-two p.m., to be precise.'

She stares at him, slack jawed. And then she laughs. And laughs. And laughs. Winding down: 'Christ, Larry. What did he offer you?'

He has held this for so long, but if he can't tell Céline, who can he tell? He says, 'Who was it destroyed the Firm in forty-five?'

'The SIS. MI6. For whom we both now work.'

'Yes, but who in particular?'

'Claude Dansey? But he died of a heart attack in forty-seven and . . . Ah.' Across her face, a cascade of feeling, none of it quite given life. 'Everyone dies of a heart attack in the end, I suppose.'

'I imagine that's the case, yes.'

'And there were a lot of people whose involvement with the Firm was not designed for public consumption. People who would owe Uncle Jeremy useful favours if their records were no longer at risk of being read.'

'That is definitely the case.'

'Strewth.' She grinds her cigarette to a thumb's-width stub

and then stands, smoothing her sleeves. For a moment he thinks she is going to walk out, but what she actually does is to walk round the desk and press a kiss to his brow. The feel of her lips lasts a long time, well past the moment when she sits down again in the chair opposite the desk. She smiles at him. 'Thank you.'

'You're welcome.'

Their smiles are balanced, united in a secret sin. Laurence relights his pipe. 'So,' he says, 'back to the point. Two things strike me. The first is that Sophie categorically did not have access to Kramme on the night you went to rescue Patrick. She could not have warned him. True?'

'True.'

'Second: after she and her colleagues joined you, Kramme did not send the Luftwaffe to flatten the mountain. He must have known you were there, and after the invasion struck, pretty much every other Maquis in France was being bombed to oblivion. They had either to move camps, or keep their fires to a minimum. You alone were untouched.'

'I thought it was down to Sophie, that Kramme was protecting her.'

'I did, too. But I've been thinking a lot about Kramme and a number of things seem clear, starting with the fact that his pride was as monstrously overblown as his arrogance. He hated being made a fool of. Look what he did to Patrick when he found out the man he had called a friend had betrayed him. In Sophie's case, she had value to him as long as she could tell him the date of the invasion and the name of the man who ran the Resistance in Saint-Cybard. Once he had captured Patrick, and the invasion had happened, both of these were redundant. She lost her value on the night of June the sixth, even if she could have contacted him, even if she might have wanted to contact him, which I really don't think she did. You didn't see her when Kramme got away. She was doing her absolute utmost to kill him.'

This is a delicate point: Céline still weeps for Fabien. 'So you're saying Kramme wasn't protecting her?'

'Quite the opposite. Bombing her to oblivion would have salved his pride, I think, but he didn't try, that's the point. He left her untouched.'

'Yes, I understand. Why?'

'I don't know, but Kramme thinks long term. As far back as forty-one, he was laying the groundwork for Icarus in case the war did not go Hitler's way, building his networks of agents behind their lines and in the communist parties of Europe as a reason for our side to keep him alive. He made contact through the Paul Mignon radio long before it was obvious to us that Hitler was going to lose. What does this tell us?'

'He planned a long, long way ahead.' Céline bites the edge of one nail. 'You think he had someone else in the Maquis.'

'Exactly so. Hold that thought, while you listen to this.'

Laurence presses the button on the tape recorder. Downstairs, someone brays a laugh. The noise knifes in over the thready hiss of the tape heads engaging. And then his uncle Jeremy is there, urbane as ever, alive, hearty:

'. . . that you fail to understand the situation as it stands. We are bankrupt. This war destroyed our empire more successfully than your Führer could have hoped. The Cousins appear to be printing their own money in ways that do not lead to paralysing inflation, which may be contrary to all the laws of nature, but the result is that they have unlimited funds and are using them to promote their own ends. Additionally, those in power on both sides of the pond feel they will only stay that way if they have a great enough enemy to ensure that our respective populations feel continually under threat, and the Soviets are the most convenient bogey man. You, by happy chance, have a functioning network of agents in the east, which is worth its own weight in promises. QED, you now belong to our friends across the water.'

There is a gap, the sound of a match on paper, the suck and sigh of a cigarette, newly lit. And then a second voice, with soft, rounded vowels.

'Let us be clear. The French desire my death and have asked for it at ministerial level on a number of occasions, as have the Poles and the Latvians, not to mention a number of your countrymen, most notably your nephew. But all that notwithstanding, you have *sold* me to the Americans?'

The voice is cultured, not quite English. If he didn't know who it was, Laurence might think it was a Scot, an Aberdonian, perhaps, but educated south of the border. It sounds, in fact, distressingly like Patrick did in the days when he had a tongue. He watches Céline close her eyes against this pain.

Uncle Jeremy: 'Exactly so. The Cousins will give you a new name and an identity of your choosing. You will be safe amongst new friends, free to build a new life. They will pay well for your services, of that I have no doubt: better than us. The only question is whether or not we let them know the *exact* extent of your help to us. And whether that help will continue.'

'You are suggesting that there are aspects of my "help" of which you might wish your closest allies to remain unaware?'

Uncle Jeremy: 'I think there is very little of which they are entirely unaware. There may be nuances, however, that escape the colonial mind. They think very literally, our Cousins, something to do with their relative lack of a heritage, I believe. Their nation remains adolescent to a great degree: very vigorous, but lacking in subtlety.'

'Whereas you and I are infinitely subtle.'

'Larry, I've heard enough.' Céline slams a hand hard on the desk. 'Stop this. Please. This is obscene. This is Kramme? And the Brigadier is passing him to the Americans? *Selling* him?'

'It is. And he is. Or was. And you haven't heard nearly enough. Bear with me. There is reason in my madness. What comes next is the key to everything.' Laurence has heard it before, but still, he sits on the chair's edge.

Uncle Jeremy says, 'We have our moments. Carpe Diem, as they say.'

There is a pause, a whiffle of a sleeve on the table, perhaps a long draw on the cigarette? A look? A nod? A raised brow? Why did nobody put a camera in the room?

Kramme: 'I, too, have my price. A life for a life. If you want continued access to that particular asset, you will have to find me Patrick Sutherland.'

Uncle Jeremy: 'That could be tricky. He died in forty-four.'

'We both know this is not true. And you know where he lives.'

Uncle Jeremy gives ground again. That's twice in one conversation. The shock of this is as real now as it was five days ago when Laurence first played the tape, even now that he knows where it's leading. The Brigadier says, 'Reaching him might be problematic.'

'Where is he?'

'In the mountains of Morez, north and east of Saint-Cybard.'

'Returned to the place of his wounding? How very English. He has friends there, I imagine?'

'More than anywhere else. And you can see that there isn't time for you to get over there, find him and get back for your flight to Washington.'

'You can move mountains when you need to, Sir Jeremy. This is my price. I will not leave Europe with unfinished business of this magnitude trailing behind. Some scores, we cannot leave unsettled. Were you to ask Major Sutherland, I have no doubt he would agree. We owe to posterity, to our prides and to each other, a settling of debts.'

Another pause. A match is struck, a cigar or a cigarette or a pipe is lit, smoke is blown out. He can almost smell it. 'In that case, I shall give the matter some thought. Moving on, I believe there might be some advantage in our sharing the product of your recent investments in personnel without our Cousins necessarily being aware of our involvement. I would like to propose—'

Laurence stops the tape. Céline stares at the reels, at the length of conversation still to go, at the length already passed. 'When did this take place?'

'Eight days ago.'

'Uncle Jeremy knew he was dying?'

'I believe he did. He left the tape in an envelope marked with my name. This note was inside.' He slides it across the desk.

Listen. And then make sure Céline does the same. My gift to you, with sincere apologies. JIVT

'One more thing.' From the drawer, Laurence brings two more envelopes, each with a name and two words:

For Laurence – Carpe Diem
For Céline – Carpe Diem

At his nod, she opens them both. In his envelope are photographs in colour and black and white of Kramme, Sophie, Patrick. In hers are three ciphers.

She sorts them into date order, earliest first:

```
SS-Stubaf Kramme: Akte: DIEM
# F3/A1.9.4-
1/6/44 2217 Std
```

An: SS-Ostubaf Klaus Weissmann

V-MANN 'DIEM': INVASION FINDET STATT 6
JUNI. INFORMATION GILT ALS 100 PROZENT
ZUVERLAESSIGKEIT. ERBITTE BEFEHL FUER
WEITERES VORGEHEN. HH CARPE

*Source 'DIEM': Invasion takes place 6th June. Information
accorded 100 per cent reliability. Request orders for action.
HH 'CARPE' (assume code name for Kramme?) CVT*

In their uncle's hand, underneath, is written:

Who is Diem?

Céline sits back, throws her hands behind her head. 'I found
these in Kramme's desk in Saint-Cybard. Minus the annota-
tions, obviously.'

'I know.'

'I really did think Diem was Sophie.'

'So did I. So did she. So, I think, did our uncle.'

'He is telling us we were all wrong?'

'I think he is inviting us to revisit our assumptions. If he
were certain, he'd have said so.'

'Then . . .'

'If Sophie is not Diem, then we have to widen our net. Whoever it is, they're not only alive, but an active and useful source
for Kramme.'

'Nobody from the Maquis is in the Russian zone.'

'If you listen again, and I have listened until I could recite it
backwards, they are not only talking about the east. We spy
on our friends as much as we do our enemies. I think this is
an agent inside a friendly power: specifically, inside the French
Deuxième Bureau. If it's not Sophie, then we have three
choices: JJ, René—'

'Or Daniel Fayette. Strewth. But Laurence—'

'They're all decent people who fought with utmost courage. I know.'

'And still do. They're the best the French have.'

'Which is why whoever it is makes such a good source.'

'Christ. If Sophie finds out . . .'

'I am rather hoping she will want to do something useful.'

The desk is stifling. The window calls, and the high, grey skies. Far below, the mourners are a mess of Brownian motion on the croquet lawn: clots of black and grey with the occasional glint of gold, silver, scarlet. Someone looks up. Laurence is too high up to see who it is; they too low down to see him. He leans his forehead on the cool glass. The pressure helps him think, however uncomfortable the result. 'I think our uncle is – was – genuinely trying to help in his own obscure, twisted, clandestine way.'

Céline lights another cigarette. 'But what do we do? Presumably Kramme is safely across the pond by now, starting a new life with a new name?'

Laurence turns, leans the back of his head on the glass. 'He's not, as a matter of fact. He was en route to a nicely hidden airfield yesterday afternoon when he vanished. Safe to say the Cousins are very, very cross about it.'

Céline blows smoke in three rings, watches them rise. 'He's gone to find Patrick.'

'He has. But this is Uncle Jeremy's parting gift to us and he planned it well. If we are clever, if we have luck and the right people on our side, we can get Kramme and Diem in one fell swoop. Two birds, one hand, all that kind of thing. The point is that whatever we do, it will have to be under the radar. Off the books. On our own initiative and our careers finished if anyone finds out.'

'That would be a fair price.' Céline nods, thinking. 'Just to be clear, this is "get" as in "kill"?'

'You think it's a bad idea?'

'Not at all.' She smiles at him as he once saw her smile at Julie. 'Not. At. All.'

He feels a remarkable lightness. 'In that case, cousin mine, we have some planning to do. I rather imagine this is all going to hinge on Sophie and her relationship with Paul Rey. Is it strong enough, do you think?'

Rising, she pats him on the shoulder. 'We have to hope it is. Because if we're wrong, we'll be risking half a dozen lives for a wild goose chase and I really don't want to die for a mistake of that magnitude.'

CHAPTER THIRTY

BERNAUER STRASSE, BERLIN
27 February 1957

IT IS DARK. THE night air smells of recent rain, of wet pavements, of winter's end. The damp street is quiet, ghostly, even. Ahead is the railway yard, and the ends of the tracks where men work on through the damp and the dark. Their shouts are guttural and Slavic; proof, should she need it, that she is in the Russian zone.

Sophie has a new Leica and the lens is good, she doesn't need to be closer, but there's an itch, a need to see and not be seen, a thirst for the sting of adrenaline in her mouth, the taste of saliva that only flows with risks met and taken. She slides into a doorway and here, now, she is not a young woman, but ancient, stooped, frail; one of those few who survived when all about her died, who foraged through the after-war hell and is foraging still. She picks up a fag end from the pavement and moves on.

A dozen paces, and nobody has stopped her. In the railway yard, they are lifting iron tracks; a dozen men to each side, unscrewing them, unbolting, crowbarring them up and then lifting them, to be walked on shoulders like a many-legged python and dropped into the trucks.

This is worth a photograph: Khrushchev digging up German train lines to ship back to Russia. Khrushchev, who is as broke as everyone except America, and who is trying to rebuild the things that Germany destroyed using German technology.

There is a rumour that when the first Russians entered the east, they stole every piece of technology they could lay their hands on, that they are rebuilding the Kremlin along German lines – but they'd have to have the materials and manpower to do it, and if they're scavenging railway lines, that's not likely. So many things to be inferred from one photograph. Or a dozen: *click. Click-cli-cli-cli-click. Snap.* Nobody asks her to smile. She lifts her face to the new rain and smiles anyway. One job done. One more to do. One for each of her handlers: the one she is paid by, and the one she sleeps with. Nobody asks too many questions. She turns back the way she came and begins a meandering walk to the American sector.

An hour later, she is safe. Safer. She keeps clear of the bars. There is rubble enough, broken buildings, broken roadways.

She waits, huddled in the doorway of an abandoned café. She is not meeting with someone, exactly, but she believes that John Nadolinsky, US citizen, will pass by shortly and she intends to be in the right place to intercept him when he does. He too, she has been told, had business in the Russian sector tonight. The boundaries are porous. They may not always be so, but for now it suits all sides to be able to cross from one to the other and back again.

She is good at waiting: she always has been. In part of her mind, she is back in Paris, waiting to make a kill. Germany has not yet been defeated. Patrick Sutherland has not yet been unmade; she has not, in fact, met him.

In the part she chooses to hide, she has met him, and he has been unmade. He cannot work, and so she must provide for two. To this end, she has joined with former

436

colleagues – Daniel, René, both now decorated heroes of the Maquis – and together they have built an import/export business that trades primarily between Lyon and Munich, although recently, branches have opened in Orléans and Frankfurt.

In the course of this endeavour, she has discovered a facility for numbers that surprises everyone who knew her before the war, herself included. This, combined with elfin looks, a nurse's empathy and an Audrey Hepburn haircut, has elevated her as high as a woman might reasonably go within the new firm, certainly far enough to make business trips to Germany twice or three times a year.

Thus she is in Bonn this week as part of a trade delegation that has come to investigate the financial implications of the expansion of the European Coal and Steel Community.

This is the delegation's penultimate day in Germany. Today, also, Madame Amélie Duval – this is the name by which the world knows her now: JJ has erased all outward record of Sophie Destivelle – has a migraine and is unable to attend. Men of several nations have sent flowers to her room on the second floor of the Hotel Vier Jahreszeiten. She has sent pretty hand-written cards to each, thanking them, or somebody has in her name: she has distinctive handwriting that is, she is told, easy to forge.

Because she is not languishing in pain in her room. She is here, in a damp doorway in Berlin, and here, however damp, however cold, however long she has to wait, she is free of responsibility and of morality.

Her gun is a Browning Hi-Power, smaller than the wartime Colt; small enough to go in her handbag or, as now, in the hand that clasps her walking stick, hidden in the folds of her shawl against the prying eyes of passers-by.

There are few enough of those, and none who are likely to take notice of an old, hunched, white-haired, broken-winded grandmother. It is amazing, really, that she made it through the war.

Bernauer Strasse is a ghost station. Trains do not run from the French sector to the Soviet one or vice versa; there is no legitimate reason to go down those steps, but someone has done, and that someone pauses at the entrance, looks left and right, sees the old woman collapsed in the doorway, coughing. In the absence of anyone else, he takes a chance.

As he approaches, she tries fruitlessly to light her cigarette. Strike ... strike ... strike: the familiar sound of a match failing to spark. A whiff of damp phosphorus taints the air.

With sad, tired eyes she looks up at the passing man. She doesn't ask for his help, and won't: her life has been one of men walking past. He pauses. His reflection shimmers on the rain-glazed road. He smiles. John Nadolinsky, soon-to-be-late US citizen, is not a bad man, just overconfident, and poor in his street craft.

In Bostonian English he says, 'Here, lady, try this,' and, leaning over, flicks his lighter.

The shot takes him under the chin, jerks him back just a little, but she is up, and catches him, sways him round and down into the doorway. There is very little mess and none of it on her. She does not cut his throat, or mark her scarf with his gore: those days are past. She searches his pockets and finds the envelope she was sent for. His lighter has fallen onto the sidewalk. She stoops to pick it up, thinks better of it and walks away. Both jobs done.

Her blood sings. She is alive.

An hour later, she is in the bar of a hotel in the American sector, drinking coffee, smoking. Her wig this time is ash blonde, tending just to the first edges of grey. Her diamanté-sparked glasses crowd her face, hiding her too-big eyes. She is a middle-aged American conducting a quiet, harmless tryst with a married countryman in a way that offends the

438

Germans. JJ will want a report, but JJ can wait until the morning. Paul Rey sits down opposite, his gaze on her face.

'You OK?'

'If you are.' The film canister is already in a dead drop, but the letter is more urgent. She slides John Nadolinsky's envelope across the table and watches him open it. He, too, has changed his appearance, but underneath, he is leaner, more lined, more patrician than he was. His gaze is harder. He laughs less, and when he does, it counts for more. He has responsibilities now, and a second wife. His hair is closer to silver than gold. Since '44, he has lost weight, gained gravitas and political acumen, and become a founding member of America's shiny new spy agency.

And he has become European. He is almost British in his sense of irony now, French in his freedom of expression. He is American only in his caution. Three of his men are already seated around the bar: Long Tall Louis from Texas, Ben from Milwaukee, Anthony from Boston, who pronounces the hard consonant of his first name softly and makes her want to slap him. They are as different as any three American agents could be, except in one thing: they worship Paul Rey with a fervour that borders on the pathological.

Sophie ignores them, as they ignore her. It has taken three years to reach this stalemate, but it does appear stable.

Paul's eyes scan the page she has brought him. He folds it, slides it back into the envelope and that into an inside pocket. She asks, 'Was he selling you to the Soviets?'

'Not just us. All of you, too.'

'You would say that anyway. You think I'll have nightmares if I discover that I've killed an innocent man.'

He regards her, chewing his bottom lip. After a moment, he takes out the envelope and slides it back across the table. 'I'm not sure anything gives you nightmares. I want you to know that I wouldn't order a death I didn't believe to be necessary.'

439

The page, unfolded, shows a typed list of seventeen names, each with an acronym after it: SIS, CIA, DB, and the name of the official position: trade attaché, undersecretary, passport officer . . . all the paper-thin covers that may as well be descriptions of their ranks in their relevant agencies. Amélie Duval is not on the list; her cover is good.

Other names jump off the page: Jean-Jacques Crotteau, René Vivier, Daniel Fayette, Theodora Vaughan-Thomas. She looks up. 'Céline is in Bonn?'

'Apparently so. I have it on good authority that she may have wind of our mutual target.'

Her guts clench, wetly. Some things have not changed at all. 'Kramme?'

'Yes. Theodora Vaughan-Thomas is going to the Canadians' reception tomorrow night under the name Susan Tomlinson. She will look suitably spinsterish: red-haired, and dowdy. You'll enjoy meeting her.'

He is smiling, but he is serious, too. She leans in, presses a dry kiss to his cheek. 'She will never be less than beautiful.'

He reaches his hand to cover hers. His thumb inscribes a circle on the back of her wrist that makes her blood sing. She turns her hand over, and catches his thumb as he draws it across her palm. 'Do you think of her, when we're together?'

His smile fades. His hand moves to her cheek and then drops away. He stands, reaches for her coat and holds it open. His gaze is grey and flat and sharply pained. In this moment, he is really very French. 'Shall we go?'

RHEINHOTEL, BONN
28 February 1957

Kramme. Kramme is in Europe. Kramme is going to hunt Patrick (she has telephoned him. He is safe). Kramme can be caught and Sophie Destivelle, who so very badly wants to do the catching, is stuck in a reception of mind-bending dullness, making conversation with imbeciles.

She is wearing a red satin-silk dress not entirely unlike the one that Kramme gave her. Her nylons are American. Her heels are stupidly tall. Of necessity, she is unarmed. The doors are too far away to be useful. JJ is nearby, standing under a ghastly, baroque chandelier talking to the Canadian ambassador, holding a champagne flute in his fist as if it were a stick of celery. His gaze flicks periodically to one of the three armed agents of the Service de Documentation Extérieure et de Contre-Espionnage, colloquially known as the Deuxième Bureau, who prowl the margins of the guests, competing with a similar number, similarly attired, from the other acronym agencies: the SIS, CIA, KGB.

This being a reception hosted by the Canadian ambassador, doubtless there are also agents of the RCMP, although nobody pays them a great deal of attention. Even without them, there are more armed guards on display tonight than diplomats or trade executives, and half of these are spies.

It would be laughable were it not that news has just reached them of a CIA agent shot dead near the Russian sector in Berlin. The atmosphere here is rarely relaxed, but tonight, it is raw, red, angry.

A hand falls on her arm. Sophie turns, briskly, crisply. 'I'm sorry, I don't think—'

It's the eyes: one platinum glance and she is lost, floating in a black night with the lights red to green above her head and the ground coming up towards her.

She finds her voice. 'Can I help you?'

'I'm so sorry, my mistake. I thought you were someone I knew.' Céline's French was perfect. Susan Tomlinson's is cloddily English. Everything about her is cloddily English; less alert, less alive, more mousy than she ever was. The spectacles are part of it, and the lank red hair, but the greatest part – the best – is her posture. Here, where England is the victor, she manages to leak a sense of defeat.

The whole construct is an instruction in cover art, should Sophie care to take it, but her attention is elsewhere – on the index finger of Céline's right hand, as it taps on her thigh. MEET MEET MEET.

How long since she last put her mind to Morse? She is fully back in the war now. Her fingers answer without her thinking. WHERE? WHEN?

YOUR HOTEL BAR 2247.

Sophie has been a resident of the Hotel Vier Jahreszeiten for the past four days, during none of which has she spent time in the bar. Such is the suspicion these days that anything out of habit will be noticed, unless she can provide a plausible reason for a change in behaviour.

The reception is winding to its natural close when she catches the eye of a man she vaguely knows.

'Alexei!' She raises her arm and her voice together, and, pushing past a tedious naval attaché from the British Embassy, strides out towards the Soviet undersecretary's undersecretary—

And trips. The floor, of course, is Italian marble. Her glass disintegrates on impact and she falls after it, into, but not onto, the shards.

There are advantages to being a more gamine version of La Hepburn. Men rush to help her to her feet, to rescue her shattered glass, her shattered shoe, the heel of which is *quite* ruined. No one asks how she managed to trip over her own feet on a perfectly smooth floor. Nobody asks where she was going or what she was doing, but when the three young officers of the Royal Canadian Mounted Police escort her – sporting a fresh Band-Aid over what turns out to be really rather a small cut – back to the Hotel VJ, it is natural that they deliver her to the bar.

442

'I will be well, Messieurs, honestly. It was a shock, nothing more. I am unhurt. I shall have a Cognac and an early night and learn my lesson. Thank you. Truly. I am grateful. I have detained you long enough. Thank you.'

Glass in hand, she finds an empty table in the furthest corner, beneath the stuffed boar's head. The Hotel VJ may be newly built, but purports to be an old-fashioned kind of residence of the sort that flourished in the thirties; the manager swears that it is built directly on the foundations of its predecessor, that some of the building stone is original.

Whether anyone believes this is irrelevant; the oak panels and dim lighting make it a haven for spies. Here, the difficulty is not the usual one of being overheard, but of unintentionally overhearing something untoward. Tonight, the atmosphere is tense.

Céline, when she arrives, is no longer a redhead, but a short-haired, rather masculine brunette, taller than she was, or perhaps less folded in on herself. Her clothes are just on the right side of mannish; just on the wrong side of casual: dark slacks and a tailored jacket in herringbone tweed with slingbacks. She orders a whisky and soda and her accent is American, which excuses almost everything.

She sits with her back to Sophie and checks the door and her watch with increasing frequency. At eleven o'clock, when nobody she recognizes has entered, she raises her third Scotch to the door – 'Fuck you, and all who sail in you' – drains it, and leaves.

There were eight words in Céline's curse and so Sophie follows four minutes later. She's easy to follow. Her short hair, her bearing, the length of her stride; all mark her out as she passes under the street lights, heading back along the Rüngsdorfer Strasse, towards the Rheinhotel and the river beyond. The night is warm and dry and there are streetlights again, which is pleasant. Bonn is sprinting towards its future in ways Berlin, and even Paris, are not.

443

They reach the Rheinstrasse and cut down the side of the hotel. It's clever, to come back to the place they left. If they are stopped, there could be reasons: a lost earring, a lover, waiting . . .

They pass down the side lane undisturbed. The hotel is dark. Beyond the gardens, puddles of light gather on the river for which the street is named. Rather late, it occurs to Sophie that if she were to fall into the water, if, perhaps, she were shackled hand and foot with iron, it would be many months before her body was found. Céline used to be a friend, but the war was a long time ago and alliances have shifted wildly since then. And Sophie did shoot a Soviet agent yesterday evening. In the grey world of their profession, she has no idea who knows this and who doesn't.

She slides her hand into her purse and grips her keys, which are at least the beginnings of a weapon. Céline turns, leans back against the white wall of the hotel with her arms folded.

'Does JJ know you're doing wet work for the Americans?'

Well, that answers one question. And yes, Céline is armed; something of similar size to Sophie's Browning weights her jacket pocket. Behind them, the Rhine slides past, slack, black and dangerous.

Into the silence, Céline says, 'Your so-daring photographs – one of them, anyway – will be used as proof that the Soviets are building a railway line, that they are a real and present threat to "Western security".'

She wondered about that, but JJ – surely he wouldn't . . . but yes, actually, JJ is ruthless and he knows how to play the Americans. One grainy black-and-white shot taken at night? It will be impossible to tell whether the rails are being taken up or laid down. If it is presented as proof of an existing argument, nobody will question it. Anybody that does will be shut down.

As if she had thought this all along, she says, 'The

Americans need an enemy so they can stay on a war footing. JJ will give them one and they will owe him a favour so big, he'll be able to ask for the moon.'

'He will indeed. If he were to stumble across Kramme, would he pass him to the Americans, do you think?'

'No.' Some lines he will not cross. 'He would never do that.'

'Good. Then we have common ground. How is Patrick? I heard a rumour JJ offered him a position in the DB, but he turned it down.'

What can one say? He is a doctor who cannot practise, and a soldier who cannot fight. JJ's offer was made with good heart, but how could a man with no tongue be a spy? He will not sit at a desk living on another man's charity, and so he is bored almost to the point of death, but his honour keeps him stoic.

She says, 'He's seen enough of war and subterfuge. He makes things, beautiful things.'

'Music boxes. I hear they fetch a fortune. Amazing, when you think about it, that there's a market for such things.'

'You'd have to see one to understand. The diplomatic services of Europe love them. There's one each waiting for you and for Laurence, if you ever get around to picking them up. Paul Rey's been to collect his.'

Céline's brows rise. She looks down and back up. 'As one friend to another, you need to know your affair with our American friend is not secret.'

'And I hear rumours of a particularly beautiful lady racehorse owner, widow of a war hero, heir to a country estate, who is happy in your company. Véronique must be inconsolable.'

The air is still for a moment. The river holds its breath. Céline looks as if she may laugh, but it is her gaze that slides away first. 'Touché.'

'I'm sorry.'

'Don't be. It's always useful to be reminded that in this

world our lives are an open book. For what it is worth, I am godmother to Véro's firstborn daughter.'

Sophie slides down the wall to sit on her heels. The scent of the river is stronger here, a musky dampness that reminds her of Amsterdam, where she made her first post-war kill, where the affair with Rey was rekindled.

She has never believed herself in love, but she has come to understand the power of raw, animal lust, and has discovered that, when backed by respect and compassion, it amounts to something similar and fills the gap her life has left.

She says, 'Patrick knows all there is to know.'

'How remarkably modern. Does he not care?'

'He says not. There are days when I believe him. He is not always an easy man to read.'

'I can imagine.' For the first time, Céline shows both her hands. She reaches for a packet of Embassy Tipped and a solid-looking silver lighter. 'Cigarette?'

Sophie releases her grip on her keys. They light up together and in the first surge of smoke is the memory of comradeship.

Céline tips her head back, blows blue breath at the sky. 'I assume you are aware that we may have a shot at Kramme, possibly our last. Are we right in thinking you would like to help?'

'Do you even need to ask?'

'Not really. But I do need to know when you last saw him, and where.'

'With my own eyes? Three years ago in Frankfurt. René got a photograph of him in the British sector in Berlin in fifty-five and Daniel tailed him for half a day in Munich that summer, but lost him. We haven't seen him since. JJ has agents across the continent keeping an eye out for him.' JJ ranks high enough in the DB not to have to give reasons for all that he does.

'They won't find him. He's had plastic surgery and a voice coach. The last we heard, he was calling himself Lincoln

Sutherland, and speaking with a slight Scottish accent.' She gives her tight, acid smile. 'We choose to believe this is some kind of compliment to Patrick.'

Sophie turns to look out at the river. Blurred memories rush at her of the Patron, of a red dress, of Cognac and conversation and laughter; of a body lifted from a ceiling hook and the savagery of what had been done to it. Her breathing is short, inelastic – a thing that has not happened since the war ended. 'Where is he?'

'We believe he's heading for Patrick, but beyond that, we are in the dark. Paul Rey may know more; the Americans, after all, have paid for him and want him back.'

She's fishing and Sophie has nothing to give. Pressing her palms to her face, she tries to bring up Rey's last kiss, the look in his eyes. Has he had Kramme in his hand and lost him and not told her? Has he got him now? If you lied to me about this, I will kill you.

She has been silent too long. She says, 'What do you want from me?'

'Whatever you can give. Time is tight. The clock is already running. In this, genuinely, hours may make a difference. We can't mobilize an assault team from the UK and get them to the cabin in time to do any good.'

Sophie raises her head. Her blood is running fast again. 'We can, though. The Maquis de Morez, such as is left of it. We're already in place.'

'Thank you.' Céline's smile says this is what she came for. 'And Patrick? Will he allow us to stake him out if it gives us a chance to catch Kramme's tiger?'

Sophie wants to say, no, just leave him alone, give him peace. But she cannot deny him this. She says, 'He'll do anything at all if Laurence Vaughan-Thomas asks it of him.'

'In that case, you can expect a visit from Larry at your cabin in the woods sometime within the next forty-eight hours.'

447

Céline grinds her cigarette against the wall and slides the stub back into her pocket. 'It would be wise not to mention this meeting to anyone outside the Maquis. The careers of a great many people depend on Kramme reaching American soil alive. They will kill us if they have to, to make it happen.'

'I will tell Patrick. I will tell JJ, Daniel and René. I will not tell Paul.'

'That's what we need. Thank you.' Céline offers her hand. 'Goodnight, Sophie.'

'Goodnight, Céline.' They embrace, coolly. Between them is a frisson of the old, ambivalent friendship. She is glad.

Twenty-five hours later, shortly after one o'clock in the morning, a dark car delivers Sophie to a passing place on the side of a hill. The driver does not remain; he never does. There are no neighbours here, no shyly parted shutters, only trees and rock and road, but still, he does not want to be seen.

She stands on the road until the car is out of sight, then walks between two pine trees that look more or less like the other pines that line the road, and keeps going along a winding, uneven, less-than-obvious path, until she comes upon the clearing Patrick Sutherland has cut in the forest, and in which, with pain and difficulty and his particular brand of determination, he has built their cabin.

Here, she has a picket fence and a gate, an archway with climbing roses that together form a small portion of England in the mountains of France. Soon, they will be in bud. For now, she can smell the first snow on the peaks, fallen while she has been away. In the orchard, pruned trees stand bare and black. Last year's crop is in the cider press; the sharpness of it textures the air, mixing with the drift of woodsmoke from the stove in the cabin. A lit candle makes a clean, sharp flame in an alcove by the door, by which she knows that the Patron has stayed up, as he always does, to greet her.

448

She reminds herself that she cares for him, which is always true, and that she does not pity him, which is not always true, but tonight, with her news, it surely is. She makes herself more of what she should be – Amélie – and less of what she has been – Sophie – and walks down the gravel path to the door, to the warmth, to the fug of tea and tobacco, to his welcome, which is always peaceful.

Inside, the kettle hisses close to the boil and Patrick leans against the timber wall of the cabin. He steps forward to meet her. He can walk now, with only one stick. His embrace is solid, assured, always careful, in case he might crush her, or awaken something neither of them wants. He lifts her scarf with both hands and hangs it over a hook in a beam above the fire, not too close that it scorches, close enough to dry.

Welcome home.

'Thank you.'

How did it go?

'Interesting. The Americans and Russians are trying to start another war. JJ is trying to stop them. The British are stirring both sides, trying to find an advantage.'

This is harder than she once thought. She told Céline that he knew about Paul Rey, which was half true. He knows about the sex, and that it means nothing. He doesn't know about the killing. Or perhaps he does. Some things are beyond discussion.

He pours her tea, brings from the oven the casserole he has cooked.

Nothing changes.

'I'm not sure it ever will.' She drops into a chair and lifts her feet towards the fire. The car JJ sent her home in was a new Citroën DS, barely run in, but the heating had broken and she lost the feeling in her feet within an hour of leaving the airport. She tries to eat, and finds herself instead watching the fire.

What's the matter?

'Céline set up a meeting. That is, Theodora Vaughan-Thomas. Laurence is coming to visit you. About Kramme.'

She is tired and it is late. She expects questions and has prepared for them. She has not prepared for the intellectual leap that lights the spark in his eyes and the questions that arise from it. *They have found him? Tell me they haven't killed him? Tell me this is our chance?*

And this – *this* – is what sets this man apart. She presses a kiss to his cheek and watches life flow into him. There is so much to tell, and not all of it safe. She says, 'He'll be here within two days. If you don't want me here, I can go into Saint-Cybard, or—'

Don't be ridiculous. He catches her, kisses the top of her head. *Tell me everything.*

And she does. Almost.

CHAPTER THIRTY-ONE

Laurence hears Sophie before he sees her, and so has time to prepare. She is singing 'The Poor People of Paris', in its original version. If this is a cover, she does it well: the carefree young wife cycling home from the station at the end of a long, cold winter's day, at the end of a long, cold winter's week in the city.

The village of Arc-sous-Montagne is bigger by far than it used to be. Once confined to the valley, now it sprawls up the hill in a surge of new cottages. Here is the new France: neat lawns and tidy laurel hedges, white-painted houses with red-tiled roofs all slushily white now, under the latest fall of snow.

Sophie doesn't see until too late that Laurence is standing in the middle of the road. He raises one arm. 'Hello, Sophie.'

'*Merde!*'

She pulls hard left. A skitter of wheels, a smear of rubber on the road, and the bike slides to a halt ten yards past him. Pulling it round, she straddles the crossbar and glares at him. 'You?' He feels surprisingly light of heart.

She is still slight, slim, dark of hair and brow, with eyes that dwarf her face and smile lines that tug at her lips, even now, when she is enraged. She wears a floral dress with sensible shoes, and has pinned a flower in her hair that might be real, although he thinks it is silk.

She has not aged. That is to say, she is nearly five years older than when he last caught a poorly angled glimpse of her in a place where neither she nor he should have been. It is over a dozen years since he hugged her goodbye in the forests above Saint-Cybard and she looks no different from then, which is, in turn, remarkably unchanged from when he first saw her standing half naked and shivering on a pile of telephone directories in the Inquisition Room in Arisaig. She was Amélie, then. She uses it again, now, sometimes. He says, 'How are you?'

She isn't in the mood for conversation. She throws the bike round, to face back up the road. She eyes him, acidly. 'Who told Kramme that Patrick is still alive?'

He can lie to most people and has done so. He is not sure he can lie to her. 'Truthfully, I'm not certain, but I think he's known for a long time, possibly since before the war's end.'

'So it might be the Americans?'

He shrugs. Céline has done her work. Sophie is not stupid. She says, 'You want me to find out.'

'It would be useful, yes. If you don't want—'

'I sleep with Paul Rey. I don't trust him. If needs be, I will kill him. I will not let him keep us from Kramme.'

He watched, once, as she bit her own tongue and spat blood at a buffer of a cavalry colonel. In Arisaig, later, in the dark: *How many men have you killed?*

Not as many as you. Never have, never will.

He says, 'Thank you.'

'I'll talk to him if he comes here. Otherwise, what he doesn't know won't hurt him.'

'That was my thought exactly.'

She steps off her bike. It has a man's frame. He hasn't seen a woman ride a man's bike before, but it's the kind of untoward thing she might do. She holds it by the saddle and shoves it towards him, so that it runs free until he catches it. 'If you cycle and I sit on the crossbar, we'll get up the hill faster.'

He laughs, surprising them both. 'You haven't changed.'

Her smile is wildly enchanting. 'None of us has. We are just better at what we do.'

Hello, Laurence.

'Patrick. How are you?'

How do I look?

What can he say? You look tired and bored. I never thought I'd see a red-haired man look dull but here, in the house you built with your two hands, you look like a caged tiger, tired of pacing the boundaries. You look like a man who has had his tongue ripped out and knows that the only person in the world who truly understands him is having sex with someone else. You look half dead, but even that is an exaggeration. You look as if you died ten years ago, and your body has not yet had the grace to lie down.

He says, 'Better than I expected.'

You're a terrible liar.

'You don't know how low were my expectations.'

Ha.

This one word is normal. And here is some life, some colour, and a reminder of all that was. Caught off guard, Laurence sits, suddenly, on a carved oak rocking chair. The cabin smells of pine resin and Gitanes, of lapsang souchong and apples. It is homely, pleasant, a place to escape to. But Patrick is not free to escape here. Therein lies the rub.

Laurence says, 'What can I tell you?'

The truth?

Sutherland tilts his head, waiting, and Laurence, who has planned a long, twenty-minute preamble to this, says, baldly,

453

'Patrick, I don't know what the truth is any more. There was a time when the Boche were bad, we were good and all we had to do was see that right prevailed over wrong. Now, even that looks naive and Khrushchev is being made out to be the enemy when as far as I can tell, we're being turned into a small and rather unimportant state off the eastern seaboard of a nation that wants to take ownership of the entire earth and might well succeed. In all of this, the Brigadier had a plan. Sadly he died before its full extent was made clear to anyone else. I suspect, but am not sure, that he believed we might be able to extract Kramme from under the eyes of the Americans, while at the same time clearing an old debt. Sophie will have explained it all to you.'

She did. So Kramme is the lamb that bleats, not me.

'I think each of you gets to bleat a bit. And you can roar if you want to, when the time is right.'

He thinks he has misjudged his man. Sutherland closes his eyes, presses his lips together. It seems possible he is going to weep.

Laurence looks down, away from whatever is happening. He hears a soft, breathless sound and thinks Patrick Sutherland has lost the battle with his grief, and the part that needs to bear witness wins over the part that needs to preserve the other man's pride. He looks up again.

And so he discovers that Patrick Sutherland is not weeping; he is laughing, big, bold, full-chested laughter, and the tears rolling down his cheeks are not those of pain.

'Patrick?'

There is a gap, a cessation, a slowing down. *Oh, Laurence, Laurence, why did you not come back sooner?*

Oh, God. He seeks refuge in honesty. 'I thought you might not want to see me.'

And now?

'And now I know I should have come a decade ago.'

454

You should. There's nothing to be afraid of here, and much that is beautiful.

Patrick Sutherland rises, slaps his hand on Laurence's shoulder. He reaches past him to a cupboard and hunts in the back of it, grunting satisfaction when he finds what it is he seeks.

Stepping back, he sets a box on the table, made of wood so dark as to be almost black. On the lid, inlaid in ghosted silver ash, are the letters *LVT MdM*.

'Patrick! That's . . . I mean, I'd heard of these, but I've never actually seen one. It's beautiful. Truly.'

I know. It's like the old days: the smell of the fire, of Calvados, of tobacco. He loses ten years just by breathing in. Patrick says, *Lift the lid. Go on. I dare you.*

And he does, and sits astonished at the first three bars, and then he, too, is laughing as Patrick laughed, and they are dancing, sedately, not very accurately, to the strains of 'God Save the Queen'.

'Oh, God. It'll drive me mad!'

With a tug and a pull, Patrick lifts out the mechanism. Lo! Underneath, Fabien's requiem:

AND THUS BY ACCIDENT WE BECAME AS GODS
BLYTHE CHILDREN OF THE MOUNTAIN
WARRIORS OF VENGEANCE
UNFORGIVING, UNFORGIVEN
UNFORGOTTEN

'Patrick . . .'

There's more. Do you remember Arisaig?

'How could I forget.'

He has heard of these music boxes, of the secret compartments that are accessed by a code in the poetry. Remembering Arisaig, he tries out SLAINTE, but it doesn't work. On the third try, under instruction, he presses IOUASCOTCH and watches in awe as some near-silent mechanism opens a drawer. Inside is a picture of Sophie, a side view, with her attention elsewhere. She is relaxed, happy. He wonders how long ago it was taken.

If you get the combination wrong three times, it will lock itself irredeemably. You could always break it open with a sledgehammer, but at least the owner will know you've been there.

'Patrick, it's too beautiful to take apart with a sledgehammer. I heard you made one for the French consul in the Congo. And another for some functionary in Bonn.'

They paid me. They weren't gifts. And they don't say the same things inside. Only the Maquis de Morez have these. One each.

'They'll become family heirlooms.'

I sincerely hope so. And now – a bottle of Talisker appears on the table, and two shot glasses – *drink up and tell me exactly how you think we can trap Kramme and unmask Diem.*

And so he does.

The cabin is too small to contain the moment.

Laurence rocks back in the oak-carved chair and watches the men of Patrick's Maquis let themselves go. Perhaps they do it all the time, perhaps there is often this much noise here, but it seems unlikely that it has ever been like this.

'I don't believe it. I don't *fucking* believe it.' René is jogging on the spot, waving his cigarette in the air like a war pipe. He is a man now, far beyond his youth, solid, hard at the edges, fierce, but young enough still to be raucous.

Daniel is trying for decorum, and failing. He keeps smacking his fist into his palm, as if word of Kramme's proximity comes afresh to him at thirty-second intervals. His face is alight. If he were newly in love, it would be hard to imagine him any different. And he *is* in love, if not newly so. He has married Lisette Moreau, who was, for four unhappy years, Lisette Andreu, wife of the Milice chief in Saint-Cybard. She has recently confirmed that she is carrying their first child. So maybe he was already a happy man. Now, he is happier. If he is an agent of Kramme's, he's exceptionally good, but then that applies across the board and is, when Laurence thinks about it, rather the point.

Patrick and Céline are deep in animated communication over by the wood burner, and here, too, there are ways in which the past is alive in the present. She is caught in the red light, tall, slim, effortlessly commanding. He leans against the wall with a teacup and saucer in his better hand, every inch an English gentleman physician. He looks almost normal. Whole. Alive.

Céline, too, is radiant. As she sinks deeper into conversation with Patrick, it seems more as if she, too, has been caught in the vortex of this place, transported back to the time when they danced the knife-edge of mortality, and felt stronger for it.

He wonders how Sophie feels about this, looks around, catches her eye, nods a greeting. At his glance, she raises her cigarette in salute, detaches herself from the wall against which she has been standing, and comes to sit on the arm of the rocking chair.

'They make a good couple,' she says.

'Except, for all the obvious reasons, they don't.' He is closest to the teapot. He pours more into her empty cup, and his own.

She shrugs.

He says, 'And yet you watch them.'

'I was watching you. Does it still hurt?'

He forgets how direct she is. He lifts one shoulder in half an answer. 'Doesn't it you?'

'I have him.'

'Not as he was.'

'Even so . . .' She tilts her cup, stares at the red-gold reflections on the surface. 'We heard of the others. However bad it was for him, it could have been worse.'

'Will killing Kramme make it better?'

'I think he may sleep more soundly. Certainly, I will.' She glances sideways. She has grown into herself; she can sustain a look like this. 'And catching Diem. That would . . . tie off a lot of loose ends. I think in many ways, it matters more. To you also?'

They are talking quietly; nobody else is listening. She really is good at this. He makes himself smile. 'One never knows until afterwards, but I think so, yes.'

There is a crash on the porch. JJ muscles in through the door, swinging a sack on his back. He is still a vast man. His head almost touches the ceiling, but not quite; it was built with him in mind.

'*Mes amis* . . . one and all' – he speaks English like a native these days – 'I come bearing gifts.' He swings the sack to the floor, opens it, draws out a bundle and unrolls it with a flourish, revealing a clutter of brand-new Colt automatics. They are matt, blued, beautiful. They smell of new gun oil. They do not yet smell of smoke. 'With the compliments of the French government, for the purposes of killing our friend. Laurence had one like it in the war. For the rest of us, I suggest we all practise with them in the next days. Out here, nobody will hear us.'

None of them is immune to the lure of a new weapon. He hands them out, one by one, and they are like children given barley sugar. Hefting his own, his gaze seeks out Patrick, and Patrick, in turn, nods to Laurence, who puts down his new toy and takes a moment to fill and light his pipe. This speech, he has definitely prepared.

'The first thing to say is that we're here running naked on this. Which is to say, we don't have any kind of official sanction. We do this on our own. Utterly, completely alone. There can be absolutely nothing to trace us back to the DB or to MI6, and' – he avoids looking at Sophie – 'definitely not to the

CIA. There are those amongst their ranks who will kill to keep this man alive. Quite literally.' He lets his gaze take in the room. 'So we succeed or fail on our own. And if we fail, there is no safety net. I hope that is clear.'

We understand. Patrick was their Patron before and has become so again. They defer to him in all things, even JJ, who is so high up in the DB that nobody knows his job title. *You have my word, for everyone. And everyone is clear that he's mine when we get to him.*

Of that, without a doubt, everyone is clear.

Laurence's pipe has gone out. He sucks on hot spittle. 'If our information is correct, he's heading for Saint-Cybard. He may have this address, but it's more likely he'll endeavour to find it out when he gets to the town. He's not stupid and he'll be on his guard. We need to get him to a quiet place where Patrick can take his shot without any risk of repercussions. We were thinking—'

'The farm,' Daniel says.

Patrick catches Laurence's eye, raises his thumb.

Laurence says, 'We didn't want to ask, but yes, that would be perfect. Your mother will have to leave for a few days, if she won't mind?'

'For the Patron, she will do anything, you know that.'

Céline says, 'Daniel, she can't know what we're doing. She can't even know it's for him.'

'She can.' Sophie speaks from the first time from the shadows. 'She didn't betray us through four years of occupation; she won't betray us now.' She turns to Laurence, to Patrick. 'You'll need someone to track Kramme down in Saint-Cybard and lay a trail for him to follow. Someone who can recognize him in spite of the plastic surgery and the voice coaching.'

'Did I just hear you volunteer?'

'You certainly did.'

CHAPTER THIRTY-TWO

ORLÉANS
Sunday, 18 March 2018
22.17

IT IS NIGHT. THE sky is clear, the stars an effervescent trail across the dark. JJ Crotteau is dead and the repercussions ping onto Picaut's phone as Rollo copies her in on some of the messages floating round the world's intelligence agencies. JJ was big in so many ways: his reach – and the shock waves of his death – stretched way beyond France.

Elodie Duval's body has not been found, although, increasingly, it feels as if this is only going to be a matter of time. Every police force in Europe and North America is on alert for sightings. Every airport, seaport and international train station has her picture. Conrad Lakoff has offered to bring in the might of the NSA to filter the world's electronic communications. The fact that he can do this says more about his trajectory towards the top of the tree than any number of speeches at a conference.

A storm is brewing, but most of it is virtual. Sitting on the shabby-chic sofa in the quiet of Elodie's apartment, with two ancient newspaper cuttings in her hand – a wedding notice and an obituary – Picaut makes three phone calls.

First, to Sylvie: 'Check for properties in the region of Saint-Cybard held in the name of Mademoiselle Amélie Devereaux or Madame François Duval.'

'On it.'

Second, to Eric, who answers on the eighth ring sounding breathless and cross: 'Do you still have Elodie Duval's hairbrush? Good. How fast can you do a DNA test to check for parentage? Twenty-four hours? Because I have a wedding notice for Sophie Destivelle to François Duval and I need to know. Can't you—? Fuck. OK, never mind. Sorry to disturb you. Give my apologies to Ingrid.'

Third, to Martin Gillard. He's in a car: she can hear road noise and the background chatter of a radio when he picks up.

'Martin, did Elodie ever take a DNA test?'

There's a pause, and the sound of an indicator. In the background, someone coughs, but it might be on the radio. Gillard says, 'No idea. Is it something she might have done?'

'If she had reason to believe she wasn't Lisette Fayette's daughter, she might.'

'Right.' The road noise fills the gap when he doesn't speak. She can almost hear him thinking. 'Where are you?'

'At her apartment.'

'Right. You'll have a visitor shortly. Be careful, Captain.'

'Martin, you don't have to come here, I'm—' He has already gone.

She hangs up, slowly. Martin, you didn't ask why Elodie might have reason to believe she wasn't Lisette's daughter. Or whose she might have been. Which, actually, when she thinks about it, is more interesting than anything else.

Have you been speaking to Laurence Vaughan-Thomas? Because *he* knew. He sent me here. What have I not seen?

461

Picaut sits in the half-dark with her whole face screaming to be itched. She sits on her hands and it's no good. She gets up and prowls down the length of the wall, makes herself focus on the photographs, on the places where the shine of the street lamps plays across them, unevenly.

Here is Pierre in young adulthood: tall, good looking in a geeky kind of way. He looks very much like a younger Daniel, but with his mother's eyes.

Right a bit and here is Elodie as a teenager, standing with her parents and behind them, her godparents, Sophie and Laurence. She is older in the next shot: standing with Lisette and Sophie. In the one after that, she is twenty-one, leaning on a powder blue Mazda MX-5 with Pierre beside her, his arm around her shoulder. They are laughing, radiant. And next along, again, Elodie, Lisette, Pierre, Laurence and Sophie in a birthday shot, all crowded round a cake.

There is a pattern here, so subtle that it's only by the end of the wall that she sees it: over and over again, Elodie is never next to Sophie. Or perhaps it might be better to say that Sophie is never next to Elodie. Even at the funeral of Lisette Fayette, Sophie has turned her head at exactly the right moment, so that she is seen only in profile, while Elodie is face on.

Oh, you are so clever, you who trained in the days when failure was fatal.

Balanced on Elodie's sideboard is the black-and-white shot of the Maquisards jumping the wall into the churchyard where Max Kramme and his new bride were killed. Here is Sophie, caught in a moment of utter passion – hate, rage, joy, action, all shining from the fierceness of her face. She is beautiful.

She is every bit as beautiful as Elodie Duval. Seeing it now, *seeing* it, the relationship is not in question.

So that's one question answered. We don't need the DNA. But who else knows?

More importantly: when did Elodie find out?

And is it enough for her to kill? Or for her to be hunted?

Who, in fact, would care, beyond those already dead?

Start with the easy ones. Picaut takes out her phone and makes some new notes:

- Who knew about Elodie? (Besides Sophie.)
- Who was the father? François Duval?
- Elodie's cipher: Paul Rey's son. Diem's legacy?
- Who is Diem?
- Who is Paul Rey's son?
- How is he Diem's legacy?
- Who was John Lakoff?
- Why did he die?

She throws the phone down and leans back, looping her hands behind her head. What difference would it make to me if I found out my father was not my father; my mother was not my mother?

My mother? I never knew her, let that one go.

Father?

Her mind is an open void in which her father's face blurs and shifts. His truth was the foundation stone of her life. It is impossible to imagine a world in which he was proved unreliable. Look at the pictures on the walls and on the sideboard; Elodie Fayette loved her parents equally – it shines from her eyes, on her face. She is the kind who loves fully, without restraint. Any mother would be proud to name her daughter.

Sophie, why did you give her away?

A knock at the door. Picaut uncurls from the sofa. 'Martin, you don't have to—'

Not Martin.

'Sup.' Patrice is as she remembers: alive, wild, electric. He reaches out as if to touch her arm, and then stops. His hand drops to his side. The smile falls from his face. 'Can I come in?'

She steps back. They stand inside the threshold, stiffly, unsure of where the boundaries are. The fire that flared between them was so brief and . . . bad metaphor. Picaut takes another, bigger step back. Patrice does the same. 'My mistake. I'll go.'

'*No!*' She reaches for his arm, pulls him in, kicks the door shut. 'No. Come in. For God's sake, come in. Have some coffee? I don't have any Red Bull.'

'I've given up.'

'Coffee?' She can't imagine that.

'No. The tins. Coffee's fine.' He fixes on a smile and she remembers this from the hospital, the sense of blotting paper in her mouth, a thick tongue, cheeks that hurt from smiling when she doesn't want to smile. He's the same. It's why she let him go. Or sent him away: it might have been that.

Not smiling, he says, 'Does this have to be such hard work? I thought we were doing OK earlier. I thought you might like to see me.'

'I do. Really, I do. Is it me making the hard work?'

'I don't think it's me. I just got off a plane from Brussels.'

'That's not the point. I didn't . . .' She closes her eyes and then forces them open again. 'Let's start back at the beginning. Patrice La Croix, I am really, really happy to see you. Really. Just surprised and out of practice at being human. Come in and sit down. It's fine. I'll make coffee and you can explain why you're here.'

'Isn't that obvious?' He follows her through to the kitchen. 'I came to help.'

'How? And . . . why?'

'Why: because I can. How . . . You tell me? Coffee first, maybe?'

He is talking, but his eyes are speaking different words. He takes his phone out, and reaches into her pocket and lifts hers, light-fingered. Holding both close to the sound of the boiling kettle, he mouths the word: Fridge?

It's concealed behind the kitchen facade, in the corner. Rolling her eyes, Picaut opens the door. He gives her a thumbs up, disembowels both phones and lays them with their batteries on the top shelf.

With the fridge safely shut, he leans against it, laughing at the look on her face. 'What? You think I'm paranoid?'

'I know you're paranoid. What worries me is that you're the one usually doing the listening, so in this case, I have to believe you're right.' She sweeps her hands over her eyes. It's been a long day and the accumulated hours are beginning to eat at her. 'It's lovely to see you, but really, why are you here?'

'Relax. It's OK.' He leans over and places a chaste kiss on her cheek. 'I found Paul Rey's sons. All of them. Pour me a coffee and I'll tell you.'

They sit in the living room, shoulder to shoulder on the sofa. It's like it used to be, almost.

Patrice pulls his laptop onto his knee. 'Paul Rey is a one-man population explosion. Three American wives, one Canadian, one Columbian, all involved in espionage one way or another. Plus a French mistress at the UN who is the reason wife number five left. He never married the mistress and the relationship seems to have lasted longer than most. From the actual marriages, he has six sons that are legitimate, all military. The eldest died in Iraq. The next down is a navy cryptographer— What?'

He's been typing his password into his laptop. Picaut just watched the flurry of letters, digits, capitals, lower case.

'Can you hack into a laptop? This laptop?' She hands him Elodie's.

He laughs again and this really is quite like she remembers it. 'Not legally.'

'But still.'

'Here—' He takes it, wires it up to his own laptop, starts typing. 'So, let me tell you what I found. Paul Rey's first six sons are all models of probity. They're boring as hell: buzz-cut forces officers who've never stepped a foot over any legal line. The seventh was the son of the mistress, the one who was a French "diplomat" at the UN.' He puts quotes round the word.

'You mean she was DB.'

'Or as we've called it for nearly forty years, External Affairs. Her only child was a son. Paul Rey acknowledged fatherhood, which was the point when his fifth marriage fell apart. The kid followed his father into the CIA.'

'But?' She can hear the but.

'But I can't find his name and there are limits to how deep it's sensible to dig into these things. I can look further if you need, but— Well, that didn't take long.' He has opened Elodie's computer. The password is D13Ms L3g4cY. Of course it is.

She says, 'Nicely done,' and moves closer. Knee to knee, they watch Elodie Duval's screen come to life. The desktop image is the now-famous still of the Maquis leaping the wall. Picaut looks at it differently now; Sophie is angled away from the rest. She is not one of them. Still, a single folder is placed over Sophie Destivelle's heart: KRAMME'S WEDDING.

Within the folder is a video file: eighteen seconds of the Maquis assault on Kramme's wedding. Picaut's palms prickle. Her hair feels static. 'Can I play this without it erasing itself or blowing us all up?'

Patrice leans back, loops his fingers behind his head. He gives her a look that used to curdle her innards and now simply warms them, which is good, probably. He says, 'What can possibly go wrong?'

What, indeed? She presses PLAY.

He's right. The hard drive does not chatter, the screen does not grow blank. In fact, nothing happens at all except that Paul Rey's film begins to play.

It is in old, wartime colour, or has been made to look as if it is. The first few frames are almost pastoral in their beauty: a wide opening shot shows a blue sky, a snow-shouldered mountain, a valley, sparsely populated, and a small church, decked out in Nazi regalia. The groom and his bride emerge from the church, radiant: he in uniform, bedecked with medals, she in white, bearing a bouquet of lavender. She does not look happy. Something startles them, they turn to their left, and—

Patrice gives a long, low whistle. 'They didn't hold back, did they?'

And here it is: the film from which the still image was taken. Picaut watches the front line of the Maquis de Morez hurdle the wall. She knows them now: Céline, Paul Rey, Daniel, René, JJ, Laurence, Sophie . . . Their guns blaze. The hate is real, and vividly alive.

At the moment she knows best, Picaut leans forward to stop the action. The image is wholly familiar, but the faces are sharper here, and while the colour may be faded pastel, it's clear nonetheless; if it were shot yesterday, this could not be sharper, or better quality. She asks, 'Can the CIA take really old film stock and bring the resolution up?'

'Effortlessly.' Patrice collects the original Maquis picture from the sideboard and brings it back to sit alongside the video. 'What's Sophie looking at?'

This is why she loved him. One of the reasons. 'René Vivier asked that and I've not discovered the answer.' Picaut restarts the action. 'Let's find out.'

The scene moves on. From Paul Rey to JJ, the Maquisards continue to charge at the camera. But Sophie darts off screen, and a few strides later, Laurence follows.

In the face of the screaming, firing Maquis, the camera swings violently away, wobbling, shooting on a crazy angle, so that Picaut and Patrice tilt their heads, following the picture, trying to keep it square. The line of sight runs clear past the church to where three figures sprint towards a line of cars. Four figures: one is up ahead, nearer the road.

'That's clever.' Patrice points to the edge of the screen. 'See the pixels at the margins? The original camera lost focus there. Cleaning that up won't have been effortless.'

And so they see Sophie Destivelle running, shooting, then kneel to take one final shot at the German staff car on the edge of the picture. They see the rifleman in the back seat of the car fall. 'Can you zoom in on that?'

'I can try.'

He tries. He succeeds. Picaut taps the screen. 'That's Toni Gaspari, the third man in the Jedburgh team. Laurence told me he was shot by a German sniper.' She chews on the edge of her thumb. 'Why would Sophie kill one of her friends?'

'Maybe she wasn't aiming for him. That's a German officer getting into the car.'

Picaut stops the film. Half a dozen frames, no more, focus on the figure by the car. They are as clear as digital wizardry can make them, but still, he is too far away, too small, too blurred to be useful. 'Can you zoom in on him?' To the right of the frame, Laurence has reached Sophie and is pointing a Colt at her head. Paul Rey is coming in on the other side. It's a captivating tableau, but still . . .

'Give me a minute.' It takes him longer than that. Waiting, Picaut studies Paul Rey, the raw passions coursing across his features as he stands by Sophie Destivelle. It's easy to see why it took the studio so long to find an actor to play him in a way that would adequately light up the screen. Easy, too, to imagine that he might get through five wives if Sophie Destivelle chose to marry someone else.

Patrice nudges her arm. 'That's the best I can do.'

His best is a miracle, or close to it. The Boche officer is in the process of throwing away his hat. The swing of his arm brings him face-on to the camera, which is, by chance – or perhaps not – looking back at Sophie and Paul. 'Can you zoom in on his head? On his face?'

He can.

He does.

And there it is.

'Inès? Inès, are you all right?'

'I'm fine.' Her head is a balloon, rising. Bright sparks float past her eyes. Her scar . . . does not hurt. 'Fine. Really.'

'You don't look it.' He's gazing at her, wide-eyed, in a way she remembers, dimly, from the hospital.

She cuffs him across the head, lightly. She says, 'Can you find me an image of Conrad Lakoff?'

It takes him longer than she thinks it might – Conrad Lakoff doesn't like to be photographed – but Patrice is . . . Patrice. He finds what she needs.

'Put it up there.' Alongside Kramme.

'Ah.' He squints. 'Think they're related?'

'I really do.' Picaut drains her coffee. The feeling of standing on the edge of a cliff is back, full of adrenaline, magical.

Patrice says, 'Sylvie's trying to ring your mobile. Do you want me to divert it to a number they're not listening to?'

She does. To Sylvie: 'What have you got?'

'Madame François Duval owns a cabin in the mountains north and east of Saint-Cybard. The Google Maps location is coming through to your phone now.'

'Thank you.'

'And Monsieur François Duval died in 1957, six months before Elodie was born.' There's a pause. Sylvie is not given to drama, so this is going to be good. 'Elodie's middle name is Céline. So you could say Elodie was the legacy of the Maquis.'

Of course she was. Nothing is quite as it seems. Where is she? Who cares who she was? To Sylvie again, she says, 'Don't go away.' She fishes Conrad Lakoff's business card from her pocket. To Patrice: 'Can you trace a phone and show where it is on the map?'

Of course he can. A minute or two later, a red dot creeps slowly down a line south and east from Orléans. He says, 'That's the—'

'A5.' Straight to Saint-Cybard. 'OK, find these.' She gives him Martin Gillard's number, Martha Lakoff's, Clinton McKinney's.

Two more dots join the first one – ahead of it, closer to the cabin that Sylvie has found. It turns out that Martha is leading the convoy, with Martin a few cars behind – he might be tailing her, he's keeping a constant distance – and Conrad Lakoff is about an hour behind those two.

'McKinney?' Picaut asks.

'He hasn't left Orléans. Or at least, his phone's still at home.'

'Right.' Too many variables. Picaut rakes her hands through her hair. 'How long before Martha reaches the cabin?'

'An hour? Bit less if she cuts across country at the end.'

'And it'll take us four hours at least. We don't have that. Sylvie, are you still there?'

'Sure am.'

'Get Rollo and Petit-Evard, meet me at the studio ASAP.' To Patrice: 'Who do you know who has a plane that can take off and land in a field, and is fast enough to get us to Saint-Cybard in under two hours?'

He spreads his hands. 'Ducat?'

'Not if Conrad Lakoff's listening in.'

'Then you need someone who knows how to get past the law. Which means either a drug runner who doesn't mind lending their wings to the police, or someone powerful enough that they might reasonably be taking off from

Orléans without anybody paying attention. And the cash for a Cessna or something like it. And a pilot.'

That's obvious then. There's only one person they know with that much money and that much power. She says, 'Lise Bressard and I went through a fire together: the least she can do is lend me a plane.' Picaut grabs her bag, her keys, Elodie's laptop. 'I'll drive. You see if you can find us a flat, safe, cow-free landing field close enough to the cabin, but not so close they'll hear us come in.'

'On it.'

'And Patrice—'

'Yes?'

'The name of Paul Rey's French mistress, was it Sophie Duval?'

'No. It wasn't her. This was a real flesh-and-blood woman who's just retired from her post in the UN. Martine Gillard.'

And there we are. The final pieces slot into place. On her cliff edge, Picaut takes a breath, leans into the wind and jumps.

CHAPTER THIRTY-THREE

KRAMME IS HERE. THE feel of him is pure intravenous opium: just walking through the door, Sophie is more alert.

Her palms ache. Her head is too light, her vision too clear. She hasn't seen him yet, but he is here.

She has spent four days in the bars and back rooms of Saint-Cybard, looking for a man whose features have been remoulded, whose voice has been coached into new cadences and dialects so that she will no longer recognize its pitch.

She has kept going, following a felt-sensed trail to this, the bar of the unimaginatively named Hôtel de Ville which was once the Hôtel Cinqfeuilles, and is now rebuilt, refurbished, reborn in duck-egg pastel paints and linoleum floor tiles and strip lights that give off a headache-inducing glare.

Outside, it has snowed again, and the streets are crisply white, tinged to amber under the glare of the street lights. In here, oil-fired radiators keep the atmosphere damp and over-warm. Women cast off heavy coats. Men shed hats and gloves and scarves.

Sophie is sober in slacks and a dark sweater, low shoes, an Italian leather jacket in a dark pewter that matches her shoes and cost more than all the rest put together. She's wearing a greying wig that puts ten years on her and make-up that diminishes her lips and eyes. Catching a glimpse of herself in the mirror, she is a hard-faced, embittered loser. Probably, she supported the wrong side in the war and will spend the rest of her life trying to forget it. France is full of these.

At the bar, she orders wine and uses the time it takes to pour to check the mirrors. Thus she finds a man behind and to her left, in the dining area, eating alone with his back in a corner so that she can only see the edge of his hair. It is red, almost the colour Patrick's was when he was whole. Céline said he'd done this and she didn't believe it, but now, her body twitches. She has not seen him this close since he proposed to her. The thought makes her intestines writhe. It is him, though, without doubt. Kramme. Here. At last. Her Browning is a living thing, whispering in her handbag. Use me. Use me. Use me.

She is stronger than the voice. Other things matter than just his death. Wait and we shall have vengeance twice over.

Another glance in the mirror. He has a short, neat beard the same colour as his hair, and his glasses are more stylish and he's wearing tweeds that look astonishingly foreign, here in the Jura, but she has visual, as Paul Rey would say, and it is entirely unambiguous.

Quietly and without fuss, she sets down her wine and leaves the bar.

In the lobby, she borrows the hotel phone and dials a number, not the Fayette farmhouse. She lets it ring three times, hangs up, rings again and lets it ring twice. Like the Morse tapped on her leg, the old code comes as instinct.

Two minutes later, Céline joins her in the ladies' convenience, dressed as a housemaid.

473

'It's him?'

'Without question.'

Céline allows herself a small sigh of happiness. She says, 'I'll let René know. If Kramme leaves before you get down again, I'll follow and send Daniel back for you.'

This is how they planned it: every eventuality covered. The spark of Céline's eyes is electric. 'He will die, Sophie, I swear it.'

They part. Sophie heads back out into the foyer and paces a while, smoking, as if lost in thought.

René arrives before she lights her second cigarette. He is her bag man in the truest sense of the word. He takes a room on the second floor and she follows him up, scandalizing the concierge. Inside, she strips down to her underwear and dresses again from the suitcase he has brought, in the maroon dress and ridiculous heels she wore to the Canadian ambassador's soirée. A new wig replaces the grey one and she becomes a brassy blonde with a surfeit of blusher and bright, scarlet lips.

Like this, she really is the lamb staked out for the taking. The Italian jacket turns inside out, and is black now, with a high collar. She takes her scarf – even now, she is never without it – but this time she flaunts it, openly.

Last in the suitcase he hauled up the stairs for her is an English-made handbag, reconfigured by the CIA and sold to the agencies of Europe. JJ has three, of which this is his finest. It contains a tiny camera, not much bigger than a couple of boxes of cigarettes taped together. A fish-eye lens concealed amidst decorative beading allows it to take in half a room. Reverse pressure on the bag's opening catch triggers the shutter.

René hands her a shoulder holster. She straps it on and transfers her Hi-Power from her discarded handbag; she has not brought JJ's Colt, lovely though it is – she needs a gun that fits her hand without her having to think about it. Two spare magazines fit into inner pockets of her jacket. She slides the jacket on and turns on the spot, raising her arms.

'Does it show, the gun?'

'Only if you know what you're looking for.'

'Which is the point.'

'Which is the point.' René is endlessly calm. He, too, has changed, swapped his red sweater for a grey one, and slid a cap on his head. He lights a cigarette and lets it droop from the side of his mouth. Like this, he is Maquis again. If he is Kramme's agent, he is nerveless.

She thinks it cannot be him, but then she thinks the same about Daniel and JJ. Curious, she says, 'Are you never afraid?'

'If someone was about to take a hammer to my fingers, I might be. Anything less than that . . . ?' He shrugs. 'What is there to worry about?'

She has many answers, and nothing is served by dwelling on any of them. One last look in the mirror: she is utterly unlike the woman who walked in. The concierge will not know her, nor the men in the bar. Maximilian Kramme certainly will, but that, too, is the point.

'Make him think he is one step ahead of us,' Laurence said in their hours of planning. 'His arrogance will lure him in, and he will be less inclined to check for traps.' She, who knows Kramme best, did not disagree then, nor does she now.

René flashes her a high-voltage grin and she feels her own mouth dry.

'Happy?' he asks.

'Very. Go now. I'll wait six minutes and follow.'

He grips her arm. 'See you at the farm.'

Sophie has never been blonde before, not like this, brazen. It's an interesting experiment. Shouldering her way through the lounge door a second time, she gives her overcoat and beret to the first man who offers, and accepts a drink from the second.

Her quarry has not moved from his seat with his back to her. She takes her white wine and moves along the bar, trailing men's attention. Her handbag rests on the counter beside her. She watches Kramme's reflection and feels in her marrow the moment when he notices her, the fractional break before that awareness shifts to recognition, the shock that follows it.

If the Diem feint is accurate in any respect, he must have known she was coming, but still, he has not been this close to Sophie since he proposed marriage and it would appear that she affects him still.

She sneezes, and fumbles in her bag for a tissue. Blowing her nose causes her to sneeze again. With a soft '*Merde!*' she closes the bag and, quite soon afterwards, abandons her wine and her entourage and heads out of the bar.

Outside, it is snowing again: a slow, soft, steady fall that will leave ten centimetres on the roads before morning. Her car is two blocks away and the pavement is treacherous underfoot. Walking on packed snow in these heels is far from effortless. She takes small steps, carefully, hands out for balance. René is off to her right. The red glow of his cigarette is full stop and question mark both. JJ should be behind, Daniel in front with René and Céline fanning out to the sides: she has the full team, the ultimate backup. The door to the Hôtel de Ville opens and closes.

She hears soft footsteps behind her. The gap between her shoulder blades feels naked. She turns right and crosses a road, left, left again, and back onto the street one block up. She stops in a doorway to light her cigarette, draws on it three times, glances back. Kramme is stooped, shuffling. He is wearing a hat. If she were going only on outline and gait, she wouldn't know him. Her spine feels ever colder.

Her car is the almost-new DS that brought her up the

mountain on her return from Berlin; one of JJ's, borrowed from his pool. It is cold and will not start. She can't pump the throttle for fear of flooding it, nor turn the key too often for fear of flattening the battery. She puts clutch and accelerator to the floor and mouths a brief prayer of a kind she has not spoken in many years. Holy Mary, Mother of—

The ignition fires.

She hauls off the wig, discards the heels for pumps and pulls away from the kerb. The fan blows frigid air at her knees and ankles and she loves it. She loves everything.

The Fayette farmhouse has not changed in any important way since she first dropped out of the sky onto its doorstep in 1944. Sophie picks out the small alterations: there is central heating in the downstairs rooms and a toilet with a handbasin has been added at the back, accessed by a short passageway from a door at the rear of the kitchen. The cattle are the great-granddaughters of those that gave milk on the morning of Sophie's first breakfast. They are in the biggest of the barns now, ahead of her as she drives in, with the cattle at ground level and hay in the upper storey. The barn to her left, opposite the house, is a machinery store.

Tonight, yard, house and barns are newly clad in snow. A torch flickers to her right. She pulls up next to it and rolls down her window. Daniel, who was ahead of her, appears out of the darkness. From somewhere hidden, he has brought his wartime Sten and is wearing it across his back. With this, he is Maquis again, younger, oddly vulnerable. Cradled across his forearms he carries his father's pre-war shotgun. Patrick is not the only one with a call on vengeance.

She says, 'Seven minutes behind.' She has stopped twice and looked back down the road to the headlights grinding slowly up the hairpin bends behind her. Three sets, a steady half-kilometre apart. 'JJ's a minute back with René and Céline two minutes behind him.'

'We're on, then.' Daniel jerks his head to their right, opposite the farmhouse, angles the torch in the same direction. 'If you park your car by the barn, he'll see it when he draws in.'

She eases the DS up to the wall of the barn, leaving a space in front, in case someone needs it for cover. A dozen paces to her right, the main doors of the barn lie ajar ahead of her with a small entrance door set another three metres further along.

She steps out and makes clear tracks in the snow, through to the gap in the main doors. Daniel rolls shut the heavy oak behind her, and clicks on the light.

Inside is Daniel's car and a host of other farm machinery, and Patrick, leaning on the wall. His eyes catch the inadequate light of the wartime bulb and reflect it back to her in all its drabness. His arms hang loose by his sides and from his left hand, the better hand, hangs a brand new Colt automatic. Tension rolls from him, but it's living tension, such as she has not felt from him since the day of Kramme's wedding.

Sophie checks her watch. 'He'll be here in five minutes. We have time for our eyes to adjust to the dark again.'

And for you to change. Her suitcase is behind him, already open. With relief, she discards the dress and dons instead the loose slacks and cotton shirt that she has kept since the mountains and that feel like a second skin. She lifts her scarf and wraps it round her neck, inside her shirt. Now she, too, is wholly Maquis.

'Thank you,' she says, and Patrick nods.

Some moments later, as if he has had to find the words, blow off the dust, stitch them together: *You might want to go into the house. It's safer there.*

She shakes her head. 'You'll need backup until the others get here.'

I have Daniel and Laurence.

If we can trust Daniel. Which perhaps we cannot. 'Where is Laurence?'

In the kitchen, by the back door. He and JJ installed a set of floodlights. He'll switch them on if we need to be able to see.

JJ's a hard, difficult man, who makes no effort to be good, or kind, or reasonable, except to her and the others from the Maquis, for whom no problem is too hard, no request denied. She can't imagine him a traitor any more than Daniel or René. She looks around.

A small jockey door to the right of the main entrance has been left invitingly ajar. It is in a direct line to Patrick, so that the door itself will cover him from anyone coming in, until they have stepped fully through. The range is less than twenty metres. Nobody could miss that close and Daniel is there with both barrels of a shotgun that could stop a charging boar. Still . . .

'I'm not leaving you now.'

Sophie—

'I won't get in the way. I won't make myself a target. But I am not leaving you now.'

Theirs has not always been an easy marriage, but from the earliest days they promised honesty, and it has survived all the vicissitudes of their life so far. His eyes search her face. She is, she imagines, as pale as he is.

Go to the other side of the car. Crouch down. Don't get involved unless you must.

Unless he is dead. This could happen. She pushes the thought aside.

'Be careful,' she says.

His right hand reaches to grip her shoulder. *And you.*

She blinks, hard. Part blind, she feels her way past Daniel's car and then a rusting horse-drawn cart that has been supplanted by a tractor.

Daniel clicks off the light. With stiff fingers, Sophie eases her Hi-Power from her shoulder holster. In the cold, still night, a single car approaches.

479

CHAPTER THIRTY-FOUR

THE FAYETTE FARMHOUSE
6–7 March 1957

L AURENCE HEARS SOPHIE'S CAR first. He knows the particular grind and grumble of the DS engine, listens as it rolls into the barn and falls silent.

Four days of waiting, and the end is here. He stands in the kitchen, by the door onto the yard, with his hand on the newly installed light switch that controls the floodlights. Marianne Fayette is upstairs in the farmhouse, lying on the floor beneath her bed. She thinks this undignified but Patrick and Daniel between them have charmed her into the understanding that she can recover her dignity in the morning if she is alive and that all the dignity in the world will not serve her if she catches a stray round in the cross-fire.

There will be cross-fire. The first, and most open plan assumes not; this plan assumes a single surgical bullet, a quick kill and the real effort put into disposing of the body.

The second plan assumes that the first plan will have been betrayed, in which case there will be a quite astonishing amount of cross-fire, but far fewer people know of this.

So everyone waits, guns out, safeties off, holding still and

480

silent for the last few moments of peace before all hell descends and Laurence, who has spent altogether too much time behind a desk of late, finds that he is not sorry it has come to this, only that it has taken so long.

Kramme's car is bigger than Sophie's, and throatier: German. It rounds the corner and crunches to a halt in the new snow. There are no lights here, not even stars. When his headlights go out, Maximilian Kramme will be alone in the dark in a strange place. He, Laurence, would reverse out and drive away, but then he would have taken the plane to Washington in the first place. In this, as in so many things, he is the opposite of Kramme, of Patrick, of Sophie, of Céline.

The car door closes. To all intents and purposes, Kramme is boxed in, with nowhere to go, and somewhere out there in the snow and the dark is Diem, who will try to save him.

Laurence eases back the hammer on his Colt and lets the kitchen door drift open one last inch.

Let's go.

Sophie hears Kramme's car door close. The pressure of waiting is barely supportable. Her fingers are bloodless sticks. Her throat is a straw, whistling. She can see almost nothing, but she doesn't need to; she can feel Patrick, his stillness, his rage. A dozen slow, snow-soft steps and the big barn door shudders as Kramme tests the weight of it, the effort it will take to pull back. The part-open side door does not move: too obvious a trap.

And yet . . . the oak is not so thick. At this distance, a Colt could fire through and still kill whoever is on the other side.

Shoot now. Now. Forget the rest, we can sort it later, just kill Kramme now. *Now!*

But Patrick won't do that. Whatever else is at stake, his decency won't let him shoot a man blind. He will want Kramme to see his face as he dies. She raises her own gun and—

481

Merde.

A spit, nothing loud, but she knows the sound of suppressed gunfire as she knows the sound of her own voice and Patrick's gun was not silenced.

A body falls, hard, against the wall and then the floor: this sound, too, she knows.

'Patrick!' She runs, crouched low. Outside, more cars accelerate into the yard. Brakes whine. Boots run on snow. Sophie gives thanks for JJ, René, Céline.

A voice shouts, 'Here! Kramme, here!'

The voice is not French, but she knows it. Fuck them – they want to play it like this, they're welcome. Raising her gun, she fires an entire magazine through the jockey door without care for who she might hit.

Following her lead, Daniel blasts his shotgun at the thin wood, both barrels, one after the other. A man cries out, but it's not a death scream: a pellet or two somewhere inconvenient, nothing more, certainly not a shattered liver, a ruptured gut, the long, slow death of which she has dreamed.

'Daniel, go!' Cursing, Daniel throws the shotgun into a pile of straw, drags his Sten over his head, kicks open the jockey door and barrels out, firing.

She shouts, 'Lights! Laurence, we need lights!'

A slight hiss, a fizz in the night and there is light. Light! Liquid silver floods under the door, through the cracks at the hinges, dazzlingly bright.

'Patrick?' He lies on his side between the barn wall and Daniel's car. She takes hold of his shoulder, then jerks back as his hand grasps at hers. He pulls himself up. His face is masked in light and shadow. He gives a strange, wry grin, but brighter than she's seen in ten years. *He is not hurt. Get Kramme. If he thinks I'm dead, he'll make a mistake.*

She squeezes the hand that lies in hers. On an impulse, she bends and kisses him on the cheek; it's that kind of night.

482

Outside is more firing, more shouting. More voices join, in several languages.

Patrick sits up, listening. *Russians? How are they here?*

She says, 'Americans trying to put us off the scent. That's one of Paul Rey's men.' Paul Rey, who is playing an exceptionally dangerous game, but then, they all are.

She says, 'If I was wrong . . .'

It won't be your fault. Patrick grips her arm again. *Laurence trusts him too.*

She pushes herself up. 'Don't show yourself until you have to. Laurence and I will kill Kramme. Céline can sort out the unwanted extras.'

If she gets here.

Even as he speaks more cars pull in, doors slam, someone shouts in English. Sophie squeezes his shoulder. 'She already has.'

With her left hand, she inches the jockey door open. Outside, the snow, which was irritating but manageable, has become a blizzard of the most debilitating kind. Nobody sane would drive in this. JJ just has – she can't see his car, but she can hear the deep bass of his voice and the stutter of his gun. He's at the yard's far end, firing at the Americans. Paul won't like that, but then Paul shouldn't have brought people he cared about if he didn't want them to be shot at.

In the silver-white whirling chaos, the yard has become a double-ended firing range. Daniel is down on one knee near the cow byre at the far end, arcing his Sten in a long angry spray across the yard. Halfway down stand the only solid shapes in the white-out; three big, black BMW 501s that look as if they might be carrying extra armour. Figures shuffle in the shelter they give. Ricochets whine.

Looking across at the farmhouse, Sophie can make out the milking parlour with the hayloft upstairs where she slept on her first night in France. In the doorway below stands a shape that should be Laurence. He is firing, shouting, waving at her.

Other, less obvious, shapes move to her left. She aims a double shot at the half-seen shoulder of a man bigger than JJ, and there aren't many of those in the world.

She doesn't make a kill, but the monster stops firing at Laurence, who signals again across the snow-driven space – arm raised, swung, made flat – movements she can see through the whirling snow; old, old signals, dug deep into her unconscious.

Her body follows the meaning long before her mind has caught up. With Laurence covering, she runs hare-like, jinking left and right, heading obliquely across to join him in the kitchen doorway. Here, amidst all the acrid reek of gunshot, is the warmth of baking and coffee, sanity in the midst of the carnage. Laurence says, 'Patrick?'

'Alive.' She looks round the corner, fires, ducks back, changes her empty magazine. Fourteen rounds left. 'He's laying low in the barn so they think he's dead. Paul Rey's here. He's brought extra men. JJ and Daniel are both firing at the Americans. I haven't seen René yet, which may be telling.' It's not conclusive, but it's a start.

'No plan survives first contact and all that,' Laurence says. 'Our priority is Kramme.'

'Where is he?'

'In the cow byre at the end of the yard, I think. We need to keep him there. He'll be trying to get to the Americans.'

'So let's stop them leaving.' She taps Laurence's arm. 'Cover me.'

He's a soldier. He stands up and blazes a full clip of his Colt at the armoured BMWs and the Americans on either side. Sophie throws herself prone in the snow with her elbows on the solid ground and takes a proper aim. Her first shot misses. The second hits. The nearest BMW's nearside front tyre collapses.

'Good idea.' Laurence stands over her, reloading. 'Keep going. I'll stop anyone who tries to stop you.'

This is a good idea that lasts exactly as long as it takes for the incomers to realize what she's doing. One more tyre hisses flat, and then she becomes the focus for fire of a savagery she has forgotten.

Patrick saves her. He appears at the jockey door to the barn, shouting, waving his stick. 'Laurence! Front and right!' He draws fire, giving Sophie time to crawl out of the kill zone before he steps back inside.

When next she looks, a snow-hazed figure is standing at the limits of the floodlights. She knows that shape, even in this light. 'Look out!' She jerks her head away, covers her eyes with her arm. 'It's Paul. He's got—'

A flare.

It soars scarlet into the night.

Laurence pulls a face. 'Paul always did have a flair for the dramatic.'

'He wasn't meant to—'

'I think we can safely conclude that Paul has not kept his promises.'

'I'll kill him.'

'Yes, but Kramme first.'

Sophie eases back out of the door. The snow spirals down, making her dizzy. She empties her Hi-Power into the havoc, wriggles back and ejects the magazine.

Laurence, ever-organized, shoves a box of shells across the floor towards her. She refills, plotting the geography of the yard. 'Where's Céline?'

'With any luck at all, she's gunning down Paul Rey.'

'She isn't. She can't find him.' Céline stands behind them, a grim, mud-soaked figure, with her hair up under a cap so she looks like a man. She started off with the Colt that JJ got for her, but from somewhere, she's found a Sten. It suits her better.

'She did see an ape of positively Slavic proportions, though,' she says. 'And if Uncle Joe really has sent people to the party, I'd be inclined to let them have him. I can't think of a better way for Kramme to end his days than in the basement of the Lubyanka.'

'He'd talk, though.' Laurence is lighting up a cigarette. He lights a second from the first and hands it to his cousin. 'We'd lose a whole nest of networks in the east.'

Céline nods, cheerily. 'Some prices are worth paying.'

Sophie takes the third cigarette. Outside, men are killing each other. She says, 'They're not Russians, they're Americans trying to confuse us. The one with the white hair was in Poland with Kramme's Einsatzkommandos: Obersturmbannführer Rudi Schäfer.'

'Bugger.' Céline frowns. 'Gehlen, then. Which means CIA. Which means Paul Rey really has dumped us in it. That's a pity, I rather liked him.'

Sophie says, 'I'm so sorry.'

'Don't be. You are not your lover's keeper.' Smiling fiercely, Céline pushes herself to her feet. 'There's still plenty we can do. The Cousins can't have Kramme if he's dead. And if we can hit Schäfer as well, I'll consider it a night well spent.'

'What about Diem?'

'If anyone looks as if they're firing the wrong way, then we have our man.'

'Right.' Laurence stabs his cigarette into the kitchen floor. 'I rather think this might have become a point of honour, don't you? Our mess. Our job to clear it up.' He offers them both his best and brightest smile. It's like the old days. They clasp hands to elbows, as they used to do before a jaunt. He nods, as if Sophie has answered a question, which perhaps she has. 'Shall we go?'

One. Two. Three. Covering lines of fire. There are textbooks written that don't capture the smoothness of what they can do when they work as a team. It's a kind of magic whose time has passed and Sophie mourns its loss even as she sprints forward to huddle in the doorway to the dairy with twenty metres to go to the uncertain safety of the byre.

Céline comes after, and then Laurence. Daniel is to their right, offering suppressing fire. More tyres have been shot out: only one car of the three BMWs is fit to drive, the one furthest away from the farmhouse.

A figure is in the driving seat, head down, gunning the engine: Paul. It's tempting to go for him. At Sophie's side, Céline says, 'If Paul gets Kramme, they've got a clear route out, between the barn and the byre.'

'So we get him first.' Sophie sprints again, nearly fires at a shape that appears from the barn on her right, but it's Patrick, running, sort of. She didn't know he could. They collide at the doorway.

He grabs her shoulder, spins her round. *Go left!*

Left leads into warmth, a dark and breathy space. The first thing she meets is the gathering yard, a clear area four metres square where the bins of hard feed are kept, the buckets, the scoops, the shovels and brushes of daily dairy use. At the back is a crush for holding single cows. A fenced partition separates the cattle from their food.

Sophie ducks under the top rung and bumps into a large, hairy body that jilts away from her touch.

She crouches down, keeping the door in view. Underfoot is straw. The waft of old urine and fresh dung is pungent, but not impossibly so. Even at the end of winter, Daniel's cow byre is well maintained. Around her move the matriarchs of the Fayette herd: thirty cows in all, progeny of ten generations of careful breeding, nurtured through war and peace. She knows this and yet, still, she wants a grenade, and she will pay for a whole new herd, because she can feel Kramme in here, in the way she felt him in the bar in town, so that her hair becomes a sensory organ and her hands sweat.

Someone else slides in through the open doorway, a felt presence, easing through the dark. Her gun hand twitches round even as her head tells her it's Céline, or Laurence, or both. She keeps from firing by a sustained act of will. Dear God, let me not kill someone I know.

She follows the prickle of her skin. Near the back wall is a place where the cattle are still, a cluster of relative calm. They are trusting of men; where one is, they will be at peace, even tonight. Sophie is easing forwards when headlights flood in and a brilliant blond head and a hoarse voice – a German voice with a shine of Aryan hair to back it up – shouts, 'Kramme! For the love of God, here. *Now!*'

She is sure that's Laurence, but he makes a convincing Rudi Schäfer. Certainly Kramme believes the figure is offering succour. He looms from her left, not her right, jumps the partition and sprints for the opening, running low, but Patrick has set himself by the door, and everyone else knows one thing above all else: Kramme is his.

He steps sideways, into the beam of the headlights, gun raised. *Hello, Max.*

For one rigid moment, Maximilian Kramme and Patrick Sutherland face each other: a man and his obscene mirror image, hunter and hunted, whole and . . . not.

In wonder, Kramme says, 'You have more lives than a cat.' And Patrick smiles.

A single shot shatters the moment, and a second after it, a burst of machine-gun fire, cut off.

Sophie drops on instinct. Patrick drops too, because he has missed – how? They were three metres apart. How could he miss? – but he has, and Kramme is running for the door and the figure in the doorway has fallen and it wasn't Laurence shouting from the door, because Laurence is here, falling to his knees at her side. 'Patrick?'

Oh, God. Laurence is kneeling by Patrick, his face a landscape of grief. And at the door, whence came the call for Kramme, a shine of blonde hair lies fanned across the threshold.

'Céline.' Sophie is up, running for the door. 'Céline . . .'

She can't think. She must not. Instinct stitches facts together and she goes down on one knee beside Céline's body, firing, firing, firing at the back of the retreating BMW, at Paul and Kramme and whoever else is in it, at the Americans and the Germans. She fires until her magazine is empty and the gun doesn't kick and the only sound is the harmless tap of steel on steel, lost in the maelstrom of shouting, and the final desperate scream of an armoured BMW accelerating out of the rutted yard, through a fence and out onto the road.

Patrick is still alive, bleeding. She pushes Laurence out of the way. 'Let me take him. JJ will help. You bring Céline.'

'In here. On the table. Marianne, we'll need sheets and hot water. JJ, get on the phone. We need an ambulance with blood and—'

Stop.

He has hold of her arm. Fabien was like this, long ago. *Sophie. Stop. It's all right. Honestly.*

'No. We can stop the bleeding. Pressure on the site and then a transfusion and—'

Sophie. We're halfway up a mountain in the middle of a blizzard and even if we weren't, the nearest clinic with transfusion facilities is an hour away. And if it was next door, it still wouldn't work. Stop. It's all right.

He is speaking fluently now, at the end. His, the shattered liver she had dreamed of for Kramme. His, the life blood leaking from a thousand ruptured veins.

But his, too, the hand that lies easy on her arm. All his pride is melted away and underneath is the man he could have been, and always was. And he is smiling, a relaxed, wry smile that takes a dozen years of brittle hardship and smoothes them to a minor misunderstanding.

Do what you're good at. His hand reaches hers; he glances back over her shoulder. *See to the living. They will need you.*

489

The living. None of them needs her. Daniel was clipped close by a round or a ricochet. He is bleeding, but not badly. JJ has it in hand.

They are to her right, near the range at the back of the kitchen. She follows the line of Patrick's gaze the other way, and at the end of it, Laurence Vaughan-Thomas stands in the doorway to the farmhouse with his cousin cradled across his arms.

Céline. The one they all loved, in their own ways. Her blonde hair fans long past his wrists. One hand flops loose. Fat, cherried drops of blood splash from her dangling index finger onto Marianne Fayette's scrubbed stone floor.

Sophie grabs the last of the white linen sheets, looks round for where else to put her.

Laurence says, 'The floor will do. She was never fussy.'

He brings her alongside the table, lowers her with care, and crosses her arms on her chest. Her features are smoothed free of the irony, the mask against the world. She is serene.

'Laurence, I'm so—'

'Don't. She knew what she was doing.'

Patrick says, *Heart of a lion. I'll tell her when we meet.*

'Tell her—' Laurence is lost. Grief has stolen all his words. She thinks he might melt, drain away into the stones and mortar. He lifts his head, pulls on whatever reserves he holds close. 'When she's found Julie, tell her to wait for me.'

Patrick's hand, fumbling, finds his. *We did our best. It was a good run.*

'More than we deserve.'

'We didn't find—'

Stop.

Sophie says, 'This isn't the end. We can track him. We can—'

No. Sophie, my she-lion, let it go. Laurence, you too. All of it. All. His gaze hooks them together, draws them in. To Laurence, he says, *Look after her.*

'Of course.'

No. Truly look after her. She will need you. Swear. Her care shall be your first concern. Say it.

Laurence drags his forearm across his nose. Snot-soaked, he says, 'Her care shall be my first concern, I swear it. Truly. Trust me. I will do what it takes.'

Thank you. That smile again. He is so peaceful. He tilts his head. Sophie?

'I'm here.'

You will take care of Laurence as he will of you.

'I don't need—'

You do. Let him do it. Be kind to each other.

'What if we're both in gaol?' This is not impossible. There are more dead out there than are dying in here. Five former Nazis lie still in the yard. Two of them have disabling trunk wounds, but what killed them was a single shot to the head. René did that, weeping. René, it seems, shot quite a lot of people, Americans and Germans both.

You think there will be blowback from killing the Americans? Having lost all his blood, Patrick is losing breath and colour. Life is leaking from him.

'Nothing insurmountable.' Laurence takes his hand. 'JJ will make it all go away.'

Sophie is not listening. She is losing him and some things matter more than dead enemies. 'I love you. I love you. I always did.'

And I you. From the moment you dropped out of the sky. He pulls her close. Really, he is gone now, the light in his eyes, the smile, the language, it is all happening in the place where the dead gather. He glances down, at her abdomen. *If it's a boy . . .*

'I shall name him for you.'

Thank you. You always were . . . a wonder. So fierce. So beautiful. So brave. He presses his lips to her hand, reaches for Laurence, who is blind with tears, and brings their hands together, links them, binding. *Forget me now. Take care of each other.*

'Patrick! Don't go. Patrick, *please . . .*'

But he is lost, slipping from between her fingers. Gone.

The clear-up happens around her. JJ is efficient and powerful. The phone lines have been cut, but it doesn't delay him by much. Men in dungarees and caps with buckets and mops and clipboards approach the mess as a logistical problem and make it all go away. Except for Patrick, who is not moved.

Sophie stands at his side until Laurence brings her a chair, makes her sit, hands her coffee and stands over her while she drinks.

She says, 'I can't do this. Whatever you promised, I can't be mothered like this.' He steps away, hurt. She catches his sleeve, draws him back. 'I'm sorry. He was yours as much as mine.'

'I gave him to you, remember?'

'You never asked him whether that was what he wanted.'

'I did, actually. A long time before you met him.' They sit together. They drink coffee. They do not move.

Some time in the night, the newly pregnant Lisette Fayette, who was once Lisette Moreau, wades two kilometres through the snow from their cottage with news that a phone call has arrived at Daniel's house. It is the third call she has taken in her life and the first from a stranger – the phone was installed at Christmas, JJ's gift for their coming child, in case they need to call a hospital for the birth. To their certain knowledge, only JJ and both sets of parents have the number. Still, Paul Rey has called.

'He wants to meet with Sophie.' She has a map reference that, when examined, denotes a road in the high mountains, close to the border with Switzerland.

Laurence says, 'Under the circumstances, it's probably a trap.'

Of course it is. She says, 'Did he say when?' And writes

down the directions, the time. To Laurence, she says, 'I will come to you afterwards, but this I will do.'

He catches her arm. 'What if you don't come back?'

'Then the cabin is yours. He would have wanted you to have it. If you'd rather not, then give it to Lisette and Daniel, for the children.'

THE FRENCH–SWISS BORDER
7 March 1957

The road bends in a hairpin hard to the left and soon after, tucked into the shoulder of the mountain, is the lay-by. A coil of old rope marks it as the right spot, and a pile of three tyres, out of place this high up. Sophie parks in gear and steps out, swaps warmth for the crisp, sharp cold of early evening.

Another storm is coming; far to the west, heavy clouds grinding on the mountains squeeze out a layer of light the colour of crushed lemons.

The silence makes her spine itch. She crouches by the car, but the *tick-purr* of the cooling engine is too loud and she has to worm out, arms extended, nerves chafed to screaming point, has to slide on her belly across the road and into the forest.

The scent of cigars draws her in, so familiar, so comfortable – just now, so dangerous. She circles round, comes in from the east and very nearly, she shoots him, but someone else has got there first. In the fusillade that followed the BMW, she thought she saw him hit, and it is true.

'Hello.' He is waiting under a tree. He looks unarmed. He lifts his hands to show them empty. His face is deathly white and full of grief. 'Patrick?'

'Dead. And Céline.' Her weapon is trained on his chest. One unclear thought and he is dead.

'I'm so sorry.'

She shrugs. Yesterday, she grieved, and probably tomorrow. Today, she is white-hot angry. 'Who is Diem?'

'I don't know. Did he not show himself?'

Really, she might shoot him now. 'What do you think?'

'Oh, Sophie.' He closes his eyes. 'I'm so sorry.'

'You betrayed us.'

'I did not.'

'You expect me to believe that?'

'Please. Please. You have to.'

There's something about his face. She takes a step back. 'What happened?'

'They locked me out of the planning. They knew . . .' What can he say?

'They knew about us?'

He gives a smile that brightens towards its end. 'Everyone knows about us. But this time, they knew – or they were prepared to guess – that I wasn't going to let Kramme leave France alive. I didn't tell them. I. Did. Not.'

'Diem.'

'Or Kramme. Perhaps it was obvious all along.'

'But Paul, you drove the car that got him out.' She did not know she could put so much outrage into so quiet a sentence. 'You could have killed him.'

He looks down at his hands. 'They had mortars ready. I had one chance – get in, get him out. If I failed, they'd have flattened Marianne's farmhouse and everyone in it. I couldn't let them do that.'

Is she supposed to applaud? Flatly, she says, 'And now they trust you.'

'Not enough. I will not be Kramme's handler when he gets to the US. I will not have access to his file. He's gone dark and I don't know where he is and I don't know who's running him and I can't find out who Diem is. It's a fucking disaster. I'm really, really sorry.'

494

He doesn't swear often; he's not that kind of man. She doesn't lower her gun, but she's not about to shoot him. They both feel the change.

He says, 'Will you sit?'

'Is it safe?' His men are around. She can't see them, but they are there. And she did shoot Long Tall Louis.

'Nobody will harm you. I swear it.'

She crouches down on the damp, cold leaves. 'Kramme lived, obviously?'

He nods, wearily. 'Schäfer didn't.'

'Good.' Patrick, when you see him, spit in his eye.

He nods. His gaze slips to her abdomen, to the first gentle swell. She hasn't told him, but he can count as well as she can. He looks at her, and the hope in his gaze is heartbreaking. 'Come with me. Sophie, please. Come with me today. I'll leave the Agency. We can make a new life.'

She laughs, surprising them both. 'You're joking.'

'Sophie, I didn't betray you. I did not. I swear this on Toni Gaspari's grave.'

That's not subtle. She rises. 'I need to go.'

He catches her arm. 'OK, so we don't have to leave the Agency. Join me. I still have leverage, I can make it happen. Kramme's in the system now. It'll take people like you and me to offer the other side of the argument, the voice of reason, the counterweight to what is coming.'

'What is coming?'

'I don't know, but Kramme's hardly alone. There are plenty of people in my country who think his cause was right and they want to spread it across the world. The assault on the Soviets is the most obvious, but they'll stifle dissent where they see it, crush anything that seeks to take power from the few and give it to the many. Come with me, Sophie. Help me fight it.'

'Paul, you can't make your own private army inside the CIA.'

'Why not? Kramme will. His family are already stateside.

He'll make a life, plan his strategies. Give it a generation, maybe two, and his people will own this world.'

'Then my presence won't help, will it?'

'It might do. Don't you see? We have to try. You'd have my patronage. He wouldn't touch you.'

'Your patronage?'

'As my wife.' He catches her hand. His pull is solidly strong. He is solidly strong. She can imagine him, a golden god, fighting the forces of darkness, and her, a bitter goddess at his side. 'Marry me. Let us raise our child in the land of the free.'

She draws her hand away. 'You've already got a wife.'

'Not for much longer.'

Oh, God. She is tired, beyond moving. She could lie here, in the forest, and sleep for a lifetime. Or she could go with him. Patrick is dead. Patrick is dead. Patrick is dead. And still, she cannot leave.

She makes herself rise. With both hands, she lifts her scarf from her neck and holds it out.

'What?' He knows what it is to her, what it has been. 'What are you doing?'

'Give this to Kramme when next you see him. Tell him to look after it. One day, I will come to collect it.'

'I don't understand.'

'I know.' She has to leave now, or she never will. She presses the old, thin silk into his unresisting hands. 'Goodbye, Paul. May your life be all you could want it to be. Tell Kramme what I said. He will understand.'

CHAPTER THIRTY-FIVE

7 March 1957

L AURENCE FINDS CÉLINE'S MUSIC box wrapped in a sleep-ing bag and slid into the spare tyre in the boot of her car. A thing of exquisite beauty, it is the inverse of his, made of near-silver ash wood with her initials inlaid in ebony in a fine, cursive script: *CVT MdM*. He lifts the lid and, expecting 'God Save the Queen', does not at first recognize 'Scotland the Brave'.

Oh, God. Come on, Laurence. You knew he loved her. Get a grip.

The mechanism slides out easily; the edges have been smoothed with graphite to make it so. He tries his own code to gain entry: IOUASCOTCH. Nothing moves. Three times, and it will lock itself. You could open it with a sledgehammer, of course . . .

He could. He doesn't want to and he thinks Céline would not have arranged things such that he must resort to destruc-tion of something so heartbreakingly precious. He goes back to her car and searches again without any clear idea of what he's looking for, only that he'll know it when he finds it.

And he does: a powder compact, hidden in the lining of

Céline's handbag, which itself is locked in a concealed compartment in the passenger door of her car.

The compact is solid silver with *J&C* engraved in bold, flowing letters on the front. Nothing else; none of the usual sworls and scrolls of ladies' accoutrements – this is the functional version. He half expects it to carry a concealed camera, or a cyanide pill.

There's an instinct to this, but even so, he might have missed it were it not for the mark on the mirror. Céline inherited the family's need for perfection more than he, Laurence, ever did; even in wartime, a flawed mirror would have been replaced. This, though, is not a chip or a scratch, but a carefully placed drill hole, designed to look like the result of careless use. Eureka!

He carries his trove back into the clean, warm farmhouse where Marianne Fayette is kneading bread dough and barely acknowledges his presence.

From the start, from back in the war, Daniel's mother has treated him with a mix of pity and disdain that he has not yet been able to unravel. He is polite. She is polite. He has tried to make conversation, to break the permafrost that lies between them, whose origin he does not understand. She has rebuffed his every attempt.

And so now, he stands on the scrubbed stone floor beside the scrubbed wooden table on which Patrick has so recently lain, and he says, 'Where is he?'

'Upstairs. He has the bed. He shall have it until they have dug the grave. And until she comes back.'

He says, 'She might not come back.'

'She will.' She's a tall woman, Marianne Fayette, big-boned, muscular, not fleshy after the manner of the farming ladies of England that he is used to. Without effort, he can imagine her wielding a Sten in defence of her farmhouse, although he doesn't know if this ever actually happened.

He imagines her a hawk, an eagle, maybe, fierce in protection of her young, and of her mate. Except she failed in that. He thinks that in Patrick's death, she has lost another hero, and the wind is blowing cold through her soul.

He says, 'He cared for you. We all knew that.'

The way she stares at him, he wonders if his French is rustier than he had imagined. She bites her lip, pounds the dough a few more times, then: 'And you for him. Yet still, you sent him to die in this foreign land.'

'He wanted to come.'

'And if he had wanted to stay behind, if he had taken an English wife, had English children, would you have let him?'

'I think they would have been Scottish.' And, at her incomprehension: 'It was war. We all did the best we knew how.'

'Is it still war?'

'I don't understand.'

'The girl, his wife. She has gone today to fight a war that is not over, yes?'

Ah. 'I think that for some of us, the war can never be over. We need it, to give our lives meaning.'

'Are you one of those?'

'Not in the same way as Sophie is. Céline was, though I didn't fully understand it until yesterday.' Her call – hoarse, so that she sounded like a man – drew Kramme out. It so nearly worked. Were it not for someone on the outside, it would have done. One day, cousin mine, I am going to find who shot you, and I am going to take him apart into very small pieces, slowly. Diem is a man: of that much Laurence is now sure.

He holds up her box in one hand, the compact in the other. 'Have you a kitchen knife I might borrow?'

It takes him some time, and a number of failures, before he works out the mechanism Céline has set up. When he does, it is, of course, both elegant and ingenious.

Tipping the compact's lid back beyond its normal range reveals a small sliding switch which, when moved across, allows him to tip the mirror out of the case. Behind it lies silk of the kind they used in the worked-out codes in the war: thin enough to burn in seconds, strong enough to take a cipher written in her neat, angled hand. It's an easy one. He breaks it in minutes. BE STRONG BRAVE HEART.

Oh, Patrick.

Blinking, he presses the letters in order and the hidden drawer in the music box opens to reveal an envelope with his name written in her hand. Inside is another coding silk, this one with a far more complex cipher.

He stares at it for long minutes: blocks of five letters, spread across the page, row upon row upon row. There are men and women with machines that might crack this open, but he does not have access to them, and in any case, he is not going to let them near it; this is family, and family holds to its own.

Come on, Laurence, think like Céline. It isn't hard. J&C engraved on the front of the compact. Julie. Julie, and all she meant. None of the others filled that gap – not Véronique, nor the new one, Felicity. He will have to tell her. Not a phone call, a visit. Oh, God. Come on, Laurence. Concentrate.

The poem codes of the war are locked in the oubliette of his memory, never to be expunged. He rummages in there now, comes up with Céline's first field cipher: a poem by an obscure American woman poet. *The hard sand breaks/and the grains of it/are clear as wine . . .*

Below the code is a telephone number: J 413868. Céline, you are a gem. Thank you. 'Madame Fayette, could I trouble you for some paper and a pencil? An eraser would be useful if you have it.'

An hour later, the obscure American poet is not the key to the cipher. Nor is it an equally obscure, rather maudlin Frenchwoman lamenting the beautiful brunette she has lost in the streets of Paris. It is not any of Celine's more recent codes, nor Laurence's own. Julie, to the best of his knowledge, never had any.

It is dark now, and Sophie is not yet back from the mountains. Perhaps, after all, she never intended to return. It is that kind of day.

Marianne Fayette has lit the fire and made him coffee and he has drunk it without particularly noticing it is there. Now she has set a glass of bright, sharp wine at his elbow and he is in the half place between past and present, drinking in the firelight, dozing on the crest of the wine, when he remembers a scurrilous ditty sung on the banks of the Cam. *Oh! Did your granny use her fanny ere your granddad came along?*

He is standing in a street in Cambridge, with the dust in his lungs and the scent of blood saturating everything, and Céline, who was Theo, weeping. He is in his uncle's house, with the scent of hot milk and distress, and Patrick, in his own old, ordinary voice, says, *So now there will be two Vaughan-Thomases who have had their hearts ripped out by this bloody war.*

Some things are only obvious when you see them. Fourth word of the first line, third and sixth of the eighth gives him Granny; Fuck; Night. He breaks them out into alphabetic order, writes the rest of the alphabet after them, and then makes his grid and runs through the first two sets of five digits.

DEARL AUREN

He has to break it without reading or he will fall apart before the end. He does it backwards, which was an old trick that he taught the FANYs in the coding room when the reports were too grim to contemplate.

Another hour, and at the end of it, a letter.

Dear Laurence,

Well done, you remembered. If you are reading this, things have gone wrong, or perhaps right . . . I am not sure I am suited to the world that is coming and there's something glorious about going out in a fire fight that the long, slow burn behind a desk will never match. You will cope better, I think: you are more adaptable, less prone to seeing everything in black and white.

Whatever has happened, I am not unhappy: unless I am incapacitated such that I cannot make a clean ending, in which case, I trust you to do what is right.

Do not grieve: I have had more life than I expected and it has been good. There is someone who will need to be informed. Her address and telephone number are in my address book under the name Yvonne Taylor. This is not her name, but she will answer to it and will know that you come from me. Treat her kindly. There will be money. Actually, there may be a great deal of money. She will not need that, but there are things of sentimental value that she will want and that I wish her to have; she will let you know what they are.

The rest, I leave to you and to Sophie's child when she or he reaches majority (please tell me her state is not news to you?), along with this box and its contents. Those who come after us will never know everything, but they deserve to know something, indeed, they must, for we are leaving to them a toxic legacy.

Unless we change it.

Think on this: Diem is one of us. By now you may know who; I sincerely hope so. You will want to kill him, who-ever he is. You must not. A moment's satisfaction now will not wipe out the pain of the past. Instead, it will remove all possibility of altering the future.

We are at a pivotal point. We have lost our war. Not the one we fought against the Wehrmacht; that was lost the day Hitler chose to assault Russia and none of his generals could stop him. We lost the war to create a balanced world. The USSR is not the enemy. It never has been. It may become so, if pushed into a corner, but I doubt if it will ever truly have the resources to combat a resurgent America. Because that is where the power lies now. Britain is dying. Our power is waning, our empire breaking apart. America's, by contrast, is waxing, and I am afraid of it.

You know Paul Rey, you trust him, and so you will scoff, but answer me this: What happens to the soul of a nation if into its body politic is injected the undiluted virus of Nazism? This is what has happened. Kramme may be a monster, but he is hardly alone. Dozens of men, hundreds, maybe thousands, have been smuggled out from under the noses of the Nuremberg judges and given new names, new lives, new meaning. They took with them wives and children, each little Wunderkind ardent in his or her belief that Hitler's only problem was that he just didn't try hard enough. They were the best Germany had to offer and they are being manoeuvred in at the highest level, not just into the intelligence agencies, but to the other arms of American government, the political life, the academic, industrial, technological, into the veins of its body politic, running its businesses and its television companies, warping its view of everything from economics to space travel.

These are not stupid men. They will not drape swastikas over their balconies, or demand that Jews be roasted in ovens, but neither will they abandon their certainty of a perfect Aryan future, free of colours, races, temperaments they don't like, purged of anyone who doesn't fit the perfect model, who will refuse to work for the greater glory of flag and nation, for the greater wealth of the dominant few. Twenty years from now, thirty, forty, what will we be, who have welcomed into our nests these vipers? How will we fight them? Will it even be possible?

And so I ask this of you: stop Kramme, stop Diem. Do not give up. However long it takes, whatever it takes, do not let their legacy be greater than ours – yours, mine, Sophie's, Patrick's.

In the meantime, you will have questions to answer back home. The high-ups may want to throw you out. Don't let them. Tell them I set this up; you will find proof in my desk. Each of us has our Rubicon and you may tell them that this was mine: that I had to prevent Maximilian Kramme from reaching the United States, or die trying. They will be happy to have a scapegoat.

It is time to stop. I love you. Never forget that. Be kind to yourself after this. You deserve peace in your world. Take care of Sophie. She is more vulnerable than she will ever admit.

All my love,

Theo. (Although if you can arrange it, I should prefer to be remembered in perpetuity as Céline.)

He is weeping. Having started at last, it may be that he will never stop.

Marianne Fayette sits down at his side. She has brought the bottle of wine and another glass. At some point, she lays her hand on his arm.

'We need to talk.'

She has read the letter. He could have stopped her. He could have thrown it on the fire, but not yet. He needs to read it again, perhaps many times.

He lifts his head. 'Talk of what?'

504

'Of our dead and how we may remember them. Of our lives, and what they are for. Of the vengeance you will wreak when the time is right. More than all of this, we need to talk about the girl who has gone onto a mountain, and the child she carries.' Her big, flint eyes hold him. 'You did know?'

'Sophie told me.' This is a lie. Until he read Céline's letter, Laurence didn't know. Perhaps he is the only one who did not. He feels a fool, but he is not about to broadcast the extent of his ignorance.

Marianne asks, 'Did she tell you whose it is?'

He shrugs. 'I don't suppose she knew. It could be Patrick's, it could be Paul Rey's. Maybe it could be someone else's— Hey!' She has slapped him. His cheek stings. 'What was that for?'

'You promised to take care of her. Is impugning her morals the way to do it?'

'I wasn't impugning anything. Who Sophie consorts with is her own affair. I am hardly one to judge.' He is cross now. It's cathartic. Reining it in, he says, 'You may judge her. I don't. She knows who she is and what she wants and I have no doubt that the men who lie with her do so willingly and feel themselves honoured. As they should.'

'Come with me.'

She takes his wrist and pulls him with her. Like a mother leading a recalcitrant child, she leads him outside and up the stairs to the hayloft above the dairy.

At the door, he baulks. The snow has stopped falling. Behind him, the world is a grey-silver dusk, a place of pewter moonlight and peace. He wants to break and run. Céline's words are looping through his head. *Twenty years from now; thirty, forty, what will we be, who have welcomed into our nests these vipers?* She should have had his job. She was so much better at this.

He says, 'Why?'

'You'll see.' She pushes open the door. The delicate, gracious scent of lavender fills the air. It does not entirely cover the first sweetness of death, but it might were he not so attuned to it.

She walks in ahead of him. Patrick lies on the bed, unclothed. His features are at peace. Almost, one might imagine a smile. His hair has been washed of blood and brushed back into shape. His fingernails, that were black rims, have been picked and scrubbed clean. A white sheet lies over him, ankles to chin.

Marianne lifts one corner, draws it back. 'Look at him. All of him.'

He grips her wrist, he who so rarely handles women. 'Why?'

'More than anything else, he wanted to be a father. When Lisette and Daniel said they were starting a family, he nearly died of the grief. He tried to hide it, but Sophie saw, and she did what she needed to. So look. And then remember your promise to him.'

But he already knows. A slow, sliding ache racks him. 'Please.' He lets go of her hand. 'Why? Why are you doing this?'

'Because nobody else will. Since the war, nobody has, and you do need to see. Believe me. There are things you will do because of this that you would not do otherwise. You are a man. It is how men think. Even men such as you.'

She takes a step back. Her gaze is all pity. 'We made Calvados in the winter after the Boche left that was like none other I have ever tasted. I have one bottle left. I will open it. Come to me when you are ready. Do not hurry. It will not hurt you to spend time with him. He would want it, I think.'

How could he want it? But it is the thought of him, watching, the dryness of his smile, that makes Laurence wait until she is gone, and then he folds back the sheet and folds it and folds it until he is holding a bulked square of white, scented linen.

He stands a long time, holding the sheet, looking on Patrick, and the final indignity that he bore with the same fortitude as all the rest. Oh, my dear. If you were angry, we knew there was good reason. When you were dull and difficult, did Sophie pity you? Or did she love you, fiercely, so that you knew you were loved for all that you are, not what has gone?

With raw intent, he brings to mind the moments of joy: the hillside on Arisaig in the driving rain; the drive back from the debrief in Hampshire; the brief joy in Cambridge, before Julie died; the long nights in the apartment with the silk sheets and the blackout blinds leaving the air clammy. He remembers Sarpedons, ciphers sent and received, the drip-feed of information coming too late, too slow, too incomplete, the frustration of it. He remembers nights spent sitting by the teleprinter, hands white at the knuckles, waiting for the all-clear. And the decision to join them.

'I'm not sorry I came. I'm only sorry it wasn't sooner. I did love you. I didn't say so. I hope you knew.'

It is time to go. He unfolds the sheet, lays it back across the man who was his friend, takes a step away. On a half thought, uncensored, he steps forward again, and presses a dry, light kiss to the dead brow, and then the lips.

And thus, by accident, we became as gods.

He salutes. It feels right. And he speaks the words that come now, more easily than he might have imagined.

'I will honour your memory, all of it, as you would have wanted, with integrity and all the shadings of truth. And I shall watch what they do, Kramme and his minions, and when the time is right, I shall destroy them, and they shall know what is being done and why, and in whose name.'

Downstairs, the heady sour-sweet notes of the spirit draw him to an armchair by the fire. Marianne Fayette has shed her own tears and does not hide the fact.

She offers him a glass. 'Sláinte.'

'He taught you?'

'The first night he was here.' She drains her glass, smiling over the burn of it. Laurence follows, holds his breath as it hits his gut. It is hot, this one, scorching.

She refills. It's such an old challenge. He is not sure he is up to it. He leans back, lets his gaze float to the fire. And drinks.

At length, Marianne says, 'Sophie's child will need a father.'

'Yes.' He reaches forward, lays another log on the fire. It is apple wood, aged and dry. It burns with a clear, yellow flame, and sweet smoke.

There is a thought, not yet fully chased down; a wisp of an idea, fragile, alert, wary. It might take flight at any moment and be lost to the world. They chase it: two children with a net, slow steps and quiet; slowly, slowly, not a word out of place.

He takes time to think about that, drinks a glass and half of another. 'She will have to choose whomever she thinks is best.'

'If she comes back.'

Paul Rey may be the father. She may choose to stay with him. Another glass later, Laurence says, 'Yes. If.'

They are there, sitting silent with the fire, when a car draws into the yard. Laurence lifts his Colt, slides the safety catch off, walks to the window. He can still walk straight, more or less, which, given the volume of Calvados he has drunk, and its strength, is a source of some surprise. It may be that if he needs to, he can shoot straight.

He doesn't need to.

Sophie is sober, thin, sad. She is enchanting, the wildness of her, the depth of her sorrow and what she does with it.

He says, 'Gone?'

'Gone. I didn't kill him.'

She drops into the chair he has just vacated. She has the feel of a fire in the last blaze before the cold. The skin beneath her eyes is too-tired translucent. He nods to the bottle. 'Want some?'

'I shouldn't.' She says it before Marianne can. There are no other armchairs. He finds a hard chair at the kitchen table and carries it through. Marianne catches his eye.

'I will make coffee.' She abandons him, his co-hunter. She is so wise.

'Sophie . . .' He leans forward, elbows on knees, knows he is too tall for this, gangly, unused and uncertain. 'I know about the child you carry. I think . . . I am sure, he – or she – will need a father.'

She stares at him. Her gaze flicks to the bottle, to the fire and back.

In the silence, the idea so carefully stalked settles. It strikes him that he should be on one knee, and he can do this, ridiculous as it might seem. He kneels before her, picks up her hand. She smells of gun oil and cinder, and blood. 'Amélie Fabron, Sophie Destivelle, Amélie Duval, hunter in the woods and on the mountains. You lost a husband. You lost a man you loved. I know I can never fully be either of these things and I will never stand in your way, whatever you want to do with your life. But I promised a man we both loved that I would care for you and now I understand why. I cared about him. I care about you. I care about the life that is growing. Will you accept me in his place, to help you raise this child in safety and love and care, that there might be a good future out of our rotten past?'

She has been so strong, and he has unmanned her. Her eyes are bright; her lips, so often strong, are weak now at the edges. She takes his hands in both of her own. 'Laurence, I can't. I can't be a mother. It's not in my nature. Surely you know that.'

'But—' Hunter in the woods and on the mountains. She is vengeance made manifest. Still . . .

'He could have been a father. A good one. I would have given him that. I would have played a role for him because . . . because of everything. But you – did you ever want children? Did the need burn in you the way it did in him?'

It has never crossed his mind. In truth, he cannot imagine it. He says, 'But what will you do? Surely you can't—'

'Daniel's Lisette had twins before, when she was married to the Milice. I delivered them: a boy and a girl. She is carrying a single child now but hers and mine will be born close together and the world will believe she had twins again. Already, I have spoken to her of this. She will do it – for him, for me, for herself, for the pain of what has happened and that she will never forget. She wants motherhood more than anything. She will have great joy in raising two children. I cannot imagine anything I want less.'

'What, then, do you want? To hunt Kramme?'

'To the ends of the earth.' She presses a kiss to his cheek. Her voice is small and tight and tired. She lifts her head and strives to smile. 'But not just him. Diem is our enemy, too. We have to find him, you and I, and kill him, however long it takes, whatever the cost. Far more than raising a child, this is our duty: to destroy them, whatever it takes. Will you help me with that?'

They are standing now, her chest to his, palms to palms, her face not far below his. If he was close to Céline – and he was – he is closer now to Sophie. He cannot imagine loving any woman more. With all his heart, he says, 'Whatever it takes.'

CHAPTER THIRTY-SIX

THE JURA MOUNTAINS
Sunday, 18 March 2018
22.52

THIS PLACE HASN'T CHANGED significantly since Laurence first saw it. An indoor toilet – two, in fact – replaces the earth closet; a television sits in the corner of the main room, and a high-speed modem; there's a refrigerator in the kitchen as tall as he is, but otherwise, the sense of home wraps around him with the woodsmoke. Still, in the furling shadows of the fire is Patrick's cigar smoke; in the sough of the wind across the chimney stack is Patrick's quiet laughter, his voice, singing Highland boat songs.

This is not new: Patrick has filled his shadows for years. What is new is that Sophie is part of the shadows, too. He is still trying to come to terms with this. The lamb staked out for the tiger. She did know exactly what she was doing, but even so . . . It may be that he never gets used to it.

He is being watched, and does not want to seem maudlin. Laying his pipe by the hearth, he says, 'You are very like your mother.'

'René said that. And Paul.' Elodie Duval is sitting on the

floor to the right of the fireplace, with her back to an armchair, one knee pulled up to her chin, her elbow resting on it. She has Paul's eyes and hair: everything else is of her mother. Almost everything.

Laurence says, 'You have his integrity.'

'We'll see.'

'You could still leave. Nobody knows you're here.'

'Please let's not have this conversation again. Sophie gave her life for this, and then my brother. I can do what's needed.'

'I'm sure you can.' Family is not only about blood. If Laurence Vaughan-Thomas has learned anything in a life of subterfuge it is this: Pierre will always be her brother. Sophie will always simply be Sophie; Paul will be Paul. Mother and Father are Lisette and Daniel, however much that may not be the absolute truth. But still, she is here.

They fall back into an easy silence. From her earliest years, Elodie was a self-contained child. She has never needed to talk to fill the gaps. They watch the clock. They watch the fire. Laurence watches the shadows in the smoke and does not know if Elodie sees her mother in any of them.

Shortly before eleven o'clock an owl calls outside. Laurence levers himself upright. 'That's René.'

'Unless it isn't.'

'Stay back.'

René taps Morse on the door: M. D. M. Laurence opens it, pokes his Colt to the crack. René's face looms over it. He grins. 'Martha's here.'

'Martha! Welcome, child. Welcome! Welcome! Let me get you a coffee . . .' Laurence holsters his weapon, throws open the door, draws her in. She accepts his embrace, and—

'Elodie! Oh my God! Are you OK?'

'I'm good.' They embrace with enthusiasm. Elodie says, 'I'm sorry if we gave you a shock – it seemed safer to hole up out here after what happened to Sophie and then Pierre.'

'Of course! Good idea!' Martha is dressed down in black leggings and a navy-blue sweat top, with a loose bag over her shoulder. She holds Elodie at arm's length, drinking her in. 'Does the studio know you're OK?'

'Not yet. We'll tell everyone tomorrow, if it's safe. Can you hold off until then?'

'Sure. Whatever.' Spinning on her heel, taking in the unstraight walls, the hand-carved clock on the wall, the clutter of equipment in one corner, Martha stares at that. 'Why is the camera here?'

'I had everything in the flat. I didn't want anyone to steal any of it.'

'But you've set everything up for a take?'

'Laurence and I were recording our memories of Sophie while they were fresh. You could do the same for JJ sometime if you'd like?'

'Yes, thank you, I'd like that.'

A coffee pot sits on the hearth. Laurence pours fresh for them all, into thick, rustic mugs with rounded lips and fat handles. 'We ate dinner long ago. I could get you cheese, though? And maybe some ham?'

'That would be lovely.'

He switches the lights on in the kitchen; they are beyond hiding now. Returning with cheese, ham, thick bread and butter, he finds that Elodie has set up the lights and Martha is sitting on a chair in the furthest corner from the door, with a drape behind her to give a consistent background.

JJ's great-granddaughter is exceptionally photogenic. Her hair is a blonde penumbra, reflecting light into the soft fabric behind, framing her face in gold. She has the perfect facial symmetry of a model, without the oversized lips and Botox-paralysis that afflicts so many of her generation.

She is animated, talking to camera about her great-grandfather. His size. His habit of throwing her high in the air when she was a child. His deep, bass laugh. His size, did she mention? He was like a great, soft grizzly bear. As she grew older, the awe in which he was held by others, while she couldn't drop the idea of his being a giant teddy bear, made just for her.

'Is the whole family so long-lived?' Laurence asks, leaning on the door frame.

'Seems that way. Grandpa Lakoff was well into his nineties when he finally left us.'

'What was he like?'

'Grandpa Lakoff?' Her eyes flick up and left, to the place where memories are held. 'Charming, very dapper. He smoked a lot; thick, black cigars that smelled like burning silage. I didn't meet him often. He was small, neat, careful, where Grandpa JJ is always . . . I'm sorry, *was* . . .'

'Martha, it's good to cry. If we don't grieve for those we care about, we don't honour the memory of all that they were.' Elodie, who has not yet wept – for her mother, her father, her almost-brother – is ready with a box of tissues. 'Take your time. I'm sorry. We had not planned to do this yet, but things are moving so fast. If we leave it, we might not be here tomorrow, any of us.' She is good at this, the bending of truth to suit the exigencies of the moment.

She hugs Martha, and so is close, holding her, when the car pulls up outside.

23.00

Lise Bressard, Mayor of Orléans, came through the fire with less outward damage than Picaut. Still, they spent two weeks in adjacent beds in a burns unit at a private hospital funded by Bressard family money. That kind of closeness is worth a lot, and nothing that has happened since has diminished it.

514

So when Picaut asks for a plane, Lise lends her one: and a pilot, Declan, who speaks French with a West Cork accent. She offers security guards to go with them.

'No, thank you. I have Rollo.' And she has her own gun. It feels good, a solid weight in the straps across her chest. Lise says, 'Please don't do anything dangerous.'

'I never do anything dangerous.' Picaut clambers up into the plane and sits between Rollo and Patrice. She feels brightly, savagely alive.

Monday, 19 March 2018
00.17

The wind is with them and the flight time is just under eighty minutes. The landing is enlivening, but not emetic. There are no unexpected boulders or cows. She had to switch her phone off during the flight, but when she turns it on again, there's a message from Kathryn Kochanek.

– Located new file on our original victim. Not sure useful, but thought you should see.

Four images of John Lakoff's body follow. Picaut sweeps across them, fast. These were taken in the pathology lab after someone has stitched shut the wound at his neck.

He looks like an old man, sleeping; nothing seems new until she comes to a close-up of his neck, taken from the left side, which shows some faint smudged marks that might be fingerprints, as if someone held his head still while the cut was made. If they are, then the killer was right-handed, but . . .

She thumbs a number on her phone.

Eric answers on the fourth ring, sleepily. She says, 'Eric,

sorry to wake you. Can I send a couple of images through for Ingrid to look at?'

Tetchily: 'Inès, I'm not her PA. You can't—' In the background, Ingrid speaks. Eric, sighing, says, 'OK. Send them now.'

'On their way. Ask her to look at the second one, below the angle of the jaw.'

The phone is passed from one hand to another. 'Inès? It's Ingrid. What am I looking for?'

'There's a ridge, a scar at the angle of his jaw. Has he had plastic surgery? A long time ago, when they weren't as good as you are now?'

A pause, and then: 'Could be.'

'Could it have been done to change his appearance? Enough to make him unrecognizable?'

'In the right hands, yes.'

'I'm sending you another picture. Can you tell me if you think it's the same man before the surgery?'

In the pause between sending and receiving an answer, she texts Kathryn Kochanek.

– Did you find John Lakoff's scarf?

– No.

– Then I know where it is.

– Then you know the killer?

– I will do soon.

– Good luck!

And then Ingrid is back on the line. 'We'd need longer with the software to analyse the underlying bone structure, but it looks like the same person to me.'

'Thank you. I owe you both.' She hangs up. In the dark, all

eyes are on her. With the sense of one revealing the secrets of the universe, she says, 'John Lakoff is Max Kramme. He had plastic surgery in the US or maybe before then. At any rate, I think Sophie Destivelle recognized him and killed him.'

'So Conrad and Edward Lakoff killed her in revenge?' Rollo asks. 'Or paid Martin Gillard to do it?'

'Maybe. Or JJ, whose daughter married Edward Lakoff – Kramme's son.'

'Do you think he knew?' Rollo asks.

'That's the real question, isn't it? Did Jean-Jacques Crotteau, demon of the DGSE, know that his only daughter had married the son of a former Gestapo officer? If he didn't, he's been made a fool of and his death earlier this evening was murder. If he did, then he's Diem and his death was suicide.'

'JJ was never a fool.'

'No, that's what I thought. Shall we prove it?'

According to Patrice's maps, the walk to the cabin should take a little under twelve minutes. They do it in ten.

Picaut's team stands in darkness at the end of a paved pathway that leads between grandfather pines. She says, 'Everyone in there is potentially dangerous. We don't know who are the good guys and who are the bad, so we go in hard, and we ask questions when we've disarmed them. Are we clear?' Picaut's gun is in her right hand and her torch in her left. The two brace against each other in a way that feels solid and safe. 'Patrice, you're not armed. Just at the moment, you're not even police. You have to stay out of the way. Promise me you will. The rest of you, come with me.'

'Wait!' Patrice holds up his phone to take a picture. She frowns. He says, 'No, be like you were. If you're going to throw yourself into the line of fire, I want to catch you like this, happy.'

She is not used to him looking so serious. She laughs, and he takes her picture, the first one since the fire, and she doesn't mind.

'Thank you.' Her face does not itch. She is alive. It was for this that she came back. Again she says, 'Let's go.'

Picaut takes the side of the door opposite the hinge. Rollo kicks it open. She rolls in. God, it's good to feel this alive.

'Armed police! Drop your weapons!'

Nobody shoots at her, which is, frankly, surprising.

And then not.

00.33

They muscle in through the front door, loudly. For seventy years, Laurence's nightmares have been regular, and they have been of this: of armed men, disturbing a sanctuary; of himself caught in a small, dark room with no avenues of escape; of the living hell that comes after. It was never truly his risk, but the fear of it leached from the men and women standing at an airfield with their parachutes strapped to their backs, and it clung to him through everything that came after. He lifts his gun.

To his right, Elodie Duval, who has her mother's wild streak and her father's integrity, who shares the courage of both, who has been trained for this moment by two generations of agents, hugs Martha Lakoff in a protective embrace.

'It's empty. There's nobody here.'

Thank you, Petit-Evard, for stating the obvious. 'Search the rooms.' Already Picaut's torch is stabbing at the separate components of the cabin: log fire – cold; ashtray – empty; light switch . . . She flicks it on. The cabin is small and tidy and homely. It has been occupied recently, say in the past month. A line of portrait photographs stretches across the walls. Here are Elodie, Pierre, Daniel and Lisette; Laurence Vaughan-Thomas and Paul Rey. To the left, above the fire, is Martin Gillard.

Martin Gillard, whose mother, Martine Gillard, was Paul Rey's final mistress.

Set opposite him is Conrad Lakoff, whose father's father was Sturmbannführer Maximilian Kramme.

If she had seen this twelve hours ago, it would not have made sense. But here, now: it is the web, laid clear.

The final pieces fall into place.

PAUL REY'S SON STOP DIEM'S LEGACY QUERY.

Fuck.

Aloud, she says, 'It's a verb, not a punctuation mark,' but nobody is listening. Rollo, Sylvie, Petit-Evard . . . they are all searching the cabin with brisk efficiency, inside and out.

'Nobody here.' Rollo comes back from checking the outhouse. 'We got the wrong place.'

'We're screwed.'

A knock at the door. They spin, weapons out. Rollo kicks back the door, gun in both hands. Nobody is there.

'It's me,' Patrice says, from a safe stance to the side. He steps onto the threshold, holding his laptop up where they can see it. 'Pierre Fayette inherited a farmhouse from his grandmother. His heir is Elodie Duval.' He looks from Picaut to Rollo and back again. 'I think I've brought you to the wrong place.'

'How far?'

'Two and a half kilometres. The ground's not great. The Maps app says we can do it on foot in fifteen minutes if we push.'

00.35

'Martha?'

'Martha!'

And yes, Martha. Martha, who is standing very, very still, with Elodie's Colt – which was once Céline's Colt – pressed to the back of her head.

To the man standing in the doorway, Elodie says, 'If she moves, she dies. If you move, she dies. Keep your hands where I can see them. Where's Conrad?'

'He couldn't come,' Edward Lakoff says. He holds his hands up, palms flat, unthreatening. He knows exactly where Laurence is, but his gaze never leaves Elodie and Martha. 'He's chairing a war game. He couldn't leave. I came instead.'

'You'll do.' Laurence is leaning on the wall by the kitchen door. The back door is to his right; beyond it is one of the new toilets, and then the door to the yard. 'I'm sure you know as much as he does of the family history, possibly more. Kramme was your father, after all.'

Martha says, 'I don't understand.' She is not weeping now. She stands carefully, as if even her hair needs to stay still, and it might choose not to.

'Your grandfather will explain,' Laurence says. And to Edward: 'You will take the seat Martha has just vacated. Speaking to the camera, you will detail your heritage, the acts of your father, his intentions and yours, and those of your son. You will leave nothing out. If you do, I shall kill Martha without hesitation. You understand, I think, that I have absolutely nothing to lose, and the opportunity to kill the great-granddaughter of both a Boche killer and a Maquis traitor would outweigh any possible regrets I might have at ending the life of so charming an individual?'

'What happens afterwards?'

'That's not entirely in our control. I imagine you will tell us that you shot Sophie; I recommend that you do. After which, we shall present the tape to the authorities. I imagine you will be arrested.'

'Martha?'

'Martha, being innocent, will go free.'

Edward Lakoff is in his seventies, but he has weathered well. He has a sharp mind, and an active one. His gaze, turned on Laurence, is unreadable, as is his face. He raises one brow, slowly. 'Your word on that? You will not implicate Martha?'

'I swear, here, now, that I will not implicate Martha. Nor will I kill her.' There's a relief in this. Even now, Laurence is not sure he could kill a young woman in cold blood. Sophie could have done. Elodie might do. Laurence is not sure what Elodie Duval can and cannot do. He is not alone in his uncertainty.

Edward Lakoff says, 'Elodie?'

She says, 'If you give us living proof that John Lakoff was Kramme, if you give us the identity of Diem, I won't kill Martha, I swear it.'

Lakoff makes the only choice open to him. 'Let's do it.' Elodie moves away from the video camera, herding Martha with her. Edward Lakoff takes her place.

'The camera is rolling,' Laurence says. 'All of this has been recorded. Face the lens. Treat this as a congressional hearing. Speak clearly. Leave nothing out. We do, after all, know most of it.'

Edward Lakoff could be reading the weather on a dull and rainy Thursday, but for the tap of his little finger on his knee.

'I am Edward Patrick Lakoff, former Senator for Illinois, former Chair of the Intelligence Select Committee. My father was John Lakoff, Assistant Director of the CIA. He was previously known as Sturmbannführer Maximilian Kramme, of the Geheime Staatspolizei. He was the senior officer in charge of the town of Saint-Cybard, in which capacity he personally tortured and killed members of the Maquis de Morez and sundry other men and women of the town. My wife's father was Jean-Jacques Crotteau, known to the intelligence services as Diem. In the early hours of this morning, JJ killed Sophie Duval.'

'JJ was Diem.'

'Yes.'

'And he killed Sophie.'

'He did.'

'Why?'

'Because he could. Because she killed my father, who was his friend. Because she had gone to the States to collect a video that could have identified my father as Kramme. But primarily because she knew who we were and, with Paul Rey dead, it seemed likely she would seek vengeance for the war.'

'You were afraid of her? She's ninety-two.'

'Nobody I know has suggested that age stopped her capacity for violence. Or her need for revenge.'

'Who killed Pierre Fayette?'

'JJ again. He could get closest. I would have done it if it had been necessary.'

To Martha, Elodie says, 'How long have you known?'

Rigidly white, Martha is holding herself, arms across the mound of her abdomen. 'I am just now finding out.' She does not look at her grandfather.

For the first time, Edward Lakoff looks discomfited. 'We didn't want to—'

A sound outside. Laurence turns from the room to the back door. He braces himself against the wall, and raises his Colt in both hands. He is not as steady as he was, but still. To the door, he says, 'They say the asparagus is best picked under the full moon.'

From the far side of the door, René answers, 'And Churchill's cigars are green in its honour.'

Laurence opens the door. On the other side is Conrad Lakoff, his hands raised to shoulder height. René Vivier stands behind him, holding him at gunpoint. From the look on René's face, Conrad Lakoff's life hangs by a particularly fine thread.

There are not many times in Laurence's experience when a plan has come together so neatly. It feels good when it does, even if it is not yet complete. He reaches behind him and flicks down a switch that has been up.

To Lakoff, he says, 'I'm sure René has explained the situation. Your father will continue to speak to the camera. You will remain where you are. If any of us thinks that you are about to move, Martha will be the first to die, and her unborn son with her. Your legacy will end. Diem's legacy, in effect, will be over, because you, now, have no future and Martha's child is your only gift to the world.'

'You cannot—'

'I am not going to harm Martha, I have said so. But you need to tell us all that you know. We have established for the camera that Edward Lakoff is Kramme's son, born during the war, and that, after his escape to the US, he married Diem's daughter, Marie. You, Conrad, therefore, are the grandson of two wartime Nazis.'

'No.' It is Conrad who speaks. 'JJ was never a Nazi.'

'He was Diem, though. All his adult life, he was Kramme's agent.'

'Yes, but not a Nazi. He was captured early in the war. Kramme threatened him. He went along with it, and was never able to stop. He kept thinking that after the war, he could walk away, but after Patrick Sutherland was captured . . . He had no choice. He—'

'Thank you. You can stop now.'

If he doesn't, René will shoot him. Laurence brings the focus back to Edward Lakoff, Kramme's son. 'Whatever JJ's affiliations, Kramme was a Nazi and he was not the only one. We need now for you to paint the broader picture. What were your plans for after Conrad entered the NSA? Are you planning a constitutional convention to overturn democracy, with the intelligence services leading the charge? What happens, what *actually* happens, when the virus of fascism is injected undiluted into the body politic of a sovereign nation? Can you tell us that?'

'Torches off.'

Picaut is fitter than she had feared. Guided by Patrice's map, her team ran for the two and a half kilometres, and she did not lag behind.

Elodie Duval's farm is ablaze with inner and outer lights that make the darkness beyond their reach all the more profound. Of the four cars parked outside, she recognizes Martin Gillard's Mercedes and Elodie Duval's MX-5. The BMW, she thinks, is likely to be Conrad Lakoff's, which leaves an aged, but beautifully maintained, Aston Martin for Laurence. As the man, so the car. You have lied to me from the start. I'm sorry. I did like you. I think perhaps I still do.

Her team gathers around her in the dark. They are fifty metres from the farm, probably more. She can hear voices through an open window, a man and a woman, both speaking English. They are too far away to identify.

'Rollo: front.' Picaut's voice is the barest whisper. Her hands, signalling. 'Evard: to the corner.' He is not Petit now, just himself. 'Sylvie: with me.'

And last: 'Patrice, stay here.'

'It might be— OK. I'm not moving.' He sits down, cross-legged, on the road. 'Break a leg.'

'Captain Picaut, stop. This is not your fight.'

That voice! She spins, and she *is* ready to shoot, but the voice came from the dark behind them and she is, perhaps, silhouetted against the yard lights. Softly, she says, 'Martin Gillard? Paul Rey's son. Are you here to stop Diem's legacy?'

He laughs, just as quietly. 'Well done. On all counts, well done. When did you work it out?'

Never let the assailant take charge of the conversation. She says, 'I trusted you,' and it is true.

'You can trust me still. I am not here to hurt anyone, certainly not you.'

'Why then?'

'I promised my father I would let no harm come to his daughter.' There's a depth to his voice, a roundness, that may be grief.

Unkindly, she says, 'How? You weren't with him when he died. Not even when he knew he was dying.'

'No.' Just that one word and she knows she has hit home. 'We couldn't risk it. We thought . . . my father thought that I was his secret, that Sophie didn't know who I was, and so Elodie the same.' If there was pain before, it is magnified now a hundredfold.

Off balance, she asks, 'What changed?'

'There was a second cipher in Elodie's email.' She feels Patrice shift, as his interest sharpens. To him, Martin Gillard says, 'It was based on Céline's poem; you'd never have got it. You weren't supposed to.'

'She wrote two ciphers in that one email? Really?'

'Really. My sister was taught by Sophie and Laurence. She's been writing ciphers since before she could spell her own name.'

'What did it say, her second message?'

'"Our father sends his love and asks that you not get in the way of what is coming."' He lifts one shoulder in a shrug. 'So this is me, not getting in the way.'

'That must be hard.'

'More than you can ever imagine. I was born for this moment.' He is striving for irony, and failing. Something is not right.

In the farmhouse, a new light flickers on. Still, Picaut cannot see him. She asks, 'What are they doing inside?'

'Filming the evidence. This goes beyond stopping Diem's legacy, or exposing the descendants of a Gestapo agent; there is a principle at stake. Kramme was not the only Nazi given a new life inside the US. There were many of them – and their children, their grandchildren, are woven through the fabric of the nation. Look at our politics, our investment banks, our universities, our science. What do you see?'

She sees corruption on a scale never before imagined, but that is not her problem. 'I will not allow you, Laurence, René . . . anyone, to shoot someone on French soil.'

'Of course not.' A crunch of gravel and at last, Martin Gillard steps into the light. He has his hands out, empty. His gun is clipped into his shoulder holster and however well trained he is, he couldn't draw in the time it might take her – and Rollo, Sylvie and Evard – to fire. He says, 'I told you I have never killed a police officer, Captain Picaut, and it is true. I will not do so now.'

'Then why are we having this conversation?'

'Timing is everything. You will have seen the lights change at the farmhouse. We can go in now. The Lakoffs have admitted on camera that John Lakoff was Max Kramme and that JJ Crotteau killed both Sophie Destivelle and Pierre Fayette.'

'You are giving us permission to do our duty?'

She is crisply furious. He takes a step back. 'Perhaps we could say I'm no longer doing my best to delay you. Also . . . I would remind you that on both sides of this confrontation are men – and women – who are not afraid to kill. They have little to lose, any of them. I would prefer not to see you hurt.'

'Then don't get in the way. Rollo? Evard? Sylvie? As you were.'

Rollo takes the front door with Evard behind him. Picaut takes the back door: slide round the side, duck beneath a window, creep along. She can hear Edward Lakoff speaking inside in much the same measured tones he used when he was describing the images in his museum.

'. . . weakness, a softness, to be extirpated. America needs a strong hand at the helm, just as . . .'

The back door hangs ajar. She signals Evard, standing at the corner of the farmhouse, who signals Rollo. *Three . . .*

Two . . .

One . . .

Go!

'Armed police! Stop what you're doing and—'

Three gunshots crack past, as if all they were waiting for was the excuse and she has offered it.

Without thinking, Picaut hits the floor. With almost as little thought, she pushes herself back up. 'Stop! Lay your guns down, I have more men outside. Martin, I will arrest you. Laurence, stop! This is over. You've made your point.'

There are no more shots.

She scans the room. Edward Lakoff has drawn his own gun, but has had no time to fire before he was hit. He is on the floor, using his own tie to bind a flesh wound on his arm. Martin Gillard, she thinks, fired the shot, but it may have been Rollo: both of them fired.

René Vivier is dead: a single shot to the head from short range. Conrad Lakoff spun, took his gun and killed him. My God, that was fast. Never again will she assume this man is desk-trained, and not competent in the field. Now he is standing with both hands on his gun in a textbook triangle, a mirror image to Laurence, who looks as if he is considering what it may cost him to fire.

Evard has Conrad Lakoff in his sights. Sylvie is covering Edward. Everyone is armed except Martha Lakoff, who stands frozen in the centre of mayhem. Martin Gillard is aiming at her. Perfectly amiably, he says, 'Same rules as before. You all drop your guns or Martha dies. Captain Picaut, I'm sorry, but these men are ruthless and there are very few things they care about. Martha and her unborn son are our only levers.'

Picaut says, 'But you have your film, you can destroy them. Is it true that JJ killed both Sophie and Pierre Fayette?'

527

Conrad Lakoff catches her eye and nods.

'Then there will be no prosecutions for those deaths. Whoever killed René will have to face . . .' It was Conrad, there is no doubt. Picaut has her entire team as witness to this, but still, she cannot imagine a successful prosecution against the man who will head the NSA.

'Exactly.' This is the Laurence she has never seen. He is not hard, but he is no longer playing a role. 'We can't let them go, Captain. You know what they are.'

'Nonetheless, I will not let you kill them.'

'Then I will be dead within a day and this film will vanish. No part of it will ever see the light of day. If you are allowed to live, you will be silenced by authorities whose will you cannot defy. They have the power to do this, and you know it.'

'Not if your video has been streamed to the web. If it's any good at all, it'll go viral within an hour. The Americans don't completely own the internet yet. Even the Lakoffs won't be able to take it down. Their reputations will be destroyed. You don't have to kill them.'

Laurence gives a rueful laugh. 'Captain, we may give the impression that we can perform miracles, but sadly, this is untrue. What you are suggesting is far beyond our technical capacity.'

'But not ours. You will all put your guns down and we will make this happen. Evard, will you ask Patrice to join us?'

REUTERS: Monday 19 March 2018

EX-SENATOR AND SON IN DUAL SUICIDE AFTER VIRAL 'CONFESSION' HITS 26.7 MILLION VIEWS

Edward Lakoff, former Senator of Illinois, was found dead in his hotel room this morning having taken an overdose of phenobarbitone tablets.

His son, Strategic Operations Director Conrad Lakoff of JTARG, was found dead at his home of a gunshot wound to the head. The police are making no further enquiries.

EPILOGUE

Picaut asked them to wait and here they are, her three wise monkeys, sitting on a bench in the Departures area: Laurence Vaughan-Thomas, Elodie Duval and Martin Gillard.

Laurence stands, extends his hand. 'Captain, you're looking well.' This is the real Laurence. She likes him better like this.

Beside him, Martin Gillard is relaxed, in jeans and a dark green polo shirt. He looks almost harmless. 'Have you come to arrest me?'

She was going to. She has ballistics evidence that the shot which injured Edward Lakoff came from Martin's gun. She took it to Ducat, but men whose security clearance gives her vertigo even to think about it have let it be known that any attempt to prosecute would lead the forensic department to conclude that the shots came from Picaut's own weapon.

Ducat relayed the message, white-faced. She has had the best part of three days to get over it.

'You know I can't do that. But you do owe me some answers.'

Martin Gillard says, 'Ask. We will answer what we can.'

She has a list of priorities, at the top of which is this: 'Did Sophie sacrifice herself to the Lakoffs?'

'Of course. They could never have killed her otherwise.' Laurence has taken the role of speaker. He gives a small smile, the layers of which she does not hope to understand. 'The bleating of the lamb attracts the tiger.' He pulls his pipe from his pocket, remembers where he is, and puts it away again. 'Please understand, this is not some whim dreamed up to make your life difficult but the end of sixty years of uncertainty. For years, we have known that Kramme had a mole inside the Maquis de Morez, but we didn't know who it was. We had lost Kramme, too. He vanished into the States in fifty-seven and as far as anyone could tell, he, his case handler and Diem were the only three people who knew who he was.'

'It can't have been hard to narrow down, surely. How many Germans emigrated to the US in 1957?'

'Sixteen hundred.' He laughs, dryly, at the look on her face. 'Not in that year alone – but sixteen hundred Nazis were repatriated under Operation Paperclip in the years after the war and, Kramme being Kramme, he had set up his identity long before he had to run. There really was a John Lakoff, lone child of a widowed mother, who really did live in Missouri and really did join a tank regiment as a lance corporal and was then seconded to the army intelligence unit as a result of his linguistic capacity, later to parachute behind the front lines. We assume he died in Sachsenhausen, but have no proof. Certainly he died before the war's end because Kramme took his place and worked his identity in the years from forty-five to fifty-seven, so that when he jumped ship, as it were, John Lakoff already had a strong and plausible legend.'

'And Diem? Did you know it was JJ?'

'Not then. That was our biggest failure in fifty-seven. We thought the Americans would trust Paul Rey enough to tell him Diem's identity.' Laurence pinches his nose. Fleetingly, he is discomfited. 'We gambled everything on that one throw. We lost. Two of the very best people in the world paid for that mistake with their lives.'

'So when did you find out who he was? And how?'

'In the summer of 2014, when Conrad Lakoff first became SOD-JTARG, an article appeared in one of the online intelligence journals. One shot, taken from one particular angle, showed a distinct similarity to Kramme. They took it down within twenty-four hours, but Sophie had already seen it and brought it to Paul and me.'

'That's the image on the wall in the cabin?'

'Indeed.' He looks pleased that she recognized it.

'You could have shot JJ then,' Picaut says. 'He wasn't particularly well protected.'

'Sixty years ago, we'd have done so, and not realized it was already too late. By waiting until now, we had a chance – not a great one, but one we thought worth the risk – to find the kinds of evidence that would bring down the entire family.'

'Destroy Diem's legacy.'

'Exactly so.'

'We needed something big enough to draw them out,' Elodie says. 'JJ always knew the ciné film from Kramme's wedding had survived. We set up the film company and used it to leak rumours that Paul was going to release it and make it the centrepiece of a television series that would shed light on the Maquis.'

'Sophie had killed John Lakoff by then?'

'Yes, but that wasn't . . . nobody planned that. Kramme was there when she went to visit Paul. They recognized each other. She—'

'If you say she had no choice—'

'By her lights, she didn't.' Laurence says this, leaning back with his arms folded across his chest. 'We grew up in a different world, Captain. There were debts to be paid. What it did was to let the Lakoffs know that we were onto them. In many ways, it added to the film's credibility; they could see it as an attempt to expose them.'

'So you were goading the entire Lakoff family into action? Men who spent their lives in a world where death comes easy. Did you ever stop to consider the consequences?'

'We knew this was a hard game. Admittedly, we didn't expect that Pierre—'

'You didn't expect the immediate descendants of a Nazi war criminal and a lifelong traitor to kill to protect their secret? You're lucky they didn't blow up half of Orléans just to cover their tracks.' Picaut is angry. The three opposite are silent.

'We thought they would come for us,' Laurence says, at length. He has lost his dry, so-English smile. 'Me, Sophie, René. In our arrogance, we imagined ourselves still relevant. We failed in many things, and I regret Pierre's death more deeply than I can say. But we have achieved a great deal that is valuable. The world knows, now, that there is something rotten at the heart of our body politic that stretches back to the war. We lost our moral direction and we need urgently to find it again before the patterns of the past repeat themselves on a greater scale than any we experienced.'

'You think it's possible to undo damage done sixty years ago?'

'I sincerely hope so, Captain. We have done our best. Others, now, must take up the baton.'

An announcer calls a flight in French and then in English. Laurence angles his elbow. Elodie slides her hand into it. They look particularly British. He says, 'We have a plane to catch. Goodbye, Captain. We may not return to Orléans, but should you travel to England, you will always be welcome at Ridgemount.'

They weave into the crowds, and are gone. Martin lifts his bag, one-handed. 'I should be going, too.'

He steps towards the gate. Picaut steps in front of him, blocking the way. He could walk through her, or round her. He stops. She says, 'Tell me why you killed Edward and Conrad Lakoff.'

'What makes you think I did?'

'If it wasn't you, then it's Elodie or Laurence, and I'm still trying to believe they are better than that.'

He laughs, dryly. 'If it was Elodie, she'd have cut their tongues out. She inherited her mother's tendency to dramatize.'

'Thank you. I'll sleep better knowing that.'

'You're welcome.' They call his flight for the second, or perhaps the third time. 'I have to go. My father's funeral is at the end of the week and I wish to be there.' He holds out his hand. 'I didn't kill them, Captain. Their deaths were as they seem. Each died by his own hand.'

'But you made them do it.'

He thinks a moment, chewing his lip. 'What did Elodie write in her cipher, the one that you read?'

'Paul Rey's son stop Diem's legacy query. You are Paul Rey's son. And you have stopped Diem's legacy.'

'Have I?'

'The legacy was Conrad Lakoff. How much more power can you have than getting to be head of the NSA?'

'That's an interesting question. Some day, we might have an opportunity to debate it. But you are forgetting the new legacy that is on its way: Martha's son.'

'Laurence said Martha and her unborn child would be left alone.'

'Laurence was speaking for himself. I have a . . . reputation and the Lakoffs know more of the reality behind the myths than most. I told them that if they wanted the child to live, there was a price. They believed me.' He flashes her a look, appraising. 'Did you ever work out who killed Pierre Fayette?'

534

'Because it clearly wasn't a man, and so the Lakoffs were lying?' Her team has debated exactly this point for most of the morning. She says, 'My money is on Martha. We have a partial fingerprint that matches hers and a woman's footprint in his garden near where his gun was fired, but Ducat won't let me arrest her without more evidence. He's under pressure from above.'

'Because Martha Lakoff was also not what she seemed.'

'CIA?'

'Far darker than that. We're moving into a world where private enterprise calls the shots. Martha belongs in that world. As, I suppose, do I. It was Martha who killed Sophie.'

Blonde, pregnant, oh-so-helpful Martha. It's surprisingly easy to imagine her dealing in murder. And yet: 'I still struggle to imagine Sophie Destivelle going quietly to her death.'

'I think if you'd met her . . . She had enormous courage. I learned a great deal from her.' He looks down at the ground for a long moment, and then up again. 'We were bred for this confrontation, Martha and I. Our lives have been shaped for it, our skills nurtured. It was always going to come to this. I am enormously sorry you became involved.'

His name is called one more time. She says, 'Will they hold the flight for you for ever?'

He grins, and is young, and very like the pictures of his father. 'Not for ever.' His grip is as dry and firm as it was when she first met him. 'Goodbye, Captain Picaut. For all kinds of reasons, I trust we never have to meet again, but you should know that I respect you highly. It's the only gift I can give. Go well. Tread lightly in your world. Do not tread into mine.'

He is gone. After a while, Picaut walks back to where her team is waiting. 'And?'

Patrice pulls a face. 'No signal. He's got some kind of white noise generator that screwed the recording. Even the CIA couldn't get sound out of that.'

Sylvie says, 'It came on when you started talking.'

And Rollo: 'Whatever it was, he had it in his bag. He switched it on when he stood up.'

Oh, Martin. Clever, clever Martin.

Wary, Rollo asks, 'What did he say?'

He said that Martha Lakoff and her unborn child are dead. And they will have died while the three most likely suspects were talking to me in an airport in full view of the CCTV cameras and with all of you as witnesses. There will be no threads, no ties, no way to connect them. You did warn me that this was how he worked.

Picaut slides her phone back into her pocket. 'He said he didn't do it.'

AFTERWORD

The experience of writing in a period of time that remains, for some, within their lifetime's memory, has been an inspiring experience. The world was a different place in the Boudican era, in Imperial Rome, or the fifteenth-century France of Jeanne d'Arc. The language and the social mores were radically different from ours and the historical record was more gap than structure. My challenge in the past was always to find ways to stitch together the small concepts for which there was reasonable evidence, and to sift them from the accretions of later mythology.

The mythology surrounding the Second World War is no smaller, but the recorded detail of the time is many orders of magnitude greater, and where there are gaps, it is still possible – just – to ask those who were alive at the time for their recollections. Even with all the usual misgivings about the fallibility of human memory, this remains a treasure trove beyond expressing for the historical writer.

It also means, however, that it is possible to offend these same people or their immediate descendants. Thus, because much of the texture of this book is drawn from personal memoirs of people whose children and grandchildren are still alive, I have, for the first time, invented places and people to populate the narrative when there were perfectly viable locations and characters available in the historical record.

Thus, Saint-Cybard is a fiction. There is a French town of this name, but it's down in the south-west and there is no counterpart that I know of in the Jura mountains; certainly not at the location of the one in the narrative. Similarly, while Max Kramme bears a strong resemblance to Klaus Barbie of the Lyon Gestapo, he is not that man. For those with an interest, there is good evidence that during and immediately after the war, Barbie was run as an agent of MI6 by men who believed that the Soviet Union was the greatest threat and who desired access to agents behind eastern lines. They kept him alive after the war when the French had sentenced him to death *in absentia*, and then passed him to the CIA, who, in due course, helped him escape to Bolivia, from where he was extradited to France in the early 1980s. He died in prison in 1991.

The women and men of the Special Operations Executive – Sophie, Céline, Patrick, Fabien, Daniel, René and the others – are each drawn piecemeal from the lives of those whose memoirs and biographies are filled on every page with acts of outstanding courage. For those with an interest I will append a bibliography, although it is worth noting that there are still lacunae in many of the accounts and it may well be that these are never filled. I spoke only last week to a woman whose late father told her only hours before he died, 'I was in the SOE. We did some terrible things.' He had lived over sixty years in silence and he will not be alone.

There is also the small matter of the fire at the SOE headquarters in Baker Street which (allegedly) destroyed many of its records; and of the complete dissolution of the SOE later at the hands of MI6. Claude Dansey really did loathe them, and although there is not the slightest shred of evidence that his death was in any way related to the SOE, its timing felt apt and I had no qualms about creating a fictional backstory linking the two.

Dansey was not alone in his dislike of the SOE: much of the Establishment disliked the 'Firm' when it was in action and were in a hurry to close it down as soon as the war was over. The shabby treatment of many of its agents, particularly the women, remains a source of national shame; in this, Sophie and Céline were unusually lucky to be able to continue with work that made the most of their skills after the war.

Like the SOE, the Jedburghs have been a source of myth and legend, and one of the sparks that ignited this book came from an exploration into the early days of the CIA and the discovery that many of its early operatives had been Jedburghs: men who had been parachuted behind enemy lines around D-Day and spent the summer of '44 in the mountains of France living like demi-gods. They had broadly good weather. They could summon food, drink, cigarettes and armaments from the sky. They had trained to be as fit as any military group of their time and they were given free rein, more or less, to kill anything in a grey uniform. Most of all, they were indisputably on the right side of a relatively black-and-white moral argument and so could hunt the Nazis and their French collaborators with a clear conscience.

Reading Colin Beavan's *Operation Jedburgh*, I came to understand that many of the global catastrophes of the late twentieth century – of Vietnam and Afghanistan, of the entire creation of Al-Qaeda and Isis/Daesh – could, in part, be explained by the fact that these men and their immediate successors spent their post-war careers trying to reproduce the heady days of that summer in France, without taking into account the fact that France was a Western industrialized nation whose political and religious foundations were broadly aligned with those of other Western industrialized nations.

One further piece of serendipity brought this book into being. I shared an agent with Nick Cook and so came to read his fascinating work, *The Hunt for Zero Point*. It was from this that I first learned of Operation Paperclip and the sixteen hundred high-ranking Nazis smuggled out of Germany under the noses of the Nuremberg prosecutors, and given new names and new identities in the United States. It was in Nick's book, too, that I first read the question voiced by Céline in *A Treachery of Spies*: 'What happens to the soul of a nation if into its body politic is injected the undiluted virus of Nazism?' The implications of this, it seemed to me, were worth exploring, and a novel is an opportunity to tease things out and look at them from new angles.

I leave you with a quote from Colin Beavan's book. It refers to the Jedburghs but I have no doubt that it applies equally to the agents of the Special Operations Executive with whom they often fought:

> Some think of Operation Jedburgh as the bravest thing they had ever done. Some see it as the most terrifying nightmare. But all marvel that, when the green light blinked on in their black-painted bombers, they'd actually jumped.

ACKNOWLEDGEMENTS

Every book floats on an ocean of other people's endeavours; of their wisdom, knowledge and forethought. This one in particular owes many debts; for the first time, I have had the novel and heart-warming experience of listening to those who lived through the times of which I write. Every conversation left me more in awe of those who lived through the conflict of '39–'45 and more aware of the debt our generations owe to those whose lives – and deaths – were shaped by their experience.

Thus, my thanks to: Patrick Ramsay and his late wife Hope, who opened many doors to England as it was during and after the war; to Alan Laurie, who took part in Operation Phantom; to Francis Suttill, whose father served in the SOE. Most especially, undying thanks to Pat and Patricia Coles, to whom this book is dedicated, for taking me to visit SOE sites near their home on the Devil's Punch Bowl (which bears a passing resemblance to Ridgemount), and for so much more.

Thanks also to the men and women of the SOE online group, who put such diligent effort into uncovering the details of the past, much of which is still classified and may remain so for many years to come. Particular thanks to Mark Stillman for help with the Q-codes, to Ben Jones and A. F. Judge for help with leaving dates, to Nick Fox for help with German telegrams and the fact that sources were known as

Vertrauensmann, abbreviated to V-Mann, and to Martyn Cox and Stephen Kippax for help with all things SOE – and for moral support with the entire endeavour.

When I needed help on STOL (short take-off and landing) planes, Ed Weatherup was there with pictures and help, with backup from Jim Perrin, Robin Carter, Doug Taylor and Isobel Picornel; thanks to you all. Tilly Calvert kept my spine from turning chair-shaped, and told me stories of her great-uncle 'in intelligence' who had a ten-foot trench dug for his telephone wires in his front garden – for both of which, many thanks.

Because my French is functional at best, enormous thanks to Isobel again, to my old school friend Angie Boinaud, to Brigitte Tilleray, and particularly to Virginie Rouxel-Halloo, who read one of the later drafts and saved me from much misspelled embarrassment. Lorant Kácsor and Amy Weatherup both read a late draft and offered their customary humour and incisive insight.

Thanks to Major Rob Pitt and Captain Michelle Roberts, both of whom showed me what it is to live in the modern army with integrity, zest, compassion, intelligence and forethought. In addition, Rob showed me what fortitude can achieve, while Michelle taught me about rolling over car bonnets in close protection duties.

Thanks to Mark Lucas of LAW Agency, for planting the seed from which the entire tree grew, and for watering it diligently through many drafts; to my editors Bill Scott-Kerr and Darcy Nicholson for the dedication to keep going through the many drafts it takes to bring two timelines into harmony; and particularly to Claire Gatzen and Vivien Thompson for astonishing acts of fortitude in the copy-editing process. Thanks also to Patsy Irwin and the entire team at Transworld for once again picking up where the writing stops and making the book fly.

To my partner, Faith, as always, my love and thanks for three years of patience and inspiration. You are the guiding light of my life.

A final thanks to the faculty and students of Schumacher College, particularly my fellow classmates in the Masters in Economics year of 2016/17, who put up with my tendency to vanish for prolonged periods with the excuse that I had a book to write. Which was true. May you all enjoy it.

Manda Scott
Shropshire, January 2018

The final draft of this work is ready for submission and I have just learned that the man for whom Patrick is named, and on whom much of Laurence's character is based – a man of absolute integrity – has died. Patrick Coles was one of my greatest and oldest friends. The epitome of an English gentleman, he was the soul of decency, courage, intelligence, tact and compassion. It is an enormous sorrow that he did not live to see this book to completion, but he helped with a great deal of the writing. And so to Patrick, my heartfelt love and thanks, may you rest ever in peace; and to his wife, now widow, Patricia, who is as full of grace, beauty and intelligence as Sophie – if not quite as lethal – my never-ending love.

1 September 2017

BIBLIOGRAPHY

This bibliography is neither comprehensive nor exhaustive, but it is a good starting point for those interested in the SOE, the Jedburghs and the evolution of the CIA into the NSA.

Bailey, Roderick: *Forgotten Voices of the Secret War: An Inside History of Special Operations during the Second World War* (Ebury Press, 2008)

Bamford, James: *The Shadow Factory: The Ultra-Secret NSA from 9/11 to the Eavesdropping on America* (Anchor Books, 2008)

Beavan, Colin: *Operation Jedburgh: D-Day and America's First Shadow War* (Viking, 2006)

Binney, Marcus: *Secret War Heroes: Men of the Special Operations Executive* (Hodder & Stoughton, 2005)

Braddon, Russell: *Nancy Wake: SOE's Greatest Heroine* (The History Press, 2005, first published 1956)

Buckmaster, Maurice: *They Fought Alone: The True Story of SOE's Agents in Wartime France* (Biteback, 2014, first published 1958)

Cook, Nick: *The Hunt for Zero Point* (Century, 2001)

Cowburn, Benjamin: *No Cloak, No Dagger: Allied Spycraft in Occupied France* (Frontline Books, 2009, first published 1960)

Cunningham, Cyril: *Beaulieu: The Finishing School for Secret Agents* (Pen & Sword, 1997)

Elliott, Geoffrey: *The Shooting Star: Denis Rake, MC: A Clandestine Hero of the Second World War* (Methuen, 2009)

Escott, Beryl E. (Squadron Leader): *The Heroines of SOE: F Section: Britain's Secret Women in France* (The History Press, 2010)

Foot, M. R. D.: *SOE: The Special Operations Executive 1940–1946* (Pimlico, 1999, first published 1984)

Fuller, Jean Overton: *Déricourt: The Chequered Spy* (Michael Russell, 1989)

Garfield, Simon: *Private Battles: How the War Almost Defeated Us: Our Intimate Diaries* (Ebury Press, 2006)

Goldsmith, John: *Accidental Agent: Behind Enemy Lines with the French Resistance* (Pen & Sword, 2016, first published 1971)

Harrison, David M.: *SOE: Para-Military Training in Scotland During World War 2* (private publication)

Helm, Sarah: *A Life in Secrets: The Story of Vera Atkins and the Lost Agents of SOE* (Abacus, 2005)

Hue, André: *The Next Moon: The Remarkable True Story of a British Agent Behind the Lines in Wartime France* (Viking, 2004)

Irwin, Will (Lt. Col. Ret.): *The Jedburghs: The Secret History of the Allied Special Forces, France 1944* (PublicAffairs, 2005)

Jacobs, Peter: *Codenamed Dorset: The Wartime Exploits of Major Colin Ogden-Smith, Commando and SOE* (Frontline Books, 2014)

Jacobsen, Annie: *Operation Paperclip: The Secret Intelligence Program That Brought Nazi Scientists to America* (Little, Brown, 2014)

Jenkins, Ray: *A Pacifist at War: The Life of Francis Cammaerts* (Hutchinson, 2009)

Jones, R. V.: *Most Secret War: British Scientific Intelligence 1939–1945* (Hamish Hamilton, 1978)

Mackenzie, William: *The Secret History of SOE: Special Operations Executive 1940–1945* (St Ermin's Press, 2002)

Macpherson, Sir Tommy: *Behind Enemy Lines: The Autobiography of Britain's Most Decorated Living War Hero* (Mainstream Publishing, 2010)

Marks, Leo: *Between Silk and Cyanide: A Codemaker's War 1941–1945* (Free Press, 1999)

Marnham, Patrick: *The Death of Jean Moulin: Biography of a Ghost* (John Murray, 2000)

Marshall, Bruce: *The White Rabbit: The Secret Agent the Gestapo Could Not Crack* (Cassell, 2007, first published 1952)

McKay, Sinclair: *The Secret Life of Bletchley Park* (Aurum Press, 2010)

Millar, George: *Maquis: An Englishman in the French Resistance* (The Dovecote Press, 2013, first published 1945)

—— *The Bruneval Raid: Stealing Hitler's Radar* (Cassell, 2002, first published 1974)

—— *Road to Resistance: An Autobiography* (Bodley Head, 1979)

Mulley, Clare: *The Spy Who Loved: The Secrets and Lives of One of Britain's Bravest Wartime Heroines* (Macmillan, 2012)

O'Connor, Bernard: *Churchill's Angels: How Britain's Women Secret Agents Changed the Course of the Second World War* (Amberley, 2012)

Seymour-Jones, Carole: *She Landed by Moonlight: The Story of Secret Agent Pearl Witherington: The 'Real Charlotte Gray'* (Hodder & Stoughton, 2013)

Sheridan, Dorothy (ed.): *Wartime Women: A Mass-Observation Anthology of Women's Writing, 1937–1945* (William Heinemann, 1990)

Suttill, Francis J.: *Shadows in the Fog: The True Story of Major Suttill and the Prosper French Resistance Network* (The History Press, 2014)

Walters, Anne-Marie: *Moondrop to Gascony* (Moho Books, 2009, first published 1946)

Walters, Guy: *Hunting Evil: The Nazi War Criminals Who Escaped and The Hunt To Bring Them To Justice* (Bantam Press, 2009)

Yarnold, Patrick: *Wanborough Manor: School for Secret Agents* (Hopfield Publications, 2009)